Four from the Witch World

Also by Andre Norton
published by Tor Books

The Crystal Gryphon
Flight in Yiktor
Forerunner
Forerunner: The Second Venture
Here Abide Monsters
House of Shadows (with Phyllis Miller)
Magic in Ithkar (with Robert Adams)
Magic in Ithkar 2 (with Robert Adams)
Magic in Ithkar 4 (with Robert Adams)
Moon Called
Ralestone Luck
Tales of the Witch World 1 (created by Andre Norton)
Tales of the Witch World 2 (created by Andre Norton)
Wheel of Stars

Andre Norton

A TOM DOHERTY ASSOCIATES BOOK
NEW YORK

FOUR FROM THE WITCH WORLD

Maps by John M. Ford

A TOR BOOK
Published by Tom Doherty Associates, Inc.
49 West 24 Street
New York, NY 10010

Library of Congress Cataloging-in-Publication Data

Four from the witch world / created [and edited] by Andre Norton.—
1st ed.
"A Tom Doherty Associates book."
ISBN 0-312-93153-0
1. Witch World (Imaginary place)—Fiction. 2. Fantastic fiction, American. I. Norton, Andre.
PS648.F3F68 1989 88-29170
813'.0876—dc19 CIP

First edition: February 1989
0 9 8 7 6 5 4 3 2 1

Contents

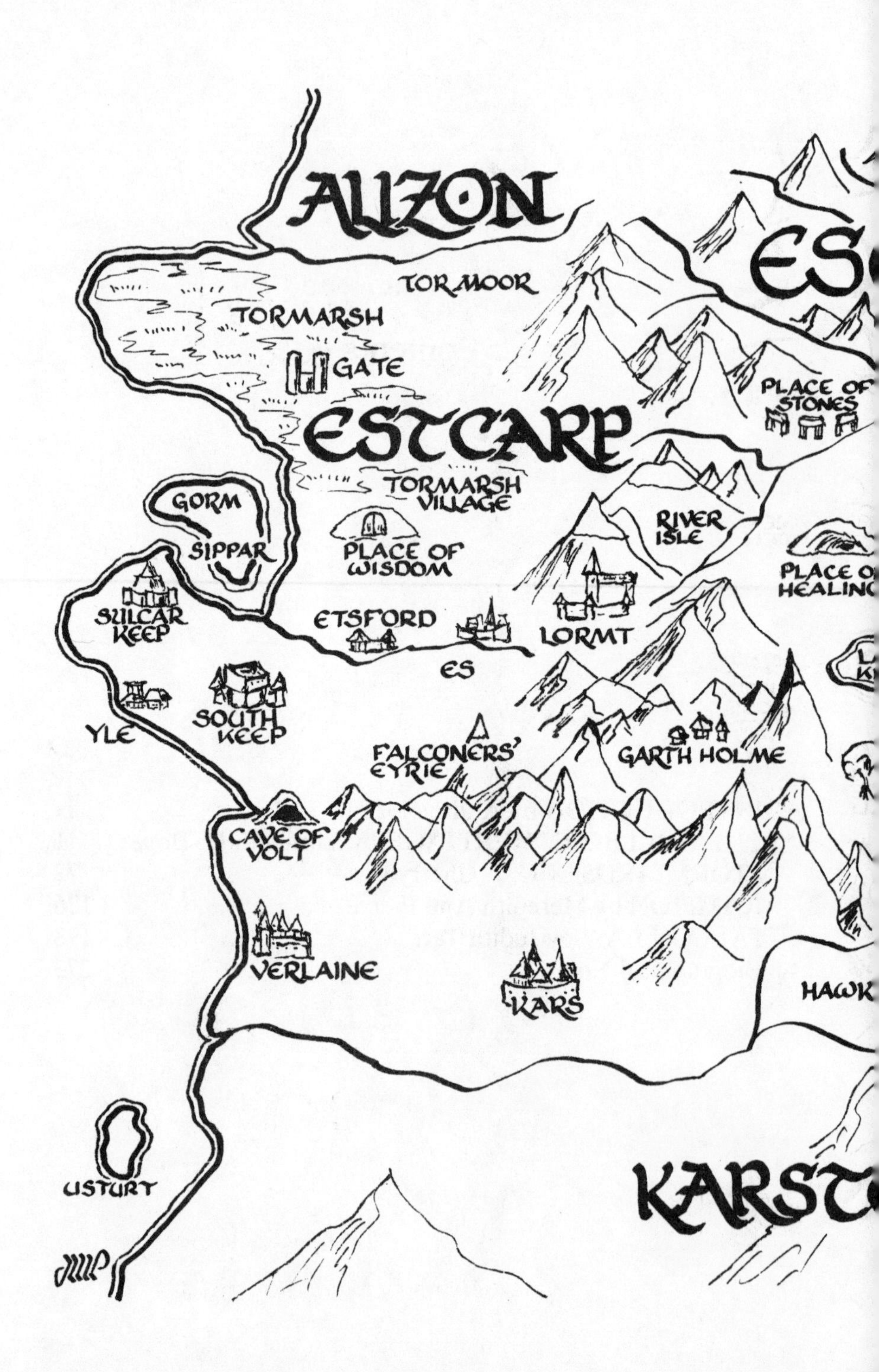
ALIZON
TOR MOOR
TORMARSH
GATE
ESTCARP
PLACE OF STONES
TORMARSH VILLAGE
GORM
SIPPAR
PLACE OF WISDOM
RIVER ISLE
SULCAR KEEP
ETSFORD
LORMT
ES
YLE
SOUTH KEEP
FALCONERS' EYRIE
GARTH HOLME
CAVE OF VOLT
VERLAINE
KARS
USTURT

CITADEL OF HILARION
GAIL WOOD
OLD PORT
RUINED BRIDGE
VALLEY OF HOT SPRINGS
DARK TOWER
STONE GARDEN
STONE FOREST
UNDERMOUNTAIN CAVES
FOREST OF MOSSWOMEN
Andre Norton's
Witch World

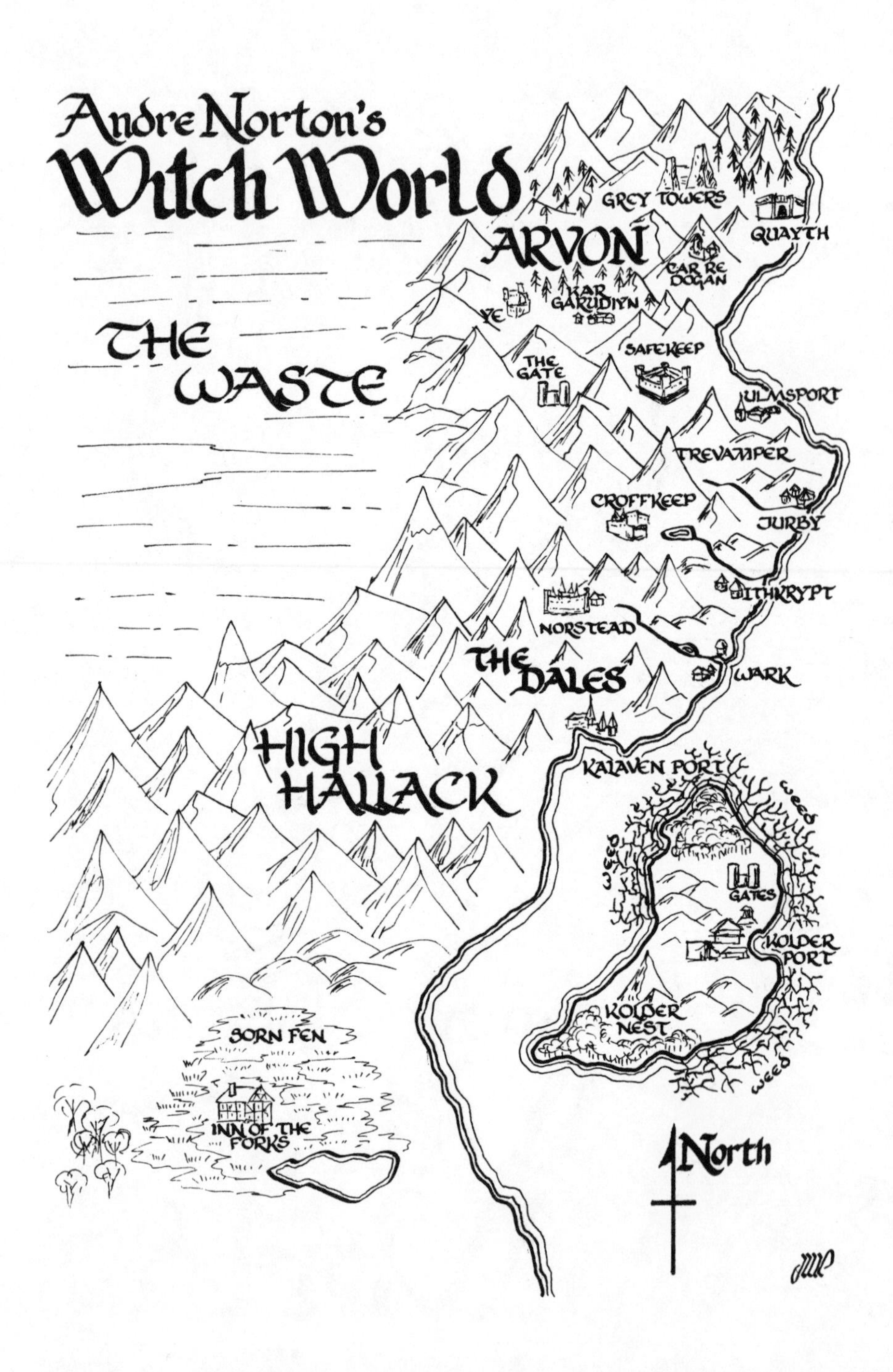
Andre Norton's
Witch World
THE WASTE
ARVON
GREY TOWERS
QUAYTH
CAR RE DOGAN
KAR GARUDIYN
YE
SAFEKEEP
THE GATE
ULMSPORT
TREVAMPER
CROFFKEEP
JURBY
ITHKRYPT
NORSTEAD
THE DALES
WARK
HIGH HALLACK
KALAVEN PORT
WEED
WEED
GATES
KOLDER PORT
KOLDER NEST
WEED
SORN FEN
INN OF THE FORKS
North

Introduction

Witch World has grown little by little; it was never carefully defined, mapped, given a formal history. In other words, it remains still wide open for voyages of discovery to this day. The map, which was at last drawn, in part shows little knowledge of the North, the South, and the western continent beyond the barrier of the Waste.

Not only does it lie historically and geographically open to exploration, but it also has inhabitants who vary widely—there are many strange pockets of peoples hidden away in the countryside, the mountains, the islands, and the marshes of illfame.

For there is one ever-present fact: the Gates. Certainly the adepts, who opened these for their own information and recreation, never thought (unless that was also a matter of experimentation on their part back in the far mists that have swallowed a great part of history) that the Gates would indeed work two ways. The adepts may have sauntered, or fled, through these, away from a world in which they had wrought much damage, but, also, there came through from other space-times unfortunates caught by the force of some one of those concealed doors, exiles fleeing the worst and believing that what lay before them might give them some small change in fortune for the better, also dabblers in powers they did not wholly understand, drawn, by their rash disturbance of the Law, against their will into Estcarp, High Hallack, Arvon, and Escore—there to be faced with what was totally strange, to try both courage and strength.

Witch World is a tapestry still in the weaving, with a most intricate patterning that alters as one weaver and then another puts hand to the shuttle and begins the *clack-clack* of a busy loom. Perhaps because of this never finished state it attracts those who see new vistas, who pick up this or that hank of thread before sitting down to add a bit here, some edging there.

To me there are still unreckoned discoveries ahead. I cannot say this is a world I have created, rather it in itself is a Gate, on the other side of which a Falconer rides on some duty unknown to me as yet, in which a Sulcar ship battles waves and sails seeking a new port as yet uncharted, in which a lady of the Dales must grasp the hard rod of rulership, in which the finding of a fragment of an ancient artifact may change life in an instant.

Because it remains an ever open land with many stories for the telling, I have asked others to fill in some of those uncharted spaces, to create people who wrought both ill and well, to make clear some point of history, or to illumine a corner of the unknown as yet secret.

I have been so very fortunate that those I summoned have been ready to add so richly to all the patchwork of former tales. I am grateful for all gates they have opened in turn. For now the Witch World ever widens. So many pebbles in which the magic of others (who have their own cherished worlds of wonder) is embedded have been thrown into a pool that has widened into a sea, sending ripples out and out to wash shores I never knew existed. I can believe now that, while I have but little Power, I can summon new adepts for the opening of Gates. Time and space are no barriers for such as seek with their own art for keys—that they have used these to enter Witch World is an honor and a joy.

To Estcarp and Escore, High Hallack and Arvon, I dare now to hope there will never come a new sealing, that Gates will not be forgotten and that this world will be enriched by other chroniclers.

So is offered further tales for those old friends to Witch World lore and those others new come . . .

—Andre Norton

THE STILLBORN HERITAGE
by
Elizabeth H. Boyer

I

Mal wormed as much of his four-year old body as he could into the drafty niche between clammy wall and faded tapestry. He had never ventured into the wing of the keep that harbored his three maiden aunts—until this peculiar secret excitement had commenced. With his finger he enlarged a mouse-gnawn hole in the fabric and watched. The screams had been going on for hours. The men were all banished below to the great hall while the women of Malmgarth dealt grimly with the crisis common to womankind. Serving women and maidservants trod tirelessly between scullery and upstairs, carrying whatsoever the midwife demanded.

Mal scowled as Ysa appeared with a steaming pot of fragrant tea and some fresh cakes old Cook had made just that day. She took them in to the midwife without once looking around to offer any to Mal. Ysa was the nicest and the plumpest of the maidservants, and she belonged to Mal and none other. In the drama of Lady Eirena's premature delivery, no one had thought of Mal's supper and bedtime. Vengefully he pulled more threads out of the priceless old tapestry and glared after Ysa. She went in and came right out, and from the look of her Mal knew she had forgotten about him entirely.

Even his uncle, Lord Rufus, would have no use for him once this new stranger arrived in Malmgarth. Mal had heard Lady Fairhona say as much to Lady Elga, who were sisters to Lady Eirena. Mal knew little of the reasons that had taken him from his own home to the south at Birkholm, save that his own mother had died of the same disease that Lady Eirena now suffered, and he had been sent to his uncle, Lord Rufus, as a fosterling.

Lord Rufus and Lady Virid had no children of their own; hence, no heir for Malmgarth would come from the line of Rufus. Any child of Eirena, elder sister to Rufus, provided a truer bloodline than did young Mal, the nephew of Rufus. Lady Eirena had not chosen to consummate her alliance with marriage, as was her right, though possible bastard offspring of Lord Rufus were not entitled to inheritance. Male or female, Eirena's child, if it survived its birthing and was not deformed, would be the heir of Malmgarth.

Mal was too young to care about inheriting Malmgarth, with its green pastures and tall stands of timber, sheltered from the north storms and cooled in the summer by breezes from the not-too-distant sea. Fertile Malmgarth meadows provided pasturage for herds of fine cattle and sheep, and clean-limbed horses.

Over generations of selective breeding, the Malmgarth horse combined the intelligence and strength of the fabled Torgian and the speed and beauty of the silver-dappled Were steeds. The result was a horse invariably born completely black, later to acquire silvery stippling in the quarters and belly, although the most prized did not change color until old age. Their necks were slender, proudly arched, their superb

heads and flowing tails carried arrogantly high. A hint of wildness always lingered in the Were-Torgians' large flashing eye and flaring nostril, yet no rider, once accepted by a Malmgarth horse, could wish for a more faithful and obedient mount to carry him over the long distances between neighboring keeps. In battle, a less common occurrence nowadays but still to be guarded against, a Malmgarth horse defended his master with teeth and hooves.

Memories still lingered of the days of wind and wolf after the Hounds of Alizon had ravaged the Dales, leaving farm and keep barren of all life, until the great ones such as Lord Trystan had taken hold to bring the land out of lawlessness into order. The father of Lord Rufus had been one such, and with him he had brought a pair of Were horses to the desolate keep of Malmgarth. Men had looked askance then at Lord Tirell, wondering at what bargains he must have driven during the war years, but glad enough at the peace he returned to the land to forget he was no lord born and forgive the expediencies of wartime.

What Mal cared about was the fat gray pony of his own named Baldhere, the tidbits Cook always gave him instead of making him wait, and the dozen or more serving women in the household who never refused him anything. Best of all were the evenings beside the fire in the great hall, sitting alongside his uncle Rufus and pestering him with questions when Rufus was in a patient mood, or watching with admiration when Lord Rufus was in a fiery temper and strode up and down shouting at some miscreant herdsman or plowboy.

Rufus was everything any boy would love—noisy, handsome, as generous with gifts as he was with cuffs on the ear, and he smelled of horses and mead and leather. Rufus often set Mal before him on a fast Malmgarth horse, and they would race like the wind together across the meadows and rolling hills, with Mal shouting for joy as the wind tore the words out of his mouth and made his eyes stream with tears.

None of this would Mal share with that troublesome stranger being born in the room across the corridor. He was cold and stiff from standing and watching, but he relished the feeling of doing the forbidden. All the women came and went without once suspecting that he was there, spying upon that which they wished no male eyes to see.

Then the screaming came to an abrupt end, but the room was not yet still. A maidservant hurried from the room, meeting Ysa in the corridor.

"The child is stillborn," the maid said hurriedly. "Send a man to the abbey for the Dame Averil. What can't be restored to life must be blessed. We don't know what evil thing might take the spirit's place."

"The poor little scrap," Ysa murmured as she turned to hurry away beside the first woman. "Too eager to come into this cruel world."

"And a girl it would have been, more's the pity," said the other.

They were scarcely out of sight when a dark, hooded figure crept out of the shadows from the other end of the corridor, where stairs descended to a thick door to the courtyard below. Mal stood very still, scarcely breathing, as he recognized in this other some of his own furtiveness.

It was a woman, he saw, but not one of those who worked in the house. This was one of the rough ones who worked outdoors, and her kind had no business here. Mal swelled with lordly indignation, and would have stepped out of his hiding place to challenge the forward creature, but his eye chanced upon the bundle the woman carried. It was a bit of old tapestry formed into a bag, and he would have recognized it by its smell alone. It had the acrid smell of pungent herbs, and it belonged to Merdice, the herb woman. Mal scarcely dared blink, lest her cat ears hear the sound, and he knew if he moved her serpent's eye would certainly see.

Merdice glanced about suspiciously, as if she sensed his

presence. He had feared her greatly since her first appearance at Malmgarth on the first day of winter. Rufus and the menfolk had burned the straw wheels to frighten off the evil spirits, but Merdice had somehow failed to be frightened away. She was homeless, a ragged wanderer begging at the scullery door, but it was a fearless sort of begging, and she had cast her dark gaze over the keep, noting with sharpness this and that detail, and finally inquiring if Lord Rufus wanted a woman to work the herbs in his stillroom. As if she had somehow known that the ancient woman who used to do the work had died and left Lord Rufus's livestock and household without the infusions and powders they needed to recover from sickness and injury. It was whispered among the servants that Merdice had the evil eye, that Merdice talked with the dead in the ruins across the beck, that Merdice could put thoughts into your head, or pick thoughts from your head; but all agreed that Merdice was one who walked apart from regular people.

Mal thought that Merdice probably roasted small children, especially disobedient little boys. From his wary spying upon her in the stillroom, he knew she talked to herself as she made her preparations, or perhaps it was invisible spirits she addressed. Once he had come upon her in the stillroom sitting bolt upright, staring as if entranced. Usually she whirled upon him angrily when she caught him snooping, and drove him away with a shake of her fist. To Mal she seemed incredibly old and wrinkled, although her hair was barely streaked with gray, and she walked with a haughty straightness in her gaunt and angular frame. Eagle fierceness burned in her acute dark eye.

Now she turned and looked measuringly at the tapestry, and Mal knew that his life was over. She punched at it, feeling the small space between it and the wall, a space far too small to hide a full-size figure of a man or woman. Shrugging, she glared at the tapestry and fumbled in her bag for a small crystal bottle. She drew it out and held it up to the light of the sconce a moment. Inside, a substance like smoke swirled around and around with the graceful, fluid manner of a living thing. A tiny face pressed against the clear surface for a moment, framed by two flowerlike hands, then it too swirled restlessly away, trailing a glimpse of pale hair. The little creature seemed to be searching for escape, rising to push determinedly against the wood stopper with delicate arms, then gliding onward around the bottle.

Mal had never seen such an engaging toy. Fiercely he yearned to possess the tiny lady in the glass—clear glass, which in itself was a wondrous marvel. Yet Mal did not move a muscle in his hiding place, only allowing his eyes to widen with yearning.

Merdice tucked the bottle suddenly into her flowing gown and turned to face a figure hastening toward her.

"What do you here, Merdice?" Ysa inquired in a tone not calculated to offend. "No one sent for you."

"The infant," Merdice said. "I have restoratives for stillbirth. I wish to see the child before the rest of you give up on her." Merdice gazed straight at Ysa, who was on the point of refusing. Her head was just beginning to shake in denial, then she stiffened slightly and her eyes did not blink.

"Very well," Ysa replied, her hand going to the door latch. As she pushed open the door, Mal glimpsed the room beyond, where several women were attending to Lady Eirena, who lay pallid and moaning insensibly. The midwife held a tiny blue-gray thing wrapped in a scrap of white cloth. They all looked up at Merdice in outrage as Ysa spoke.

"The wise woman is here with a restorative for the child," she said, speaking as if by rote.

The midwife started to heave her massive bulk to its feet, and the other women turned indignantly, but Merdice lifted one hand and all their actions were stayed.

"Good," Merdice said. "That's much better."

She glided into the room and took the baby from the midwife. With one hand, she slipped the bottle from her gown and loosened the cork with her teeth. Holding the bottle under the baby's tiny nose she removed the cork, and the smoky fluid substance inside vanished. Almost at once the infant drew a breath and began to cough and sputter, its voice rising in a querulous wail.

Merdice returned the infant to the midwife and swiftly stepped out into the corridor. It had all taken just moments. Ysa remembered to shut the door behind Merdice, and Mal heard her voice cry out "The child lives!"

Lady Eirena spoke wearily. "Her name is Aislinn."

Then Mal again faced Merdice, who halted beside the tapestry, her head turning warily as she surveyed its length. This time she spied the hole Mal had picked in the fabric, and she pounced like a cat. Mal scuttled along behind the tapestry, with Merdice pouncing a split second after him. He couldn't very well cry out for help, even had his throat not been paralyzed with terror, since he was an intruder in Lady Eirena's domain. There was no one to save him, and he was speedily running out of tapestry.

A projecting abutment suddenly shunted him to the left into darkness, and he tumbled a short way down a flight of narrow steps. Below, he could see a light and hear voices, so he stifled his frightened sobs and crept downward. Pressing against the wall, he slithered down the stairs as fast as he could go with his short legs reaching down doubtfully for each step. He expected a clawlike hand to grab him at any moment, or perhaps Merdice had changed shapes and would come after him as a wolf, a great rat, or even a spider.

The stairs ended at a narrow door, which Mal pushed against frantically. It opened, and he tumbled into a closetlike room that he recognized immediately as belonging to the realm of the kitchen and the wonderful, kind female deities who reigned there. He scrambled out of the pantry into that fragrant haven of firelight and roasting meat. The kitchen deities flocked around him, and Cook took him on her billowing, comforting lap and soothed him with a sweet cake and held a cold knife to the rising knot on his forehead.

"He's been up that musty bolt-hole to the ladies' wing," observed Cook, wiping cobwebs out of his hair. "Spying on the birthing, I have no doubt. Is that where you were, my little lordling?"

"They'd have his hide if they knew," said one of the others with a nervous titter.

"It's no matter now," Cook said. "We won't tell them and they'll never know. A pity the poor baby never drew breath. And Lady Eirena cheated after all. Went to such a deal of trouble, she did, to get that child. We'll have little Mal for a lord after all, it seems. Well and good enough for me, instead of Eirena's spawn."

Mal looked around at their faces and sat up straighter on Cook's lap, knowing he had something to say that was portenteous.

"The baby isn't dead," he said solemnly. "Merdice came and the little lady in the glass went into the baby's nose."

"Merdice?" Cook repeated, and the kitchen women all looked at one another uneasily at the mention of her name. "What a fanciful tale. He must still be frightened. Little Mal, old Merdice wouldn't come into the house. The outside doors are all locked and nobody would let her come in. You don't need to be frightened of her."

Mal cuddled once more into Cook's ample lap and bit into another cake, letting the crumbs fall on her greasy apron. He was getting sleepy now. He drummed his heels against Cook's knees to keep himself awake, and squirmed, but within minutes he was asleep, with the half-gnawed cake still clutched in his grubby hand.

II

Mal saw Aislinn infrequently, when the nurse carried her, squalling, up and down the courtyard, or, once she was bigger, as she staggered around on the rough flagstones of the great hall, closely attended by a nurse so she would not fall and hurt herself. No nurse could be always so vigilant, and Mal was secretly pleased when Aislinn fell down, or when she hugged a big muddy hound and spoiled her fine little gown. Always the secret fear nagged in the back of Mal's mind that, because of Aislinn, one day Rufus would send him away, as the serving women had said he would.

By all accounts Aislinn was a pretty child, and all the women cooed over her when they got the chance, a treasonable disloyalty that rankled Mal exceedingly. She was a troublesome little brat, and as she became larger she attached herself to him and followed him about, and he wasn't sure how to get rid of her. Mud and water was no deterrent; she came paddling after him with no regard for the hem of her embroidered dress and thin beaded-satin shoes. He could get on his pony and leave her, but she always waited for him, and looking back at her gave him an uncomfortable guilty feeling.

When she was six and he was ten, Lady Eirena's half-hearted and usually futile attempts to govern Aislinn were abandoned. If Aislinn was decked out in the morning in a rich gown of fine fabric encrusted with beading and twining embroidery, the child abandoned the heavy dress somewhere in the meadow or byre in favor of her undersmock, which did not interfere with running and climbing walls and riding horses. Stiff shoes met a similar fate, never to be found again, unless she gave them away to some other child, and dainty slippers were ruined after a day of play-hunting. By the end of the day she looked like a woods nymph in her short smock, girded about with vines and leaves, her loose long hair crowned with flowers and hanging in a pale, tangled cloak around her shoulders.

Mal was not aware of the particular day when he became thrall to her. Perhaps it began the day when he let her ride behind him on his horse—old Baldhere long ago forsaken in favor of a gentle, tall mare. They raced with the wind, laughing as the mare leaped across streams, letting the wind snatch away their shouts. It could have been the day when Mal crept up on her in the woods to frighten her away from following him, and he had found her lying on the ground surrounded by mice and voles, and other little furry creatures were coming from their burrows as she called to them. Her voice was strange and low, and the words she spoke made no sense to Mal. When she saw him watching, she laughed and banished the small animals with another word. Then she called again and a butterfly settled on her outstretched finger, and yet another, until her hand was covered with butterflies and a cloud of them circled over her head.

Mal edged out of his hiding place to look more closely at the bright-winged little creatures.

"How did you do that?" he asked suspiciously.

Aislinn smiled and waved her hand so they scattered once more. "I say their names and they come to me. Oh, Mal, show me the place where Tavis saw the big cat—or are you afraid the cat is still there?"

Mal certainly was not, and they spent the day in the old ruins, where they caught a glimpse of the great silvery cat retreating from them into a dark place between the fallen slabs of stone. Aislinn started crooning to it in her peculiar voice, and the cat replied with its own throaty crooning, coming into the sunlight again, blinking with lazy curiosity as its head swung from side to side, searching for the source of Aislinn's voice.

"Stop!" Mal whispered urgently, his every hair standing

upon end in utmost horror as the cat padded slowly toward them on its huge, silent paws.

"What's wrong? Are you afraid?" Aislinn asked in great surprise, a gleam of merry devilment in her eyes.

"Yes!" Mal blurted. The snow cat could see them now, and the tip of its long tail flirted interestedly as its slitted golden eyes dwelt upon Mal.

"I'll send him away if you promise to let me go with you wherever you go," Aislinn said reasonably. "If you don't, I'll tell everyone how frightened you were when we saw the snow cat."

"You'll tell anyway, and everyone will laugh."

"I won't. You can tell them you touched a snow cat." She reached out and clasped Mal's hand in her own; then she stepped into the clearing, pulling him after her. The great cat padded toward them, its huge head slung low. As Mal gazed at it, all the menace he had been trained to see left the beast. He saw a creature of wondrous strength, a lord of nature among animals, who crouched at Aislinn's feet and gazed up at her with lazy amiability. Mal felt its curiosity as she touched its broad, furrowed head, its willingness to do her bidding. At Aislinn's insistence, Mal touched the snow cat's head also, taking care to keep a tight grip on Aislinn's hand. For a brief moment he had the disturbing feeling that the Dalesmen and their kind were excluded from a force as mighty and ancient as the land itself, where all beasts were united in a common knowledge. That knowledge was denied to Mal and his kind.

Aislinn spoke another word to the snow cat, which got to its feet and moved away with no haste, pausing to look alertly toward the garths and byres of man below before vanishing once more into its grotto.

"Now you can tell the herdboys you touched a snow cat," Aislinn said.

Mal shook his head. "They wouldn't believe it. And you'd

better not tell anyone either or they'll think you're just boasting. Where did you learn his name?"

Aislinn was kneeling in the midst of some flowers, talking to them as she chose a handful of blossoms. "Everything has a name," she said with a shade of annoyance. "You just look at it and know. Even people have names, but they keep them secret."

"My name is Mal, and I don't keep it secret."

"That's not your only name. You mustn't ever tell that one. You must know that! The creatures don't hide their names from me." She looked up at Mal, her pointed face suddenly sober. "Do they tell you their names, Mal?"

"No, of course not," he said disdainfully. "It's a girl-thing to know names."

Nor did it seem unusual that Aislinn could speak to plants, coaxing berries out of hiding so that the branches swung into her reach, or calling the fruit and nuts to drop from the trees when she was hungry. By speaking a name, Aislinn could even banish the pain of cuts and scratches and close a wound so it bled no more.

In the way of all children, these things became commonplace, as much accepted as part of the world of Malmgarth as the huge disc of the red rising sun, the dew that came from nowhere each morning to water the grass and flowers, the glossy-coated new calves and foals that magically appeared at their mothers' sides, young creatures like themselves.

Aislinn liked to be outside before dawn, barefoot in the dew. Long ago her mother and her servants had abandoned their attempts to keep her within the ladies' wing of the keep, teaching her useful things like sewing and embroidery and gossipping. If Mal did not come out, Aislinn sent a bird to twitter in his window, or a hound to jump on his cot and lick his face, treading on him with huge feet all the while.

Then they crept into the kitchen, where the cooks were

starting their work, and Mal carried away what cake and bread they would let the children have. Next they stopped at the dairy for dippers of fresh, warm milk. Then they visited the horses in the mews and ate their breakfast in the hay mow, watching the men harnessing the draught horses. Hitching a ride on a wain would take them far afield for the day, from which point they could range in any direction, pretending to be outlaws of the Waste plotting to pillage Malmgarth, or Rangers exploring the Dales for the first time.

Rufus was content with the situation, if Lady Eirena was not.

"That boy is getting no education," she pointed out frequently over supper in the great hall at night. Mal and Aislinn should have been in bed long before, but they often availed themselves of the opportunity to spy upon their unsuspecting elders.

"That boy," Lady Eirena continued, "is running wild like a hare and he's teaching Aislinn all manner of wicked tricks. She never wears her shoes and she rides a horse with her shift pulled up over her knees and she's forever among the servants and animals, acting as if she were no better than they are. That boy is a young savage, not suitable company for a young lady of the keep!"

Rufus grinned. "You should get her some riding clothes, then. That boy is learning more about this land than if the gamekeeper walked him around it every day. Let him have his freedom a bit longer, and by himself he'll come around to becoming the landlord. The Lady Aislinn will not regret it one day, when she is ruler here. She'll need a landlord who knows Malmgarth's every stone and pathway."

"Her future husband will be lord here, not your fosterling," Lady Eirena replied acidly. "Although I suppose," she added with ill grace, "as our brother's son he may stay as long as he wishes."

"A stranger cannot rule Malmgarth," Rufus said. "A landlord must have his heart in the land, or it will not produce for him. It's a born gift."

"Nonsense," Lady Eirena said. "You speak of the land as if it were alive."

"And it is, my lady sister," Rufus replied.

The idea of Aislinn's future husband coming to Malmgarth only amused Mal and Aislinn. They knew what they would do with any unwelcome intruder—Aislinn would call upon the vines to bind him up, the clouds to rain upon him, and the wolves to chase him away. Always in their minds this unwelcome stranger named Hroc of distant Brettford was inextricably linked with the marriage proxy, a wispy little man of beyond-middle years named Chlodwig. Next to the burly and noisy Rufus, Chlodwig appeared as a withered leaf shaking in the blasts of Rufus's humor. At the wedding feast he scarcely had picked at the food placed upon the plate that he was to share with the bride, Aislinn. With a shudder Aislinn pushed the meat to his side of the plate, with other things she did not like to eat, and drank deeply from the glass that he only sipped at, like the anxious elderly rooster that the other roosters liked to pick at. Aislinn had laughed secretly during the celebration meal, exchanging glances across the table with Mal, who was squirming and uncomfortable in new clothes.

The proxy marriage was promptly forgotten by Aislinn and Mal. In eight years the groom would appear to claim his bride and her land by marriage-right, but eight years was eons to children. The birdlike Chlodwig and his proxy groom, Hroc, were soon ridiculed into nonexistence.

Nothing could frighten Aislinn and Mal into what Lady Eirena considered proper behavior for children—much as she knew about the subject of children or their behavior or how to control it. Her best attempt had been to employ fear, but its effects were not long-lasting. When Aislinn was old enough to start following Mal around on her short legs, Lady Eirena had told the sepulchral tale of the black wain. Mal heard it often himself, with Lady Eirena's sharp nails digging into his arm as she gripped it, her eyes boring into him to emphasize the awfulness of the fate she foresaw for both him and Aislinn if they didn't mend their ways.

"There's a great black wain covered with strange writings of the Old Ones, and it has two great wheels that turn with a sound like thunder. An enormous flayed ox draws the wain, dead these long years but still the evilness of little children keeps him walking and walking, going from house to house where there are evil little children living, who fret their mothers to distraction. Then the ghoul in a long gray cloak who drives the ox and the wain gets down from the wagon with his great hay hook and catches the children with it and carries them away to the black wain, where they can't get out no matter how much they scream and cry. He carries them away to be eaten later by wolves and ravens and evil things who like the taste of wicked children. Would you like for the black wain to come to Malmgarth after you, you heedless little imps?"

The story gave Mal waves of gooseflesh whenever he heard it, even when he thought he was far too old to be frightened by such fancies. But Aislinn always listened open-mouthed, her eyes upturned to her mother with rapt attention no matter how many times Eirena thought to reprimand her daughter with the horror of the black wain.

Inspired, Aislinn almost always sought out some fresh source of trouble, something particularly forbidden to her, and the more horrific it was to Mal the better she liked it.

"Let's go to the ruins of the Old Ones," she suggested after a severe scolding for losing yet another fine dress, this one washed away in the river. "The ruins where I once showed you the snow cat."

"That's a forbidden place," Mal objected. "The Old Ones left a spirit there to keep people out."

"It's a good place," Aislinn said firmly. "Now come, or I shall go alone."

Mal was helpless to protest any further. His only worse crime than accompanying Aislinn was allowing her to get into trouble by herself. Leaving the walls of the keep, they crossed over the bridge that could be withdrawn against possible attackers. On the far side, against the foot of the woods, were the huts of the servants and laborers, who lived beyond the walls of the keep in these times of peace. Within the wood itself, where the trees were most dark and mossy, old Merdice had a hut of stone held together more by moss than by any visible mortar. A winding path led from her house to the keep, where she went each day to the stillroom to dispense the needful cures.

Mal groaned. This was another strongly forbidden pastime: the spying-out of Merdice. Today, luckily, the door was shut tight and no smoke came out of the hole in the roof. A large cat of mingled colors sat washing its face on the stone that served as doorstep. Hearing their approach, it looked up warily, one paw still poised in midair as it studied the intruders. As Aislinn stepped forward, speaking coaxing cat-words Mal was familiar with, the cat turned and vanished into the underbrush.

"He's gone to tell Merdice what we're doing," Mal said. "She always knows everything we do, with that evil eye of hers."

"Nay, she doesn't," Aislinn replied. "She's just a dusty old thing. I'm not afraid of her."

"Yes you are. You always run past the stillroom as fast as you can."

"Not anymore. I think I should like to talk to her sometime, Mal. You're not afraid of her, are you?"

"Afraid of her? I'd sooner be afraid of old Chlodwig." But beneath all his bluster lurked a deep memory tainted with fear and misunderstanding, and Merdice and Aislinn were somehow strongly linked. Mal did not remember much except the tapestry and Merdice flailing at it as she hunted him. If Aislinn had run past the stillroom as fast as she could go, it was to keep up with him.

They did not visit the ruins often, unless they were on horseback in the midst of a longer journey. The site was on a hilltop, and the dressed stones of shattered walls had tumbled down as far as the bottom, leaving a maze of obstacles to thread between to reach the top. Little remained to help them judge the character of the buildings that had once stood there—except a jumble of ornate doorposts and lintels, and fallen pillars adorned with fine carving, all made of a bluish stone that had withstood weathering so well that the cryptic symbols were still easy to discern.

The symbols and the signs of the previous dwellers of the land now called Malmgarth were disturbing to Mal. They made him feel that men were newcomers to the Dales, and temporary newcomers at that. If the builders of such a grand edifice had come to an end, then Malmgarth might too lie waste one day.

Aislinn felt no such qualms. She climbed among the ruins with a fierce intensity, as if she were looking for something she alone could recognize, rather than merely exploring. Mal clambered after her, lest she get out of his sight and disappear into one of the many dark holes that offered themselves to the imprudently curious for inspection. He had not forgotten the snow cat who had laired here two years ago.

Aislinn was not content to explore in the usual areas. She beckoned to Mal and climbed to the top of the hill of broken stone, where they looked down into the area that had once been the courtyard of what seemed to have been a small keep.

"An awkward place for a keep," Mal said. "Too far from the meadowlands and grainfields."

"This was no keep," Aislinn said, her eyes busy with the

scene below. "This was a place people came to and went away from strengthened. Come, there's something down there."

As they went around a shoulder of shattered stone, they looked down into another courtyard area. A circle of pillars still stood, although some of them were broken off short and others stood crookedly. Within that circle was a pavement of patterned colors forming the design of a large, five-pointed star. Someone had cleaned away the rock and rubbish, which now formed a low, crude wall beyond the circle of pillars, that must have covered it. As they watched, a dark figure appeared among the rubble and approached the star pavement, pausing at a point of the star to heap up a small pile of firewood before moving purposefully toward the next.

"It's old Merdice!" Aislinn whispered, and they both crouched down to watch with bated breath.

At first sight of the place Mal had known this was something he did not understand, and the awful grip of fear clamped down upon him. Aislinn, however, had gasped with rapturous delight, as if she greeted the appearance of something lovely and welcome.

Merdice moved from point to point of the star and then took a position in the center, where she placed a silver urn. From her untidy bundle she took a peeled wand. To Mal's horror Aislinn stood up and started climbing down the slope.

"Nay, Aislinn!" he gasped. "That's old Merdice! She must be working evil in such a strange place! The Old Ones made that star . . ."

But Aislinn never hesitated, her bare feet finding the way down the faint path as if by instinct, and Mal had no choice but to follow her. She did not seem to care whether he followed or not; all her attention was for Merdice and the star. Mal reached the bottom of the slope and slipped behind a large rock to watch what Aislinn was going to do. Merdice was certain to report it to Lady Eirena, and there would be more trouble blamed upon Mal, who was supposed to keep Aislinn from harm.

Merdice looked up from her secret works, scowling as was her habit. Aislinn approached her fearlessly and stood gazing at her as if awestruck, or paralyzed by her own temerity.

"What do you here, child, without a guardian?" Merdice demanded sternly.

"You are my guardian," Aislinn said.

Merdice nodded her head once sharply and edged a step nearer Aislinn. "And you are one of the Stillborn, who need no teaching. All things will come to you at the right time. Or you will be brought. My duty is merely to ensure that no evil thing comes near you."

"I have Mal to protect me," Aislinn said.

Merdice shook her head. "Mal will do you no good at the time when you most need someone to defend you. He will abandon you, out of his foolish mortal pride and fear."

Mal's pride was sorely stung. He came around the edge of the rock, mustering as much anger and dignity as a thirteen-year-old boy could muster.

"Aislinn!" he called commandingly. "Come away from there! We should go back now!"

Merdice cast her eye over him and chuckled dryly. "I remember you, poking and prying where you had no business, and I have a warning for you. Don't interfere with things you cannot understand, little mortal. And this girl and her fate are two things you shall not interfere with."

"She's only trying to frighten us," Mal said to Aislinn. "Let's leave her to the Old Ones. Perhaps the snow cat will find her and make a feast of her old, dry bones. Now come, let us go."

Merdice spared him a withering glance before turning back to Aislinn. "You needn't listen to him, my fair one. He can command you in no way."

There was an unpleasant glint of triumph in her dark eyes, but Aislinn drew back toward Mal.

"Mal is my friend," she said, "and I like him better than I

like you, guardian though you may be. Mal will keep me from harm, as he always has done."

Turning quickly she came toward Mal. For a long moment Mal and Merdice stood eye-locked, glaring at each other in mutual dislike and distrust. Then Merdice turned and snatched up the silver cup and thrust it into her bag, muttering angrily.

Thereafter, Mal began to watch more closely the comings and goings of Merdice, and with uneasy surprise he noted how often she seemed to be attending to some ill creature or harvesting some plant within sight of Aislinn. The windows of the stillroom gave her a view of Aislinn's window in the ladies' wing of the keep, as well as of the lower door into the courtyard.

Lady Eirena became more grim as Aislinn bloomed into a tall young girl of lithe stature and long clean limbs and disturbing steady gray eyes that often gazed unblinking at nothing for long periods of time, as if Aislinn were considering matters of grave importance. Supposedly, young girls of the keep had nothing more important to consider than looking as pretty as possible, or perhaps what color of wool to use next in a tapestry or embroidery.

Aislinn questioned where she should have remained silent and ignorant.

"Mother, where did we come from? Before, I mean—the world before the Dales."

"Before the Dales? There was no world before the Dales, child. Our ancestors came here long before the war with Alizon and they made the garths and keeps, and there was no before. Who put such a notion into your head? Was it Mal, or was it Merdice?"

"Mal does not know, and neither does Merdice. If she does, she doesn't tell me. But I don't believe she knows. She's merely a servant."

"A servant indeed, and you shouldn't talk with her so

much. It isn't seemly for the lady of the keep to be too familiar. If I had my say, Merdice would be gone long ago."

"Merdice is a guardian. She must stay. No one knows the fields and groves as she does, and where the good herbs grow. You need not fear Merdice, Mother. There's no harm in her."

"What peculiar, fanciful notions you have, child. In three years you'll have no time to brood about such foolishness as secret powers and spells. You'll have a husband to take care of, and children soon enough after. If only I had taken you in hand better as a child, and forbidden you to run about like a wild thing with Mal—"

"You could not have stopped me then, Mother, any more than you can stop me now from doing what I think fit."

"Such talk! Do you want to break my heart, after all I've done for you?"

"There are things I must do, Mother."

"Nonsense. You are a young lady of gentle birth, and there is nothing you must do except marry and produce an heir to Malmgarth."

"Nay, Mother. I have other things."

"Indeed! And who decided you must be so high and mighty and important? You're just a girl, my dear, and one day you'll discover of what little importance you truly are."

Aislinn smiled her strange, rare smile, a smile of secrets and hidden sadness. "Mother, none of us is of little importance."

Now that Mal had turned seventeen, Rufus began taking an earnest interest in teaching him the duties of a landlord, and many times Aislinn could not go with him. Rufus took him to the fairs in the fall to sell or buy grain and livestock, flax and nettle for weaving, fine cloth for the ladies, and innumerable other wares all displayed in tented booths for sale or barter.

As many of the household of Malmgarth as could be spared rode to one particular fair in a procession of wains to carry the ladies and the bartering goods. Aislinn and her mother and her two aunts had a wain to themselves, but as soon as she could escape, Aislinn bestrode her horse and rode alongside Mal. When they reached the fair, she went with Mal and Rufus to look at animals and tools of the farming trade. She was now thirteen and growing into a young lady, but she still had no use for a long, smothering gown stiff with embroidery, nor any use for the company of other keep ladies and their daughters. Nor did she any longer shed her confining clothing in the meadow to dance airily free in her thin shift; Lady Eirena had conceded so far as to allow her shorter, divided skirts for riding and tall boots to protect her feet and legs. Aislinn, however, never lost her relish for running barefoot in the dew with her pale hair streaming free of the nets and combs and pins thought appropriate for ladies. And Mal did not like to see her bedecked in fine gowns, with her hair tightly braided and coiled, any more than Aislinn enjoyed such confinement herself.

In the company of Mal at the fair she walked along looking as much at the other people as she did at all the wares offered for her perusal. Still wearing her plain riding skirt and boots, she eyed the other young girls in their elegant gowns, put on especially for the fairing and the chance glances of possible young suitors.

More than a few curious glances came her way, and Mal saw industrious whispering going on behind hands and fans, and sly eyes turned in her direction. He began to seethe, although Aislinn was interested only in the wares in the traders' booths—silver spurs, bridle ornaments, bells for harnesses, and fine saddlecloths of bright colors.

"That's the lady Aislinn, who is to marry Hroc of Brettford," said one of the whisperers from a clump of ladies gathered beside a weaver's stall. "A plain, pale thing she is, is she not? The young lord will be happier with the land than he will be with such a wife!"

"Will Brettford come to the fair this year?" queried another woman. "If they do, this will be the old lord's chance to see what sort of wife his son is getting. No one knows what the sire is of that child. The lady Eirena never chose to show him to anyone."

"Hist! Here she comes! Be still!"

If Aislinn heard, she gave no sign, but Mal bestowed a fierce glower upon the gossipping ladies as he passed.

"There's a deal too much cackling from these geese here," he growled loudly to Aislinn as he hurried her along.

Aislinn, however, was not to be hurried when she wanted to see something. Standing apart from the merchants' booths, a ragged booth where a juggler was entertaining a sparse group seemed to draw her eager feet toward it. A dark-eyed youth played a stringed instrument as accompaniment to the juggler's amusing chatter, and it was to this youth Aislinn was attracted. She pushed her way through the small crowd to face him directly, her manner quick and her body trembling with eagerness. A swift beam of recognition passed between Aislinn and this ragged young minstrel, who lived upon the road and from the bounty of strangers. He was nearer to her age than Mal's, and his smile was bright and quick in his sun-browned face, as if he had any right whatsoever to be so forward to a lady so much his better.

Mal smoldered, tugging Aislinn away. "There's a better show on the other side," he said. "These fellows are nothing but wandering beggars—and impudent to ladies besides."

"Oh look, Mal!" She halted beside a booth, her countenance suddenly clouding. "He's got birds in cages! I'd like to buy them all and set them free! Do it, Mal!"

Mal gripped her arm and tried to hurry her away from the twittering captives. "Come along, Aislinn! Let him sell his birds. They'll live much longer as ladies' pets than they would on their own in the wild."

"How would you like to exchange your freedom for a long life in captivity?" Aislinn demanded angrily, her eyes flashing.

She planted her feet and glowered at the bird seller, not minding the curious and amused onlookers.

She was going to be headstrong; Mal knew all the signs. He stifled a huge sigh and felt for his purse. It wasn't fat, but he could probably induce the bird seller to liberate all his captives for as much as he had.

"Little birds are good companions for ladies," the bird seller began indignantly. "There's no reason to take on about keeping them in cages. They don't mind a bit, being fed every day and kept safe from hawks and weasels. It's a life lots of us wouldn't mind ourselves." Nevertheless, he took the purse and began opening the cages.

The men waiting for their wives chuckled. Mal flushed scarlet, darting a murderous glance at Aislinn. Or rather at the spot where she had stood a moment before. She was gone, probably drawn away by some other gaudy attraction of the fair.

Or perhaps that ragged fellow from the juggler's tent had followed her and kidnapped her, thinking to ransom a pretty pile of gold from Rufus for her return. Any lascivious fellow in the crowd would covet her if his lusting eye fell upon her. The evils that could befall Aislinn without his protection were legion. Mal plunged through the thickening crowds, cursing the darkening sky. Straight to the juggler's booth he went, but the juggler and his son were yet entertaining the ragged crowd. Mal searched around their tent and wagon and saw no sign of Aislinn. The juggler's wife sat clutching her baby, terrified into silence by the fury of his manner.

Mal rounded upon her at last, demanding, "Where is the young girl? She wore a red jacket and riding clothes!"

The woman stared at him in growing fear. "I saw her," she whispered. "She's another one of them, as is the boy. His mother died when he was born, and I wish he'd gone with her, and him that juggles, too. Your lady is like the lad. I'd know another one of them, after what I've seen—"

"Is he your husband—the juggler?" Mal demanded.

"Aye, and that is the worst of my luck. Stay away from that juggler, lad. He's not—" She ended with a gasp as a shadow loomed against the tent suddenly. In the light that remained, Mal recognized Merdice. The sight of her chilled him, and he had the feeling that meeting her at such a time was not a good omen.

"Idle tongues do a lot of rattling," Merdice said, and the woman took her baby and slunk away. To Mal she said, "Come you, and I'll show you what you seek. A fine protector you are."

"You know where she is?"

Merdice nodded a single sharp nod in the direction of a nearby booth. "I always know where she is."

"What are you doing here?" Mal demanded. "What would your sort care about a fairing?"

"Nothing at all," Merdice replied.

Inside the booth, Mal found Aislinn in the midst of a company of four other young ladies, with their mothers and attendants looking on. They chattered like a flock of birds, delighted with the company of one another as they talked about their homes in distant Dales. Mal looked in but did not enter. Merdice stopped outside, as if she intended to wait there.

"Now are you satisfied?" Merdice inquired.

"No," Mal answered. "How does she know those girls? She likes talking to them, yet there are other girls she refuses to speak to. She thinks girls are boring and stupid."

"And so she should, because they are," Merdice replied maliciously. "Have you met her future husband yet? He's here at the fair, and Eirena is arranging for them to meet."

"I don't care," Mal snapped.

"Why should you be jealous? You've always known she wasn't for you."

Mal heatedly strode away a few paces, then he came back for Aislinn, stepping into the tent.

"It's getting late, my lady," he greeted her politely. "Your mother will be getting anxious."

On the way back to the Malmgarth tents she looped her arm through his and sighed happily. "I've never had such fun," she said, her eyes still feasting on the treats they passed. "We must come here every year and see the ones we met before."

"Who were those girls you were talking to?" Mal asked. "You'd never met them before."

"Oh! Mearr and Lilias and Ana!" She skipped as she walked. "I feel as if I'd met them before. They're friends. Does it seem to you that you know friends at once when you meet them, and no one else seems that way? No one else is the same, or ever will be. I have four friends—Mearr, Lilias, Ana, and you. And Merdice. I've decided I want to make her my fifth friend. She walked all this way just to be where she could guard me. I want you to go back to the juggler's tent and tell her she is to come and share my mother's tent."

"She won't do it," Mal said. "And your mother won't like it. Merdice smells."

Aislinn considered. "Perhaps you're right. Merdice wouldn't like my mother. But I shall win Merdice over to my side somehow, see if I don't."

Mal secretly breathed a sigh of relief, but his sorest trial was yet to come. On the morrow, Lady Eirena brought about the long-awaited meeting of Aislinn and her legal bridegroom, Hroc of Brettford.

Hroc was no withered sapling, as was the much maligned Chlodwig. Mal was certain he would hate him on sight, and he was not disappointed when Hroc and his father's retinue approached the place where Rufus was tented. Hroc rode a mincing white stallion, magnificently caparisoned—and Mal thought hotly of the fine silvery Malmgarth horse Rufus had sent the young rogue as a wedding gift. Beside Hroc rode his father, Lord Brettford, on a chestnut horse, and behind came the ladies on horseback. Brettford was too far away for people to travel comfortably in wheeled vehicles, so everyone rode and carried their trade wares on strings of packhorses.

More fine gifts were exchanged between Lord Brettford and Lady Eirena and Lord Rufus, while Aislinn and Hroc stood by stiffly, waiting for the formalities to reach the point of formal introduction of the bride to the groom. If the meeting had taken place at home in Malmgarth, Mal would have slipped away to hide his raging jealousy, but here in the open meadows of the fairing place, he was forced to stand still and glare his hatred at Hroc from the ranks of Lord Rufus's eleven men of arms.

Aislinn made her curtsey and immediately subsided into wan silence, doing her best to look pale and listless and drooping. Mal knew she was sulking in the rigid dress she had been forced to wear, which could have stood up by itself without a reluctant young girl inside it. Lady Eirena had supervised the elaborate dressing of Aislinn's hair, which looked unnatural on such a slender girl, robbing her of her own fresh beauty and attempting to invest her with something far more guileful.

Hroc was a simpering youth near Mal's age, glossy with a superficial politeness that did not extend much further into the Malmgarth hierarchy than Lord Rufus and Lady Eirena. He scarcely acknowledged his introduction to Mal, who had not ceased to look as menacing as he possibly could. Mal did not care if Hroc saw his hatred; he would have slain him on the spot if looks were daggers.

Before the fairing was over, Mal heard through the gossips that young Lord Hroc was not displeased with his bride, however had he not approved the bargain it would have made no difference. As the youngest son he was forced to be content with what fate had dealt him. An invitation to Malmgarth was strongly hinted for, but Rufus extended no such and they rode back to Malmgarth with the lady Eirena livid with rage at her brother's rudeness the entire way.

III

Aislinn sought out Mal's company when she could, more shyly now than in the past. To her silent hurt and dismay, Mal seemed remote and even unfriendly, where once he had possessed almost her entire affection and wholehearted trust. His manner was so cold and stiff that she feared she must have unforgivably betrayed his friendship in some unconscious manner. In company he was severely polite to her, but when she found him alone he virtually rebuffed her, falling into sullen silences punctuated by the shortest of answers to her speech.

So it had seemed to Aislinn since the fair when Hroc had been presented to Malmgarth as its prospective lord. Or perhaps the cause of Mal's hostile behavior was her discovery of the voices on the wind, which had come to her the day after they returned from the fair as she was riding with Mal near the ruins. So plainly had she heard the short snatch of speech that she turned to Mal, thinking he had spoken to her.

"Nay, it was not I," he said rather crossly. "I heard nothing. Is it a crime if a man wants to be silent?"

"Only when the so-called man is only seventeen," she said in jest. "Truly, Mal, I heard a voice."

"The voice of your husband, Hroc, perhaps," Mal snapped.

Aislinn's heart turned cold at the mention of Hroc, who would appear in Malmgarth altogether too soon at the end of three short years to claim her as his wife and Malmgarth as his home. All the joy went out of her in an instant, and to make matters worse Mal was angry at her for some unknown cause.

"Why are you angry? If I said something wrong, I didn't mean it as an unfriend. You know there's no one in the world I like better than you, Mal."

"Don't be such a child, Aislinn. You're the betrothed wife of Hroc and I don't think we should go about alone together anymore." He rode his horse away from her a few paces, leaving her gazing at him, stricken and white.

"Are we no longer friends?" Aislinn's voice trembled, and a great stab of pain gripped her throat and crushed her heart until she could scarcely breathe.

Mal's shoulders rose and sagged in a long sigh. "Yes, but not as we once were. You belong to him—and not anyone else."

"I belong to myself and to Malmgarth," Aislinn said fiercely, blinking back tears that were now angry. "Hroc is neither friend nor enemy to us. Who are you to tell me who I belong to? I belong where I please!"

But she had not reckoned with Mal's pride, or Mal himself. She could attach herself to him and ride out with him and follow him around as usual, but Mal held himself remote from her. He spent more time with Rufus in the fields and meadows, and Aislinn realized how lonely the keep could be without the warmth of Mal's friendship. Always before he had found time for riding with her, or for simply talking by the kitchen fire. Now, instead of warm hopes, there was a cold knot of loneliness in Aislinn's heart.

Merdice went about her business as usual, seeking out the good herbs to replenish her stores, preparing them for the easing of man or beast. She noted with satisfaction that the interfering Mal was taken away more by Rufus to be instructed in the duties of his status as landlord, and that Aislinn was left to her own devices. From the beginning Merdice had worried about Mal, finding him spying upon her as she had. But no one had listened to the little brat's tale, and Merdice had breathed a sigh of relief. By now, a dozen of years later and longer, he would have forgotten completely what he had seen.

The artful little minx began coming around, even as Merdice had suspected she would, when the time arrived. From that day on the ruins, Merdice had known the curiosity was there and she secretly rejoiced. Aislinn would be everything Merdice had hoped—everything the Old Ones had planned.

Aislinn began leaving things she had come across in her solitary wanderings—a handful of fresh-picked burnbalm with the dew still on it, a snakeskin, the teeth and bristles of a wild boar killed by one of the huntsmen. Merdice waited, knowing what was stirring in the girl. She also watched, following when Aislinn never suspected. She saw that the girl still called the creatures and plants by their true names, instead of forgetting them as she grew older.

Some of the other Stillborn, Merdice knew from their guardians, had forgotten their ways when they became old enough to know they were not typical children. The wise ones had foreseen that the use of mortal bodies would have strange and sometimes unwelcome results. As Merdice read the sendings, she learned that some of the children betrayed themselves innocently and were set aside as lunatic. A few were indeed badly torn between their two heritages, and not to be relied upon. Some had died of illnesses or accidents. Only ten of the original twenty were thriving, unsuspected among their mortal families, grasping eagerly for the keys of knowledge as they gradually came into their hands. In them would repose the knowledge, and the responsibility of maintaining the ancient knowledge.

Aislinn's curiosity about Merdice increased as she was left more to her own devices. In short, she was often lonely, not caring for the company of her mother and her aunts, nor did she care about the distant cousins who were sent occasionally to Malmgarth. The advent of company in the house was excuse for Aislinn to slip away, and increasingly she went to the stillroom. At first she watched Merdice working and was silent. Merdice tested her knowledge of the secret names, not suspecting that before the end of a year it would be she who would listen more often while Aislinn talked.

"The little redwort is more powerful for stimulating the heart than the witch's thimble," Aislinn would observe gravely, "and harder to find. I shall show you where it grows, and we can bring back a root for your garden."

Not always would she tell Merdice the secret names.

"There is too much Power in that name," she would say.

"Do you think I can't use it wisely?" Merdice demanded angrily when some such was refused her. "Have I not been a guardian of the Power for all my life? Is this jewel I wear merely a bauble to enhance my beauty?"

Aislinn, though young, gazed into the face of Merdice without fear. "It is forbidden for a reason. I know no other answer. What am I, Merdice, that I am placed somehow above you, who are so wise and old?"

Merdice sighed, her temper forgotten. "My dear, I know not the answer. It is within yourself and will be revealed when the Old Ones deem you ready for the knowledge. Until then, I am your guardian and you are the vessel of a power greater than anything created by mortal man. Your purpose will come to you, a thing which you do not now dream. Now is the time for preparation. You know the names of all things, greater and lesser. You can cure wounds, this I have seen. You must learn to hear the voices and understand them, and one day you will learn to speak to those far distant from you."

Aislinn accompanied Merdice to the Place of the Voices, as the young girl named the ruins of the Old Ones with such a sense of certainty and rightness that they both knew it was the true name of the fallen fortress.

"Who are these voices?" Aislinn asked impatiently. She sat within a small circle of broken pillars, turning her head from side to side in the wind, hearing faint scraps of speech blowing past her. She had grasped only the most tantalizing of scraps at first, after Merdice had shown her where to sit. At once she had been gripped with a sense of belongingness, and she had stayed in the sending seat until she was on the point of exhaustion.

"Ones like you are speaking," Merdice replied. "You must learn to hear only one voice at a time."

"Can you understand them, Merdice?" Aislinn asked.

"Only when someone is sending directly to me. I have not the power that you will have one day."

At last the day arrived when Aislinn, straining her senses to hear the voices, suddenly cried out, "It's Mearr! I can hear her! She's speaking to the juggler's boy, and his name is Hwitan!"

She stayed in the seat until sundown, with Merdice watching nearby and holding the restless horses. Merdice made intermittent feeble attempts to tear Aislinn away that were ignored.

"There are others like me!" Aislinn said, when she finally noticed how dark it was getting and realized they must go back to the keep. "We are ten in number, Merdice, and that is all that is left."

Detecting a note of sorrow in the girl's tone, Merdice replied, "Perhaps the other Stillborn will get another chance someday—perhaps there will be more beings such as you. We don't know what the Old Ones intended by placing their spirits within human mortal frames."

Aislinn rode in silence, her silvery hair glowing like rays of the moon itself. "I am learning more about my Purpose," she said slowly. "The Stillborn speak of the Waste and what lies within it. We don't know yet what is there, but it is something important to the Old Ones—and to us, since we are of the Old Ones. Merdice"—she hesitated long before speaking—"I never knew before how alone I truly am."

"Tush, child. I shall always be with you, whatever comes to pass. And there are nine others like you."

"But what about Mal? And my mother. And Rufus? I'm not as they are. I'm apart from everyone—except the other Stillborn."

"You owe them nothing. If not for the intervention of the Old Ones, they would have had nothing but a stillborn child. You would be nothing but an essence in a bottle. The Power created you, child, and it alone will sustain you. These others will soon pass away from you when they learn what you are. There is no future for you except the Power."

"Mal will not desert me," Aislinn said.

Merdice sniffed. "Mal is no different from the others. He'll turn his back when he discovers how different you are. No man would want a wife with a soul from the Old Ones. Our fancy young Lord Hroc wants healthy children with no blot upon them—or tie to other powers. He wants a wife who stays in the keep and attends to the home fires. That's not the life for you. Nor do we know what powers you might lose in the coupling with a mortal man. All could be lost."

"Or perhaps nothing," Aislinn added. "I don't much like to think about living your sort of life, alone with your Power, feared and despised by almost everyone. Are you never lonely, Merdice? Do you not wish for just one other person in the entire world who will be with you as a staunch, true friend as long as you live?"

"Pshaw," Merdice snorted. "That's a lot of girlish nonsense. I think you're acting very human."

"And feeling very human," Aislinn said. "It's very well to live your entire life in service of the Power, but I don't want to be alone."

"Then be with your own kind, who understand you."

"But even the Stillborn cannot replace my lady mother, and Rufus—and Mal. Did you never love anyone, Merdice?"

"I was taken away from my mother and family when I was six years of age and I never saw them again. Loving mortal beings will lead you only to distress. They are by nature intransigent, and inconsistent, as well as inconstant. Save yourself the grief and devote yourself instead to the Power. It will never fail you."

"And I must make my human feelings die? How will I be happy if I do that?"

"It's a human mistake to think overmuch about happiness. There's not much of it to be found among your human family that I've noticed."

"But there's the hope of it, the memory of it, and the idea of it," Aislinn said. "I don't think the Power has much to do with happiness."

"Certainly not with the trivial kind you're thinking of. You will be complete only in the Power, and completeness must be happiness. The choices are made for you, Aislinn. There is nothing you can do to alter your fate."

"We shall see about that," Aislinn answered stubbornly. "Is it human to believe you control your own destiny?"

"Very human," Merdice replied in exasperation. "If I did not know better, I would say you were completely one of them. I fear I shall have to discuss this with the other guardians. I hope the other chosen ones aren't similarly infested with human emotions."

Aislinn found increasing comfort in sendings from the other Stillborn, until the tenor of the messages abruptly changed. From the south, Mearr reported strangers who said they had come in ships from the land across the sea. Despite their engaging tales of adventure and ingratiating manners, Mearr did not trust them. They asked too many questions and seemed far too interested in the numbers of men-at-arms stationed at the keep.

Lilias reported other strangers, and Ana, and the rest of the Stillborn in scattered holds across the southlands and up the seacoast toward Malmgarth. Hwitan and the juggler saw more strangers and travelers than was usual for the roads of the Dales, and all the strangers had the seeming of outlanders, and all asked a great many questions concerning the land between coast and Waste.

"Is this the Purpose?" Aislinn asked of Merdice. "Do the strangers know the secret of the Waste?"

"Even you with your knowledge cannot answer that," Merdice replied. "How do you expect me to know?"

Aislinn laughed nervously and paced up and down the length of the stillroom, pausing to examine this or that infusion or dripping bag extracting juices. Her eyes were brilliant when she looked at Merdice, and her entire body radiated tension.

"It is the Purpose for which we were sent," she whispered. "It is almost time. Do you know," she added with a strained laugh, "last night I dreamed of the black wain my mother used to try to frighten me with. I saw it just as plainly as if it were real, and I got into it, and went away. I always thought that wagon was death, coming for me."

"It was only a dream," Merdice said. "You are too fanciful—another of your unfortunate human characteristics. The other guardians have the same problems. If you do have a Purpose, I fear for its success, as long as you cannot set aside your human fears and fancies."

"It's no fear or fancy that a strange force is coming into the Dales from across the sea," Aislinn replied, gazing with unseeing eyes into the sunny courtyard beyond the coolness of the stillroom. "And I cannot rest with any comfort until I know why they are here. They must not go into the Waste, Merdice."

"What is in the Waste?" Merdice asked.

Aislinn shook her head and moved toward the courtyard. "I cannot say, Merdice, but it must be protected."

When they finally arrived in Malmgarth, the strangers were as Aislinn had foreseen in Merdice's scrying cup. There were four of them, dressed well enough in traveling cloaks and chain mail, but to Aislinn they had the air of hired men outfitted and paid for a purpose. To Lord Rufus and the others, the strangers were fair-seeming and courteous, and plausible in their story of seeking unoccupied land for settlement. It was only sensible that men on such a mission would want to know how much protection Malmgarth thought necessary, and what threats might arise from the direction of the Waste.

They stayed at Malmgarth three days, and by the beginning of the third Aislinn sought out Mal. It was a foggy morning, and she waited on her horse on a rise of ground, knowing Mal would soon be riding by her position.

She nudged her horse forward to meet him halfway.

"Mal, there's evil abroad in the Dales," she greeted him. "The strangers beneath our roof are no friends to us. They are the harbingers of war and death. Once the Dales were overrun with men from over the seas, with strange weapons and wains that moved with no horse pulling. More bloodshed is coming to the Dales, and the threat is already upon our soil."

"How do you know all this? Did Merdice give you these ideas? It sound like something an old crow would cark about. She's not a clean one, when it comes to strange taints. I wonder that Lord Rufus has tolerated her so many years."

"Would it astonish you to know that I am as unclean as Merdice? If not more so? You should know it well, Mal, seeing me call creatures and plants by their names, and a host of other gifts given to me by the Old Ones. I am not as you are, Mal. That which I was to be perished in that stillborn babe. It was the Old Ones who put this life into that body made by Lady Eirena. You should know it well. You were there and you saw what Merdice did."

"I thought it was a nightmare."

"It was no dream. Nor is it any dream that the Dales are being invaded again, and the strangers from Alizon are again searching for that which is hidden in the Waste. Even now the spies are under our roof."

"What would the Old Ones have us do? Kill them?"

"It is what they deserve. We are not murderers of guests,

so they should be captured and taken back to their ships. If this were done throughout the Dales from north to south, the invaders would know we are ready to defend that which is hidden. They will not walk through us burning and pillaging so easily this time."

Mal was silent, ominously silent. Perhaps she should not have told him all that she was.

"How do you know for sure they are coming from the south, through all the settlements?"

"There are ten Stillborn such as I am. Mearr in the south speaks to everyone through sendings, and Hwitan the juggler's boy has traveled from south to north many times. What they have seen makes their warnings very dire indeed. Please believe me, Mal. Everyone in the Dales is in the greatest danger."

"What would the Old Ones have us do? Call together an army?"

"Yes, but it must be done before it is too late. Last time the invaders came searching, the Dalesmen quarreled among themselves too long. We must not be afraid to raise up leaders over ourselves this time."

"We? Are you certain you wish to include yourself in our number, my lady? If what you say is true, then you are not of the Dales, but rather of those Old Ones."

"I am a Daleswoman first, and this is where I belong!" Aislinn snapped.

"Then you plan to live here at Malmgarth with Hroc and raise up his children as a Daleswoman for the rest of your life? Is that what you intend to do?"

Aislinn hesitated. "I cannot say. To tell the fate of a man is forbidden."

"I thought as much. You will leave Malmgarth to be with those others like you. You wouldn't care for this narrow life, after knowing what the Old Ones can give you."

"Mal—you and I must be together. Either I will follow

you, or you will come with me when the call comes. I can't exist apart from you—even knowing you're angry at me. You are my one true friend, and I'll never have another."

"You'll have your husband, Hroc."

"Don't be foolish. I know nothing of him except his name and his face, and neither is important to me. Without you near, I'll be lonely for the rest of my life. You are like the other half of my soul, Mal."

"Your soul came from a bottle out of Merdice's old bag," Mal said. "What need can it have for me, a common Dalesman? What do you Old Ones care about the people of the Dales, except as fodder to protect whatever it is that is hidden in the Waste?"

"I am not an Old One," Aislinn said.

"But you are. You know the real names of all things. You can heal wounds. You command the storm clouds. You speak with your people many miles away. The gulf that separates me from you is so wide and deep that we will never see its sides and bottom. You are one of them. You will never be one of us. But your warnings will be heeded. The Old Ones have the gift for stirring men to battle."

He swung his horse's head around and sent the animal plunging back toward Malmgarth, leaving Aislinn behind. She started her horse forward, letting it carry her where it would. The pain in her heart was like the gulf Mal had described, so huge it threatened to swallow her, and achingly empty and hopeless. In his own hurt he was a stranger to her.

The horse carried her as if by habit to the Place of the Voices. Aislinn dismounted and approached the sending seat. At once the voice of Mearr was in her ear, questioning. "What is the source of all this grief?"

"I love a mortal man," Aislinn replied heavily, "and a love such as that is doomed."

"Are we not mortals?" Mearr asked. "These bodies are just as theirs, with the same dreads and desires. Why should we not love mortal men?"

"The Power sets us apart," Aislinn answered bitterly. "We can never be ordinary Daleswomen, with our knowledge and the Voices whispering in our ears. We were created for a Purpose—the protection of that which is hidden in the Waste. How can we be ordinary with such burdens?"

"The burdens will be greater or lesser at times when there is greater or lesser need," Mearr answered. "In times of lesser need we will be almost ordinary."

"But will Mal come to see me as almost ordinary, or will he always see me as one apart? If we were so great and wise, would it hurt so much?"

"We are also human, sister, and with human nature, nothing can be truly foretold. It is a fearsome mixture. Even the Old Ones cannot foresee our fates."

"Why not? Perhaps the Old Ones are not so great and wise either! Why must we suffer?"

Mearr was silent a moment, and Aislinn could hear the voices of some of the Stillborn. Ana had hurt her leg falling from a horse when she was a small child, and the pain had never left her since, and others had hurts similar to Aislinn's. A storm of complaints rose in Aislinn's head until she had to break away. Rising from the seat, she took a single step, then a single clear voice pierced the din of voices, piercing Aislinn's hurt with a single word.

"Asmerillion!"

Always the sudden gift of knowledge had made Aislinn tremulous and weak for a short space, but this was the sort of knowledge that staggered her. She dropped to her knees on the green turf, gasping, her heart laboring until she thought it might burst. She had been given a Name in which there reposed as much power as the knowledge of her own Name. She trembled in fear and humility, knowing afresh the burden of Power and its imperative for proper use. The Name she had been given was Mal's, and she now had the power to command him as if he were a puppet in her hands, if she so desired.

There was that within her which would exult in his domination, and it warred with her knowledge that misusing her powers in this way was an evil that would lead her to misery.

"Merdice!" she called, and the guardian answered with a mind-touch from the rubbly hill above, where she had been waiting and watching. She came down to the sending seat as if she had been expecting to be sent for, crushing a pungent herb between her hands.

"Smell this. It will clear your mind."

"Merdice, I know Mal's name."

"You must never use it or you will destroy any love he has for you."

"This I know, but I'm afraid to lose him."

"Do you want to keep him in a cage? Do you not remember the cage birds at the fairing, and how it hurt you to see them imprisoned?"

Aislinn stopped her restless pacing to and fro, standing still to gaze into her own memories a moment with a faint smile softening her lips. Either the soothing herb or her own wisdom calmed her turmoil. In a more gentle, if sadder tone she said, "So it must be. I will never use his Name to bind him to me, if he wishes to go. Mal is no cage bird; he's a hawk no fetters can bind."

It was evening, and a heavy dew had settled by the time Aislinn and Merdice reached the keep. Aislinn's feet and hem were soaked, as she had insisted upon Merdice's riding her horse while she walked. On the morrow, Aislinn had a fever and kept to her bed, attended by Lady Eirena and Merdice, an unlikely pair, but resigned to the fate that had thrown them together in the joint custodianship of Aislinn.

Aislinn fretted at the wasted time, sending Merdice for this or that concoction to reduce her fever, but after a short space the fever always returned. By night Aislinn tossed in her bed, plagued by dreams of the black wain and the flayed ox.

"Where is Mal?" she asked on the third day. Her face was

pale and her eyes shadowed by the fever's wasting. "I must see Mal—before I go away."

Lady Eirena attempted to soothe her, but Aislinn did not cease to call for Mal.

"Mal is gone," Lady Eirena confessed fearfully. "Gone with Rufus to join forces with Lord Brettford."

"Brettford!" whispered Aislinn, closing her eyes and sinking back as if the strength had left her. "Ill-fated Brettford! He must be stopped—before the black wain . . ."

Lady Eirena and Merdice stared at one another. They had never liked each other, but their disliking was now forgotten.

"Is there nothing you can do?" Lady Eirena whispered. "My daughter is dying!"

"This is no fever of ordinary cause," Merdice replied slowly. "My lady, this child is not wholly your daughter, and there are forces that hold sway over her which you can scarcely understand. She was brought to you for a Purpose, after the life of your child had flown. The Old Ones do not wish for their knowledge to vanish. There is that which is hidden in the Waste, and it must be protected from wrong use. This child is one of ten whose Purpose is to defend that secret. If she chooses to fulfill her Purpose, she must leave you and Mal and all she loves. She struggles between the pull of her two natures—mortal and ancient. It is this struggle that gives her fever. She is yet only a child, with such a choice as this to be made."

Lady Eirena sank to her knees beside Aislinn's cot, gazing into her daughter's face. "Was I too proud, too greedy? I wanted Malmgarth for her, and a rich husband to bring her fame. I should have let her choose Mal. Mal could have kept her here. There is no one she loves but Mal, and I was envious. Now I will lose her completely, won't I, Merdice?"

"I know not, my lady. Such a one as I is unable to read her future."

"My daughter, can you hear me?" Lady Eirena bent closer.

"I will release you from the marriage contract with Hroc. You must become strong again. There is something you must do—the Purpose for which you were sent. If Mal is your destiny, then you must go after him. No one will interfere. You are still my daughter, whatever else you may be. Let the fools and cowards say what they will; I am proud to call you daughter."

Aislinn's sleep became easier. The two women watched over her until just before dawn, when even the vigilant Merdice dozed away lightly. Aislinn awoke and crept softly out of her bed. Her mother slept uncomfortably in a chair, cheek pillowed upon one hand. Aislinn gently kissed her, then touched Merdice on the shoulder.

"It's time," she whispered, taking up only her shoes and her cloak. "The black wain—it's coming."

Merdice awoke and followed her from the room and down the stairway to the door to the courtyard. The door was securely barred and bolted with heavy locks, but they all slid aside soundlessly and the door fell open to let them pass. It closed silently after them.

Aislinn stopped in the center of the courtyard, her loose hair catching the moonlight in a pale nimbus around her head. Her head kept turning, as if she was listening to sounds Merdice could not hear.

"Child, you are ill," Merdice began.

"It comes!" Aislinn whispered suddenly.

A distant rumbling of wooden wheels sounded almost like thunder. The sound grew louder, punctuated by the cracking of a whip. Aislinn turned toward the great outer gates of the keep, which were safely locked and would remain so until Lord Rufus returned. Nothing could come through that portal—yet a cloud swirled there, filled with bits of whirling light that gradually resolved into the form of a great black wagon with two high wheels carven with symbols familiar to Merdice. The wagon was drawn by a giant ox. Its naked form was gray and glistening, streaked with blood, and it moved toward them inexorably as in a nightmare. The hooded driver raised his whip and cracked it with a sound like lightning striking, and the power of it rushed by Merdice and Aislinn, tearing at their cloaks and hair.

Merdice clutched Aislinn's arm, trying to pull her away, but Aislinn could not be moved. The wain rumbled to a halt and the driver beckoned with his whip. The hay hook stood in the whip socket, its sharp edges gleaming with blue fire. Aislinn pulled Merdice forward, ignoring her babble of protest, which was snatched away in the torrents of wind.

IV

The rest of the Stillborn were in the wagon. A ripple of excitement passed through the other nine and their guardians as Aislinn took her seat. They communicated without a sound, yet Merdice found herself in the center of a sea of excited chatter. She was not conscious of leaving Malmgarth behind in a mighty crashing of wind and thunder and an eerie flaring of lightning, as was witnessed by those who were left behind. The wain traveled not by conventional means; instead of lurching along over a rutted Dales road, it somehow soared, with nothing to be seen distinctly through clouds of swirling mist.

Aislinn strained her senses to find their direction with growing unease. "We're going north into the Waste, Merdice—away from the battle at Brettford. Mal and Rufus won't have enough time to come to terms with the other lords before the invaders land on our shores. Why are we going north, when the conflict is in the south?" She spoke loudly enough for all to hear, ignoring Merdice's attempts to hush her.

The gray-clad driver turned. His face was a hollow shadow beneath his hood. He replied, "If the Dalesmen will not be able to agree on their leadership, once again all will be destroyed. Singly, their weapons and troops cannot stand against the weapons of the invaders from Alizon."

"We could help them, instead of going into the Waste," Aislinn persisted.

"This is their fate, since they have chosen to be stubborn and foolish. They make as much war among themselves out of pride and distrust of one another. Mortals are born to fight and die in wasted causes. They will keep the invaders occupied while we take up our position to defend that which is hidden."

Aislinn thought of Mal, and the surge of her emotion playing upon the sending powers of the others rippled through them like a stiff wind among leaves, lifting them from their blind acceptance of the driver's will.

"My parents and my brothers will perish unless I do something to help them," Mearr said. "They would never turn their backs upon me!"

The others seconded her in a rising tide of resistance.

Aislinn spoke to the driver. "Turn your wagon around and drive it south."

"Would you oppose the will of the Old Ones? I cannot turn it around. I was commanded to bring you to the Place and I must do it."

"I command you to turn southward, or I shall name your Name," Aislinn said. "I know you and I am not afraid!"

The guardians cringed at her audacity, and Merdice tried to pull her down into her seat.

"Aislinn! This is rebellion! No one fights against the Old Ones in this way! You cannot change what they have decreed."

"Do the Old Ones determine the fate of mortal men?" Aislinn demanded. "Are men not free to determine for themselves their own choices and take the paths their choices lead them to? Not even the Old Ones have the right to say that the

Dalesmen must die to save that which is hidden. I say they will not die, if we turn around and go to their aid, as we should. We are just as mortal as they, despite that which sets us apart. By turning our backs on them, we betray ourselves!"

"Aislinn!" cried Merdice. "You can't do this! You don't know what you do! You might destroy yourself and all the Stillborn! All the careful work and planning of the Old Ones will come to naught!"

Another of the guardians answered, "Perhaps it should! It was a mistake putting such spirits into the bodies of mortal man! What an unholy conjoining of Power and emotion!"

"Be silent!" Aislinn said. "We shall turn the wagon around. We all know the Name of the driver, and I shall be the first to speak it."

"You are a travesty of the Old Ones' Power!" the driver hissed. "You must not command this wagon to turn!"

"But I shall," Aislinn replied calmly. "Your Name is Weard, and I command you to turn about."

"It is as you command," Weard replied grimly.

"Turn about, Weard!" called the Stillborn, while their guardians cowered in the bottom of the wagon.

Weard lashed the air with his whip, scattering deafening bolts of lightning. The wain pitched and trembled like a ship at sea, finally grinding almost to a halt as it swung around. Then the great ox lunged forward again, snorting a spray of foam.

"We're turned southward, Merdice!" Aislinn exulted, giving her guardian a shake.

"Such a thing has never been done before!" Merdice gasped. "You have opposed the Old Ones!"

"No," spoke Mearr. "We are the new Old Ones. We have decided for ourselves."

The wain carried them onward until it was light, but they could see nothing through the clouds that swirled around them. At last, Weard turned and spoke over his shoulder to

Aislinn. "We are near your destination. I will leave you soon, and you can try your skills against the fate that rules these mortals."

"You will stop in a sheltered place and wait for our return," Aislinn said.

The place Weard chose was a ruin on a hilltop overlooking Brettford and the seacoast not far beyond. The keep lay surrounded by green fields and meadows, defended by ditches and earthworks, where sheep and cattle grazed. The only sign of great events afoot were the bright banners flying over the fortress to announce the presence of the visiting lords there. Lord Brettford's retainers on horseback in full battle attire were escorting a delegation from the invaders toward the keep.

"Brettford treats with the enemy," murmured the Voices of the Stillborn uneasily.

Aislinn made a sweeping scrutiny of the surrounding hills. The Dalesmen of various holdings held aloof in their encampments in the hills, waiting for the word of their lords inside the keep while the enemy unloaded men and weapons from their ships.

In the harbor were four ships, not of the like any of the Stillborn had ever seen. They were all of the same gray color, riding low in the water and mounted with inexplicable devices instead of sails and masts. Gaping maws spewed forth into the shallow water of the harbor men, who waded ashore to a large encampment where marching companies were forming up. As Aislinn watched, four small ships plowed into the water and came growling up onto the beach, trundling away with no visible means of locomotion. As Aislinn gazed at them, a part of her recognized the ships and the menace they carried. Among those strangers lurked an ancient evil that she sought for with her mind-powers, stealthily, lest that evil one become aware of her presence.

"They have summoned a Power," she whispered. "A coldness is there, a thing I cannot name. Something not of mortal man, nor of the people in the ships."

She touched Merdice with one hand, and Merdice uttered a stifled cry as she shared the vision. It had the feel of ancient evil, and it was a living thing that suddenly became aware of them, as a bear awakens suspiciously in its den. It cast around warily, then Aislinn suddenly closed it out of her mind contact.

"We must go back," Merdice whispered. "We can't face that alone! It's old and it's evil!"

"We are old also, and we are not evil," Aislinn replied. "Hwitan," she called to the juggler's boy. "Do you know the names of the storms and the giants of the air and of the sea?"

Hwitan surveyed the harbor and the ships, his dark eye kindling with a speculative light. "To be sure I know the Names of the sky and water rulers," he said. "It is time they were awakened against these ships that trespass."

"Not yet, Hwitan. Take with you Hagan and Ehren," Aislinn said. "Mearr, Ana, Adalia; you will go along the shore to find the war camps of the men from the ships. Lilias, Eanraic, Kining; follow the roads leading from the harbor and overtake those who are already advancing into the Dales. We know the Names of all creatures and how to assume their shapes, and we can turn the elements of air, earth, and sea against our enemies. Every stone, every leaf and stem, must turn against these invaders. On the land we must meet them with disasters, and succor those they meet with in battle. We will turn them back to their ships, and drive the ships far from our shores. Merdice and I will go into Brettford and enlist the united aid of the Dales."

"My lady," Merdice addressed Aislinn, with deference for the first time, "I would not want to see one of the Stillborn fall into the hands of Alizon and that evil that they serve. They would be glad to capture and make use of the power that resides within you."

"Are you afraid, Merdice? If you wish to go with the others, you may, but I must go into Brettford. Mal and Rufus are in there. They must be warned that there can be no truce with these strangers."

"My place is to watch over you, wherever you go," Merdice answered staunchly. "If you go there, then I shall also—though it be to our deaths we go." She slipped a sharp dagger from its sheath inside her sleeve. "They will not capture us alive."

Aislinn did not wait for dark, as Merdice repeatedly and doggedly advised. They approached the keep openly, meeting a contingent from the enemy encampment that eyed Aislinn and Merdice wolfishly, their weapons held as if they expected trouble. Merdice made a soft, contemptuous sound, and Aislinn had no difficulty reading her guardian's thoughts. These were common riffraff, blank shields from Alizon who would do anybody's killing for the right price.

"Here's a pair of geese for the plucking," one of the Hounds of Alizon sneered, his evil laugh echoed by the others. They surrounded Aislinn and Merdice, blocking the way with their horses.

"Get you gone!" Merdice snapped. "This is the lady Aislinn of Malmgarth, and it will go ill with you if you attempt to distress her."

The Hounds laughed rudely, and one reached out to touch Aislinn's hair with a grimy hand.

Aislinn eluded his offensive touch and named the collective name of horses, "Hesturfljott!"

Their mounts at once began to prance and curvette restlessly, while their riders tried to bring them under control with shouts and whips.

"There's witchery in this!" snarled the leader of the Hounds. "We came in peace to negotiate, and we've been attacked with witchcraft!"

"Hesturfljott! Strjuka!" called Aislinn, adding the command to run, and the horses bolted away wildly, snorting, every eye white-rimmed.

Knowing the Hounds would not return while she could speak to the horses, Aislinn advanced to the earthworks surrounding the fortress.

At the main gate, standing confidently open, they found a mixed guard of Alizon and Dalesmen keeping a suspicious distance from one another. A pair of Hounds with lances barred the path, their hairy, weasel faces suspicious.

"Stand aside," Merdice ordered. "This is the lady Aislinn, betrothed of the young lord Hroc, and you dare not deny her entrance."

"You can't pass here," the foremost of them said roughly. "No one else is permitted to enter while our chieftain Beorg and the priests are within. We don't know what sort of treachery you might be planning."

The Hounds laughed unpleasantly, casting their eyes over Aislinn with villainous leers.

Brettford's men listened, watching with disapproval written on their features. Exchanging a glance, they approached, their weapons held ready.

"Allow the lady to pass," spoke their leader. "We'll take the responsibility if she menaces your chieftain and his wizards. I see nothing to be so frightened of in her aspect."

"No one will pass," the Hound snarled, barring the way with his lance. "I find it suspicious you'd let her pass. I don't like the look of it."

"We'll hold to our truce if you will," retorted the Dalesman. "Are you accusing us of breaking it?"

The Hounds gripped their weapons and moved slowly into defensive positions. Aislinn knew the metal of their weapons and spoke to it, and the weapons were hurled from their owners' hands with a fiery crackle of sparks.

"Witches!" spat one of the Hounds, clutching his seared hands in pain.

Four of the Hounds seized their longbows, but Aislinn named the name of the trees the wood had come from, and all the arrows flew wide. Some even arced backward upon the ones who had released them, when Aislinn was able to concentrate adequately upon the command, with Merdice tugging urgently at her cloak.

The Hounds backed away to a safe distance, their hairy faces incredulous. Silently Brettford's men opened the gate for Aislinn, staring at her with startled eyes as she passed within.

Outside the main hall doors six Hounds of Alizon skulked, glowering as Aislinn approached and barring her way. One of the main hall doors opened a suspicious crack and another Alizon guard peered outside around the edge of his shield. Aislinn named the wood of the doors, causing them to fling outward wildly with a crash and stand open, as if a monstrous hand had seized them. Four Hounds within scuttled backward, gazing incredulously at the form of the advancing foe—a girl, slight of build, with pale hair streaming past her shoulders in tendrils that stirred as if they possessed life of their own. Her image shimmered, mixed with a myriad of other faces and forms and accountrements until her opponents knew not the nature of their foe. They backed away before her advance, and she crossed the threshold into the great hall.

Among others seated around the great table were Lord Brettford, Hroc, Rufus, and Mal. They rose to their feet, aghast at her intrusion and her method of gaining entry into the hall.

Aislinn spoke, her voice echoing against the stone walls. "Lord Brettford, Lord Rufus, and the other lords of the Dales, you must not form any agreement with these invaders. How can you have forgotten so easily what passed in the time of your fathers when last these Hounds harrowed the Dales and laid it waste?"

Hroc and his father muttered the first accusations.

"What manner of woman is this? Is it a Witch among us?"

"She has powers!"

The Alizon chieftain and his three gray-cloaked wizards scowled at Aislinn. Again she probed with her thoughts, and she encountered the lurking darkness redolent of evil.

"These wizards traffic in unclean powers," Aislinn said, "besides coming under the protection of those strangers in the ships. Everything about them augurs ill for the Dales."

"We won't be ensnared by strange powers from any quarter." Angrily Lord Brettford rose to his feet and beckoned to his men. "Take Malmgarth and their sorceresses out of our gates and see to it they don't gain entrance again. I hereby sever all bonds with Malmgarth and release all obligations and deny all future alliances. At Brettford keep, Malmgarth has ceased to exist."

Mal turned to face Aislinn's accusers like a wolf at bay. "You fools," he spat. "The lady Aislinn speaks the truth and you know it in your hearts. We can make no truce with Alizon and those shipmen when all they wish for us is doom. Know all you present that I stand with the lady Aislinn, and any who attacks her, attacks me."

"Put her outside the walls," Brettford commanded. "She doesn't belong here, where she can bring more harm upon innocent mortals with her vile powers. To think my son nearly allied with such a one!"

"She's tainted by the magic of the Old Ones," Hroc said. "Those of stillborn birth are said to be inhabited by the unknown forces."

"Aislinn is a gift of the Old Ones," Mal retorted. "To save us from our enemies and our own folly."

"We want no gifts from the Old Ones," Lord Brettford said. "Take your witch and go back to Malmgarth. There can be no alliance with those who consort with evil powers."

"Evil powers!" snorted Rufus. "There's nothing evil about the lady Aislinn, who is heiress by birthright to Malmgarth.

I've known her since her birthing hour and she's never done anything of this nature until now. If this be your idea of evil, then Malmgarth is better not to rally under your flag!"

"I say the same!" echoed Merelow, lord of Wealdmar. "I join with Malmgarth and the lady Aislinn."

"And I," added the lord of Traedwyth, stepping forward to ground his axe on the floor with a resounding clang. Six others and their principal retainers stepped forward to announce their loyalty to Aislinn.

This took nearly half the assembled lords, and the two factions eyed each other warily. More tension mounted in the hall as Beorg and his contingent took their leave with scowling faces and menace in their manner. The chief wizard, Duru, paused a moment to stare at Aislinn, his thoughts probing, testing her strength. She shuddered at his unclean prying, and barred his attack.

"We'll meet again," he murmured, passing by.

Aislinn stepped forward, sweeping each side of the table with an angry glare.

"You are quarreling yet," she said. "The invaders are baying at your doors and you should be unified! There are only nine other Stillborn, and they are in the hills turning back the enemy in the way they know best, and others are striving to keep shipmen from landing more warriors."

"There's not many of them," Brettford said contemptuously. "And they have few horses. What can they do, when each of us has fifty men waiting behind him?"

"They are not many, but they have weapons such as we have never seen," Aislinn replied. "All of you must call your men down from the hills at once before these strangers and their rolling ships move across our land. How can you have already forgotten what happened in the time of your fathers, when Alizon rent the Dales with murder and bloodshed and destruction?"

"While you argue," Merdice said, "Beorg is rallying his

men to attack us. How much longer do you intend to sit and bandy useless talk, Brettford?"

Grimly, Rufus said, "Half of us are ready to defend our lands. You who are not afraid to fight for your lives and freedom, rally under your flags and Malmgarth will lead you to victory!"

Wealdmar, Traedwyth, Ulfmaer, Faerwold, and their principal retainers shouldered their weapons and strode into the courtyard at the heels of Rufus and Mal, sending part of their number to saddle and bring forth the horses.

A shout from the battlements halted their cavalcade.

"They come! Beorg and his Hounds and a war engine!"

Merdice gasped, "Too late! We're trapped!"

"Not trapped," Mal answered. "They are fewer than we are. We'll drive them back into the sea. Not so much as a foot of Dales land will be given them."

Aislinn commandeered a horse for herself, swinging onto its back before Merdice or anyone could say nay. With a soft word in its ear she sent it cantering after Mal. None of the warriors moved to oppose her—except Mal, who scowled in disapproval, but he knew it was senseless to attempt to alter her mind once she had resolved to do something. He moved his horse near hers protectively, watching alertly as the enemy approached.

A dark knot of men and one of their unfamiliar engines of war moved toward the main gate of Brettford. Ten Alizon warriors rode in the fore, their shields and helms bearing their symbol, a lizardlike creature. Behind them came ten others on foot, followed by one of the strange engines, unfamiliar in aspect but clearly deadly in purpose. It moved like a small ship with no sail, with sinister growling and grinding sounds.

Malmgarth and its allies rode forth from the gate and halted, watching the advance of the enemy to the first earthwork barrier. Had the fortress been properly manned, a body of armed skirmishers would have ambushed them there and made short work of such a small number.

Aislinn watched their advance, the restless wind plucking at her hair. The Voices of sendings whispered insistently in her ears.

"The enemy has landed at Arnwold," she said, nodding to the south, "and a band of twenty is moving inland. More are eastward, already as far as Waleis."

"What of these who are coming?" Mal asked her.

"Ordinary enough men and horses. But their war engine that comes on wheels of its own power is different. I know not the names of its metals. It is all nameless to me. There are two men inside." Briefly her questing mind touched two minds, which reacted at first with curiosity, than sudden anger and withdrawal. A wave of cold passed through Aislinn that was not cold of the real world around her. It was as menacing as the darkness she sensed in Beorg's wizards.

The war engine halted, its snouty forward end pointing toward the mounted riders. The Alizon warriors fell to each side of it, and Beorg rode forward to approach Rufus and Mal with a swaggering air of smug self-confidence.

"This fortress will be ours before nightfall," Beorg said with a leer. "Take yourselves and your Witch into the hills to hide, unless you are ready to die today. Wherever you go, we will ferret you out like rats on the threshing floor."

Rufus replied, "It is you who will be winnowed this day, and the chaff of Alizon will blow away on the wind!"

"You will rue your decision," Beorg said, reining his horse around to move out of the path of the war engine.

For a long moment nothing moved. Inside the engine, the men were making subtle clicking sounds.

Suddenly Aislinn spoke a single word, and the war horses beside her and beneath her sprang as one out of the path of the war engine, just as a puff of smoke issued from it, followed by a thunderous explosion. The stone gatepost behind them exploded with flying shards of rock. The horses no longer needed Aislinn's warning; they fled in snorting, eye-rolling terror, with their riders struggling for control.

Aislinn's horse plunged wildly to the side, crashing down the road's embankment in a spray of gravel, and plowing to a halt on its knees. Jarred from her seat by the precipitous descent, Aislinn flew over the horse's head and landed hard in a pile of rocks. Stunned, she lay gasping with pain, hearing only a senseless roaring in her ears. She struggled to rise to her hands and knees, but the earth swayed dizzily beneath her.

"Mal!" she called desperately, striving to recognize him among the blurred figures swinging around her.

Mal and the others were gradually regrouping their frightened horses in the shelter of the earthwork when Mal heard her cry. Seeing her, he sent his horse charging toward her, while the war engine rumbled forward once more. Then it halted, pointing its snout toward the gates, now standing securely closed. With another great explosion, the gates shattered into flying pieces, sending the horses plunging in terror once again. Mal leaped from his bolting horse and raced toward Aislinn. The Alizon warriors perceived his intentions and charged to meet him with swords and axes bared. Behind him, Mal's allies urged their reluctant horses forward, but were not in time to avert the end of the short, fierce battle. A sword struck alongside Mal's helmet, sending him reeling as if poleaxed. The Alizon attackers then turned on the Dalesmen and drove them back, and would have pursued them but for the command of one of the three gray-cloaked sorcerers behind the war engine.

"Beorg! Let them go," commanded Duru. "Let's see what we have captured here." With a jangling of his belt apparatus, where an assortment of symbols and pouches dangled, the sorcerer halted near Aislinn, who could sit up steadily enough to stare back at him in defiance. A bruised and lacerated lump was rising on her forehead.

The sorcerer passed his hands through the air, making signs that glowed momentarily, casting unsavory light upon his raddled countenance. To Aislinn, he had the look of one who had tampered unwisely with the forbidden secrets of the earth.

"I am called Duru. What do you here, Old One?" the sorcerer simpered maliciously. "And in such a vulnerable form as that? Do you not know how easily mortal bodies suffer and perish? Or were you merely curious to experience pain?"

Aislinn commanded a mighty effort of will and rose to her feet, subjugating the agony of her bruised body to face this opponent. Opponent he was to Malmgarth and to all that she held dear, as well as to the Old Ones' powers inhabiting her fragile mortal frame. She recognized Duru for what he was, and for the powers that governed him. He was one who served the evil forces, as Merdice served the Old Ones, yet he did not possess pure Power as Aislinn did.

"You are an unclean thing, Duru," she said with contempt. "You have no dominion over me."

"Do I not? Are you not flesh, and mortal?" Duru beckoned to the warriors. "Bring this one along with us, and don't be deceived by her tricks into letting her go. She'll soon see that the form she is in is prison enough."

Two men grabbed Aislinn's arms and dragged her along, not realizing that her resistance was due in part to the bruises and swellings incurred in her fall. Biting her lips, she refused to utter the least admission of weakness.

"What of this one?" asked one of the warriors, prodding at Mal's inert form with his foot.

"Bring him," the sorcerer replied after a knowing scrutiny of Aislinn's pale face. "He came to rescue the lady. Perhaps he is important to her. Weak mortals often attach misplaced importance to other mortals."

Aislinn made no sign to gratify his suspicions. Mal's unconscious form was thrown over a horse, and Aislinn was hoisted onto another. Duru rode beside her and held the reins, precluding her escape in the short distance to the fortress.

The war engine rumbled ahead. The Alizon warriors followed in its wake with shouts of savage triumph as it crashed into the remains of the door, finishing the job of ripping the gate from its hinges. The few defenders inside rained arrows and lances down at it, which bounced away without doing harm. Once the war engine was inside, more explosions followed in quick succession, and more shouting.

Rufus and the remaining warriors milled about, torn between the desire to rescue their companions and the need to obtain reinforcements.

"Some one of you must carry the battle sword to the others." Rufus held up the sword, already tied with colored strands. "Tell them it is the time of seige and battle. Beorg and his shipmen may hold the fortress, but much good it will do any of them if no one can get in or out. We hold Beorg and his sorcerers virtual captives. Their advance inland will fall into confusion if we can hold them."

In three days' time the warriors of Wealdmar, Traedwyth, Ulfmaer, Faerwold, and Malmgarth were united to lay seige to the keep of Brettford. They came down from the hilltops suspiciously at first, alarmed by the tales of earthquakes, floods, avalanches, and flash fires carried back by their spies. Barriers of fire on the ridgetops blazed by night, and lightning walked there by day. All nature seemed to be in revolt, hemming in the invaders wherever they turned, except seaward, the way they had come.

V

Inside Brettford keep, Aislinn paced the narrow confines of her prison—a circumscribed area within a five-pointed star, with a vile-smelling candle burning at each point. When she tried to pass the invisible line, a force halted her as if she had walked into a wall. Duru watched his prisoner gloatingly, disturbed from his self-congratulatory glee only by the unfavorable reports from the battle outside the walls.

"Your Dalesmen have us surrounded," he sneered. "Their efforts are paltry and useless when compared to our superior force. We have two hundred trained fighting men, besides four of the war engines you saw. Each is as powerful as a hundred men with longbows and swords."

Aislinn replied, "Their might is nothing if all nature opposes their passage. Rocks, trees, water, the air, and the earth itself will gape to engulf them and the earth will tremble in warning. The sea and the giants within it are waiting for our command. We Stillborn were formed for the defense of that which is hidden. Now we defend that which we love. This time these invaders will not pass."

Duru snorted angrily, galled by the truth in her words. He had heard the earth's grumbling, and seen with his own eyes the fires and lightnings in the hills. The harbor, usually placid, had turned rough and windy, and the ships were unable to disgorge more men into the dangerous water. Great finned and spiked backs often broke the surface of the water as something large and unknown circled the ships.

Duru continued arrogantly, "You must send to these others and command them to let us pass, or you shall die, and that one with you. A great many of your Dalesmen will die if our troops turn to deliver Brettford keep from the seige. All their blood will be upon you unless you command them to surrender."

"They will not be so commanded," Aislinn replied. "I would deserve to die if I gave such a command."

"I wonder how arrogant you will be when I decide to have that one with you put to torture—or death."

"Do what you will, but the result may not be what you expect." Her eyes flashed with a dangerous light, and Duru winced as if some invisible force had struck him. Aislinn gave no betraying sign of surprise, and he hastened to conceal his reaction as an impatient turning away.

"We wish only to pass through your lands on our way to the north," Duru continued when his composure was regained. "Perhaps we could come to an agreement. Safe passage for us all to the Waste, and no blood will be shed. I believe you could guarantee us this—even without your cooperation. You would be much more sensible to agree to take us to that which we wish to find, so no harm will come to those you value."

"And afterward, when you have found that which is hidden?" Aislinn questioned.

"You would be freed, of course, and your companion. All those we captured in Brettford would be freed," he added expansively. "It's your foolish hesitation that keeps them in the dungeon below."

Aislinn spoke slowly, her concentration turned within on the voice of warning she heard there. "Those men inside the war engines and the ships are not as we are. They have come from a far place through a strange gate. They seek another strange gate to bring more of their own kind into this world. Do you not know that you will be destroyed along with everyone else when the shipmen move into our lands? They are different, and powerful with their strange weapons. They won't let us live among them in peace, even if we wanted to."

Duru uttered a sharp bark of laughter. "You won't frighten any of us with that sort of talk."

"It would be most wise," said one of the other sorcerers,

pulling on his gray beard, "to show the shipmen our goodwill by taking them willingly to the gate in the Waste. And if not entirely willingly, then seemingly willingly."

"I won't show you that place," Aislinn replied. "It is forbidden to such unclean ones as you."

"Nothing is forbidden if you have enough power," replied Duru, signaling to the other sorcerers. "We'll go into the great hall. It is almost time to appease the powers that dwell within with another life force. Get that old woman we captured; she's a small loss to anyone. Bring the Lady Aislinn, so she may see how vain her protests are."

The wall of unseen force around her was broken by a word, a name Aislinn did not recognize. The sorcerers gestured with their staffs, also unfamiliar wood, and Aislinn felt herself pushed forward. It was a helpless feeling she did not like, not knowing the nature of the force that bound her.

Duru opened the doors to the hall and stepped inside, beckoning the others to follow. At once Aislinn knew she had entered the domain of a power as great as her own. The great hall was nearly dark, except for narrow slits of light coming in from windows above. Sullen, smoking candles of unsavory hue burned at the five points of a star marked on the pavement. Her eyes swept the hall, searching for the source of the evil emanations that beat against her, prying, searching for a weakness in her defense. Her birthright protected her as if by instinct; she was invulnerable to the strange voices that swirled around her, coming from the dark, formless center of the pentacle, where something darker than the dark hung wavering.

The three sorcerers gained in strength with proximity to their source of power. Grizzled of beard and raddled of countenance, they burned with the fever of their search for the greatest of powers. Aislinn felt their thoughts prying at her, trying to read the secret they knew she possessed—the secret of what was hidden in the Waste.

One departed and returned with Merdice, pushing her along roughly.

"This is a paltry offering," the wizard remarked. "There's scarcely any meat on her bones to speak of."

"The Voice does not care for meat," Duru answered, his eyes burning with fervid heat as he lit a brazier. "It wants the essence of life that all living things possess. It feasts upon the power released when a life is taken."

He drew a long sharp knife and stood gazing toward the center of the illuminated pentacle, repeating words of invocation. Aislinn sought to touch Merdice's mind and was sharply rebuffed with the words "Don't feed it your fear!"

The darkness gathered itself almost into a recognizable form. Duru beckoned, and the others brought Merdice forward.

Aislinn flung back her head and commanded them, using the powers of her voice. "Halt! Release this woman! You trespass gravely in this wanton slaughter, and forces are rising against you as I speak."

Her voice flattened the flames of the candles, driving them backward, but not extinguishing them.

The centermost of the three sorcerers jerked forward a step. His withered lips parted to speak in a voice not his own, which strained his throat with harsh rasping.

"Who are you that dare defy my servants?"

"I shall remain nameless. You don't belong in this place. I command you to depart, by the power of the Nine Great Names!"

"I was summoned," came the resonating answer from the center of the blackness, thrumming through its human medium, shaking him in its grasp.

Aislinn darted a look at Merdice. Seeking forbidden knowledge had somehow led Duru to the discovery of the name of this ancient malignancy, and thereby he gained a small degree of control over it.

"What folly!" Merdice hissed. "Duru, you're a fool to have raised this thing from its sleep!"

Duru smiled coldly. "Bow to my will and live. Resist and you perish forever, swallowed by the Voice."

Aislinn was drawn a step or two nearer, then she halted the pull that drew her forward. Contemptuously, she said, "I am not yours to command. The vermin who called you are your slaves, not I. Command them to your will."

She swept the gray-cloaked ones with her gaze, feeling more of the cold evil radiating from their glittering, soulless eyes. The Voice they had summoned had taken them over completely.

The Voice spoke. "Seize her and bring her to me."

They moved forward with clawlike hands reaching for her, waves of overpowering strength beating at her. For an instant Aislinn dared hurl her mind probe into them, searching for something in them whose name she knew. They resisted fiercely, but not before Aislinn was able to pick from the mind of the weakest of them a single frightened thought: "Power and emotion! Does she know?"

"I am not afraid to approach this creature of my own volition," Aislinn said, shying away from the touch of their yellowed, evil hands.

Turning her back upon them, she moved forward toward the dark nothingness hovering like a cloud within the pentacle. She signed with one hand, creating a glowing blue image that hung in the air before her.

"That will not protect you here," spat the sorcerer medium, trembling again with the force speaking through him. "It is commanded that you reveal the hidden gate in the Waste, or your fate will be that of those who thought to oppose my might."

The dark force permitted her a brief glimpse of the other captives held in a dark place, ringed about by fire and cold. Among them she recognized Mal, and her probe leaped out to him like a spark from a pitchy log bursting asunder, brilliant with all the power of her need for him. She glimpsed his startled face for a split second, time enough to whisper his secret name, "Asmerillion!"

Then the Voice broke around her in a wave of thunder, a roar of pain and fury that shook all three sorcerers. They gripped their skulls, convulsed in pain. The Voice lashed out at Aislinn in a withering blast of life-destroying abnegation. Merdice gripped her arm, whispering, "Use your anger as a weapon! Emotions are nameless to this creature! It has never been human!"

Relentlessly, Aislinn summoned her fury and will to live, and the blackness retreated. She probed with her mind power, finding Mal again in some dark corner of the fortress. He was on his feet now, raging at the door that barred him and the others from escape.

"Asmerillion, come forth!" Aislinn called with a fiery surge of wrath.

The mediums jerked like puppets, stumbling forward, then reeling back in the gust of Aislinn's anger.

"Release your prisoners and depart!" she hissed, her rage honed to razor sharpness by the glimpse of Mal. "I am Stillborn of the Old Ones, double-protected against all Nameless!"

The Voice growled, selecting Duru for its punishing grasp, shaking him as a dog shakes a rat. Aislinn felt his fear as a rush of emanations, which the Voice seized upon with greedy hunger. The creature expanded, threatening to burst through the protective wall of candle and flame. Now it had form, many forms, mostly bestial and distorted.

"Asmerillion! Come forth! Speak!" Aislinn commanded again, silently speeding the true name of the wood to Mal.

In the dungeon below, in the most ancient part of the several keeps that had stood on that site, Mal stood transfixed, his essence pouring around him like steam from the body of a sweating horse. Then he spoke to the door, and the wood burst from its iron bands. Brettford and Hroc and the others still stood flattened against the wall, not moving, staring at him and the door in stupifaction.

"Asmerillion!" came the quavering cry again, and all of Mal's being answered that call. He plunged through the wreckage of the door, meeting the Alizon warrior set to guard the prisoners. Still stunned from the explosion, the warrior reached belatedly for his sword as Mal hurtled into him with a catlike leap. It was as if the fanciful dreams of his childhood had come true—his strength was limitless; no enemy could touch him, so great was his speed and power. He tore the warrior's weapons away from him, hesitating only long enough to command Lord Brettford and the others: "Follow me if you want to live!"

The power of his voice brought them out of their shock; they hastened to follow him, inflamed by his own strength to deeds past their reckoning. They overtook more Hounds of Alizon in the subterranean corridors of the keep, taking their weapons and leaving them broken and wounded in their wake. As they gained the stairway to the surface, they battled relentlessly with twice as many Hounds, ever pressing their way forward with Mal in the fore, swinging his sword with tireless ferocity.

Ever in his mind he heard Aislinn's voice calling, "Asmerillion! I summon thee!"

By the time the short, sharp battle of the stairway was done, eight Hounds lay dead and dying, and three were fleeing to spread the alarm.

"After them!" panted Hroc, fired with bloodlust, but it was Mal's command he waited for.

"Let them go," Mal said. "It's the hall we must take now. Aislinn is there!"

They had yet the courtyard to cross, which seethed with Hounds taking up battle positions. Mal counted fifteen of them remaining, not including the two men inside the war engine. It sputtered into sudden life, rolling forward with its snout swiveling. Below the snout was a slot from which protruded the smooth black weapon that issued a puff of fire, a sharp explosion, and instant death to one of Brettford's men. The force threw the man backward, clutching his breast where a deadly gushing of blood poured relentlessly over his hands. More sharp cracking sounds came from the war engine, causing the stones to explode where an unseen projectile struck, and splintered holes appeared in doors and pillars. Mal and his followers flattened themselves behind abutments and walls, scuttling desperately to escape the death-dealing machine as it revolved around the courtyard. The Hounds of Alizon cheered nastily, nevertheless maintaining their hiding places as if they also feared the thing.

Mal's small force retreated from the courtyard, their hot fury subsiding quickly into bafflement and fear.

Within the hall, Aislinn and the others heard the battle raging outside.

"Your barbarians have escaped," Duru said. "Bring them into submission at once, or they will all be destroyed!"

"I have come to free my people!"

"Your people!" the Voice repeated, speaking through one of its mediums. "If they are not your slaves, they are not your people. You are of the ancient breed, as I am, even though you appear in human form."

"I am human also," Aislinn flared pridefully.

"These people are nothing," the Voice persisted.

"I will destroy you to save them," answered Aislinn, darting another searing mind probe toward the darkness in the pentacle. In her wrath, she summoned the Names of the loose objects in the hall, creating a storm of flying cups, stools, benches, firewood, and loose weapons. Even the fabric of the tapestries on the walls flapped frantically. Strains of wild music tore through the air, dischordant harps and lutes and flutes clamoring in protest. Aislinn's image shimmered, giving her a hundred faces and forms of attire in the space of moments. A flickering nimbus of light hovered around her.

The Voice thundered sharply, "We are old enemies, you and I! Do not attempt to deceive me with these idle tricks! Your human nature pollutes your powers with these strange manifestations! This is abomination!"

"Go back to your well of darkness," Aislinn commanded. "Only the wisest ones will hold the secret of the gate place, and the wisest ones are not the most evil ones." The nimbus flared like black smoke, roiling with anger.

"You will die, and your Dalesmen, and your brothers and sisters in mortal flesh," hissed the Voice enticingly. "All you own will be mine then, and you will feel no more pain."

Like a whiplash, Aislinn's bruises and aches flared into agony. With enormous stubborn pride she bit her lip and vowed inwardly to give no sign of her pain. The nimbus surrounding her turned red, shot with swirls of black.

Then the Voice showed her a brief vision of the courtyard, with Mal and the Dalesmen cornered by the triumphant Hounds, with the war engine growling like a ravening beast over its prey.

"They will die, unless you save them," the Voice whispered. "Speak the word, and they will be delivered. Hesitate and they are all lost."

As Aislinn gazed, another of the Dalesmen was caught by the projectiles hurled by the war engine, and she watched his life expire before the Voice barred her sight.

"Don't weaken!" Merdice snapped. "Rage! Weep for those who die! These are your weapons! Use them!"

"Asmerillion!" Aislinn's thoughts directed the Name guardedly, and she was rewarded with a sudden bright flash as her mind touched Mal's. She felt his wrath directed toward the Hounds and their engine, his fury at the death of his companions, and his fierce will to survive sweeping all fear and doubt before it. At the sound of his true name he leaped to his feet, again radiating the mesmerizing power that heartened his companions and strengthened every fiber of his being.

Mal heard her voice whisper as if in his ear. "Take the lance to the war engine. Speak the Name Jurtsprengur!"

Mal gripped the lance at the mention of its name and felt a tremendous surge of power in response. It moved like a living thing in his hand, finding its mark twice in the flesh of the Hounds during his rush across the courtyard. No hand or weapon was able to touch him. He charged at the engine and drove the sharp metal point into the slot, crying out the name of the wood: "Jurtsprengur!"

The lance exploded into splinters and greenish mist. Mal leaped away, eyes watering with the acrid sting of the mist, gasping a little at its choking smell. The war engine continued rolling forward, scattering the Hounds and crashing blindly over obstructions as if it had gone mad. Then it shouldered up against a wall, partially knocking it down, climbing sidewise up the rubble in a drunken manner, and then it rolled ponderously over onto its back. Its multitude of wheels kept turning with the same grinding noise, but no more explosions issued from it.

The remaining Hounds, perceiving that their guardian was helpless, mounted a determined defense of the main hall. Mal scarcely saw the men he battled; they bobbed into his view for a few moments, then were hewn down by his sword, mortally wounded. When he reached the door, he remembered the word that had broken the door of their prison. Speaking it again, he was rewarded with a shuddering explosion of splinters and shards of wood flying away in all directions. With his men at his back, he thrust his way into the dark hall, somewhat lighter now by the loss of its two great doors.

"Aislinn!" he roared.

"Asmerillion! Mal!"

"Good!" hissed Merdice. "Think of Mal, child! You love him, don't you?"

Triumphantly, Aislinn's power surged forward, pouring out

all her defensive fury and loyalty and passion and indomitable human will, from the depths to the heights of her scale of emotion. Shapeless images gathered around her, each trembling with a different color: angry black, courageous red, blazing yellow, white, pure quivering blue, and the malignant fury of green. Aislinn summoned them, gathering them, honing them into darts, which she hurled at the blackness in the pentacle.

The Voice winced away from her bombardment of nameless forces. The mediums raised a unified shriek of agony and terror as the bolts struck the center of the star. They collapsed like empty sacks, convulsed and clawing.

"This is anathema!" the Voice wailed, already distant. "These powers are nameless!"

Duru gasped. "The Voice is retreating!"

Trailing colored auras, Aislinn strode past them without a glance and smote off the flame of the nearest candle with a spattering of grease and sparks. With a howl, the Voice fled back to its hiding place, a distant dark region Aislinn glimpsed in one last hurled thought probe.

The warriors surrounding the fortress waited for the expected attack. One of the ships in the harbor disgorged another of the war engines into the churning waves, only to watch it being engulfed and overturned by a huge dark green wave that some watchers insisted was a mighty beast of the sea with glistening scales and a spiky spine.

"Hwitan is doing his job well," was all Aislinn said.

All the forces of nature seemed conjoined to bring to pass the battle at Brettford. The retreating forces of Alizon struck toward the fortress and found it ringed with the besiegers. At the end of the third day, when night should have fallen, which might have aided their attack upon and retreat into the keep, the light stayed in the sky, a red, lowering nimbus that bathed the keep in lurid light. Baffled and not a little dismayed, the enemy forces staged a series of rather ragged attacks upon the siege-holders, harrying and retreating. Always the unexpected fire sprang up for no cause, obscuring clouds of fog divided the enemy into smaller bands, lightning strikes heralded the stealthy approach of the foe, and the sea in the harbor threatened to devour the ships anchored there.

Near dawn, one of the ships attempted to negotiate the rocky mouth of the harbor and was ground to pieces against the rocks, ending in a series of fiery explosions and billowing clouds of roiling black smoke. The warriors of Alizon, perceiving themselves in the desperate situation of being deserted on hostile shores by the ones who had brought them there, abandoned their ambition of capturing the keep and pushed toward the sea. Another war engine guarding the harbor encampment grumbled into life, advancing toward the water at a speed fast enough to be construed as cowardly flight by the besiegers, leaving behind the Alizon warriors who once so confidently had followed it. Some of them plunged into the water, risking their lives to reach the open maws of the ships, but the rough waves and that below them greatly reduced the number that managed to crawl safely out of the water and into a ship.

Once in the water, the war engine was easy prey for another dark green wave sporting scales and fins, which rolled it over several times almost playfully before taking it under and keeping it. The water exploded many times, but the war engine did not resurface.

The three remaining ships weighed anchor and drifted seaward past the wreckage of the fourth ship, leaving behind the tattered remnant of an Alizon host, suddenly with no place to turn on shores unmistakably hostile. Battle horns were sounding in the surrounding hills. Beneath snapping banners, Rufus and Mal led the united forces of Dalesmen to the attack, finishing the war that Alizon and its strange allies had thought to bring to the Dales. The prisoners taken were held securely until ships could return them to Alizon, and the dead were heaped up and burned; the burning lasted seven days and seven nights.

At Aislinn's orders, the Black Wain rolled away empty, except for gray-cloaked Weard morosely cracking his whip. Only a select few watched it depart and vanish into the mists that accompanied it. The Stillborn and their guardians, including Merdice, and Mal and Rufus, watched it disappear like a banished nightmare.

"I did not dream it was real," Mal said uneasily when it was safely gone. "Not even when Lady Eirena tried to frighten us with it. How did she know?"

Merdice replied, "It was an easy matter to put such a dream into her head, to help prepare Aislinn for the day it would arrive."

"Nor will it return," Aislinn continued Mal's thought, "until war again threatens that which is hidden."

"Then you will go with it again?" Mal questioned.

"Yes, we all must," Aislinn replied. "But it will be long years before any of us return forever to the place where the Wain is kept. Long enough for me to be lady of Malmgarth, if you will be its lord."

"But your mother, Lady Eirena, and Hroc—"

"All barriers have been removed, Mal, except, perhaps, your fear and distrust of my Stillborn heritage."

"Let the others fear," Mal replied. He lifted her up on his horse to ride before him. "We'll send word ahead for Malmgarth to prepare to receive its Stillborn bride. There'll be such a feasting and a celebrating, and every holding will be invited."

Turning away, Merdice almost smiled, quickly hiding this irregular impulse with her hand as she thought of a night fourteen years before when a small boy had eluded her behind a tapestry. All her regrets about that escape left her. Aislinn had a new guardian and would not require her protection, but soon there would be more young ones of the Stillborn heritage for Merdice to teach the lore. So far, the unholy conjoining of Power and emotion had proven strong, and bright with promise.

Afterword

"The Stillborn Heritage" was my first serious attempt at a short story, although it didn't turn out very short. Since I hadn't read any of the Witch World *books up to that point, I got busy and read them all in a relatively short period of time. It was impressive to watch the unfolding of the entire Witch World panoply. As I read, I gradually picked out the details I liked the most, the neofeudal fortresses, characters with differing levels of psychic abilities, conflict between technical and nontechnical cultures, and especially the idea of the secret gates into other realms.*

To me, these are prime ingredients for fantasy literature, which is perhaps the oldest form of storytelling, leading back to the earliest oral traditions. People with special gifts of powers mental or physical have long been the subject of folklore and adventure tales.

Once I had separated the complex strands of Witch World possibilities into my favorite story elements, I cast about for interesting characters to involve in a Witch World–type adventure. The concept of the Stillborns evolved from my own interest in spirits and predestinies and in coming to grips with one's own spiritual destiny, which is, in my opinion what life and literature are all about.

I wish story development were as easy as eating bad mayonnaise—although sleepless nights can be helpful in mulling over ideas that coalesce into something wonderful, sleep deprivation and gastric experimentation are generally not recommended methods of creative enhancement. There's no real substitute for the spontaneous inspiration that lights on you gently, after hours of terrible mental flogging.

—*Elizabeth H. Boyer*

STORMBIRDS
by
C. J. Cherryh

Dry grass and gorse, knolls alike except for the occasional limestone outcrop, and the loneliness of a vast and widening sky: that was all the land round about; and Gerik rode with now and again a glance behind him, or toward the hills—Gerik of Palten Keep of the Dales. But Palten Keep was fallen, the Hounds of Alizon were victorious there and elsewhere, and war was the rule of the world—the Kolder-driven Hounds crossed the sea to attack the Dales, a diversion for Sulcar while the Kolder themselves beset Estcarp, and no word had come to the Dales of any success Estcarp had. There was no surety that any human men were faring well in the world, or that humankind would live beyond these years: so it seemed to Gerik. But he had heard that the south still held. His mother's kin were there, and if rumors were true, hard-beset. So he set free his aging sorrel in the high hills, took everything he owned—which was his kit, his war gear, and the bay horse that his lord had given him—and set out to travel light, toward the coast, where the rough land and the lack of habitations made less attraction for the invaders, and where he hoped that he might pass through the thinnest region of their lines on his way south. It was a narrow chance. But it was a narrower one to stay where he was. So he left the deep Dales for this place where, against a clouding sky, he saw white wings of gulls that promised a change of land again; himself and the horse—himself and so little left of home.

Sunel was the bay stud's name, the greatest of the horses that Palten Keep had bred in its pastures: Sunel had been his lord's own warhorse at the last—even Palten Keep's creatures had been taken from their peace; but Fortal of Palten Keep was dead . . . oh, far back on this course, not in battle, but quietly, in the high hills, for he was old and sick and his wounds had festered. "Take Sunel," Fortal had said. "Ride." "Where, my lord?" Gerik had asked, there at that last campfire he had insisted to make for his lord's comfort. "Ride," Fortal had whispered a second time; that was all, a last little gusting of breath and a diminishing of his body, that still, still sleep that Gerik had seen too much of in his years of battle and retreat, harry and retreat again. Palten Keep was ashes, and their little band of survivors had diminished and diminished again, till at last there was Fortal and young Neth and the twins and himself; till Neth took an arrow through the lungs and the twins died one at Petthys and the other at Greywold, where Fortal took his last wounds.

"Ride," Fortal had said. And meant that it was over. Paltendale was lost. Fortal's war was done. There was no counsel beyond that.

What did a man do then but seek kindred, and what kindred did he have but his mother's folk? Gerik did not know them; but they were human men, and in a failing world, a warm hearth and a human voice was the most a man could hope for, till the world failed altogether. He was thirty-eight. And if there would be anything after him, except the Kolder, he did not know. "I am sorry for you," his lord had said, while his mind was still clear. "O man, it is you I am most sorry for."

He had not understood then. Had not felt solitude till Fortal died. Now it was gorse and the dry grass and the wind among the hills. He tended the bay horse. He talked to the beast and thanked the gods there was something living and friendly to talk to and lay his hands on. He made what speed he could and moved either by night or day according to the land. And at last there were the gulls, which came to the inmost Dales only driven on great stormwinds.

"You too?" he muttered to the birds, white wings against the clouds. "Now it is us driven to the sea." But not loudly. Only for himself and Sunel.

The bay horse flicked his ears and tossed his head. Snorted then, in that way that had nothing at all to do with the gulls, not considering that sudden tensing of muscles and flattening of the ears. Gerik's heart did a little skip and quickening. He patted Sunel's neck to steady him.

"Where?" he whispered, taking in on the reins, a feather touch, and Sunel, already slowing, moved slower still, flicking his ears and angling them to this side and the other and sifting the wind with a lifting and turning of his head. A second time Sunel made that anxious little sound, and every muscle in him was tight: Gerik felt it, and freed his helm from the thong that held it at his shoulder. He took up his shield from where it hung at Sunel's side—all this without dismounting or delaying.

The fitful wind was quartering now at his back and off the hills, now across the trail, which ran as a flat, grassy track between the low knolls. It was a gray full daylight, and the occasional limestone outcrop and clump of gorse gave no great amount of cover. *Mistake,* his instincts told him now, with the clarity of hindsight: he had paid attention to the gulls and not to the clouds, not to the windshift that a few moments ago had come skittering along the grass. Now a cold fear ran through him, and self-reproach: *Fool.* Men died of such things as a moment's carelessness—and he had remarked only the winds aloft and not the one that had suddenly shifted to his cheek and to his back by turns.

Fool, fool, and fool. He reined Sunel aside, looking back in chagrin at the clear trail he had left in this grassland—and it would be worse if he took to the hills, where such a trail would be evident to any casual glance. Full daylight and nowhere to go to cover; and the traitor wind carrying scents one way and the other—*something* was near him.

He found a limestone outcrop to shelter him from that wind, and drew a distance up between two hills to wait a firm windshift or the breaking of the storm. The Hounds could be careless. They counted on terror and brute force, and Kolder weapons where they had them; but the men of the Dales used the land they had known from birth. That evened the odds somewhat.

Gerik waited, seeing the first spatters of cold rain on the grass and bright pockmarks kicking up in the dust that coated his armor and his gear. That would, he thought, drive the Hounds to cover if they had not pitched camp already; gods knew he had ridden through storms before this, and the chance of the enemy reading his scent or finding his trail through the grass was far less once the rain started. The storm that had almost betrayed him bid fair to shelter him and give him a chance to pass, if it lasted into dark, and by the darkening of the clouds it might.

It would—

But Sunel snorted quietly and threw his head, and Gerik scrambled up to steady the horse and to see what it was.

Hound patrol, out on the road. He patted Sunel's cheek and tugged down at the bridle, hard, urging the bay's foreleg with his knee—*Down, down, friend*—for the last few of Paltendale's warriors had learned a new kind of fighting, and the last of their horses had learned tactics other than body-check and swinging sword-side in a melee. Sunel grunted and sank down, lay flat to the ground, and Gerik did the same, there in the scant cover of the gorse, the two of them spattered by raindrops and his arms desperately holding Sunel's neck. "Hush," he whispered to the horse, for canny as the beast was, that head would come up at some noise, and instinct would claim him. It was unnatural, what men asked; but reassurance helped. "Hush, hush, my lad." He held with all his strength now, patting Sunel's cheek, for the riders were near: Gerik could hear them on the trail below.

Gods, that they not come up here for a camp—for the rain was pelting harder, and there was little better shelter to be had than this rocky outcrop and this fold between the hills.

The Hounds came into view. Four of them, riding in the rain, on dark bay horses—

No. Three. The one in the middle was no man, nor bulked in armor and horsehair plumes, but slender, clad in pale yellow and white, and with hands bound, skirts kited up as she rode astride. She was bowed so he could not see her face, but she looked no more than a child, dwarfed by the dark-armored men. Gerik trembled as he stared down through the brush; Sunel strained against his arms.

"Gods," he whispered against Sunel's neck. "O gods."

Three of them. And well armed.

Coward, something else whispered, and stung his pride and his memories, the while he pressed himself the closer against the ground. Then: *Curse it to the dark*—as he felt about him with one hand for his sword and pressed on Sunel with his body to keep the horse's head down. He found his shield and thrust his arm through the straps—no hope of his bow in this cursed weather and with the wind blowing and a hostage in the midst of the enemy: he was never that good a shot.

He got the reins over Sunel's neck, his foot in one stirrup and a grip on the saddle before he hissed a signal to the horse.

Sunel scrambled up under him, turned under the rein and headed downslope at the enemy's flank.

"Hyyyyyaaaaaaaaiiiii!" he yelled, as if there had been all of Palten Keep behind him, charging in amongst the Hounds as pandemonium broke out. It was not the outermost man he went for: it was *through* that defense, taking the man who thought to hold the hostage. "Get away!" he yelled at the girl, and whirled to defend himself with his shield as he heard the second rider at his back and saw the third coming.

That was when he caught sight of the rest of the patrol—a score of foot soldiers, coming up the road.

He slashed wildly, jammed his left heel into Sunel's ribs, and turned with a clash of shield on shield. Archers back there. Twenty of them. The girl had gotten aside, out of the immediate fray, her horse sidling nervously out of harm's way. A wolfshield came up in Gerik's face, old device—old enemy, this band. "Paltendale!" he yelled, perversely, so that these two would know who they had to thank; and got in one blow with all the strength of his arm before he gave Sunel both his heels and shot clear of engagement with the third rider.

"Girl!" he yelled, kiting past, and hit her horse on its rump with the flat of his sword, headed for the hills. Her horse bolted with his: it was all he could ask for. He held Sunel back a little, thrust his sword into its sheath, and made a try for the reins that were flying loose from the captive's horse, leaning from the saddle as he heard arrows whistling about them with that sound no Daleman of these times could ever forget.

The girl's horse stumbled, faltered, a shaft jutting from its hip—he saw it going, and reined back hard, grabbed a handful of cloth and hair and pulled with all he had in him as the girl left the saddle—he was going to drop her, he thought, could not haul her whole weight up one-handed.

He leaned far to the other side and made it in a rending

effort, her body across his saddle within the compass of his shield arm. She was only weight to him, was only a six-stone flurry of skirts and hair flung across him he could not tell which way—he had no time to see, for there was a wall of wolfshields forming across his path, foot soldiers and archers running up against the hillside that was his escape route unless he turned—they *wanted* him to turn, and to no good for him, he reckoned. So straight on he went, his shield covering both himself and the girl, his sword a second time drawn. "Go!" he yelled to Sunel, laid both his heels first one and then the other to the warhorse, and swerved from the clot of wolfshields that formed to bar his way. The foot soldiers surged back—he took one with his sword, took a blow on his shield, and felt Sunel trample a man and stumble his way clear.

They were running then, running free, down off the hillside and onto the road in a gathering patter of rain that stung his face and his eyes and washed blood in sheets down his hand and sword.

The girl struggled and moaned; by that he knew she was alive. But there was a pain in his side he had not felt till now, and a dizziness growing on him that had nothing and everything to do with the way his heart was hammering and his limbs were shaking in the ebb of battle strength. He was hit. He was afraid to look down to know how badly; and when he felt Sunel slowing to a bone-jarring trot and then to a limping walk, he knew that his plight might be worse than a cut in his side.

He rode a little farther. He thought that Sunel could go that far, where the steepening course of the hills beckoned to rougher and more confused land. The crack of thunder and the sheeting rain were friendly violence; the rain closed like a curtain between him and an enemy who might, he prayed, believe that no Dalesman was fool enough to attack a patrol single-handed. They had done it deep in the Dales—hit a patrol with a small force and lure it into a trap—they had taught the Hounds to suspect gifts from the gods and Dalesmen who acted the fools.

And if those were Lord Cervin's men, they had learned it well at Paltendale.

So Houndish suspicion defended a man who had been a true and thorough fool; so the powers of the Dales saved a lostling son and an orphan daughter.

"Are you all right?" he asked the girl, when he had cut her bonds and gotten the sword in sheath. He helped her in her struggles, gathered her up, careful of her tender skin against his bosses and buckles, and cleared sodden blond hair from a pale and half-drowned face.

"Dalesman," she murmured through chattering teeth. "Dalesman."

"Gerik," he said, "of Palten Keep." She was all of twelve. No more than thirteen at most. She was shivering in spasms that left her weak between. "Are you hurt, did they hurt you?"

A great shiver and she shut her eyes tightly.

Fool, he chided himself, and hugged her hard, her temple against his cheek, the rain beating down on them, and his own head spinning between blood loss and panic for their situation, for what he had roused and what he had done back there. "No one will hurt you," he said. "By the Lady and the Lord, no one will hurt you again. I swear it."

She clung to him then like the lost child she was. And he drew Sunel to a halt and slid back in the saddle, settling the girl with her hands on the saddlehorn before he slid down to see to the horse.

The stretch of his ribs cut like a knife, and he fell against Sunel's side with a gut-sickened loss of balance. "O my lad," he muttered, patting the great, warm shoulder, "I have made a fair muddle of it."

The bay horse hung his head and shifted his weight. From where he was, Gerik saw the cut along flank and belly, a sheet of red on rain-drenched brown. "Fair cursed muddle of it," Gerik said, patting the warhorse's shoulder, and felt a knot of despair in his throat as he looked up at the girl. It was in sheer panic that he took up Sunel's reins and began to lead the horse.

There was so much of silence, finally—the unsteady hoof-falls of the bay horse, the whisper of wind in grass the sun had dried. It was cloudless, clear day in this rocky stream cut, and if the Hounds were near, if they moved amid such silence, then they were easy prey for them; Gerik knew as much, but flesh had its limits: he was dying and the bay horse was dying, the two of them together, which was meet enough—if the child had not been fevered, if she were not raving what time she was awake. He had had to tie her to the saddle, which awoke her worst nightmares and made her confuse him with the Hounds.

"Ride," Fortal had said. And it came to this, at last, wounded man and wounded horse and a poor waif he would leave defenseless in a world of enemies.

He had buried Fortal. He had given his lord that much. He had brought stones heavy as he could carry, and made his rest secure from predators—even from the Hounds, he suspected, straining bone and sinew and bloodying his hands with his labor—for no petty effort would topple the cairn he had raised, no idle whim disturb Fortal's rest.

But when it was done he had sat there in the dark, directionless. *Where, my lord?* And never an answer. Against the Hounds, perhaps? Take Sunel and make one grand gesture, and perish, then?

That was a young man's answer. That might have been years ago, when he had more of hope in things. But he had seen a score of such self-destructions in his soldiering, most of which he counted foolish, and none of which had stopped the Hounds or saved much at all for a time that Fortal had truly and desperately needed them.

No, Fortal had no respect of heroes. *Ride. Choose your own way. Live.* What else would the lord of Palten Keep want of him, of the last man of his guard? Fortal had wanted a survivor, that was all. Wanted his beloved Sunel safe and wanted at least one man of Paltendale to ride out of there, no great man, no hero—only the last of his soldiers and the one who, he knew, would bury him.

But it came to this finally, this rocky streamside, in the silence, with the wind and the uncertain steps of a wounded horse, and his own blood darkening the leather of his armor from his ribs to his knee. Sometimes a jolt in his step would break the swordcut open again, and bright blood would leak out from the wadding he had put there: at such times the hills and the sky would waver and reel about him, and the rocks shimmer in his vision.

He shut his eyes from time to time as he walked, lost in the pain, and lifted his head at the jolt of a misstep on a peeling stretch of stone, a sudden catch in Sunel's pace that sent a stab of fear into his heart. "Easy, go easy," he whispered as the horse stumbled. He patted Sunel's neck. He must stop, he thought, he must rest the horse, but he had staunched the bloodflow with salve once the rain stopped; while the enemy—the Hounds—would recover themselves, would have scouts out now that the storm was over. There was no time to rest; and his head spun, he could not lift the girl, not against the pain. Still, the horse—if they pushed him too far . . . "Stand," he said, and let the reins slack, went back and stopped Sunel with his shoulder, patting the drooping neck. "Whoa, my lad, rest awhile."

Sunel shifted weight, and moved again, fretfully pushing him aside, a few more steps toward more level ground, Gerik thought, and then saw the stagger, the unsteadiness in the hindquarters. "O Lady," he murmured, lunged after the horse to stop him, but Sunel gave a tottering step, threw his head, and wandered a triple step more before his right foreleg wobbled and gave way. Bound to the saddle, the girl fought to keep herself upright. Gerik scrambled after her as the warhorse went down kicking—he drew his knife and cut the cords that tied her, trying to disentangle him and her from Sunel's struggles to rise. There was a great deal of blood suddenly—was a horse's grunt of pain as he turned himself from the fallen child to the struggling horse. He flung his arms about Sunel's neck and tried to keep him from breaking the wound wide open. The struggles faded; and Gerik, who had not wept when he buried his comrades or his lord, leaned on Sunel's shoulder and stroked his neck and felt his heart broken like the horse's, just finally broken, not by one thing, but by many, and by the choices that he had made, that had killed the last thing he loved.

O my lord, he thought wearily. *I think that this is as far as I can go.*

Then he thought that quitting was a fool's act, that perhaps he could staunch Sunel's wound, that perhaps if he tended the horse and if the Hounds did not find them—

But Sunel began to fight again to lift his head, battering his cheek and jaw mindlessly against the rocks. Gerik swore and clasped him tight about the neck, clenching his teeth against the pain the horse's struggling sent through his side, holding him still as he could; he talked to the horse and patted him in the quiet moments, and when finally he could not deny that Sunel was dying, he gave him the only mercy he had left to give.

He sat there with blood all over him, and lifted his spattered face to meet the girl's horrified stare. "I had no choice," he said, and put the knife away. "I had no choice."

She made a strangled noise, shook her head, and edged backward on the rocks.

"Come here," he said, and swore again at the pain of reaching for her. "O gods. *Come here!*" He got to his knees and to his feet and snatched at her as she scrambled up and struck at him. He caught her, crushed her tight against him till the pain eased and he had his breath; then he patted her fevered cheek with a grimed and bloody hand. "There," he said, reasonably, urgently, "they are coming, do you understand? They are coming; you have to walk for yourself. I cannot carry you."

She gulped air and clenched her hands on the leather of his sleeves. Tears were running on her face. He gripped her arm for fear of her bolting in fright, and turned and started walking down the stony course, steadily as he could.

Well down from that place where he had left the horse he washed his hands and his face in the little rill of water, and wet the hem of her overskirt and washed her face for her, and straightened her hair with passes of his wet hands, and cooled her brow. But he was bleeding again, and when he investigated the wound, the wadding was soaked and wet; that sent the cold fear through him.

He said nothing about it. He said nothing when he looked back the way they had come and saw the black birds circling, plain as writing across the sky for any Alizon trackers that might be on their trail.

"Come," he said, and stood up and braced his feet wide to catch his balance. He offered his hand, was dully surprised that she took it and used it to gain her feet. She did not let it go. Their steps wandered apart and together again like two drunken soldiers, him in armor, her in her torn frock, mumbling now and again in fever, tending ahead of him at times, walking in slippers that were already in rags.

Fool, he thought then, in the long trek downland—he had his sword, his shield was banging away at his back where he had slung it, but his kit and the canteen he had left with Sunel's gear in his delirium. He had set out among enemies and with a fevered child in his care and no Lord-forsaken canteen nor any provisions or field gear—but he could not have carried its weight. The sword swung at his side and hit his legs, the belts gone askew, and the helm that made his head ache was only one Lord-forsaken more thing to rattle if he took it off and slung it with the shield—but he had no impetus to set his gear aright, had nothing, now, but the more and less of pain, walked with his eyes shut against sunglare—sank down to his knees only where there was a rock or some lone, twisted tree to lean on to get him to his feet again.

No canteen. Stay with the stream. Stay with the water.

Keep moving.

Between one time of sanity and another, the sky turned dull. Between that time and another, the stars grew bright. He fell once, and got up again, stumbling on the rocks. He fell a second time and got to his feet with the girl shaking at him and crying. Beyond this he was only aware of a dull kind of pain, and a general downward slope, the girl holding sometimes to his arm, at last to his fingers, like a child, tugging him along as if she were the one who knew where they were going.

Then the world turned giddy and he was one time under stars and the next that he remembered waking on a rocky hillside with the sun on him and the flight of gulls above him.

It was the height above the sea. He had followed his stream and it had brought him to land's end, world's end, a coast that he had hoped for as a road to lead him south to Jorby. That was what he must do. His head seemed clearer now, after sleep. He drew a breath, lying there on his back on this vast slope of grass, with the girl curled against his side. He stirred, patted her shoulder. "Little rabbit. Wake, wake." Was it his voice, that weak sound? "We have to walk."

She lifted her head. She leaned on her hand and looked down the slope with jaw slack and wide eyes staring on the day. Then she got up and began to walk without him, with the dazed wandering steps of a dreamer.

The child managed for herself. It was harder for him. He levered himself to his feet by degrees and in pain that blinded and dizzied him, and started off again behind her, no longer thinking which way he went until he remembered to wonder, and knew that it was the right way, the way to the sea—*Follow the gulls,* he thought. Birds betrayed him and birds guided him. The black ones and the white. Follow the stream, follow the land till it gave way to the sea, pale illusion of salt water beyond the hills.

He might have fallen once again. He could not remember. The child was with him again, holding to his fingers, tugging at him to go on, and he stood in a windy gap of the hills and saw the sea spread before him, made out in the distance a boat ashore, drying nets beside a homely house of weathered wood.

"People," he murmured to the child. "Human men. Some fisher family."

It was fresh water that linked them, the dwellers by the sea, the fool who had lost his provisions, the wise child who correctly followed the stream downhill despite her delirium. Water brought them both to safety, to a refuge he had never hoped for—honest folk he needed, whose help he would repay with warning—

Steps sounded on his right, where the hill sloped at his back, steps heavy and hasty in the grass-grown sand; he turned in fright as the child screamed, saw a dark man, a blade aflash in the sun, the look of the enemy—

He drew his own blade too late, the hostile sword already swinging, smashing into his arm and his wounded side. He went down, sprawled half-stunned from the pain and the jolt of the fall. The Hound came down on him with his knee in his belly. He fainted then. He knew that he was going under, and for his life, for the child's, he had no strength left to prevent the hand at his throat or the grip that pinned his sword hand.

Least of all he had planned to wake, naked beneath a blanket, within sight of twilit sea, and with a shadowy figure sitting between him and a fire. That fire glanced off the ends and edges of a woman's dark hair, it edge-lit robes and the curve of a cheek, an arm and hand that the robes did not cover—a woman sitting by a rack of fishnets with the dimming color of the sea and the slow roll of the surf behind her.

It was a mistake, perhaps, that he stared and betrayed his waking. But it was too late to mend that. The firelight was on his face. Besides, he had been a fool too often in past days to feel much chagrin at another turn. He should be dead. He was here, and the pain was gone, leaving behind only a general lightness of the brain, a weakness in his limbs that said they would not respond to any asking.

But he thought of the child then. Of the dark man on the hill. And panic ran cold through him.

"Well," the woman said. "Awake."

He blinked for answer. To speak cost too much.

Her robes shadowed him as she leaned forward and her hand brushed his brow. Her fingers were chill, and he did not want to be touched at all, but to protest anything was far beyond his strength.

He tumbled away into dark. He thought that she was speaking to him, but he was not sure. Perhaps he was dying after all.

But he heard the sea again after a while, and waked to the stars overhead—he was sure that he waked, and that his shoulders hurt and his hands were numb, held remorselessly above his head. He was in no pain but that, and he tried to relieve it, discovering then that he was tied at wrists and ankles.

But he was wise, and smothered his panic: best to do nothing without thinking, and his mind was clear again. He remembered everything—the Hounds, the child, Sunel, the attack that had come on them. The waking and the woman. All of which came to this. Where had the Hound gone? Was there a connection, the Hound and the woman? Where was the child?

Was the woman from Alizon? One of the enemy's? Had the Hound brought him here—alive? And the child?

Or—

He held himself very still, and heard from time to time, above the roll of the sea, the night sounds of a stabled horse—on the other side of the hut, he thought. So there was a way of escape. There was a means a weakened man could outrun pursuit. His heart beat the harder then, his breathing quickened. But the girl—

He remembered her with him at the last. Remembered her screaming. He had brought her back to the Hounds.

Fool.

His eyes misted. He quieted his breathing, blinked his eyes clear, cast careful glances about him, at the sea, the beach beyond his feet, the hut that was all silver boards and shadow in the starlight. Of the woman, of the Hound if they were together, there was no sign.

The Hounds had taken this fisher hut, perhaps. Lived here. It might even be the point from which the patrols rode out; and gods knew what the woman was—dark-haired and robed in costly stuff, if plain; that had been the look of her. If she was some fisherwoman held captive, she was a delicate sort of fisherwife. No. Not of the shoreside. Not, perhaps, of the Dales at all.

She was asleep inside the hut, surely, with what company he did not know, but well guessed; and stopped at that. The masters of this place had retired for the night and had tied their prisoner hand and foot to have an untroubled rest, that was beyond doubt. That his pain was eased, except the cramping of his back and shoulders, meant something ominous if anything: that they wanted him alive and hale enough to question at some length.

But there remained the chance that a weapon might come to hand. They might be careless. The woman might stay alone with him, if the men in this place went to report to their fellows: that was the greatest hope. If she was a Daleswoman she might be brave enough to help him or if she was not she might make a mistake the men would not. In womanly pity she might help the girl, and keep the men from her—if the girl was here at all, if there was a chance for her . . .

O lords.

To be meek and quiet was the best thing, in all events. To play at fear—that was no hard thing. To play the fool—well, he had had experience of that, in coming here. To speak them softly and make his first attempt at escape when he was able to put distance between him and them—that was the best course.

So he stayed very still and let the night pass, counting past the turn of the stars in snatches of sleep and longer periods of misery, till the sun seamed the horizon over the sea, and the stars faded, and there was a stir of life inside the hut.

It was the Hound who came out to him, a towering broad shadow in the halflight, who bent over him without a word, turned his face to the light, and slapped him on the cheek, at which Gerik flinched and drew in his breath. In the same silence the Hound went on to try the cords that tied his hands—freeing him, Gerik thought with a wild hope, and then reminded himself that he dared not flail out, no matter what happened, with numb hands and feet that could not bear his weight.

Wait, wait, and wait. No matter what they did with him. He had to be able to run. To find the best chance, and know it was the best.

"Hassall will see to your comfort," the woman said out of the shadow, and he turned his head in that direction as she stepped out of the doorway, wrapping her robes about her. "He does not speak. Do not expect harm of him."

"The child with me—the girl—" It was dangerous to mention her. Having discovered that he had some care of her, they might take worse notions into their heads.

"Leisia," the woman said. A name. The girl had given him none at all. He was dimly distressed at that, and at the woman's easy tone. "She is sleeping. Have no fear, I say."

The cords fell away. His hands fell dead beside his head as the Hound moved down to untie his feet. It was a disadvantageous position, gazing at the woman upside down, having to drag his own arms down like something dead attached to his aching shoulders, and remembering that he had not a stitch of clothing for his dignity except a borrowed blanket. But one or both of them had seen whatever they wished to see of him. He thrust an elbow under him and rolled onto it, testing how much pain there would be, and the lack of it dazed him as much as the pain might have.

There was no wound. He dragged a dead wrist down over his ribs and moved the blanket down, finding no wound at all, only the tender ridge of a scar.

Then he knew what one of them was, at least. He leaned on his quaking arm and looked up at the woman with the profoundest dread that she was by no means the weakness in this pair.

They had wondered, they of the Dales, whether Kolder lords directed the Hounds, or whether those who led the brute ranks were hirelings all.

"My name is Jevane," she said then, but he did not believe for an instant that it was her true one.

"Mine is Eslen," he said, because Eslen of Palten Keep was long buried, and beyond all harm. He felt his feet free, and moved to take the strain off the arm that was shaking perilously under him, as the Hound rose. But lying there helpless as he was, a sort of craft came back to him. "I should be dead," he said in a dull, dazed tone. "I should have died, except you found me, I owe you that." And he looked up with a worshipful gaze he might have given his lord. "I owe you that, my lady."

"So," she said quietly. "Of what hold, Dalesman?"

"Palten Keep." He leaned and fumbled after the blanket,

having discovered a little feeling in his right hand, painfully returning. So an urge of nature came on him, acutely painful in itself, and a gut sickness knotted up in his throat to add to his misery. "O lords," he murmured, beyond feigning anything after that one injudicious move; he held out an arm to the waiting Hound, for there was no one else a man could in decency appeal to. "Help me—"

"Hassall," the woman said, and withdrew into the hut, at which the Hound dragged him up naked as he was onto legs that would hardly bear him and took him out aside from the hut, beyond a hummock of sand. The Hound stood then with arms folded while his prisoner emptied all his gut. He offered no help, no blows, only a sullen patience when Gerik fell half-senseless on the sand; eventually he prodded Gerik with his foot and made a sound deep in his throat.

Gerik moved, cleaned himself with handfuls of sand as best he could, and sat there a moment with his head on his knee until the Hound prodded him again. *No wound,* Gerik thought in all that dim haze of spinning sea and sky. *No wound.* No scar where he had thought the Hound's blade had sheared his arm and side; and only a healing, angry ridge where some blade had cut his side. He had bled, o Lord and Lady, he had bled—what Wise Woman of the Dales could have brought him back and healed a killing wound?

More than Wise Woman. Witch. Witch of Estcarp.

With a Hound for company? Estcarp and Alizon was a pairing unimaginable.

Except the Kolder—

The Hound's fist clenched in his hair and pulled his head up. The other hand grasped his arm and twisted, bringing him to his feet. He walked. He made no struggle and the Hound let him go, holding him only by the elbow as he brought him back to the hut.

The woman waited by the door, cold-eyed and disinterested in his shame. Gerik clenched his jaw and thought to look up, stare for stare, but no, that was not the game he played. He felt his face hot and kept his head bowed when she indicated a pail of water for bathing, a blanket for drying, and his own clothes lying folded on a rail above his boots.

He knelt down and did as he was told under the Hound's watchful eye. And his clothes when he took them up were clean and dry in a morning when sea-damp had made the blankets clammy.

It was that small, unexpected gift that made him look up toward the woman in curiosity. But the doorway was vacant. And in the Hound he saw only a foreign look and a bitter look, the same with which Hassall had favored him beyond the hill, and despised him—*Run,* that look said, mocking him and his nakedness with a dead cold invitation to try what he would.

So he ducked his head and quietly dressed in brown breeches and brown shirt, on which the blood was washed to a faded stain of many edges—that small domestic task the Witch had failed, when the wound itself she had mended; she was not all-powerful. In a strange sense that comforted him. And the dryness was likely only because the clothes had been drying on the hearth of the hut all night. No purposeful kindness. The Hound was the real truth of matters, and it was a fool's persistent hope that saw mercy in what Hounds did.

He edged closer to the door in what he meant to be a sickly stagger, as far as the doorframe with the intention of looking inside, one quick scan to find the child; but the Hound's hard grip closed on his shoulder and spun him about with his back to the wooden wall.

He did not resist. Did not resist when the Hound drew him with him down and away from the hut, past rails and hanging and rotting nets, down toward the sea, though his heart was beating in panic. Not today, fool, not weak, not shaking in every limb, no hope, no hope, no hope in the world.

The fisher-craft was beyond, up on blocks and braces, its

hull skeletal and stripped and with many a plank missing, next the net frames and the hanging rope. Against one of the posts that supported the frames the Hound shoved him, facing the hulk, and pressed down on his shoulder so he should sit; there Hassall bound him in a twist of net and rope.

Then the Hound went down to the boat and its blocks, and took up an adze, at which Gerik despaired, and sat sweating in fear of the Hound's intentions with it. But the Hound arranged a length of wood across a brace and applied the tool to that in businesslike and skillful strokes, sending bright curls flying.

A Hound at carpentry, blessed gods. There was no sanity in the world. A Dalesman sat tethered to a seaside net frame and a Hound of Alizon worked like a fisherman, boat-mending, while the sun rose and passed its zenith.

The Hound gave him water once at midday, bringing it down from the hut. At evening the Hound let him free at last, and led him up to the hut, from which came the smells of cooking, and from which Gerik saw the child come, her ragged yellow dress all clean, her hair combed—she stopped still in the doorway with her eyes wide and her mouth open in horror till the woman appeared behind her, and laid a hand on her shoulder, and said something Gerik could not hear.

Then he was walking free of the Hound, with no hand on him, a little distance that the girl halved, running forward to throw her arms around him and hug him for dear life.

He was shaken by such a demonstration. He looked beyond her to the woman in her fine robes, then took the girl's face between his hands. "Leisia?" he asked, that being the name the woman claimed for her. The girl blinked and stared at him, not denying the calling. "Are you all right?" he asked.

"Are you, lord?" Leisia's lips quivered. Her eyes went beyond him half a breath and came back again, signifying the Hound. There was no fever. It was a wise, Dales-bred girl of thirteen that held his hands and asked him questions with her eyes.

"Of course," he said. And did not look beyond her at the lady. "For Hounds, they are very mannerly."

"Leisia." The woman's voice.

And of a sudden the girl's fair eyes seemed to gaze through him, on something far and difficult.

"Leisia. Come."

"Leisia!" he said, for her hands slipped listlessly from his and she turned away, toward the door. "Leisia!" he shouted, forgetting all his intentions; but she did not hear. The Hound's grip descended on his shoulder and he flung his arm to free it.

So the Hound took another grip, spun him about, seized that arm and twisted it in a lock that sent a stab of pain through his side. Gerik remembered his resolution then, and prepared to go down to his knee as the Hound pressed him to do. But the Witch lingered in the door in which Leisia had vanished, and signed the Hound otherwise. The Hound let him go.

"For her safety," the woman said, "do no rash thing. Your dinner is ready."

It was a night like the other night, only he did not sleep his way into it. The Hound put him to bed, and let him wrap himself in his blanket there beside the hut before he tied his hands and feet again; and Gerik bit his lips for the misery of shoulders and back still stiff from the last such rest he had had.

But he was stronger, for all that. He counted away the last hours of the night in immobility that sent fire through his spine and shoulders with every little shift he made to relieve his discomfort; but his head was clear, his muscles had some strength in them, and the lingering twinges in his side seemed less than before—in all these things he took hope.

But in the girl's face. In the listlessness, the vacancy in the eyes that was like the fever—

Like the fever in which she had walked to come here . . . to this place . . . to the Witch . . .

He thrust that thought away. It kept returning. The Kolder, they said, had such power over minds. The Kolder turned the men of Alizon into—what they were and created the Hounds. If witchblood ran in Estcarp—was Kolder not its neighbor? Might there never have been prisoners, Witches, whose chastity might be violated, whose offspring—female—might be Witches too?

Were the Hounds alone sufficient to direct the attack on the Dales, and had Kolder no agencies this side?

Gunnora save them. Children. Children taken by the Kolder and the Hounds. Innocents who had no knowledge to fight with.

Captive of the Hounds he had found her. And taken her straight to the center of their power. They were saving him until their patrols returned, or they saved him to keep the child docile—who knew but the Kolder and the Hounds? For some reason at least they did him no harm, and for that same reason the Hound was being careful of him.

How many days until the patrol tired of hunting him in the hills and came here for their revenge?

And after that—

He lasted until morning. Until the Hound came again to take him out beyond the ridge of sand. And he limped as he moved, and moaned when the Hound took his arm. "It hurts," he said in a beaten, weary voice. "Gods curse you, it hurts. Let me be. Let me walk. Have you ever spent a night with your hands like that?"

The Hound grunted some sound. But never a word. The Hound. Hassall. Faithful as a shadow all the while, and, gods curse him, never letting his guard down either.

Gerik slipped once on the loose sand of the dune face, went to his knee with a gasp and an unfeigned moan of pain when the Hound dragged him up by the elbow. He brushed sand off and limped his way down to the house, where a breakfast was set out beside the door. A shaggy bay pony was having its own breakfast in the pen, and Leisia was outside, standing barefoot on the bottom rail, reaching over to pat its dusty back.

Homely scene. It might have been any steading-daughter with a pony. The chances within it set Gerik's heart to pounding like a sledgehammer.

He limped his way aside to the fence, under the Hound's watchful eye. He saw the driftwood piled there, that was for their cookfire. He staggered and he leaned against it, and his hand found the stick that would serve.

He whirled on the Hound with all the strength that was in him, and the stick broke when it hit the Hound full on the side of the head.

He was half amazed when the Hound fell—merely fell, like any enemy, whatever his companion's sorcerous powers. Gerik dropped down on his haunches and searched the Hound over for a weapon, found nothing, and sprang up to seize Leisia by the wrist as she stepped down off the rail in shock. Her mouth opened. He covered it with outheld fingers and forbore to bruise her. "Hush," he said, "listen. Come with me. Quickly."

He ducked low and pulled her through the fence of twisted rails, as the shaggy horse sidled off in alarm. He scanned the lean-to shed in hope of tack and found only rope. He snatched that up and caught the pony's mane and looped the rope about its neck. "Up," he hissed, and caught Leisia by the waist, flinging her up astride with an exertion that sent a stab of pain through the scar. He gave her the two ends of the rope for reins and in feverish haste slipped the loop off the gate on the far side of the little pen, then came back and heaved himself up behind the girl belly-down on the pony's rump—got turned about and upright on the moving animal with an effort he had not used since he was a boy, and caught wildly past Leisia at the pony's mane as the pony protested such unusual goings-on. With the other hand he took charge of the rope, Leisia between his arms, as the gate swung ajar.

He drove his heels in hard, and a second time, into the flanks. The pony jolted forward, knocked the gate wide, and at a third blow of Gerik's heels, hopped into a run and bolted, careening over the side of the dune and onto the low-lying flat—a surefooted pony, the shaggy breed the Houndish cavalry rode. Gerik shifted his weight and used his heel in that way a sword-and-shieldman's horse knew. It answered those commands more readily than it answered the rope, veering toward the hills and more solid ground, avoiding the last of the stream that made a sandy bog and vanished into beach sand, finding firmer ground on the reed-grown margin and the stony sand and the sea-grass. Free! Gerik saw the hills ahead, be they aswarm with Hounds and enemies; the pony was under them, the south coast was open, and there was the way to Jorby, with all that he had learned.

The pony dropped its hindquarters suddenly, braced its shoulders, and skidded into a halt in mid-career, scattering stones, sending the world spinning in one wild gyration. Gerik tried to keep Leisia aboard, kept his one-handed grip on the mane a heartbeat longer than the girl did in the animal's plunging spin, and lost it as the pony reared up and aside in a panic fit. The stony ground came hard, and he rolled to clear the hooves that pounded near him, gathered himself up, and spun aside in horror as the shaggy beast charged him and struck him a glancing blow with its shoulder. He shouted at it, shouted at Leisia, who rose shakily to her feet and stood as if dazed; he charged the creature, waving his arms to frighten it from her, reeled back again as he saw it turn and threaten him with bared teeth—no natural pony, nothing natural, which would not turn from his shouts or his hands. He evaded its teeth, slipped on the stones, and rolled to save himself, feeling one and a second sharp-edged hoof drive down on his leg as it trampled him.

A whistle sounded. The horse shied back then, and shook itself, as Gerik caught his breath and raised his head to see a human shape coming over the rise. It was Hassall, alive and moving all too fast; and Gerik, lying windless and covered with sand, gasped after breath and cursed himself twice over that he had not stayed to break the man's skull.

But it was not Hassall who had stopped them and driven the horse into frenzy. It was not Hassall who kept the beast hovering over him now, stamping and blowing in fretful menace. It was the Witch who had beaten him, and the Hound who came on him now with his face all bloody and scowling was only her servant.

He heaved up to his knees and to his feet, legs braced too wide for defense, but it was all he could do to stand at all, with the breath driven out of him and one leg cut and shaking under him. "It was my doing," he said, shifting between the Hound and the stunned girl.

But Hassall stopped a little distance away and pointed the way back to the hut, that was all. Gerik looked into that sullen, bloodied face and did not object that the pony had lamed him or that he did not think he could walk ten steps. "Leisia," he said, motioning back toward the house, and Leisia shook herself as if waking from trance and came to him. "No," he said. He shook her hand off, turned his back on her, and found the strength to walk, albeit slowly, no matter the difficulty of the sand or the grating sensation in his twice-injured leg. He walked, and the Hound mounted up on the pony and rode behind him, herding him and the child home like any strayed beasts.

Gerik collapsed at the front of the hut, there on the crest of the slope. He lay down where he thought the Hound was willing that he stop, at that place he had measured with his eye and promised himself that he might reach. The Hound might ride him down, or not. He had ceased to try to fathom

Hassall's motives, and only watched through sweat-blurred eyes as the Hound rode quietly past him on the reinless horse, doing no harm. Leisia reached him, and tried to rouse him and to comfort him.

"Go away," he said.

"Leisia."

The lady had appeared in that moment, standing in the shade of the net-frames by the side of the hut. Gerik lifted his head and looked her way, and, to Leisia: "Go back to her. Understand? Go back to her for now. Only for now."

The gentle hand left his shoulder. Leisia walked away to the house. He lifted his head again and watched the whole scene, till Leisia vanished into the hut, and the Witch went after her.

Then he rolled onto his back and stared at the sky until the Hound came back and shadowed it with his dark bulk.

Gerik cursed him in a quiet, reasonable tone and rolled onto his belly to get up. He made it as far as one knee when the Hound grasped him by the collar and the arm and ungently helped him the rest of the way.

And in front of the hut Hassall let him go, and walked inside.

Gerik stood a moment out of breath and numb, then limped a few futile steps toward the support of the woodpile. The pony, back in its pen, regarded him with a dark and wary eye.

But there seemed nowhere to go, no hope in horse theft, no hope of gaining even a hundred steps down the beach before Hassall should come riding down on him a second time, to worse hurt. He thought of going down to the sea, for the salt water to ease his cuts and bruises, but the chill of the wind was already enough to bear, and the water's edge was a far walk. It was warmth he wanted, warmth of fire, warmth of comradeship, warmth of shelter—the sense that the girl's touch had brought him; only she was inside, with *them,* with the Witch, with the Hound—gods knew what they might do to her, what purpose they had for her, and he was powerless to help her or himself.

In contempt of him, the Hound let him free. He knew now, that was it; and the Hound knew that he knew. He was as thoroughly a prisoner as he had ever been.

More so. For now he believed it himself.

He slammed his fist down on the wood, and walked to the rail and leaned his arms on it, staring at the pony.

Prisoner too. Both of them. One inside the pen because it had no understanding. One outside because he had enough to know his situation.

But the Witch who controlled the pony had her hold only on Leisia. Why stop the horse and the child and not the man who was responsible?

Could she not?

Could she not throw that net over him, and take what she wanted, more surely than any torment, if she could do that much?

Some difference in the mind of a child and the mind of a man? Or was there a limit, and was a wary adult that much harder for the Witch to manage?

If that was so—if that was so, was it possible to break the girl free, if the Witch had too much to hold?

Not if there was the Hound to hold him by brute force.

Gerik sat still, leaning his back and his head against the rails of the pen, his arm along the fence, suffering the more and less of pain in his leg, wondering were bones broken and fearing that there were—he tried to work off the boot on that leg and gritted his teeth and shoved at it with the other foot until his vision came and went. It began to come off. He made it, and afterward sat trying to work his toes in the sand, which shot lines of fire up his calf. He could not tell if they moved. He leaned his head against the rails again, mortally afraid. He had removed a great many of his choices. Too many of them.

And Hassall, he thought, owed him no little matter of personal revenge, whatever the Witch's opinion.

At length the Hound came out of the hut, and stopped there, staring for a moment, so that Gerik's muscles tensed all across his belly and down his arms and legs, though he did not stir. He did not trouble to hide that fact, or to keep apprehension from his face. If the Hound would pay him for that blow he had taken, then the Hound would do as he pleased: *Be no fool; be no fool,* Gerik told himself. *Take what comes. Stay alive.*

The Hound beckoned him. Gerik pulled the other boot off, since he could not get the one on, gathered himself up, and hobbled over till he and Hassall stood face-to-face, or near as a man his stature could with Hassall. The Hound moved; Gerik flinched; and with perfect solemnity Hassall laid a hand beside his neck, patted him gently, and seized him by the arm.

Down away from the hut the Hound dragged him, Gerik stumbling and limping along as best he could, down the slope toward the boat. There by the net frames Hassall made him sit down, but there was no rope this time. Hassall merely walked off to the boat, stripped off his shirt, and picked up the adze that was lying there beneath the blocks, setting to his day's work.

Gerik leaned his head back against the pole and breathed carefully until the pain ebbed and his heart stopped hammering and the ground steadied again under him. But he watched from slitted eyes, and saw an answer to Hassall.

Next time, he thought, watching the metal blade peel curls from the wood, *next time—I make it here . . .*

Let him put me to work.

A fisher-boat. Lord and Lady, what insane whim is this, that drives him?

Was it wrecked? Do they need it to some purpose? But the Kolder supply them ships—what need of this poor hulk?

Everything seemed mad, the lady and the Hound chiefest in their madness, himself only a passerby, snared in this place madder than all the crumbling world, in which evil fared far better than good, and the gods turned a blind eye to justice.

Blasphemy was dangerous for a dead man. He did not want to think on that either, how the Kolder were winning, and if there was any other outcome of it all he would not live to know it. As none of Palten Keep would know it.

The sun moved in the sky, the shadow traveled off the place where Gerik sat, and the sun baked him, sending little trails of sweat down his sides and raising perspiration that stung in the cuts. But that was nothing to the ache that attended the swelling, that beat in the arteries of his leg and in strained muscles and stretched skin; the heat helped, somewhat. But there was thirst. There was a misery in knees and elbows where he had hit the ground. He discovered stiffness in injuries he had not felt yet, and he dared not stir. Hassall, he thought, was waiting for an excuse.

He watched Hassall wipe his brow and then trek up the slope to the hut—as if he had no prisoner to guard. Hassall was after a drink. Gerik leaned around the pole enough to watch Hassall reach the water barrel, and leaned back again—to stare at the sharp-edged adze and the hammer left by the side of the boat.

To stare at them and think that this Hassall was not the dull brute that he had taken his kind to be, and to suspect that it was with design that Hassall had left him free with the tools there. He. Sitting here. Knowing full well that he was too lame to avail anything, knowing by that gesture that Hassall knew what he was thinking, and that Hassall enjoyed a jest at his expense.

Frustration welled up, tightening his throat, misting his eyes so that sun and sea shattered. *No hope,* a small voice said. *No hope, no hope; this will not be here when you can reach it, if ever you do walk after this—or live long enough to heal . . .*

Hassall returned down the hill. He brought a clay cup. He shadowed Gerik from the sun and sank down on his haunches to offer it. His face was dour, but there was a lightness about his eyes that Gerik had not seen before.

Gerik took the cup and drank, and gave it back. "Thank you," he said. It was self-discipline.

The Hound's lips curved. Hassall patted his shoulder, offered him a little bit of fish and bread in a frayed napkin. Gerik took it, ashamed that his hands were shaking. The shadow fell again as the Hound rose and went back to work, and Gerik broke off bits of the tasteless fish and swallowed it past the knot of anger in his throat, down onto the sickness the pain made.

There was mockery in all of it. *Be strong, my enemy. Try me.* But he ate it, and kept it down, and thought of the hut and Leisia, whether she waked or slept in the Witch's keeping, or when the rest of the Hounds would come riding in, discover him, and take exception to his attacking them on the road.

He had seen the Hounds' vengeance. That recollection did not improve his appetite.

Planks filled the sunlit gaps in the boat's hull. The Hound had a good eye. They admitted no light at all.

Hassall took him up the hill at sunset, gently held him by the arm and helped him on the bad side, for the leg was so swollen that it would hardly bear his weight, and climbing the sandy slope unaided was beyond him.

At the door the Witch met them with bowls of fish stew and a loaf of bread. Gerik sat down to eat, his legs stretched out before him, his back against the wall of the hut, and Hassall sat down cross-legged by him, putting down his food with great zest; Gerik did the best he could, and did not look at the man more than he could avoid.

But Leisia came timidly out the door and sat down by him,

her face all worried. "M'lord," she said, "Jevane says she will help you."

"Does she?" He swallowed a lump that grew suddenly too large. "I am not 'my lord.' I am not anybody's lord." Perhaps it was not well to admit that. Perhaps they confused him with someone. Perhaps it was all that had kept him alive. He took another morsel of bread and dropped it into the broth, and looked at the girl, whose face showed only concern for him. "Have you slept today?"

"Sometimes." Leisia's lips quivered. "Gerik—"

He invited whatever she would say with a tilt of his head; and winced at that use of his true name.

"I love you," she said.

That he had not expected. It went right through the armor. He moved his shoulders, gave a breath of a laugh. What else could a child say of a grown man who tried to do better for her than the world had done? Even if he failed at it. "You are a brave girl," he said. "Go on being brave."

A quick flush came to Leisia's face, a shining in her eyes. Hope. It hit him like a dull blow. "I want the lady to help you. I want . . ." Her voice died away, like the hope. "I want you to be safe."

He did laugh. It seemed a preposterous wish. "So do I." He wanted to reach out and hold her. But that betrayed too much to people who had no good intentions toward either of them. He quietly finished the bowl.

"When the boat is done," Leisia said, "we will sail away, to a place outside the war."

He set the bowl down and did not look at the Hound, whose ears seemed to work far better than his tongue. "How do you know that?"

"The lady showed me. In a dream. I can see that place."

"And will I go?"

Leisia shook her head, a small movement. Tears welled up in her eyes. "I am trying. I want you to go. Please do what the lady says. Do everything she says. She might let you then." The tears spilled. "The lady says you are a man; you can take care of yourself. But they kill everyone. They killed m-m-my—"

He snatched at her and hugged her to him, frail, hard little body racked with weeping. He hugged her till her shudders stilled, and rocked her, and squeezed his eyes shut along a seam of tears. "There," he said, when he had gotten his throat clear. He sighed and felt her sigh, and shivered and set her back before she could sense fear in him.

Her fingers brushed his eyelashes, the skin beneath them.

"Men cry," he said.

"I know," she said.

And all the while the Hound's eyes were on them. Gerik pushed her back from him, holding her arms and then her hands. There was nothing to say. There were no promises.

He thought of one. "I will try to come," he said.

It seemed to comfort her. He smiled at her, touched her chin. "There might be shells," he said, "on the shore. I had one once. No matter how far you are from the sea, if you put your ear to it, you can hear the waves. I thought it was magic. But the Wise Women said you can hear it in any shell. Do you think you can find me one? This great lump of a Hound is not likely to oblige me."

She turned an anxious glance toward Hassall, who made no move at all, then looked at him again, searching his eyes, whether he was telling her something secret in his whimsy. Wise girl.

"Leave me with the lady," he said.

She was afraid. She wanted to say something she dared not. Perhaps it was a warning.

Go, he shaped with his lips.

She slipped her hand from his, not without a look at Hassall, who sat with his arm over his knee and an empty bowl, his second, in his hand. She got up then and walked down the slope toward the shore.

"I want to talk with the lady," Gerik said to Hassall. And when Hassall made no move toward him or toward the girl, he braced his hands against the side of the hut and the ground and levered his way to his feet. A sweat broke out on him. It might have been the food, which lay like lead in an unwilling stomach. It might have been the movement of the small bone in his leg, which grated when he turned it and sent him blind a moment, leaning his shoulders against the boards as he stood.

Hassall gestured with his empty bowl toward the door of the hut. And got up, to walk behind him.

He had thought that would be the case.

But Leisia was out of the way. He hoped on that account there might be truth. He hobbled to the doorframe and grabbed for it, and looked back down the sandy slope where Leisia was.

And was not. She walked—and simply vanished.

"O gods!" he cried, and stumbled in that direction, but Hassall caught him as his swollen leg failed to bear his weight. He shoved at the Hound all the same, but there was nothing on the beach but sunfire, a fading twilight. *"Gods, bring her back!"*

The Hound wrapped him in his huge arms and turned him about again, to face the doorway where the Witch stood, wrapped in her dark robes. "She is safe," Jevane said quietly. "Hush, be still."

It was Hassall's grip kept him sane, till he had caught his breath and thought to himself that if Leisia was anywhere he would not learn it except of the Witch, of Jevane herself. He took another breath and a third, and slumped against the Hound's restraining hold. So the Hound pushed him forward, and as the lady would have it, took him inside the hut, half dragging him from the door to the hearth, where a fire lent light to the shabby interior. Jevane walked slowly to that hearthside and made a sign with her fingers.

Hassall let him go, carefully, and with a grip on his collar pulled him back against the stonework, off his balance. Gerik caught a hold on the rough stones, caught his breath again.

"Where is she?" he asked.

"As safe as I am," Jevane said. "Does that warn you, Dalesman?"

It did. He leaned his head back against the stones, his right arm still in the Hound's grip, his right leg refusing his weight. "Is she yours?" he asked. He thought that if that were the truth he would have no more reason to fight. Everything would have been a lie. Perhaps the Witch would sense as much and lie to him, for her own reasons. But he tried her honor, and his own sanity.

"No," the Witch said. "She is everything she seems. Sit down. Sit!"

The Hound let him go. He slumped toward the hearth, lost a convenient hold, and needed the Hound's help to make the last of the descent without jarring his leg. It still sent the stars flashing through his vision, and sweat stood cold on his skin. He caught his breath, resting with his head against a projecting stone and stared sidelong at the Witch, who sank down like a peasant with her arms about her knees, her fine robes in the dust and the fire lending her pale eyes a disquieting chatoyance.

So the Hound crouched down directly in front of the hearth, armored darkness in which the fire found points of metal and light.

The Witch searched among the clutter at the side of the dusty hearth, and moved several small pots in front of her. She dipped up a pannikin of water and set that among the rest, meticulous in her preparations.

"Where is she?" Gerik said, hoarse and harsh. Pretensions seemed vain now, and all on their side.

"You have lied to me," she said. "What is your name?"

"Eslen."

"A lie, Gerik of Paltendale."

Panic flowed through him. He did not move at all.

"Leisia told me," the Witch admitted the ordinary truth.

It hurt; but he had trusted his name to a child, and delivered that child to the enemy. What better did he deserve? She had betrayed him even recently, outside, without a thought. "So, well," he said, and shrugged. "That might be so. Or might not."

"Gerik," she named him assuredly. "Where do you fare?"

Again he shrugged.

"With what purpose?" she asked.

"Are you," he asked, hard-edged, "of Kolder or of Estcarp?"

"I am not of the Dales," she said. She disturbed the water with her finger, making rings. She drew her hand in a circle. He looked at her throat, amid those robes, for some Witch's jewel, but he saw none, only the silver ring on a fine-boned hand, the stone of which was colorless in the firelight and tawdry as peddler's glass.

"Where, then?" he asked. "Are you Kolder-bred?"

"You were going to your kin," was her answer, her voice soft and insistent as the sea-sound outside. "But there is no hope there. From south and from north the Hounds come. From Ulmsport and Jorby. There is no hope."

Such firm insistence was in that voice. It crept into the bones like other pain. And she could *not* have learned his intent from the child. He had never spoken it. He finally broke the spell. "Do Kolder ever tell the truth?"

"I can show you the truth," she said.

Scrying cups and witchery. He shook his head again, conscious of the Hound close to him, assurance that he would go nowhere against their will. "Or you might show me anything you choose," he said. "*That* is the truth, lady. Do not trouble yourself for petty tricks."

"You are no fool," the Witch said. Jevane. Or whatever her true name was. Then: "But I will not prevent you. You lost your horse. You stole Hassall's. But more, you stole the child, else I had let you go. This one more time I will spend effort on you. A third time you come to grief; do not come asking me for help."

"Kindness?" He did not believe it for an instant. The Witch told him there was no hope of his kin and told him in the next breath that she meant to help him.

"Hassall will gift you with the horse. Your armor is there in the corner. That is a choice you have."

"Where is she?"

There was long silence. At last Jevane took off her ring and dropped it into the bowl of water. The surface shimmered in the firelight, and steadied, became sunset, and sea, and children playing on the shore.

"Leisia," Jevane said, and one stopped, and left the game, walking toward the eye, toward the surface. Leisia's face shimmered within the bowl, her eyes wondering, as if she listened to something far and strange.

Jevane's hand plunged within the water and destroyed the image, retrieved the ring; Gerik thrust himself up on his hands, stopped instantly as Hassall's hand met his chest.

Answers. Lord and Lady, answers. What has she done?

"Was there grief?" Jevane asked. "Were there tears? No, Dalesman. They were happy."

"What have you done to them?"

"Sheltered them. Given them refuge. Did I not say it was Leisia guided you? Else you would have seen nothing here."

"You and this Hound—"

"Hassall is no ordinary sort of Hound." Jevane returned the ring to her finger, and laid that hand on Hassall's leather-armored knee. "The Kolder fail—at times. Rarely. But they do fail. He does not speak. Perhaps I might mend that, but it would be perilous for him. And we do understand one another."

Hassall inclined his head and looked Gerik's way. The almond eyes showed less of sullenness of a sudden, glittering with disturbing intelligence below that uncombed mane.

"The children—" Gerik said.

"Such ones are precious," Jevane said. "Such as could hear me, such as could come to this shore—such as are born with the gift—"

"The Wise Ones."

"Those. Would they were ten thousand. They are seventeen."

"With this . . ." Gerik moved his hand toward the Hound. "A Witch of Estcarp, with a man of Alizon—"

"A remarkable Hound, I say."

"A Kolder trick!" But it was not what he wanted to believe. He leaned there against the stone and hoped for answers. "Witch," he said in a voice not his voice. *"Kolder Witch—"* For they said that Estcarp battled for its life; Alizon had gone to the Kolder, and now it seemed that the Kolder took more than Alizon, and that more than the Hounds had sold themselves. "Where else could you match the two of you?"

"On a common border. In old quarrels. No, not Kolder, I. We have our quarrel with the Kolder, both—" There was for a moment something forbidding in Jevane's eyes. "But that is an old matter. This one involves the Dales. Do you understand? These children who have the gift, too young to wield it. Those with the Seeing, and the Healing—Leisia's kind—that boat will carry them. When the morning comes to the Dales—and it will come, Dalesman!—that boat will fare back again. No sword will come near them. Not one will perish. And they will have dreamed a dream. That is what you have seen. That is where your Leisia is, and there you cannot be."

He drew long, slow breaths. He clung with his hand to the projecting stone and felt its age-smooth heat, painful on that side. Coals chinked down in the fire. Such small things went on, despite the shifting of all the world. It seemed strange that they should.

"You have pressed me hard," Jevane said, "you, in coming here. Best you had never come. But Hassall will have no need of the horse. That much I can give you. I can heal your hurts. Do not think *that* comes without cost to me, or danger to all we do. The seeming that shields this place is very fragile. Still, we will manage, Hassall and I. Soon we will have finished here. And you will ride where you choose. South and west, by my advice; I did not lie about Jorby."

"The enemy is in the hills," he said. Truth spilled out of him. Perhaps it was be-spelling. He was afraid and he did not trust any future for himself, but young lives might be in the balance, as she had said. "The Hounds, wolfshields, Cervin's men. I know him from the north."

There was a sound from Hassall, a feral thing that touched the nape-hairs.

"Many of them?" Jevane asked.

"There will be. You take your reports from a child—Leisia would not know. I attacked them. That delayed them. But it also means Cervin will not come down our track with any light patrol. We taught him too well at Paltendale. But we left a dead horse behind us—carrion birds and a trail no tracker could fail—"

Hassall looked toward Jevane a long, long moment. Jevane nodded then, and opened certain of her tiny pots, and sifted herbs into the water. Often enough Gerik had seen a Wise Woman's healing, several times had that grace done him, in boyhood falls and sword-cuts and sprains in war. But she had not the homely aspect of Paltendale's Wise Woman, was forest fire to that woman's candle flame. There was a trap. Surely there was a trap. It was for him she prepared, he knew that it was by the things that she did, and the Hound sat there silent, unmoving.

"They are coming here," Gerik said again. "Have you a magic against that?"

"None to spare," she said. "Move his leg, Hassall."

Gerik edged the other direction and winced at the subtle grate of bone. "None to spare. Then give me the horse. Forbear your help. I will ride out of here."

"Do you believe me, then?"

He did. He did not. He caught a ragged breath against the throbbing in his leg and the buzzing in his skull, and shook his head. "No. But what *they* will do, I believe. Give me my armor. Give me the horse."

"And you will do great battle. You cannot sit a floor, man, small chance you can ride. Shall we leave you for them? Move him, Hassall."

He held up a hand in his defense; but Hassall put a gentle arm about him, eased him down on the hearthstones with tenderest care, and propped the leg on a folded blanket.

Jevane passed her hand over his shin and heat flowed beneath it, the whole swelling seeming fit to split the skin. She did the same with his whole body, which sent heat out from scrapes he had not reckoned. Then she drew back and dipped her fingers in the bowl, humming to herself—perhaps part of the magic, Gerik thought, perhaps high sorcery and not the sort Daleswomen knew. Or perhaps—his head spun as she worked and strange thoughts came to him—perhaps it was only idle preoccupation. He felt as if he drifted. He was lost, and heat and cold flowed through his wounds. "Hassall," Jevane's voice said from the bottom of a well, and he felt a harder, duller touch close about his leg; he suspected pain to follow and clenched his jaw and clenched his hands, wanting desperately to faint away as the Hound pulled and turned. Bone grated and snicked into place, a hot flash of pain became warmth, then cold. Lights ran fine trails through his vision, stars flashed and smelled of herbs and sulphur. He was falling. He felt all his life rushing along his veins wherever her hands hovered, this way and that, like winds. His command of his senses was threatened, his will undermined as if he stood on some crumbling cliff—no more of Gerik in the void below his feet, no more of him than she willed, no more could return than she was willing to surrender back again.

True, true, true. He knew it in that moment, all unwilling; he knew the scope of the disaster in High Hallack, the extent of the enemy, the fall of villages and keeps and holds throughout the Dales, saw the dead and the dying, the pitiful lot of refugees overrun by the Kolder-driven Hounds—the faces of his dead, of Fortal sinking away in his arms, of his parents, his sister—torn and bloodied—his mother and his brother—

He flung himself away. Pots scattered, spilling herbs and water, and hissed into the fire; it was Hassall who snatched him from harm, and caught him and held him fast.

"It is done," the Witch said.

The vision lingered. He saw it with his eyes open, saw it there and not there in the close dark of the hut and the night, in the shadows of her robe. He heard it in Hassall's harsh breathing and his own, the tramp of feet and the snap of banners.

"I counsel you go tonight," Jevane said.

"They are coming." The presence was about them like nightmare. He recognized the pass that flickered in his vision, though he had never seen it in the dark. A man did not have the Power. He flung his arm to free himself and to shake away the illusions. Her doing. Everything he saw was lent him, was a trick, was what she wished him to see; and in his mind he saw the boat standing bare and unfinished against the starlit shore. "Curse you!"

"Provisions. A canteen. Speed will help you most. I have the Farseeing, that only. The future is a trap and the past is a web of judgments." Sweat stood on the Witch's brow. Her skin was white, and hectic flush stained her face like the marks of fever. "There is peril in such Seeing now. Not in their seeing us. But the veils that shield this place have no substance against a chance intrusion."

"The Lord-forsaken boat is a wreck, a rotten hulk; for the

love of the Lady, woman, they are a day away from here at best—" The vision left him. The hut was about him with aching clarity, every imperfection, every ugliness of age and decay. "In the pass. Up there in the hills."

"You have lent me that. Yes."

"You cursed fools! Get out of here!"

She shook her head and gazed at him—Estcarp Witch, with nearly a score of young lives wrapped about her finger, with the Power to cast shapes and blast her enemies—only so they were not too many.

Power to shape truth. That too.

He swore. He tested the leg, whether it would bend. He got to his feet as Hassall did, springing up warily and between him and the seated Witch. Faithful Hound. Man of absolute loyalties.

"I am a Dalesman," Gerik said. "Curse you, ask me about horses, not boat building."

"Hassall's skill," Jevane said in a faint, faded voice. She did no more than lift her eyes to him. "Your willing hands, Dalesman. I have given you the strength. No more can I give you, but to tell you the choices."

They slept when they exhausted themselves, he and Hassall sprawled by their weapons on the sand near the blocks; they waked and worked by dimmest torchlight; for, Jevane warned them, fire and sound were both hazards to the illusion. Fire to light their work, fire to heat the pitch for caulking, and the soft sound of the mallet as Gerik worked seam after seam in the hull, the louder strokes of adze and hammer as Hassall did the exacting joining work in the fitful light.

"She did this," Gerik muttered, sure that Hassall heard him. "She meant this from the beginning." But it was unfair to harry the man about his loyalties, when the man had no voice to answer him. Tap and tap of the mallet. "We met

Cervin at Paltendale. We bled him. We bled him twice. You know him?"

There was a grunt, that much of a word. Gerik looked along the pitch-smeared hull and caught a look at Hassall's face in the torchlight. Hassall's mouth twisted and clamped in a grimace. He made a rude gesture common to both sides of the sea, and jerked his hand back toward the hills, toward the way the enemy would come.

"*Not* a friend of yours," Gerik said.

No. He was not.

Gerik dipped a new length of cord and applied it to the seam, cursing the heat and the stickiness of the pitch that made them both grotesque, he and the Hound streaked and crossed with black wherever cord or hull had touched them, wherever a hand had wiped sweat from face or chest or arms. The torchlight made them both demons.

"The lady will be sleeping," Gerik surmised. "Keeps the veils while she sleeps, can she?" A glance at Hassall, who betrayed nothing. "Or have we got them while she sleeps? Do you know?"

If Hassall knew, he kept that to himself.

Seam after seam, till hands were numb and the mallet slammed knuckles all too often. Gerik gnawed his lip and leaned up against the hull to work, with the tide curling up close to them.

"How in the sweet Lady's name do we get this thing to the water?" Gerik asked when that thought came to him. "Carry it on our backs? Push it, the two of us?"

A look and a two-handed shove at the hull from Hassall. Gerik spat pitch and sweat and blinked the salt that stung his eyes.

Leisia, shimmering away under the Witch's fingers. Spurt of blood from Sunel's neck, from a killing wound, from his brother's side, blood standing in puddles in a muddy and trampled field. He tapped away at the hull until he smashed his knuckles hard enough to bend him double and send the breath out of him. He swore when it came back, then staggered over to the blanket he had borrowed from the hut and threw himself facedown on it, to nurse his hand and shut his eyes until the gulls came crying overhead and he heard the sea again.

The sea was farther now. He had never marked the differences a tide made. He remembered then, things about launching ships on an ebbing tide, riding the outbound surge.

And landwind and seawind and moons and weather. Hassall might know these things. A man who could shape a boat would know such things.

It was not a case of launching at whim. He had not understood that. He reckoned with it now, and got up and joggled the can of pitch against the coals, stirring it with a stick to take down the scum that had formed. He attended a call of nature and came back to work, not thinking about breakfast, but Jevane herself came down in a cloud of swooping gulls, bringing them mealcakes and a little wine, which tasted all the same of pitch.

Three more planks went in. They were the last. Gerik wiped sweat in the morning sun and tapped away at the caulking, while Hassall hammered away at the tiller assemblage, iron muffled in leather—little to choose, Gerik thought, whether the hammering and the lights at night were worse, or this, by full light when they knew well that the enemy was that much closer.

Of Jevane there was no sign now. Of what she did up at the house Gerik had no sure knowledge, but he imagined her at the hearthside, scarcely stirring, spying on what might be spied upon, doing things into which he had no wish to inquire. Perhaps she could do something to muddle hearing as well as seeing. Perhaps she knew very well where the enemy might be. It was maddening that the one who might know was inaccessible and the one who knew her mind could not tell him what he knew—only a look, a grimace, a small sound or two.

He stopped to eat a bite of the leftover cakes that they protected from the gulls beneath a pile of canvas, had a drink of tepid water, and grimaced as he surveyed his blisters.

A thump sounded overhead. He looked up and saw Hassall come overside onto the shaky scaffolding that surrounded the bow. The Hound dropped again, landing on his feet in the shadow of the boat, came and motioned impatiently at the planking that lay by the net frames.

Up the scaffolding, then, scrambling up and down with lumber on boards that quaked and bounced under the weight. They both left bloody handprints on the boards, dropped spatters of sweat on old wood and new, as they fitted the decking and pegged it down.

"Deck," Gerik muttered. "Lord-forsaken boat needs a deck. The enemy is out there—do you have to walk around in this thing? Just make it float, for all that's holy—does the lady want pillows and brass fittings?"

Hassall pointed at a square down in the well as if it answered the matter.

Answer it did when the Hound insisted on larger timbers braced from under that deck, timbers hauled up that same scaffolding and handled over the side and down into the well; and decking fitted with a pit matching that below, while the sun sank lower down the sky and the heat lingered.

It was the mast that arrangement would support, the footing for that great timber that lay weathering on blocks over beneath the far side of the boat. Hassall fitted various trailing ropes about the mast cap in arcane purposes of his own, lifted the heavy foot of the mast on his shoulders, and Gerik raised scaffold braces under it; Hassall climbed the scaffold and lifted again, and the structure grew more precarious still under the unwieldy weight. The mast foot reached the rim of the boat, and both of them clambered up and hauled and heaved and braced their backs to step it into the socket; it slammed in with a thunder that rang through the wood and off the hills, and Gerik leaned there panting, embracing their unwieldy accomplishment and blinking through sweat as Hassall caught one of the heaviest of the trailing ropes and went to the bow.

"Tent pole," Gerik muttered, gazing up at the clutter of ropes that were still to fasten. He seized one that matched the forward stay and went to the stern with it, wrapping it about the stern post as Hassall came back to see to it.

The sun was low in the west now. They heaved and tied, tautened and wrapped, stem and stern and two ropes to the sides.

But Hassall stopped at the last, lifted his face as if he had heard a distant voice, and scrambled over the side as if that voice had said something that he had no wish to hear.

"What is it?" Gerik followed him to the side and leaned over the rim, but Hassall was looking toward the hills. "Are they there? Does she see them?"

Hassall made a furious gesture to come down, turned, and ran as much as walked across the sand, where the canvas was piled. Gerik clambered down the scaffolding, dropped to the ground, and, arriving to help, found himself hauling back heavy tackle and cable that made no sense to him, except he knew it was the rigging. Hassall brought other pieces; more of climbing and balancing on the tottering scaffolding until the gut ached and the knees went to water, as Gerik transferred the heavy items aboard.

Then the great boom had to be lifted aboard, and last came the unwieldy canvas, in a struggle across the sand that brought them to their knees more than once. Then the scaffolding collapsed. Gerik threw himself clear and looked up where the roll of canvas disappeared over the side like some monstrous white snake. Hassall's head and shoulders appeared above it.

Gerik waved a hand that he was unmaimed, and fell backward on the sand a moment to take his breath, drew several gasps unimpeded, and gathered himself up again to restore the scaffolding. He found himself mindlessly cursing on every breath, a kind of litany of the doomed, and glanced now and again toward the hills. He wanted to ask Hassall about saddling up the pony and bringing it around in the case they needed it; but why they might need it was too much to explain.

Instead he walked off from the work, took his sword, and cut the bindings on the nearest of the great net frames. He threw it down, dragging it and its rotten nets across the bow of the boat. Whether Hassall understood in his turn what a Dalesman was about, Gerik did not know, but he had in mind the good bow and the large supply of arrows that Hassall had brought down with his sword and his gear. He knocked down another of the frames and dragged it a little farther up and over from the last, struggling in the flutter of the rotten nets and the resistance of the sand. He took a third, and, sweating and sucking at a splinter in his palm, looked up at a whistle. The Hound clambered off the scaffolding and landed in the sand. Pointed back toward the hills.

Gerik turned. He could see nothing, yet. He strained his eyes toward that distant cut where high hills gave way to shoreside, remembering how the land lay, and how a force must come out there on that long slope.

Hassall arrived beside him and he looked back again, in the gathering twilight, seeing how the sea had moved in again, how the rollers came in and the wind blew stronger and stronger from the sea.

Lord, the tide goes out in the morning. They come too soon. Or we are a day too late.

"The lady—" He gestured up the hill.

Hassall gripped his arm, drew him back in the direction of their weapons.

"Do you know that she knows?" Gerik asked. He went beside the Hound, half running. "Man, do you plan on her holding them?"

The Hound said nothing, only ran ahead of him and took up his harness and his weapons.

Gerik took his own, gazing backward where the enemy must come. The light was at that treacherous time, colors fading, be it shore or hill, under a sky clear and leaden dull. He fastened buckles to the familiar tension. He felt over that split in his armor that he had not had time to mend. He saw Hassall heading back to the boat and felt a rush of panic, a sense of secrets he did not know, mundane things of the sea and the tides, sail and canvas and work he did not understand. Matters slid beyond his grasp and beyond his control.

He looked up to see the Witch descending the hill with bundles of cloth and baskets, refugee like all the thousands of his people, a power of Estcarp driven like the rest of them.

She came down to him in the twilight. Her hair was uncovered. Her robes fluttered and snapped about her in the sunset like so much smoke and night.

"There is the horse," she cried over the wind, fighting free of her hair. "There is time—there is time. Ride out of here!"

"And leave you to what?"

"There is no more shield! There has not been, since this morning! Get clear, I say, get clear."

"It is not finished!" he shouted at her. "Lord, woman, it is not finished. Can your Power weave cable and tie rope? If you have Power, use it on *them*!"

"*That* is my spelling!" she said, and thrust her hand toward the heavens, her face pale and terrible. "The weather I can hold—do you ask me the rocks and the hills and the enemy? *Get you gone! Twice and three times I give you your life. Do not waste it; we will manage with the sea!*"

"Lord-forsaken fool, woman! Tend to the enemy—they will be here before the tide floats her, even a landsman can reckon that—"

"Tend to the enemy and do *what* with the tide? I have said! There is no more shield—I cannot do one and the other—it was my strength I spent in you, that was the time I bought, you have paid your debt, man, now *ride.* Get off this shore and leave the matter to me!"

She swung her bundles beneath her arm; she shook the hair from her eyes and began to run. He stared after her, open-mouthed with what else he had meant to say, that she did not know the enemy, or the speed with which their cavalry moved—a woman, and no more apt to tactics than a fish to feathers. A woman with a damnable habit of waving a hand and having her way with one man and another.

Excepting the Kolder, who beset her kind in Estcarp. Excepting the Hounds, who, if she had the Power she vaunted, could not have harried her and her companion to this shore and cornered them and backed them to the sea.

Power enough to snare children, to lure them from across the Dales, through war and dangers the like of which Leisia knew—

"Damnable fool!" he cried at the winds, the gathering dark, at no one within reach.

And ran, taking his helm and shield as he went, for the house and the pen where the Alizon pony circled and stamped in rising disquiet at the wind.

The tack was there—that much foresight Jevane had had. The pony's gear was hanging over the rail, and Gerik slipped through and snared the pony with a rein, calmed him enough to get the blanket and saddle on his back. The pony rolled his eyes and sniffed the wind—danced and fretted when Gerik opened the gate and shot free as he came up in the stirrup and landed astride.

Rein and heel—not southward. It was the hills he aimed for. It was the downslope of the pass out of the Dales. He gave that wild shout the folk of Paltendale had given the Hounds cause to know, sent it ringing down the wind.

It had worked once, gods knew. Once before they had delayed off his track because they suspected more than a single man. He shouted, high and clear, and rode into the wide open, far, far up on the grassy heights.

"Haaaaaiiiiiiyyyyyyiiiii, Cervin! Come and fight me; do you dare?"

A darkness appeared at the top of the slope, a thin rim, like the rising of some vast black sun. It grew, and grew in the halflight, and became a line of riders from horizon to horizon. He heard them, that muttering and yelling that gave the Hounds their name. He heard the thunder of their horses above the howl of the wind.

"Haaaaaaaiiiiiiii!" he yelled, and lifted his sword to them, holding the pony tight reined.

He heard the arrows loose, saw the stain of shafts across the sky.

"Haaaaiiii," he yelled to the pony, and wheeled and fled pell-mell down the height.

Every shaft fell short. The wind was gusting in the archers' faces. The slope lent speed to the pony in its flight—creature half wild and surefooted in the dark.

They were following. They were doing what Dalesmen had prayed the Hounds would do a score of times, and now, *now,* the blackguards turned reckless and pursued, with the wide shore in their sights and the surety that in that broad beach and that rustic fisher hut and ship, there was no peril but prey.

They were Hounds. *Some* of them would stay for plunder, no matter how poor the pickings, no matter how many others of them he could draw off behind him. Enough of them would pull off his track for easier and less suspect prey—O Lord and Lady, to sweep through the fragile defense on the beach toward the ship that lay straight before them.

He had failed his intentions. Again. Fool that he was. He was not in danger. He could veer off south and up in the hills again and through brush and over game trails in the dark till the best of their trackers were confounded.

But there were costs of being a fool. A man who was a man knew that.

They would see him, Hassall and the lady Jevane; they would see a cursed fool out on the beach before them, and perhaps he would buy them time for the Witch to do something to save herself. And Leisia.

Leisia. And the others like her.

He had sorted the pursuers out. Houndlike, they rode without discipline. The fastest had come the farthest as they rode onto the beach, and that put the archers out of the business—their own front lines were within the arrow-fall; and chasing him had sorted them down to a handful of the foremost and the fleetest—two of whom found the bog in the gathering dark and foundered.

He did not press the pony now. He let himself be overtaken; and when he heard the hooves come thundering up, he whirled the pony about and met the rider with shield and sword, tumbled the wolfshield from the saddle in one shock of encounter as another rider came screaming in, leaning from his saddle.

Young Hound. Early mistake—against a veteran. Gerik turned and met flesh with sword's edge, and the enemy's sword went flying off in one direction, the rider and the horse in two more.

"Hyya!" he yelled at the pony, seeing riders coming in a closing crescent. He veered out of the arc and rode into the wind that came now as a hammering gale. The horse shied from it, threw his head, and spattered him with froth as he drove it straight on, gaining more room, more of the broad sand. He saw the boat black against the reflecting sea. He saw water closer than it had ever been, glistening under the blocks that held the boat.

"Jevane!" he shouted into the witch-wind. He saw the

chance of their safety, if that water swirled the sand into a froth beneath the boat, if it made ground the horses would not venture. The Witch had, after all, known what she was about—and the veteran soldier had lost the dice throw. He wished them well—he with his narrowing expanse of beach between the Hounds and the sea. He expected the riders behind him. He lifted his sword to the Witch and the Hound, knowing it was, after all, victory for the Dales. "Good luck to you!" he yelled, and hauled on the reins with his shield arm, to face about then, turning the hard-breathing pony to face the charge.

The Hound bearing down on him spilled out of the saddle, and the riderless horse veered off from the wind. Another saddle emptied, of the riders oncoming.

Their own fire, he thought in disgust for them.

And heard a keen, sharp whistle down the wind at his back.

Hassall!

Arrows flying *down* the wind, lent range and sorcerous accuracy. A whistle, loud and clear on a gust.

"You great fool!" he cried, and reined the pony about into the wind and the darkest end of the sky, full tilt for the boat. Great flapping monsters rolled and tumbled into his path, black shapes he recognized for the net frames, rolling in the windstorm. The pony whinnied terror and pitched, and he slashed the reins, pulled back and slid off, sending the terrified creature free in the dark, free as many another pony running loose in the night. A net fluttered at him as a frame rolled past. He cleared his shield of it and ran, dodging through the tumbling masses, letting the shield trail him in the wind.

The boat loomed ahead, moving on a surge, clear of its blocks. A light glowed along its bow, a shining beacon that snaked down to the side that turned to him as he waded and splashed into the treacherous sands. The hull bore down on him like a dark and perilous wall, like as not to bear him under.

He thrust his sword through his belt. He grabbed one-handed after the shining rope and lost his footing as a surge carried the boat against him and boiled the sand from under his feet.

But the rope drew him above the water. He used his shield hand on it as well, desperately, as the rope, in the small jolts of a great strength pulling it, lifted him to the rail. He flung one arm over, clung as the boat heeled and rolled, and a strong hand found purchase among his belts and gear and dragged him over the rim.

He caught his balance, face-to-face with Hassall in the dark. Jevane was clinging to the rope beside him, her hair flying straight out.

"Did I not say?" she shouted at him. "You mistake your directions, Dalesman!"

"I can go back to them!" he shouted back, waving a hand toward the enemy.

The Hound's hand rested heavily on his shoulder, a massive arm flung about him, steadying him as the boat heaved and he reeled for balance. The sea was under them. The sea was rolling far up, toward the Hounds. He saw chaos in the starlight beyond their bow, heard screams and panic.

Jevane flung up her arms and an illusory fire ran along the rim of the boat, up the ropes, up the mast. The wind died into sudden hush.

Then, which touch lifted the hairs at Gerik's nape, a new wind began to breathe outward from the land, the merest whispering of a wind.

"Get the sail run up," Jevane said. "On this one we can ride."

Afterword

When I read the Witch World *books, I was rather intrigued by the Kolder: perhaps it's my fascination with the alien . . . but that particular enemy and that particular period always seemed to me the most idea-producing. So when I was asked to do a story set in the Witch World and involving part of that war, I had little trouble visualizing my characters: figuring the land had to have survived the Kolder assault somehow, I came up with several of the more unlikely survivors and some of the odder allies—and got the notion that Estcarp or certain forces within it might have taken direct action in the situation my briefing sheets described . . .*

Some of the most effective actions in any war are carried out on a very small scale—the pebble that changes the course of a river, preserves or destroys things far downstream.

—C. J. Cherryh

RAMPION
by
Meredith Ann Pierce

I: Sif

The place I remember best about Castle Van is the women's garden. It was set in a little niche off the main courtyard, an open square of earth in the pavement, and it was planted with rampion. That was what we called it, anyway, after a similar herb that grew on the mainland. This herb that grew here in the garden was not native to our little island, or even to our world. It had been brought to the castle five years before my birth by Zara, the witch. The stranger. The madwoman. The woman who had come through the Gate.

Our little isle was called Ulys, and we lay off the coast between Jorby and Quayth. On a clear, very fine day, you could sometimes just see the hills of High Hallack beyond the haze. Most days were not fair. We were a stormy place of rough tides and submerged rocks, a magnet for every squall. Few ships docked at our tiny port. We kept aloof.

My father, Halss, was the lord of Ulys. Originally he had been a man of the Dales, the second son of a second son, who had left his clan and gone adventuring. He found his fortune here quite by accident, when the Sulcar merchantman he was passenger on began taking on water and had to put in to the nearest land they could—even if it was a nothing-place like Ulys.

What a stir he must have caused among the fisherfolk: they had seen Sulcarmen before, but never a highborn man of Hallack. He must have been gorgeous to look at then. Even in later years, when I was old enough to take note of such things, I could see how glorious he must have been, with his fair, flushed skin and sandy-coppery hair—though by then age and wenching, drink and despair had thickened and coarsened him.

He had been taken in by the lord of Ulys at once and housed in the finest guest chamber, while the captain of the Sulcar vessel and his men were left to find what lodging they could in town. The lord of the keep had only one child, my namesake, Alia, and she of marriageable age. When the Sulcar ship moved on, my father stayed to court the lord of Ulys's daughter.

Such a prize her dowry must have seemed! I have been told the weather was unusually fine that year, with hardly a storm. The winter, for once, was truly cold and dry, producing a fine crop of seafoxes, those small, thick-furred water dogs that visit our rocks. In winter, the keep men all go out with clubs and kill as many as they can. We sell the pelts to the Dalesmen merchants of the mainland.

My father married the lord of Ulys's daughter in spring, and when the old lord died a year later, became regent for the lady Alia. But she died childless, of the coughing sickness, barely three years after. That left him in a fine mess.

He could have left us then, gone back to High Hallack, but he did not. Shame or pride, I don't know which motivated him. Perhaps it was only inertia. Or greed. The seafoxes brought in a good income. His family had cut him off penniless when they had heard of his marriage outside the Dales.

The dowager Lord Halss spent four years improving the island then. He formed a small militia of castle guards and took charge of the fishing fleet. He repaired the boats of the fisherfolk and rebuilt the castle's crumbling outer walls. He even had a sea-chain stretched across the narrow harbor as a defense against pirates. Poor as our island was, raiders had been known to land—but only at the harbor. Reefs protected the rest of our shore.

These were the prosperous years for Ulys. It was during this time that the outland woman Zara came. I remember her a little, dimly. She was very tall, with dark red hair and dusky skin. She was not Sulcar, and she was not of the Dales. She would not say where she was from. Some called her mad or witchbrede. My father, it seems, was fascinated with her.

But he married Benis in the end, she who had been the lady Alia's cousin. Once more he could rightly be called the lord of Ulys. It was not a love match. I was born a year later and named Alia, though called Alys. But it was sons my father had been hoping for. Lady Benis managed the castle contentedly enough, stitched tapestry in the evenings, and ordered the servants about by day.

My father, with only the one daughter and no heirs, was not a seafaring man either by birth or inclination, so there was no escape for him from this little prison he had entered into by marriage. How he hated the rampion! I remember it growing in squat clumps of jagged, fleshy leaves. In spring, clusters of cone-shape flowers appeared on top, smelling pungent, like leeks. My father complained that they reeked, but to me the scent was rich and wonderful.

My lord wanted to dig up the garden, throw out the rampion, and plant something useful. He had no need of women's herbs. But my mother said no, to his face, quite definitely. It was the only time I remember her standing up to him openly and winning.

"I won't have you undoing the garden. I don't care where it came from—it is the only herb on this island that helps me. Once a month I send the girl to pull the leaves and make a salad for me."

She didn't mean me. She meant her maidservant, Imma. I hadn't known that, about the rampion. All I had known was that sometimes when my mother was ill, she shut her door and would not see me. Her women moved quickly and quietly then, and told me to go away.

I tried eating the rampion once, when toothache was making me flushed and feverish. The taste was sharp and peppery, almost bitter. It made my eyes weep, but it didn't do any good. I learned later that that was not the sort of illness it relieved. I was not old enough to have that sickness yet.

My earliest clear memory is of confronting my sister in the women's garden. It was summer, but the sky was cloudy, the air hot and damp. My mother was ill and had sent Imma for the herbs. I had followed secretly and stayed behind, and now stood among the miserable little clumps of rampion in violet and bluish bloom, each stalk blossoming like a mace among the glossy, dark green leaves. I was glaring at my sister—of course, I hadn't known then that she was my sister. I must have been about four years old.

To me, she was only Sif, mad Zara's child. My eyes were not good, and I recognized people more by shape and coloring than by details of feature. Sif was a lanky girl, with straight hair, long and yellowish, never combed. Her face was always smudged with grime, as were her patched, ill-mended clothes. I could see just well enough to note she had a long, strong jaw with a definite cleft to the chin and eyes that might have been any shade between blue-gray and sea-green. The day was dark, with storms coming. The light was bad. I had never been this close to her.

"What are you doing?" I cried, stamping my slippered foot and bunching the gores of my gown at the hips. "Stop that at once."

Not a moment before I had seen her empty a bag of kitchen scraps over the garden plants.

"Throwing rubbish on my mother's rampion," I shrilled. "Stop! Pick it up."

Sif looked up with a start, then squared her shoulders, obviously caught by surprise but unwilling to run. She was wearing trousers like a peasant or a boy. She didn't say anything. I was a cheeky brat, much spoiled, and seeing my advantage, came forward.

"Pick it up," I said, in the tone my mother used with washmaids, but Sif only looked at me. I flew at her in a fury of fists, shrieking, "I'll tell! I'll tell! My mother will send for the boatman, and he'll box your ears!"

Sif didn't fight me as I kicked and buffeted her, but she did catch hold of my wrist and whispered fiercely, "Very well, then, *do,* you little slut. See if I care. He can't do worse than he already does."

I stopped hitting and looked up. I was close enough to see her face almost clearly now, and I realized that what I had thought was a smudge on her one cheek was a bruise. She had another on the same side, just at the jawline near the chin. Her fingers twisting my wrist hurt. I jerked away and fell back a step. We stared at each other for a few moments, panting.

"It's not your mother's garden anyway," Sif said after a moment, still angry, but not so fierce. "It's *my* mother's. She started it."

I squinted, trying to see her better. "Your mother's dead," I said, doing my best to sound contemptuous. The truth was, the bruise on Sif's face had shaken me.

She answered without nodding. "Yes."

"She died on the rocks," I added in a moment.

"Yes."

Six months before, mad Zara had stolen a boat and tried for Arvon. It had been a foolish thing to do. Women were no use in boats. She had broken up on the reef and washed back, drowned. Her body and some of the wreckage had been found on the beach two days later.

I had heard my mother talking to her maids about it, little edges of disdain and horror and triumph in her voice. When Zara's body was found, my father had bolted himself in his chamber for two days and refused to come out. I was too young to understand these things. Old Sul, the boatman, kept Sif now.

I stared at her across the rampion. I could not see her well enough in the murky light to tell if her face had any expression. It seemed expressionless to me, a chalky blur.

"And it isn't rubbish," she said, toeing at something among the fleshy plants. Her voice was low for a girl's, like a sounding horn. "See for yourself. It's fish bones."

I knelt down and peered at the little white skeletons. They stank. "Why did you dump them here?" I demanded, looking up, still feeling righteous. I wrinkled my nose. "Can't you throw them on the midden like everyone else?"

Sif was kneeling across from me. "I didn't dump them," she answered, calmer now. "I put them there on purpose. For the rampion. They're good for it. Can't you see the plants are dying?"

I squinted at the fleshy, flowering clumps. They looked well enough to me.

"They need bones," Sif was saying. "Something in the bones nourishes them. And oyster shells. I put down crushed oyster shells when I can get them."

I rubbed my wrist and looked at her. My gown was already muddied. There was nothing I could do about it now—perhaps my mother was so sick the maids would not notice, or if they did, would not make a fuss. I knew I should be getting back, but strangely, I wanted to stay with Sif.

"Why?" I asked her. "Who told you this?"

"I *told* you," she answered. "My mother started the garden when she came to Ulys, ten years ago. She told me."

I had been born in the Year of the Salamander; Sif, some three years before. That would make her about eight at this time of our first meeting. If she spoke true, her mother had come to Ulys three years before Sif's birth. Before the lady Alia died—I had not known that.

And Zara had lived at the castle once. I knew that somehow, had heard it somewhere, whispered. My mother could hardly abide hearing her name mentioned. Sif's mother had been brought here by Sulcars, who had found her in the sea, and since she had no money, only a watertight bag of healer's herbs and cuttings, they had put her ashore at their first landfall. She could not get off the island then. My father would not let her go.

But she had left the castle when he married Benis, gone down to the beach and built a little hut. She had lived by scavenging, beachcombing, and as a sort of healer woman, practicing the herb craft. Some called her a witch, but the fisherfolk and even sometimes the keepfolk went to her. My mother would not have allowed her to set foot in the keep—if ever she had presented herself at our gate. But she never did. And she went mad in the end. Ulys drives many of us mad. Sif's mother never wed.

I wanted to ask Sif about her mother then, where she had come from and why she had stolen the boat. Why she had wanted to go to High Hallack, or Arvon, or wherever she had been headed, and had she truly been a witch, like those nameless women with their jewels across the sea?

I had no inkling then that she had not been of our world at all, but from another place, beyond our world and time, beyond the Gate—but I heard my nurse calling me, and since I did not want her to come looking and find me with dirty Sif, I ran away.

After that, we were not such enemies. I slipped away from my nurse as often as I could to meet with her. I had never had a friend before. Sif took me down to the wide, deserted ribbon of sand below Castle Van. All the sea wrack washed up there—nothing valuable, only bits of driftwood and shell. Once we found the blade of a Sulcar oar, broken off from the handle and partially burned, and once a harpoon head made of bone. Sif liked that. She put a string through it and wore it around her neck.

Sif showed me how to find shellfish under the sand, and how to skip a flat stone over the waves—I could never see well enough to watch it go, but my wrist soon gained the feel of the flick. I showed her my secret place at the top of the tower. It had been built long ago as a lookout for warships and pirate raiders, but High Hallack had long been at peace with us, and since my father had devised the harbor chain, pirates no longer troubled us. No one used the tower anymore.

Save Sif and me. We stayed in the tower often, crouched on the highest landing, three flights up, whenever Sif could get away from the boatman, Sul. He gave her all the hard work to do, she said, scraping the hulls for barnacles and hauling the catch from the hold to the gutting tables. My mother and her maids taught me mending and needlework.

Sif told me tales, tales her mother had told her of the land beyond the Gate. Impossible tales, mad tales that grew more marvelous with each telling, of a land where people lived ageless till the day they died. Everyone there was a witch with a house the size of Castle Van. Hundreds of castles built side by side made up vast cities of shimmering stone. People rode ships that sailed the air. Carts pulled themselves. Sometimes, I think, she was making it up.

"If your mother lived in such a wonderful place," I said once, scoffing—I must have been seven or eight by then, and Sif eleven or so. "Why ever did she come here?"

We stood on the rocky slope above the beach under a dark autumn sky. Arms spread like sea gulls for balance, we picked our way forward, hopping from stone to stone, looking for hegitts' eggs. Sif took my arm and heaved me over a wide gap. I was still much smaller than she, and wearing a keep-woman's voluminous gown that beat about me like wings in the wind.

"She said her world was very old, very crowded," answered Sif, bending to pluck a blue egg twice the size of my thumb from a crevice. She put it in a little bag with the others. "The witches had all had too many children. And some people were tired of the witchcraft, the palaces, and the carts. They wanted to come to a new place, and try to live without them."

She straightened. I stared at her, astonished. "They wanted to come here, to Ulys?"

Sif laughed and shook her head. "Not *here*. In the north somewhere. Where the Gate is. Her people have been coming through, she said, in little groups, for years."

Still staring, I lost my balance and caught Sif's arm to steady myself. We had legends of the Gate, even here, even in Ulys—brought in snippets and fragments from the mainland. It was a place in Arvon, a terrible place, where monsters came from and men disappeared. It was guarded by unspeakable horrors. It did not exist. It existed, but there were more than one. It moved about. It was impossible to find except by accident.

"Why did your mother come to Ulys, then?" I persisted.

Sif gave an exasperated sigh. "She didn't mean to. She'd been on her way to High Hallack when a storm caught her. She'd been in the sea three days when the Sulcarmen found her."

"Why?" I asked. We were picking our way carefully now.

"Just to see it!" cried Sif. "She said her people had stayed in one place four generations without exploring. My mother decided to see what the world was like. She was a great traveler. She told me she had already been across the sea to the Witch Land when her boat went down."

I scoffed again, clutching Sif's arm once more against the wind. Sif was strong. "Women don't travel," I said. "Except to marry." Sometimes girls on Ulys contracted to marry on the mainland. It was a rare and wonderful thing. Then their mothers gave them semroot to make them sleepy and bundled them onto brideboats to be ferried across. "Women don't travel," I said again.

"My mother did," said Sif. There were no bruises on her face today. Old Sul had not been in his cups the night before.

"They're useless on boats," I said, coming after.

"My mother wasn't," answered Sif, leaping the gap.

Your mother died on the rocks, I thought, but didn't say. I jumped, and the tall girl caught me.

"And neither am I!"

I looked up. "What do you mean?"

Sif just grinned, looking more like a boy than ever, thrusting out her long jaw with its cleft chin—not ducking shyly as a woman should. Her teeth were long and even, and her brows, which were darker than her yellow hair, met above the bridge of her long, straight nose. I poked her.

"What do you mean?"

She helped me down off the rocks. We had come to the strand. "Old Sul is teaching me the handling of boats," she whispered, and then squeezed my hand.

"He isn't!" I cried. "He can't. Women can't. It's . . . *bad.*" Women in boats brought sickness and storm. Everybody knew that.

Sif set off down the beach with her long legs striding and pulled me after. "He is. He has to!" Her voice was rushed with excitement. "He gashed his hand with a bait hook a half year gone, and it's been numb in three fingers since. He needs someone to help, and all he has is me. He treats me like a boy, anyway. It doesn't matter."

I stopped then, simply staring at her. The hegitts and the robber gulls wheeled overhead. Sif reached out for one. It veered away. She watched it, and laughed.

II: Woman's Plight

Sif and I spent what time we could tending the rampion. She still brought fish bones and oyster shells. I saved bones and brought the shells of eggs when I could get them away from table. The rampion struggled on in our loose, sandy soil. It was stubborn—but Ulys kills all things in time.

One day Sif brought a rampion leaf up to our landing at the top of the tower. We were still young, too young to know the true use of it yet. We had the vague feeling that it would make us women. Sif drew the long, jagged leaf from her sleeve and brushed the dirt from it. We stared at the dark green thing, and then Sif, very carefully, folded it along the vein and broke it in half. The juice was clear and colorless.

Silently, we ate—as I had eaten once before, before I knew Sif—grinding the leathery skin between our teeth to reach the wet within. The taste was strong and green, the smell like onions. Our eyes watered. We waited for a month after that: proud, expectant, secretly terrified. But nothing happened. We were too young.

Once, in the tower, Sif told me more of her mother, red-haired Zara, who had worn her hair cropped short and trousers like a man.

"Was she really a witch?" I asked.

Sif chafed her arms and shrugged. It was full night, the window in the wall above where she sat full of darkness. I crouched on the stairs. The candles guttered in the cool evening wind. Sif tore at the heel of bread I'd brought her. It was summer. She would not freeze in the tower that night. Old Sul had been in his cups again and had left a red weal across her shoulder that would last for days. She had shown it to me. She would spend a night or two in the tower, then go back to Sul, and things would go quietly for a while.

"I don't know," she said at last, and it took me a moment to realize she was replying to my question. She was silent a few moments. She was always silent after Sul had raised his hand to her. Then she said, quietly, "But I know the place my mother came from. It's north of here—I know that much. If I had a boat, I could find it."

She glanced at me.

"I made my mother tell me the way we were to go."

"Go?" I said. The tongue of flame on the candlewick made the stone walls jump and dance. "She left you behind when she tried for Arvon."

Sif shook her head and gnawed at the bread, moving her shoulder as she did so and wincing. "It wasn't Arvon she was heading for. And she took me with her."

The candle guttered.

"Down to the shore to say good-bye," I said, not believing what she was telling me.

Sif shook her head. "Into the boat. She put me in and shoved us off from shore. The water splashed about her legs, then up to her hips. It was early morn, the clouds obscuring High Hallack gray as dragons' breath."

She spoke calmly, as was her way. Sif rarely let passion overrule her—as I did invariably. I came up the last two steps and stood by the window, gazing out at the far, black, moonless sea. The starlight shone on it, a moving white blur to my eyes. But I could hear the sound of it, the crash and wash of distant waves, and I could smell it.

"It was a light boat, no draft at all," Sif went on, "the shallowest she could find. She hoped it would ride high enough to pass over the reefs. I didn't know anything about boats then. I must have been about six. She waded out, shoving the boat, with me in it, before her until the water was up to her waist; then she hauled herself aboard. I wanted to help, but she bade me stay where I was or we'd overbalance. Then she took the oars and rowed."

Sif nibbled at the bread.

"I'd never seen a woman row: long, even strokes. I thought it was wonderful. I thought my mother must be the strongest woman in the world. We drew near the reef. The sun was coming up, a white glare behind the shadow of Ulys in a gray-streaked sky. The tide was high, but going out. There was a gap in the reef she was making for, a little gap."

I saw Sif's hand tighten where it gripped her knees.

"But she had misjudged the depth, or our draft, or the time and tide. She could have made it, I think, in a smaller skiff, built only for one, or even in that boat if I had not been there weighing it down."

Her voice was very quiet now, bitter and deep.

"Our hull caught on a jagged rock. My mother tried to use the oar to lever us free. I started to stand, but she told me to sit and cling tight to the gunwale. The bottom scraped and grated. Mother leaned against the oar. A swell lifted us. We seemed to float free for a moment. Then a cross-wave struck the boat, spinning it, and we broke against the reef."

Sif stared into the candleflame. I could not think of anything to say.

"My mother was thrown beyond the rocks, I think, or onto them. I did not see her again. I was pitched shoreward. The currents are strange around the reef, with a fierce undertow going out with the tide. But I was so light, and rode so high in the water, that the waves carried me along parallel to the land for a while, then closer to shore. Old Sul was coming along the beach. He fished me out."

Even in the bad light, I could see Sif had grown pale. I touched her arm, which was cold. "I didn't know that," I said softly, able to speak now. "That she took you in the boat with her."

Sif shrugged into the sailor's blanket we kept in the tower against the wind. "No one does," she answered, "except maybe Sul. He guesses, I think."

She had finished the bread and now sat looking about as if there might, somehow, be more. There wasn't. Cook had been in a foul mood that evening, and half a loaf had been all I could beg.

"Your mother washed up on the beach two days later," I added, not asking.

Sif nodded, tucking the blanket more closely about her. "Yes."

Some years passed. Sif grew taller, while I gained barely an inch. She told me tales she heard the fishermen tell, of people and kingdoms under the sea. Sif was better at talespinning than I. I told her what the fishwives in the market said, and the gossip from the kitchen and my mother's maids. My father's hair got silver in it. My mother bore my father another short-lived son.

Then I found Sif doubled over in the tower one afternoon, not up on the landing, but below, near the bottom, on the steps. She was on her knees, bent forward, her forehead pressed to the wood.

"Sif, Sif," I cried, dropping the napkin of bannock I had brought for our supper. I ran to her and knelt.

When she lifted her face I could see she was very pale. Dark circles lay under her eyes, which had a wild and hopeless look. She was panting and shaking, and I could see where she had been biting her lip. She was twelve now. I was nine.

"What is it—has Sul hit you?" I asked. I could see no bruises.

She looked at me blankly, then turned and put her head down. "No. No, it isn't that."

I bent closer. "Are you ill? Is it fever?" I touched her arm, but the flesh felt cold, not hot and damp. Sif twitched.

"I . . . no—don't touch me," she panted. "I can't stand to be touched." Her teeth were clenched. I felt baffled, helpless.

"Something you ate?" I tried. We were seafaring folk, and

every one of us knew to eat fish fresh or not at all. But Sul was a lazy sloven these days, Sif said, and who knew what he might have given her?

She shook her head. "No, no." Her hands resting on the wood of the steps were fists. Silence a moment, then, softly, "Go away."

I sat back, startled, staring at her. She had never said such a thing to me before. I frowned hard, tracing the grain of the wood on the step, thinking. I had no intention of going. That was out of the question. Sif needed help, and I must think what to do. I gazed at her doubled figure, listening to her shallow breath, and then, suddenly, I knew.

"It's woman's plight, isn't it?" I asked her. Sif panted and said nothing. "Has old Sul told you what to do?"

Sif made a strangled sound. I couldn't tell if she was weeping or not. "He doesn't know anything—old fool, and wouldn't tell me if he did."

I chewed on that for a moment, feeling strange. For the first time, I knew more about something—something important—than Sif. A pale spider ran across the step beside my hand, jumped, and floated down on a thread of silk.

"Do you have any things?"

"No!" gasped Sif. Her teeth were clenched. "I hate this," she whispered. She was weeping. "I wish I were a boy."

I rose. "Stay here," I said, idiotically. Sif was not going anywhere. I unpinned my cloak and put it over her. She didn't move or turn to look at me. I put the napkin of food on the step near her hand before I left.

I went back to my mother's apartments and stole some of her bloodlinens. No one was about. She and her maids must have been down in the kitchen or the spinning room, or out of keep altogether at the market in the village. It didn't matter. I went down to the women's garden and tore up a handful of fat, dark green leaves. Clutching them and the bag of linens to my breast, I went back to the tower and Sif.

She hadn't moved or touched the food. My cape was slipping from her shoulders, and she hadn't bothered to pull it back up.

"Sif," I said, kneeling. "It's me, Alys. Eat this."

She looked up, her face pasty. "I can't eat," she whispered. "I feel boatsick."

"It's rampion," I said. "My mother uses it. Eat. I promise, it helps."

She stared at the leaf I held out, dully, as though she had never seen such a thing before, as though she had no idea what it was. Slowly, she moved her hand toward it, then stopped. "My fingers are numb."

Her voice was a ghost. I fed the leaf to her, bit by bit. Her lips were cracked and dry. I made her eat two more. Then we waited. The tower smelled of dust and seashells. The summer air was warm. I played with the ants that were carrying bits of chaff down the tower wall. The wind murmured. An hour later, Sif slowly straightened. She still looked pinched and weak, but her breathing had quieted, and some of the color had come back into her cheeks.

"I feel better now," she said quietly. "It still hurts, but it's bearable."

I gave her the last of the rampion, which she ate without complaint. Then I handed her the bloodlinens. She stared at them.

"They're my mother's," I told her. "Put one on."

Sif kept staring, and then looked at me. "How?" she said finally, so blankly I laughed. I showed her. We fumbled, but managed. I was too young yet to be wearing bloodlinens, but I had seen my mother's maids putting on theirs.

"How long. . . ?" I started.

Sif blushed to the bone. "It began last night. I felt ill this morning and couldn't haul the nets. Sul tried to box my ears, so I ran." She shrugged. Now that the pain was past, she seemed more her old self. "But running made it worse."

I sighed and mouthed a phrase I had heard my mother use. "We're born to suffering."

Sif gave a snort and picked at the crumbs of bannock in the napkin I'd brought. "My mother never said that." She shrugged again and gave me back my cloak. "I'll wager it isn't like that, beyond the Gate."

The winter I turned ten, my mother put a woman's gown on me, one that dragged the ground, though I was young yet to be called a woman. The garb was so heavy it slowed my steps, like a gown of lead. She kept me inside with the women then, saying I must learn to spin and weave and wait on my lord at table if I was to marry well. I found it all absurd. Who would marry the ten-year-old daughter of a tiny island lord? I wanted to know.

"Whoever'd have the fur trade hereabouts," my father laughed, stamping the snow from his boots and holding his hands out over the great hall's fire. My mother cleaned the blood from his fingers with a warm, wet cloth.

It had been a good clubbing that year, the foxpelts thick and soft. We would do well in spring when the fur traders came from the mainland. My father laughed again.

"Goddess knows, that's why I wed. And truth, no one'd have you for your looks."

I could not tell if he was joking or not. He boxed me across the backside as I passed, hard enough so I nearly dropped the pitcher I was carrying. He smelled of ale and the blood of seafoxes. My mother said nothing. She never crossed my father in public—or in private, either, for that matter.

I missed the outdoors and my freedom, the wind and wave smell, and the running on the beach with Sif. I hardly saw her anymore. Old Sul kept her working breakback at the nets and boats. He hardly lifted a hand himself anymore, and Sif had to do it all.

On rare occasions we met in the tower. She looked brown

as a boy, her shoulders straining the seams of the narrow shirt she wore. I made her a new shirt. She had never had much breast—unlike me, who my mother wrapped tight lest I look older than my years. Sif didn't show beneath the baggy front of her blouse. When she rolled back the sleeves, her arms were corded and hard. She spoke like the fisherfolk. I scarcely recognized her anymore. More often than our meeting, she left me presents in the rampion: a bright shell, a seastar, the speckled claw of something crablike and huge.

Then came the night when I was nearly eleven; Sif must have been about fourteen. It was the very end of winter, near fullmoon feast, but already warm enough for spring. I had seen the strand of kelp draped over the seaward gate: our signal to meet in the tower. It was nearly dusk, and I would be due in the supper hall soon. My mother always scolded when I was late; sometimes she pinched. But Sif had hung the seaweed, so I went.

I found her on the landing, pacing—not sitting at her ease as was her wont. Her shirt was torn at one shoulder, and she held it up, striding, striding the narrow space. She was two palm widths taller than I was—I realized that with a start. For the last year, when we had met, it was always crouching in secret, not running and walking the beach as we had used to do.

The look in her eye stopped me short on the last step: it was fierce and burning, half wild. I had never seen her so. Her face was flushed and bruised.

"Sif," I started.

She cut me off. "I'm going. I've got a boat."

I just stood, speechless. The candle in my hand, flaring and guttering, made the tower walls jump and dance. I shook my head, not understanding. My heart was pounding from climbing the steps.

"I got it out of the castle shed last autumn," Sif was saying.

"Sul let me take it. He said it was hopeless. But I've patched it. It'll hold—long enough to get me to Jorby, anyway."

"What are you talking about—what do you mean?" I started to say that, but she wouldn't let me speak. Her free hand clenched, the knuckles white.

"Sul was in his cups again—had been since noon. This morning he found a keg of the red washed up on the sand unbreached, unspoiled. Never a word to my lord, mind you. Kept it all to himself, and not a drop to me, either."

Her words fizzed, popping like the candleflame.

"And then a couple of hours back, he says what a pretty thing I am and how he's always liked them tall and fair. He told me I reminded him of a lass he once knew—save for being so skinny—and didn't I like his hand on me? I'd come under his roof so long ago, he could hardly remember if I were a lass or a boy, and he'd see for himself if I wouldn't show him."

She fingered the rip where her shirt's shoulder seam had parted. She was shaking with fury.

"I hit him with the gaffing hook. It drew blood. He fell—maybe I killed him. I didn't stay to find out." She chafed her arm a moment. A trickle of ice bled through me.

"He can't be dead, Sif," I whispered. "You wouldn't hit him that hard."

"Could and would," she muttered, then pierced me suddenly with her eyes: sea-green, green-gray. "Even if he's not dead, I can't stay here. I must get off Ulys, or I'll go mad."

The trickle of ice in me had become a torrent. I started to shake. "No, don't go," I said. "I'll tell my father. He'll punish Sul—make him leave you alone. I'll get Cook to give you a place in the kitchen . . ."

The words trailed off. Sif had stopped pacing. She leaned back against the stone wall beside the window, looking at me. Then she laughed once, a short, incredulous sound. "Do you think your father cares one tat what happens to me?" she asked. "If he'd any honor, he'd have taken me in himself when Zara died."

"I don't know what you mean," I stammered. "My father is a just and noble . . ."

"Oh, don't talk to me of your 'just and noble' lord," spat Sif, suddenly furious again. She straightened and stood away from the wall. "It's his noble justice left me in Sul's care all these years." She was close to shouting now. "Your fine lord father would have *married* my mother if I'd been born a boy!"

I found the wall behind me with a hand and leaned against it. I needed that support. I stared at Sif. She did not approach.

"I don't know what you mean," I whispered at last.

"By Gunnora," choked Sif. "Who did you think my father was?"

I did not answer, could not. I felt myself growing very pale. I had never, not once, ever imagined such a thing. I suppose if I had bothered to think of it at all, I would have guessed Sul.

"He promised to see she got safe to High Hallack," Sif was saying, "with money enough to buy her passage north—he promised to take her north himself, but later, once his position as lord of the island was more secure," Sif leaned her head back. "She grew to love him. He was kind to her. She told me that. But she didn't bear him an heir—only me. So he wed *your* mother and left mine to find her own way home."

"That isn't true," I whispered. My voice was shaking. I was close to tears. "My father would never . . ."

"Be so dishonorable?" she finished for me, then gave a sigh like one very weary. She spoke softly now, but the words were fierce. "Be glad he was, chit—for your sake. Else it'd have been me trussed up in those fine mucky skirts of yours, and you'd *never have been born.*"

We were silent for a while, looking at each other. The spring night air was cold. Her eyes implored me at last.

"I'll need food, Alys. I've already got the boat."

I did weep then. I couldn't help myself. She couldn't mean it. Not Sif. She couldn't truly mean to be leaving me.

"Where will you go?" I managed at last.

Sif turned away, started pacing again. "I don't know. To High Hallack, first. I'll sign as a seaman. They'll think I'm a boy."

"They won't," I said. "They'll find you out."

"I'll move on before they do," growled Sif, "I'll go north. I'll find my mother's Gate."

It was all absurd, as if she could really go.

"They'll never let you out," I said. "Even if Sul isn't dead, they'll never raise the harbor chain to let you pass . . ."

"I'm not going by the harbor," my sister snapped.

Panic seized me. "You'll drown like your mother—you'll die on the rocks!"

She stopped pacing and came back to me, stood above me on the landing. I stood on the steps. She reached out and touched my shoulder.

"It's midmonth, Alys," she whispered, and eyed me, wondering. "The full moon's in two days' time: spring tide. The water's deep. Don't you know that?"

I shook my head. I had lived on this little island all my life and never once sat in a boat. I knew nothing of tides. Sif's hand tightened.

"You have to help me," she said. "Sul kept no stores, and I've had no time to lay any in. I'd wanted to wait a year. But it must be now, tonight. I can't get into the kitchen, but you can."

I could indeed, but I didn't want to. I didn't want to help her leave me. Yet at the same time, I knew that Sif would do what Sif would do, as she had always done, with or without my help. Then I realized she needn't have told me at all. She didn't really need me; she wouldn't starve between here and High Hallack. She had come to say good-bye.

For a wild moment I wanted to go with her, wanted to beg her to take me along—anything to keep her from leaving me. But I remembered her tale of her mother's boat catching the reef because of too much weight. I would only burden her. I was just a girl. Women in boats were bad fortune. Everyone knew that. I was just a girl, and Sif . . . was Sif.

That was part of it, part of the reason I did not beg her, simply stood there with her hand on my shoulder and held my tongue. The other part of it was that suddenly I knew, with a certainty beyond all doubts and shadows, that full moon or no, high tide or no, spring tide or no, she would never succeed. Sif would die on the rocks.

I brought her everything she asked of me and more—though I had to wait till after supper. All through the meal I waited on my father's table. I stared at him as he ate his fill, laughed with his men, and played games of chance, till my mother pinched me and asked what made me so walleyed. Both of them looked like strangers to me. I didn't know them.

When I was dismissed, I lingered in the kitchen until Cook and her maids were at their own fare in the adjoining room, before seizing everything I could lay hold of and wrapping it up in an oiled cloth for Sif: roast fowl and hardcake, seagranates, and two pouches of wine.

I brought them to her in the tower, along with a little bag of sewing floss. I mended her shirt by candlelight and helped her carry her journey fare down to the seaward gate. No one saw us. My father's guards were slack and full of their own importance and never kept good watch. The reef and the harbor chain were all the watch our island needed.

I gave her my good green cloak, which was closewoven of seahair to keep out the damp, and the gold brooch my mother had given me the year before, when she had first put a woman's gown on me. The month after Sif left, when I told her I had lost it, she gave me a slap that bloodied my nose.

Standing there by the seagate in the darkness under the high, near-full moon, Sif bent down and kissed my cheek, a thing she had never done before, and passed the bone harpoon head that she wore on a string around her neck into my hand. I got my last good look at her face. She was smiling.

"You're not afraid, are you?" I asked.

She shook her head. "I know the way as far as Jorby—I've made sailors at the inn tell me as much. It should not be too hard from there."

I hugged her very tight, holding the bone harpoon head till it cut my hand. I never wanted to let her go. But I did at last, when I heard her sighing and impatient to be gone. She really wasn't afraid. I released her and stepped back.

She bent and gathered the things I'd given her and was off—striding down the steep, narrow, moonlit path toward the sea below. She had eyes like a cat in the dark, and I had the eyes of a mole. I didn't stay to watch her go. I would not have been able to see her long anyway. I shut the seagate and turned away, back to Castle Van. I knew that I would never see her again.

III: Seasinger

It's strange sometimes how the scent of someone lingers, like smoke in a still room after the candle's out. Sif's presence lingered with me for months. I kept expecting to see her, striding along the beach below Castle Van, or ducking into the tower, or to see a strand of kelp draped over the seagate—but I never did.

They never found her body. Sometimes the sea does not give up her dead. Old Sul turned out not to be dead after all, and I could not help feeling bitter that he was not. It meant my sister had died for nothing. She could have stayed.

That spring when Sif disappeared was the start of Ulys's long misfortune. All the luck seemed to wash away. The weather turned bad—a constant, dismal, murky, damp wind so cold that it cut the bone, but no snow drying the air. Fishing fell off, and the red dead-men's-hands got into the shellfish beds. Shore fever took many of the fisherfolk—but not old Sul. He lived another three years before expiring of an apoplexy. Inwardly, I rejoiced.

But worst of all, the seafoxes dwindled. Perhaps they found another place to winter. I hoped so. Every year my father's men came back from the clubbing with fewer pelts; almost no white or speckled or silver anymore—only the black and the brown, and those thin and small. Second-rate fur—the Dalesmen paid little for it.

Castle Van went into debt to the Hallack merchants from whom we bought many of our goods. Certain valuable heirlooms about the palace quietly disappeared, sold on the mainland, I think. My father made the crossing more than once to secure us loans, always smaller than he had hoped and at exorbitant rates. He lost a good deal of that money gambling and, probably, wenching.

My mother, in a white rage, whispered—but not to him—that he ought to ask his Dalesmen kin for help. He was too proud for that. They had disinherited him years ago. At last, there were no more loans to be had. My father, resourceless, prowled the confines of our small, gray keep and our small, gray isle, and began to go mad.

My mother, with a kind of desperate determination, refused to despair. All would be put right, she vowed, when I married. She and her maids got me by the hair then and took charge of my rearing—a task she said they had grossly neglected before.

Got me by the hair quite literally. I was no longer allowed

to trim it off just below the level of my shoulders, but must let it grow and grow, a waterfall of reddish gold that was heavy and, in the summer, hot. Why couldn't I cut it? I wanted to know. Why must it be so long?

Because that was what a woman's hair was for, my mother said, parting the strands along the center of my scalp with a comb—to be a beauty to a husband's eye. But I didn't have a husband, I protested. *Yet,* she countered, brushing, brushing. It would be sooner than I thought—didn't I want one? No, I didn't want one, I answered, but only to myself, silently. I wanted my childhood back. I wanted Sif.

When I was thirteen years old, my father betrothed me to a minor lord of a minor clan of High Hallack, one Olsan. A brilliant stroke, he called it. Not for sixty years had the daughter of the lord of Ulys actually lived upon the mainland as a lady of a Dale.

I was to remain on Ulys until I was fifteen, then go to join my lord. He wrote me letters I could not read. My mother read them (or pretended to) and summarized. I had the impression he must be older than my father. No one would say, but he already had children, sons. His first wife was dead.

When I was told that the arrangements for my betrothal were being made, the envoys with the marriage axe already on their way, I went down to the beach and looked out at the rocks. I wondered what it would be like to drown, to be torn apart by the gray and heaving sea, to die on jagged stone. I wondered whether I was brave enough to follow Sif, to wade out to my death rather than marry an old man whose household would probably laugh at me.

I was not brave enough. I was a coward at heart—or perhaps I was only practical. I knew that freedom was impossible for me. It was only a question of death or life. And I wanted life, even as the plain, untutored, provincial young wife of a stranger. I turned away from the rocks, from the storm-gray sea, and went back to the castle to face the axe.

* * *

After my betrothal, I was taught how to pin my hair, how to walk, how to speak, how to wear my clothes. My mother sent to the mainland to learn how Daleswomen's gowns were cut. I was made to recite poetry. (They gave up on singing—I had no voice.) I could dance a little. My mother was passionate to impress on me all the arts and graces she fancied a matron of High Hallack would know.

My husband even sent a dame, one of the religious women of the Dales who live without men in sacred houses and worship the Flame. This woman was to instruct me in my husband's religion. (My father's clan had followed other gods.) I could make little of what she told me, but was able to rattle off the phrases quickly enough by rote.

I think Dame Elit sensed my reluctance. She did not stay long: two months. The unrelenting gray of our weather grated on her. She gave me a pat on the cheek and told my mother she would instruct me further when my lord sent for me. Then she went down to the harbor and took passage on the next boat to the mainland. My mother was furious, saying I had driven her off with my stupidity.

The rampion died. Without Sif, I had not the heart to tend it. I came to womanhood not long after my betrothal and suffered the woman's plight my mother had always complained of without relief. Nothing grew in the garden anymore. At regular intervals thereafter, whenever the moon turned dark, it was the same. I thought of Sif, and dreamed of the dark leaves' green and bitter taste.

My betrothed, Lord Olsan of High Hallack, died when I was fourteen years old; some border dispute among the Dalesmen, and he was killed. We had mourning. For three months my mother tied black ribbons in my hair. I was told to look sad. Secretly, though, I did not mourn.

Then I learned that my father had not even waited for the days of mourning to elapse before offering me to any of

Olsan's sons who would have me. He was soundly rebuffed. They were all but one married themselves, to good Daleswomen. I had been but a toy for their father in his age, but they had heirs to get and needed no beggars from Ulys to do it on.

So my father demanded that the part of my dowry that had been sent ahead be returned—and was laughed at. The sons of Olsan knew we of Ulys had no friends or armies to insist on justice. My mother raged. My father suffered fierce headaches and fits of temper. I crept about dejectedly, like a whipped dog, until it occurred to me that what passed between the Dalesmen and my father really had nothing to do with me.

When the castle's debts fell due, he offered me at large in High Hallack. Few lords even bothered to reply. Some of their scorn was for me, I think, as a pauper's daughter—but mostly for him: the madman who would sell his kith so openly. There were delicacies to be observed in the barter of daughters, and he had not observed them. Ulys became a laughingstock, and some of the fisherfolk began to say it was a curse that had driven the lord of the castle mad and chased the seafoxes away.

My father began to be too much in his winecup then, and to gamble in the evenings with his men. When castle stores ran low, he sent men-at-arms to seize the fisherfolk's catch. He ordered the people to gather oysters and search for pearls, though our shellfish are not the kind that bear many pearls. His headaches grew worse. The gates of the castle began to be barred in the evenings, a thing that had never been done in the history of Ulys.

Eventually he began to revile my mother. I remember once we sat in the hearthroom just off the kitchen after supper; my father, my mother, me, and a few of their men and maids, there together for the warmth. It was winter, and we were short of fuel. My lord and lady had been arguing about something, some little thing, over supper, but had been silent since, when suddenly my father looked up from his cup and growled,

"What is wrong with you, woman, that you never gave me sons? Sons to bring commerce to this little spit of rock, sons to sail and find where the cursed seafoxes have gone?" He looked at the wine dark in the bowl of his cup and muttered, "All you could give me was a chit."

My mother, tight-lipped and hemming a handkerchief beside the hearth, could take much from my father and had done so over the years, but his saying that she had not done what women were made to do—that is, give their lords an heir—was too much. Before I could even blink, my mother was on her feet, crying.

"I gave you four sons, live out of the womb." All this from the time I was two till I was nine. "They were your seed, my lord, but they died." She had pricked herself with her needle, and the cloth held a bright red stain. "Do not complain to me that you have no sons."

At which, my father cast his cup away with a shout and gave her such a blow it put her on the ground. He was seized with one of his headaches then and was not fit company for days. He was clearly mad. We were all afraid of him.

My mother grew to loathe the sight of me, my father as well. I came to move between the pair of them furtively, like a shadow. My weak eyes did not help. I could not always tell what expression sat their faces. I stayed out of reach. I thought of Sif dodging old Sul, and looked back on her plight with new understanding.

There was no one on Ulys high enough or rich enough to marry me, and no one in High Hallack would have me. My mother spoke once—only once—of sending me to dwell with the dames in Norstead, but my father shouted that by the Horned Man, he'd not send even a worthless girl to serve the superstitions of the thrice-cursed Dalesmen and their Flame.

It was not, I think, that he had forgotten he had been a

Dalesman once himself, but rather that he remembered and at the same time knew beyond all shadows, to his bitter rue, that he could never be one again. Ulys had got him by the hair, too. He could never go back.

I was seventeen, unmarried and unspoken for, when the seasinger came. The girls on Ulys wed at thirteen and fourteen. I was an anomaly, a quirk. A jinx, some said. No man would have me. I had learned not to go down to the market anymore, even with my mother's maids. The looks some of the fishwives gave me made my blood cold.

Perhaps they thought I was the reason the catch and the seafoxes were all so scarce. Or perhaps it was just that I was my father's daughter. He took their labor and their goods, calling it his due, and shared none of the castle stores with them, even when they were starving. They had begun to hate us, I think.

But the seasinger changed all that. He came on a ship of Hallack merchantmen come to look at our meager crop of furs. It was spring. He was not a merchant himself, that much seemed plain. He spoke more like a Dalesman than not, but the cut of his hair was different: bangs across the brow in front and long down the neck behind. It was fair hair, dark gold, though his beard was reddish. A fine, thick beard—no boy's—so he must have been late in his twenties, surely. His face, they said, was neither lined nor weathered, though well-browned by the sun.

Not a common seafarer at all, perhaps? Higher born than that, perhaps? That was what some of the maids speculated. I got all my information from them. They invented excuses to go to the market to see him, to gather news of him.

He played in taverns down by the wharves, songs of High Hallack, and other songs such as none of us had ever heard—though he knew the Ulish fishing songs as well. His accent was good. He picked up the way of our speech very quickly.

All my mother's maids were wild for him. He paid them polite attention and nothing more. They mooned and sighed over him shamelessly, I am sure, while he—never cold, never aloof—yet never seemed to favor one over another, or return a sidelong longing glance, or answer an urgently whispered plea to meet behind the tavern, or in the cow shed, or on the strand.

When the furriers went back to High Hallack at week's end, he stayed. That sparked great interest among the fisher-folk—among my mother's maids as well. Another four days passed, but none seemed to know what the stranger's business in Ulys might be. He would not say.

One of my mother's maidservants came to me when the seasinger had been on our island a week. It was Danna, a saucy girl with dark brown curls. She was younger than I by a year, unmarried, but spoken for. That did not stop her flirting. I sat making tapestry by the open window, bending close and peering so I could count the threads. Danna was a good enough sort. I did not dislike her.

"He asked about you today," she said, her voice pitched low, conspiratorially.

I sighed. "Did he send you to fetch me?" I asked, grown used to my father's whims, but unwilling to go before him without some accompaniment to help insure my safety. "Where's my mother?"

Danna laughed and slapped her hip. "Your mother's below, with Madam Cook, else I would not be telling you this. And it's not your father I mean who asked of you. I mean the stranger, down by the tavern. The singer—*he* asked."

I frowned and looked up. "What do you mean?"

Danna was not close enough for me to see her face well. I could not tell if she was teasing me. As it turned out, she was, but by telling the truth, not otherwise.

"I was at the market," she said, "buying the fleckfish your lady and Madam Cook are now discussing. And I saw him, leaning against the inn wall and looking out over the square, eating a fat carnelian fruit in slices with his dagger. So I called out to him, bold as hegitts. I said, 'Ho, singer, why are you not singing in tavern, as that's what you do?'"

She gave a nervous titter at the thought of having been so brash.

"And he said, tossing me a slice of fruit, 'Not all the time, my lass. A man must eat.'"

I sat looking at her. She had covered her mouth with her hands and was blushing—I could see that well—but her tone told me she was more delighted than ashamed.

"And then he said," whispered Danna, "then he said, 'You're Danna, aren't you—Uldinna's daughter?' Truly, hearing him say that, I nearly jumped out of my hair, and I didn't eat his fruit. I came to myself. I said, 'And how do you know that?' And he said, shoving away from where he was leaning. He was smiling—oh, he does have a foxy smile: all his teeth straight, and none missing. But truth, I was a little ware of him by then.

"But he said, soft and courtly as a lord, 'Oh, I've learned many things, Danna, in the little time I've been here—about you and about this place. For example, I know you work in the lord of Ulys's keep.'

"'I do,' I said. 'I am maid-waiting on the lady Benis.'

"'Ah,' he says, 'and I hear the lady Benis has a daughter, a famous daughter, one all Hallack speaks of . . .'

"And I said, forgetting myself, I said, 'Hold right there, you. It wasn't the lady Alia's fault, her Dalesman lord dying and my lord all in debt. She's a fine, *good* girl, and all this talk of a curse is nothing . . .'

"But he laughed! 'No, no. You mistake me. That is not what I have heard at all,' he said. 'Word is, where I am from, that she is a handsome lass, fair as morning light, with all the virtues a highborn maid should have. But she is proud as her father is rich, and spurned the lord she was betrothed to, till he died of grief. Then she spurned all the other desperate suitors that clamored for her hand.' He smiled at me. 'At least, so they sing the tale where I am from.'

"'Where are you from, sir?' I asked him, but he only laughed.

"'Ah, that I cannot tell you just yet, my lass.' He sounded so like a Dalesman then. But not like a merchant—more like your father speaks, like a lord. I'm sure he cannot but be some highborn noble of High Hallack, and the way he speaks to sing us songs in tavern all pretense."

Danna was gazing at me earnestly now. I did not know what to make of her words, nor whether she might be gaming with me. Flustered, I tried to turn back to my tapestry, but the threads kept tangling. My mother's maidservant went on.

"'But how is it,' the seasinger now says, 'in all the days I've been here, and all the ladies of Lord Halss's keep'—imagine him calling maids such as I *ladies*—'all those that have come down from the keep to hear my singing, that I have never so much as glimpsed this celebrated girl?'

"'Well, she never comes out of the keep,' I said.

"'What, never?' the young man asked. He seemed truly surprised. 'Does she not walk along the beach of a morning, or come down to the village on market day?'

"'No, sir, she does not—my lord and lady keeping such a close watch on her as they do, not wanting her to fall in with mere common sorts.'

"I said that, looking hard at him, for suddenly I couldn't tell anymore whether he seemed a common seasinger or a highborn Dalesman lord—and the moment before I'd been so *sure*. But he never so much as blinked."

I gazed out the window then, at the blur of nothingness beyond that was the sky. Danna's words ran against my ears like water for a little space, meaning nothing. "Close watch" indeed! I was a prisoner of my father's keep and my mother's isle; withering and dying by inches, like the rampion. I felt frozen, and old.

"He seemed to think on that a while," Danna was saying as I began listening again. "And then he said, 'Might this young lady be in need of music lessons? Every fair daughter of a high lord surely must . . .'

"'Oh, sir, she's hopeless,' I cried. 'The lady Benis tried and tried . . .'"

I glanced at Danna, and the dark-haired girl had the grace to stumble to a halt and blush. I sighed again and turned back to my weaving, satisfied that I knew this seasinger now for what he was, a fortune-seeker, and one who clearly thought my father richer than he was. We had no gold to spare on fripperies like music. But even my glare had not silenced Danna.

"Well, then, all he said was, 'Commend me to the young lady Alia and tell her I stand ready at her service,' and I said I wouldn't, he had a fair tongue, and that I had it in mind to tell the lord Halss himself that an impertinent talesinger had been asking after his daughter.

"But—and here's the odd part, my lady—he only just smiled at me. He didn't seem angry or frightened at all; any common man would have been. And his voice grew all High Hallack and noble again suddenly. He just smiled and said I'd do no such thing—didn't I want to eat my slice of fruit that was dripping all over my hand?

"And then, truth, I just didn't want to tell my lord, or anyone, save you, and I was ravenous for that bit of fruit. So I ate it quick, and when I did, it was the sweetest thing."

A strange sensation ran through me, hearing that last which Danna said. I began to wonder if there might be more to this mysterious seasinger than just fortune-seeking. My mother's maids continued their silly speculations that he must be some prince of the mainland traveling disguised, adventuring, or—here they sighed—even bride-seeking.

But the more I pondered Danna's tale—of his causing her, with no more than a word and a smile, to forget her intention to report to my lord and savor a fruit she did not want—the more the strange fear grew in me that he must be some conjurer, about what game I could not tell. I resolved to stay wide of him; not that there was any need, with him safely barred from keep and me safely prisoned within.

To my surprise, I did have need of my resolve, and soon. The very next afternoon, the seasinger presented himself at the castle gate. My father was ill with headache and could receive no one, and so my mother was sent for. She was suitably indignant at this mere entertainer's cheek and kept him waiting an hour before donning a fine, fox-trimmed robe and going down to the audience hall, a crowd of maids and ladies revolving around her like satellites.

I was instructed to remain out of the way and on no account to show my face in the audience hall. This I gladly did, having no desire to don a formal gown too tight in the bodice to breathe in and too voluminous to walk in with ease. I dawdled in the kitchen, helping Cook make tarts. I had no wish to see the seasinger. I hoped my mother would send him away.

But she did not. She entertained him for two hours in the hall, listening rapt to his songs and stories. Twice she sent to the kitchen for refreshments, first for cakes and candied eels, and shortly after for the good yellow wine—not the common cellar stock, either, but my lord's private store.

Cook was astonished. I went back to my mother's chambers to await her return with a sharp sense of misgivings. She returned at last, she and her maids all in a flutter, their faces flushed from the strong yellow wine.

"Oh," my mother said, clinging to Imma for balance while another of her maids helped her off with her slippers. "Oh, he is an impressive young man."

A third assisted her with her outer robe. They were all a little unsteady on their feet.

"Such wit, such courtesy. Surely Ulys has never seen the like—saving only my lord husband, of course." She hiccuped and sat down suddenly. Her maids, some of them hiccuping themselves, giggled. My mother joined them.

"And wasn't it clever," she added, "wasn't it clever of me to call for the wine? It put him in a garrulous mood, did it not?"

"A fine mood, m'lady," Imma echoed her. I could see Danna just beyond them on a footstool, dozing where she sat.

"The thing or two he let slip after the second cup!" my mother laughed, worrying with the pins holding her hair. Imma stumbled to help her.

"The way he talked, m'lady, I wouldn't be surprised if he was a prince disguised, a prince of High Hallack come adventuring."

My skin prickled and drew up; he had them all believing it now, and even saying so in front of my mother. I glanced quickly at Danna, but she never so much as stirred in her sleep. My mother nodded.

"I am sure he is of the Haryl clan," she answered. "He mentioned their Dale."

I blushed. The scent of yellow wine was strong in the room, like spilled cider. Imma and her fellows buzzed around like bees. Clearly they had all had several more after the second cup—and probably done no better than make fools of themselves before this common conjurer. My mother laughed again.

"Surely he is rich."

I looked up sharply. What could she mean—a seasinger, rich? My mother seemed to catch sight of me then for the first time.

"Look, Alia; look," she exclaimed. "See what the young man presented to me."

She beckoned her other maid, Rolla, forward. The girl held an oblong something covered with coarse brown sacking. She laid it on the bed. My mother awkwardly pulled the sacking off, and I saw a bolt of cloth—but such cloth as I had never seen.

The threads were very fine and slick, the weave tight, not the least bit sheer. I ran my hand over it; it was soft, yet strangely crisp. It made many tiny wrinkles but did not keep them, springing back from the touch. I sensed water would bead on this stuff. It rustled. It whispered. But the oddest thing about it was its color, appearing from some angles pearly blue-gray or silver, and from others pink.

I stared at it. The cloth had left a witch feel in my hand. All the fine hairs along my arm were standing up. My mother held a length of it up to her, fingering it.

"Oh, we must make him welcome, that we must," she crowed. "One who knows where they make this cloth—he could make us rich! Alia, have you ever seen the like? How much would even a yard of this bring in High Hallack? Wealth!"

The hairs on my head felt charged and alive, the way they did before a storm. I felt strange, troubled. I could not think of anything to say. My mother dropped the cloth suddenly and frowned a trace. "What a pity he declined my invitation to stay at keep."

She glanced at me.

"Well, no matter," she said. "Alia, my dear"—she spoke very distinctly now, against the slurring of the wine—"we must make you ready. I have invited this young man to fullmoon feast two days from now. Your father will be over his headache by then, and we must be certain you are looking your best."

I drew back, my heart dropping like a stone. My throat was suddenly tight. The cloth on the bed snapped and sparkled where my mother stroked it. I began to fear more than wine and flattery had had a hand in my mother's change of heart:

inviting strangers to table and calling them lords. Conjurer—warlock, more like! I wanted nothing to do with him.

"Must—must I, mother?" I stammered. "The time of the moon is wrong. I shall be ill that night, I know it." It was a lie. My time was always at moondark, not fullmoon feast—but it was all I could think of. My mother's lips compressed.

"Well or ill," she snapped, "you'll make yourself ready and be glad on it. The young gentleman—who is calling himself Gyrec at present—has expressed a particular wish to see you." She glanced away, her eyes a little unfocused. "Imma, my patterns. We must see my daughter has a new gown."

I shuddered then and could have wept. So they were offering me up to seasingers now. Who would it be next—Sulcars? Seacaptains? I had begun to think myself safe from this bargaining at last; my father too ill and indebted, my mother too resourceless to try again. I had been a fool to hope. I thought of Sif, tossed and dying on the rocks, and envied her.

IV: Fullmoon Feast

I was made ready for fullmoon feast: bathed and scented and bundled into a many-gored, fur-trimmed gown of russet and olive. I had never had a fox-trimmed gown before. My mother had meant to make me a gown of the seasinger's silk, but my father had seized the stuff as soon as he learned of it and, above my mother's protests, sent the bolt to the mainland to be sold.

It brought a staggering sum, enough to pay half a year's debt and more. He was in a fine expansive mood by the time of the feast, chucking my mother's cheeks and telling her what a clever thing she was, arranging for this excellent young Dalesman to come sit at our table—they'd have me married yet.

What a banquet it was that they laid. We must have gone through stores to last a month in that one meal: sweetgrain and date sugar, honey and nutmeal for cakes and cozies. Broiled fish and baked bird, eels fried and spitted and dressed seven ways. Shellfish in bloodsauce and succulent pincushion fish, sea currants and ocean plums, apples stuck with spice pricks and steamed in cider. New butter brought over from the mainland in tubs. Cook was a madwoman and beat the kitchen boys for pilfering.

At last the board was laid and the guests in place. My father sat in a high-backed chair at the center of the table, bedecked in all the finery of High Hallack he had left. The garb was old, a little shabby, and tight across the belly even where the seams had been let out.

But he wore it with such an air of unfeigned pride that for a moment, approaching him, I caught a glimpse of what he must have been like when he was young. My mother sat on his left. She had never been a beautiful lady—her hair was graying, her eyes surrounded by tiny lines—but that night she was a regal one.

The stranger sat on my father's right—of middle height for a man, so far as I could tell, well proportioned, with long legs. He was dressed in a tabard and breeks of blue and dark red, gold-chased, finer far than anything anyone else in the hall had on, thereby reinforcing the rumor that he was some disguised lord of High Hallack, as I was sure was his intent.

His hair was indeed dark gold, as I had heard tell, with bangs across the brow and the ends curling under at the shoulder, much longer than the hair of a man of Ulys. And, unlike a man of Ulys, he was bearded. A thick fringe of curly reddish hair ran along his jaw and upper lip and chin, but left the cheeks for the most part bare. The effect was strange to my eye, both enticing and oddly menacing at once.

I dropped my eyes as I approached—as my mother had instructed me to do—curious as I was. I did not have a seat at the table, of course, being only an unmarried girl. My task was to serve the wine and other victuals. I was not to speak unless directly addressed, and then to answer softly with a bob—any other response being a breach of maidenly modesty.

I filled my father's cup, and then my mother's, but as I bent near to fill the stranger's I became uncomfortably aware that he was watching me. I knew that I must not look up, but his gaze on me was so fixed, so intent, it made my skin prick.

I did look up then, and found him staring. His eyes were gray, dark-looking by candlelight. The hall was ablaze with torches and candles that night—another store we were using recklessly in ostentatious display. The seasinger's eyes, like a steady-burning flame, never wavered. He said nothing.

I backed away from him and dropped my gaze, and, my first serving duty done, retreated in confusion to the kitchen. He had been looking at me as though wishing to see into my very soul, or impart some urgent message. Surely it had been those eyes, conjurer's eyes, that had made Danna eat the fruit.

I began to be afraid then, and cowered in the kitchen until the guestcup was drunk and the next course ready to be served. Every time I went into the serving hall, I felt those eyes on me. My lord and lady did nothing to discourage it. I sat trembling in the kitchen between times and could not eat.

Soon enough my parents began openly to encourage him by discussing the merits of their lovely daughter, a mere child, trained for the life of a lady of High Hallack—until the unfortunate demise of her intended lord. They spoke as though it had been only months, not years ago; as though I must be heartbroken. The young man Gyrec spoke to them wittily, absently, and stared at me.

He had a fine voice, a bit light, but he used it well. He did not quite have the accent of the isles, but his way of speech was close, very close. There was about it, too, a hint of something I had heard before—Sulcar speech? I could not say. It troubled me, making me at once want to listen more closely and run away.

My father and mother began to praise my virtues one by one. Lord Halss went on about my youth, beauty, modesty, obedience, and sweet nature. He might have been describing a stranger. Then my mother held forth about my skill in all the womanly arts: how well I sewed and cooked and could mend a legging. She told him I recited the pious offices of the Flame and sang like an idylbird in spring.

At that the stranger suddenly laughed, a surprisingly deep-throated, likable sound. He covered this breach with some pleasantry to my mother that if her daughter's voice was half so sweet as her own, I must be a jewel indeed. My parents nearly killed themselves for smiling then, but I knew with certainty that the singer was well aware I had no voice. Danna had told him so in the market square. And he did not care.

When I brought in the next course, the candied fruit between the soup and the meat, the singer's fingers brushed my hand. I shied away and made myself gone as quick as I could, but when I brought in the meat and was taking the soup plates away, he actually caught hold of my wrist, quite unobtrusively and not hard, but I was so startled I jerked away and nearly dropped the dish.

He did not seem angry, only perturbed, and when I next entered the room, he ignored me. My parents were not amused, however, and my mother caught me aside to hiss, "Do not be so standoffish, you silly chit. Smile and be receptive to the young man's attentions. Speak to him if he should speak to you."

Fear bit into me to hear her say that. Desperation made me bold. "I won't!" I whispered. He was no Hallack lord, I *knew* it. "He's some conjurer—"

"He's none, and you will," my mother snapped, pinching me hard enough to make my eyes sting.

"I can't," I gasped, half weeping now. A sidelong glance showed me my father and the long-haired warlock deep in some convivial talk. "I don't like him!"

"That's nothing," my mother said fiercely under her breath. She gave me a shake. "Do as you're told."

A strange, sudden calm that was nearer numbness descended on me, and I stopped weeping. I realized then that I would not marry, ever, any man at my parents' behest. I would live in Castle Van all my life a withering maid if I must, but I would not anymore do as I was told. I would fling myself from the tower first. I'd die on the rocks.

But how to survive this evening was my first concern. Once more I retreated to the kitchen. Once more I emerged to serve a dish. This time when I approached the table, I found my father and his guest at a game of chancesticks. My mother sat watching, seemingly rapt.

She did not know how to play, chancesticks not being considered a suitable game for ladies, but I did. Sif had taught me. My father was a fair enough player, but the seasinger was better. Nevertheless, twice during the next few rounds, I glimpsed our guest surreptitiously discarding a counter to give himself a losing score.

"So," my father said, rubbing the pieces between his palms for luck, "tell me where you found this marvelous cloth you gifted my lady with. Somewhere north of here—Arvon, perhaps?"

He cast the sticks. The stranger laughed.

"Ah, my lord, were a man to divulge such a thing, he'd not long keep his monopoly." He shook the counters between cupped hands. "No, my lord, I am not looking for a confidant. I am looking for a port—preferably an island off the coast of High Hallack. I've already surveyed your neighbors to north and south."

He threw, but the score was low. My father won the round.

"What good's an island port to you?" my father asked, marking the tally and gathering up the sticks.

"As a place to display my wares to the lords of the Dales," the seasinger replied.

My father threw. "Why not take your goods directly to their ports?"

The seasinger smiled and collected his sticks. "Because they would tax me, my lord."

He breathed upon the sticks. My father took a cup of wine, eyeing the other meditatively. Most men were uneasy in my father's presence, if he chose to make them so. But the sea-singer showed not a trace of unease. His hand was steady, his air relaxed. My father fingered the stem of his cup.

"And would I not?"

The singer threw. "Think, my lord," he murmured, watching the counters fall. "Think of all the fat Hallack ships coming into your port—Sulcarmen, too. Tax *them,* my lord, when they come to buy my cloth."

My father roared with laughter, and set down his empty cup. The round was his again. My mother ran her linen napkin through her fingers, watching, watching. The gold the bearded man counted out to my father was new minted in High Hallack. *Ting, teng,* it rang. My father's eyes glittered.

But I caught a glimpse the seasinger stole at him while handing over the gold: unsmiling, narrow-eyed, calculating. Suddenly I had the uncanny feeling that he disliked my father—no, more than disliked: *hated* my father for some reason I could not even guess. My parents, I was certain, sensed nothing of this, and the seasinger's look was gone in a moment, as if it had never been.

I had been lingering, watching and listening to what the two players said. I had drawn closer to the seasinger without realizing it. This time he caught not my wrist but my sleeve. My lord and lady conveniently studied the board.

"Ho, gentle maid," the stranger murmured—and again his eyes were on mine with an alarming urgency. "Stand beside me and bring me luck."

Surreptitiously he pressed something small and crumpled into my hand and made to draw me nearer, but I passed on quickly, alarmed, blushing to the bone, determined not to stand long enough to let him get hold of me again.

"Leave me alone," I muttered, just low enough that my parents might not hear.

Safe in the kitchen, I looked at what he had pressed on me:

a little slip of brown parchment covered with tiny scratchings and signs. They meant nothing to me—surely some witchery. I threw it in the kitchen fire and scrubbed my hand with salt.

I didn't want to go back into the banquet hall then, but Cook made me. It was the last course. After that, I could flee. The full moon shone down through the open windows of the hall. The evening was wearing late.

Even as I entered the dining hall, I dropped my eyes. I would not look at him. Conjurer, warlock—doubtless eager to see if his scribbled spell had made me pliable. I squared my shoulders defiantly. I was bearing a basket of spotless goldenfruit, so sweet and ripe that it bruised if so much as breathed upon. Eyes still downcast, I began serving my father. He caught me about the waist with seeming affection.

"Not so fast, not so fast," he laughed—there was an edge to it, though. I had grown deft at hearing such undertones. "Bide a while, my duck. Do not hurry off. From your haste, one would think you eager for this night to end."

A smile, another laugh, a less-than-gentle squeeze. He was very angry with me and would seize an opportunity within the next few days to box my ears, I could be sure. I didn't care. I served my mother then, and she looked daggers at me. She did not speak, but I could fairly hear what she was thinking: *Chin up, now, girl. You've got his eye. Toss your hair and swirl your skirts a bit. Show your meager gifts off to the buyer at their best.*

I tucked my chin and held my neck perfectly rigid, glowering fiercely, but the stranger would not stop looking at me. My father rose, cup in hand, and began offering a toast, going on about it so as to give the singer some cover to talk to me. I fairly hated my father then. I think I had hated him all my life, for not once had he ever consulted me about my fate as he went about arranging it. At that moment, I could gladly have put a dagger in his heart if I could have done so and lived.

The stranger took my father's cue and bent near me as I passed, taking hold not of me or of my sleeve this time, but of the basket's edge, as if to examine its contents. He pretended to, and I stood trembling in fury. Warlock or no, I was tired of being afraid.

"You read the note?" he said, very softly, lifting a fruit from the basket and turning it in the light.

"I threw your ensorcelled scrap in the fire," I hissed.

He looked up, startled, nearly dropping the fruit. I saw the bright red bruises his fingers made in the smooth golden flesh.

"What—why?" he gasped, astonished. I felt a little surge of triumph.

"I wouldn't have read your spell even if I could," I said in a low voice. "I can't read."

"Can't. . . ?" he started. "But your mother—"

"She lied," I murmured, with relish. "I can't sing, either. You know that much from Danna in the market."

"Sweet Gunnora . . ." He swallowed the rest of the curse. "There's no time. Meet me on the strand tonight, before midnight, after the feast. I must—"

But I cut him off, wrestling him for the basket. "I won't. I'll not go anywhere with you, warlock."

"Alys," he said then, and I gasped that he could have discovered my secret name. Both my parents had been naming me Alia all night. Surely he was a warlock if he could know such things.

I got the basket from him then and stumbled back, hard into my father as he stood making his toast. The wine supped from his cup as I jostled him, sopping his sleeve, and the goldenfruit spilled, to roll bruised and ruined among the platters on the white tablecloth.

"Stupid. . . !" my father burst out, and raised his arm as if he meant to backhand me there before all the hall—it would not have been the first time. But the stranger leaped up suddenly and got between us under the pretext of steadying my lord's cup. He was as tall as my father, nearly, though lighter built.

"My lord," he cried, his voice hearty, not a trace of alarm

or anger to it. He never so much as glanced at me. "My lord, you have offered me a worthy welcome this night, and for that, my thanks. My resources are, at the moment, meager, but allow me to repay your hospitality as best I can."

He kept my lord's eyes square on himself, and I seized the opportunity to retreat a few paces, out of my father's reach. I dared go no farther. My father's stance, as he eyed the young man, was angry still. If I had not known better, I might have thought the seasinger was protecting me. *No.* I resisted the thought. This was all part of his game somehow.

"The time has come to breach that keg, my lord, with which I presented you earlier this even, when first I arrived."

His voice had a fine ring to it. It carried well, commanding the attention of everyone in the hall. My father began to look a little mollified. Already the seasinger had him under his spell. Already he had begun to forget about me. Slowly, my father smiled.

"Indeed," he cried at last, and motioned to two of his men standing across the hall. "Bring it up."

My father's soldiers knelt and lifted something that had rested between them, and came forward with it. As they set it down before the table, I realized it was a wine cask. One of the guardsmen knocked a bung into it. The stranger spoke.

"My lord, lady, good company of the hall, I am a seasinger. I have been far over the ocean wide, seen many places, and drunk many fair wines—but none is finer than the stuff they call seamilk, which is made in a place far north of here, where I have lately done some trading."

He motioned to my father's men. They hefted the cask and came forward again. The singer held out his own cup, which was empty, and let the liquid splash into it. It was amber gold, with a strong, aromatic scent. I was standing close enough to note all this—but under the gold there seemed to be a darkness to it, a blueness like smoke or a shadow in the depths, for all that the surface sparkled and shone like fire.

"A sup, now; a single sup for every person in the hall—for

luck," the stranger continued, and I noted a quickening in his tone, not fear, but an eagerness that had not been there before. Holding out my father's cup, he let the soldiers splash in a measure to mingle with the wine already in the bowl.

My father stood, seemingly a little perplexed, as though not sure how he liked the singer's presumption now that he thought upon it. The guardsmen moved down the table and poured a little in my mother's cup. She stood holding it, looking at my father uncertainly. He ignored her, but when the men-at-arms paused, he gave them a nod to go on around the hall.

"Drink, drink up, my lady, lord," the seasinger urged, his tone commanding yet convivial. Smiling, he raised his cup as in salute. My father brought his own cup to his lips and sipped. I saw his eyebrows lift in surprise, and then his whole face eased.

"By the Horned Man, that is good," he exclaimed, and downed the strange wine in a draught. "Give me another. Let the whole hall have it!"

The stranger gave my lord his own cup, untouched. I saw my mother sipping now, and the same reaction of surprise and pleasure on her face.

"What d'you call that stuff again?" my father asked, taking the full chalice from the seasinger eagerly. My mother eyed the bottom of her cup in disappointment.

"Seamilk, my lord."

"From the north—where in the north?"

"The same spot the silkcloth comes from—but you'd have to offer me a fine bargain indeed to make me tell you that," the stranger laughed. This time I saw him glance at me, and my father, following his gaze, laughed, uproariously, with him.

"Got any more with you?"

"Not this trip. Drink! Drink up, the hall!" cried the seasinger. The soldiers had made their way a quarter of the way around now, and I could hear the sighs and soft exclamations as people tasted each their splash. I saw servers and kitchen boys scrambling—for cups, I guessed. No one was to be denied a sip, not even servants.

And the hall was full, packed to overflowing. I realized that in some astonishment. I had taken no note of it before. All come to see the seasinger, I guessed, or to steal a bite of that magnificent feast. Probably there was not a stablelad or chambermaid in keep who had not come. Now they all held out their cups as the men-at-arms made their round with the smoky seamilk, and still the singer talked. "But my lord, my lord—your health and the lady's. The seamilk is only the first part of my gift. Here is the second."

V: Werefox

Reaching down, the seasinger caught up a little harp hardly bigger than my hand—I could not see where he had been keeping it. It almost seemed he plucked it from the air. Then in one swift striding sweep, the singer was around the table's end and standing in the middle of the hall, in the open space between the other tables. He faced about.

"Let me tell you a tale of the seafoxes, my lord—a song that they sing in the spring in that lonely northern place whence I have lately come. You will find this tale of interest, my lord, for I gather you know something of seafoxes here."

Again my father laughed, and half the hall with him, though I thought the stranger's jest—if jest it were—a feeble one. The soldiers had made half the circuit now, and it seemed to me that that half of the hall was very merry. The singer put his hand to the strings, and the little harp, for all its tiny size and shortness of string, had a surprisingly full, rich sound. The soldiers continued their task, and the aroma of seamilk pervaded the room.

"Once was there a prince of the seafoxes, good people, on a tiny isle far north of here. A man he was upon the land, a silver fox upon the sea . . ."

He told the tale of that seafox prince, and his beautiful sister who swam south one year and disappeared. She had been captured by a cruel lord who kept her prisoner in his keep until she lost the power to become a seafox. When she tried to swim away from him, she drowned.

It was a haunting tale, skillfully sung. The singer had a fine, full-throated tenor voice that soared to the high notes with no trouble at all. The men-at-arms completed their circuit with still a little seamilk in the keg. No one offered me a cup, and I was strangely glad.

I glimpsed a kitchen maid bearing a full chalice through the kitchen door—for Cook and her minions, I supposed. I wished that I, too, might slip from the hall, but I could not have done so without attracting my father's eye. He was sitting now beside my mother, intent upon the singer, seemingly in a fine mood once again, but I could not be sure. The two men-at-arms stole quietly from the hall with the last of the keg—to share it with their fellows on watch, no doubt.

"That prince, he waited long years for his kinswoman to return," the seasinger sang. "But at last he said, 'I fear the worst. Some evil has befallen her. I will trade my human shape for a fox's skin and search for her.'"

The hall should have been very still by then, out of respect for the singer, but it was not. A constant ripple of low laughter ran through the crowd of banqueters; there was much grinning, a chuckle, even a guffaw now and again—though I could find nothing mirthful in the strange, sad tale. The seasinger, however, did not seem to mind. I could not make out his face well at this distance, but he seemed to be smiling.

"It was years; it was a very long time that that prince of the foxes searched, but at last he found the isle where his kinswoman had come. He put on the shape of a man once again and entered the town as a seasinger. Thus he learned her fate."

It seemed half the hall was laughing now, a little madly, like men drunk at the sight of land after a long voyage or a storm. There was an odd sound to the hilarity, an eerie wildness—as though the listeners laughed less at what they heard than because they could not help themselves. Unease danced a feather down my spine.

"Then, after a week's time, the lord of the keep called him up to his hall," the seasinger sang. "'Come sing to my people; come sit at my board.' And the prince of the seafoxes sang them a song, and gave the lord of the castle two gifts: a cask of seamilk sweeter than honey on a lying tongue, and a bolt of silkcloth that glimmered like fishskin, or pearlstuff, or oil."

My hands and feet had grown very cold. I stood staring at the seasinger, unable to move. He had turned, gazing intently at my father now, no longer facing the hall, no longer making any pretense at a smile. That edge I had heard before in his voice returned.

"The lord offered him his daughter's hand, saying, 'Take her, good sir. You seem an enterprising young man. And I need an heir.'"

The hall had quieted a little now, but no one seemed in the least alarmed. The half of the hall that had drunk the seamilk last were laughing the loudest now. The first half were nodding and yawning, even the guards. I saw my mother bowed over her cup and my father resting his jaw on one hand and rubbing his eyes with the other.

"'I will take your daughter,' the seasinger replied, 'and your wealth, lord, and the good fortune of all these people here—for I have learned that not only my kinswoman perished here. Scores of my people have lost their lives upon this rock. In winter, you and your men go out hunting—bat the seafoxes' heads in and steal their skins . . .'"

His voice had changed utterly now. He was not singing anymore. Abruptly, he stopped speaking, turned and surveyed the hall.

"But enough of songs," the stranger barked, returning his attention once more to my father.

He came forward and tossed his harp upon the table with a carelessness that frightened me. I shrank back against the wall. Once again those piercing eyes looked at me and pinned me where I stood. My father took no note of any of this, still rubbing his eyes.

"My lord, the seamilk and the song were but the first parts of my business here. There is a third part. Do you know what that might be?"

My father looked up, bleary-eyed. He licked his lips. "Eh?"

I wanted to cry out some warning—or run—but the warlock's eyes had paralyzed me.

"Do you know the third part of my business here this night, my lord?" the singer repeated, sharply. My mother snored over her cup. At the other's words, my father's head snapped up, but quickly sagged.

"Oh . . . my daughter," he muttered. "Benis says . . . must lose no time, contract you to marry her. Before you leave the isle."

I could not swallow. The seasinger laughed.

"Your daughter will be coming with me, never fear," he answered lightly, his tone all darkness underneath. "After this night, you will never see her more. But she will not depart here as a bride, my lord."

My heart twitched in my breast. I leaned back against the wall. The stone was hard and cold. I hardly felt it.

"What?" my father cried, half rising, but his torso seemed somehow too heavy for his legs, and he had to rest one arm upon the tabletop. With the other hand, he clutched his chair. "The girl . . . the chit goes nowhere . . . till she's wed and bred me an heir." He squinted, peering at the bearded young man before him. "You're no Hallack lord . . ."

"I never said I was," the other snapped. "Nor am I a common seasinger. Did you think it was only some singer's tale I told? It was a true account. *I* am that prince of the seafoxes I sang of. This is the isle where my kinswoman perished. You are the cruel lord that held her here."

Once more he turned and seemed to appraise the hall. It had grown far quieter at last. I saw people, some slumped where they sat, others still upon their feet, but like sleepwalkers, gazing vacantly. I saw a serving boy very calmly give a great yawn and lie down upon the floor. A soldier staggered and leaned against the wall. My father had slumped back into his seat and sat looking stupidly at the stranger as though he were speaking a foreign tongue.

"Kinswoman?" my father muttered. "Kinswoman?"

Again the stranger's cutting laugh. "Can you not recall her name, my lord—has it been so long? *Zara.*"

My father choked and shook his head, as if to clear it. He whispered. "Zara."

I saw two of my father's men try to rise from their seats, and fall. The seasinger's hand went momentarily to his sleeve as if to draw something concealed there. A weapon? A dagger? But he left the motion uncompleted as both my father's would-be defenders fell. He turned back to my lord.

"Yes, Zara." His voice was low, furious. "You kept her prisoner on this crag—ten years."

My father shook his head again, his speech thick and difficult. "No," he muttered. "No." Then: "Zara."

"You promised to take her to the mainland and buy her passage north," the seasinger answered, advancing on my father.

"How did you know that?" my father whispered. "Warlock."

The seasinger smiled, leaning nearer. My father's eyes rolled. I had never seen him afraid.

"You broke your word," he said, very softly.

"I told her . . . told her that I had to . . ."

"Had to?"

"To keep her. To keep her with me!" My father's words were a moan. That frightened me still further. I had rarely known him to express any strong emotion but rage.

"She wanted nothing more to do with you," the seasinger half shouted.

For a moment, the grimace on my father's face vanished. His head fell back. He smiled, clumsily, remembering. "No, not after. But those first years—those first years, she loved me."

"Why didn't you marry her?" the seasinger demanded. He had regained his composure, spoke quietly now.

My father's teeth clenched. Again the look of pain. "Wanted to. If she'd given me a son. . . !"

"But she didn't. So you married Benis."

"Had to! They'd never have kept me lord here without an heir—my claim was by marriage. Oh, it was all Benis. Old lord's niece; she wanted it. She forced it—if she'd married someone else, *he'd* have been lord."

He seemed unable to stop talking—part of the seasinger's spell, I knew. My father rested his forehead on his hands. They curled into fists. His voice shook.

"If I'd had a son, a son by Zara, I might have resisted. With an heir, perhaps no one would have cared if I married Benis or not. I held out, hoping . . ." His tone darkened, no longer shaking. His jaw tightened. "But all I got was that brat, a girlchild: Siva."

"Sif." The bearded man's voice dropped, low and dangerous. "Also my kith. Why didn't you let my kinswoman go?"

A moan. "I wanted . . . I thought she'd come back to me."

"With you wed to another?"

My father's head snapped up, his voice a wail. "I didn't think the cow'd live forever! Her cousin, Alia, the first one, died young." A moment's silence, then, softer, "I thought I could get a son on Benis, and Zara would take me back."

"Ten years," the seasinger hissed. "And what became of the brat, the girlchild Sif?"

My father shook his head and swatted the air as if to slap away a relentless fly. "Dead. Dead."

"You left her in the care of the old boatman, Sul. He'd have worked her to death if she'd let him—or worse. Nearly did."

My father gazed ahead of him, at nothing. "Trapped," he murmured, not making sense. "Prisoner."

"You could have raised her in the keep," the seasinger persisted. "She was your daughter—would that have been so hard?"

My father shrugged, petulant. He was growing more sluggish. "Benis'd have killed her. Shoved her down steps or poisoned her in kitchen." He sighed, frowning, scratching his arm and looking about as though he had lost something. "If Benis could have had a son," he murmured, "she'd not have cared a whit about the girl. Or Zara."

"*You* didn't care what happened to her."

"I needed a *son.*"

My father's last spark, gone in a moment. The seasinger was very quiet then, for a long breath, fingering something in his sleeve. "Did you. . . ?" he started, then stopped a moment, as his voice caught. "Did you ever love her, lord?"

My father blinked, slowly, confused. "Alia? Married her for the keep."

"Not Alia," the seasinger said.

"Benis. Had to. To keep my hold on Ulys—all I'd got. And for sons."

"Sif?"

"Brat."

"Zara," the singer said finally, and my father murmured, "Zara."

I thought at first that was all he would say. But he drew breath in a moment, with difficulty. "Only one I ever did. Love. Only one . . . never did a thing I wanted, unless it suited her. And I loved her . . . moment I saw her. And those first years . . . she loved me."

The words trailed off. My father's eyes were vacant, his head tilted slightly askew. The seasinger seemed to consider a moment more whatever he was meditating on, but then he straightened and his expression, though fierce and determined still, eased ever so slightly. He left off fingering whatever it was in his sleeve.

"I'll not kill you, then, old man."

He looked away, raising one hand to his cheek, but his face was turned, and I could not tell what he was doing. All at once, he broke off, turning completely from my father's table and going to inspect the other guests.

I gazed, frozen where I stood, while he took their measure—mostly just by looking at them, but one or two by shaking and tapping lightly upon the cheek with the back of his hand. All stayed as they were, staring vacantly, except one girl, a kitchen maid, who moaned. The seasinger raised her cup to her lips and guided her to drink the rest. She did not resist or move again.

The guards he was especially wary of, shaking them roughly. One he slapped hard—but they did not stir. They must have drunk deep of the seasinger's draught. That would be like them. Only the stranger himself and I had drunk nothing of it. Like everyone else in the hall, the guards stood or leaned or slumped or lay—motionless. The seasinger took their swords and threw them in the fire.

I found myself thinking stupidly then that I was just standing there, waiting for whatever the warlock might do. And I realized I must not, must not simply stand—as I had stood waiting all of my life, waiting for others to do what they would with me. I wanted to scream, shout for help, but I dared not draw the warlock's eye. Perhaps I had stood so still he had not realized I was not under the influence of his dram—it was a slender hope, but I seized at it. Perhaps he had forgotten me.

I tried to think. What could I do? I had heard somewhere that a warlock's spell is like a circle or a chain. If one link could be broken, one person roused, then the magic might weaken, the others become easier to free. I realized I must try to wake someone, rouse them from this witch sleep. Dropping to a crouch, I crept forward, trusting the table to hide me from view. Still crouching, I caught hold of my father's sleeve and tugged at it.

"Father," I whispered, terrified of speaking too loud. "Father, wake."

He sat like a man stunned, his body holding its position and balance, but his eyes were empty, his jaw slack. I shook harder.

"Father," I hissed. "Throw off this spell. The seasinger has cast some witchery on you. Wake!"

He never stirred. I let go his sleeve, and his hand slid from the chair's arm to dangle limply. I seized him again, by the shoulders this time, and shook him roughly, my breath short. I could see the seasinger across the room, his back to me. He was holding an empty plate onto which he was throwing food snatched from the banquet table. I stared at this, astonished. My father did not move.

"Rouse, my lord!"

The seasinger turned and cast about the hall. I ducked behind my father's chair, my heart in my throat, afraid that he had heard me, was looking for me. But he was not. He spotted a wine pitcher on another table and went to fetch it. Once more his back was to me; stealthily, I crept to my mother's chair.

"Mother," I whispered, desperation edging my voice. "Mother!" She remained as she was, head bowed over onto her arm resting crooked on the table before her. The breath snored and guttered in her throat. "Wake and help me rouse the others—help me!" I entreated, my voice turning to a squeak. I bit back the sound, shaking her vigorously till her head slid from her arm onto the table, and there it stayed. I was close to panic.

"Alys!"

The cry brought me sharp around and into a crouch again. I saw the seasinger, pitcher in one hand, his platter of food now full in the other, casting about the room. His call had not been loud.

"Alys, where are you?" His use of my name made my skin prickle. I stayed motionless. "Alys, I know you're here," he cried—softly. "Don't hide from me."

He saw me then. I tried to duck, to get out of his line of sight, but it was useless. His tense stance eased. He seemed relieved—I did not stop to wonder why. As he started toward me, I sprang up, shaking my father furiously, no longer bothering to whisper.

"Father, help! Hear me—please!"

The seasinger halted in seeming surprise. "Let him alone," he said. "Do you want him to wake? He sold you to me for a bolt of foxsilk and a cask."

I stared at him, terrified, and fell back as he approached. He was not really looking at me, though. His eyes were all for my father now. His expression clouded as once more he came before my lord.

"Know this, lord," he said quietly, but very clearly, as one who speaks to penetrate a dream. "I have much reason to hate you, but I will spare your life, and all the people of this isle—upon a condition. There is indeed a curse upon this place, because you are killing the seafoxes. You must kill them no more, never again."

He set the pitcher down.

"The seafoxes must be allowed to regain their former numbers, for it is they that eat the red dead-men's-hands that are ruining your shellfish beds. When your shellfish come back, they will seine out the little toxins and bitternesses in the waters about this isle that drive the fish away."

He spoke calmly, but full of urgency. Then his tone eased. His face quieted. He leaned back a little, sure of his triumph, a man well satisfied.

"I will take only one thing from you, my lord, in payment of my kinswoman's life." He nodded toward me with hardly a glance. "Your daughter. One kinswoman for another. That is a fair exchange. You will have no heirs, and there will be an end to the lords of Ulys."

He tossed the plate of food down onto the table in front of me then, still not really looking at me. He spoke to me, but his eyes were on my father yet.

"Here, eat this. We've a long journey ahead of us, and you haven't touched a bite." He nodded over one shoulder. "That kitchen boy there looks about your size. Trade clothes with him. Then I'll cut your hair."

I couldn't move. The seasinger glanced at me with a snort of disgust.

"Alys," he said. "We haven't much time."

He reached across the table, for my hand, I think. Suddenly, my father's table dagger was in my grasp. I didn't remember snatching it up, only of shrieking as I lunged with it. I had no intention of going anywhere. I felt the point just graze the seasinger's arm.

He fell back with a startled cry and brought the pitcher down on my hand with force enough to knock the knife from it. It skittered away across the floor. But I felt a momentary triumph. Warlock or werefox he might be, but he was afraid of sharp metal like any other man and bled red blood. And I had gotten him away from me and off balance for a moment. I ran for the kitchen door.

VI: The Rocks

He was after me in less than a moment, vaulting the table instead of going around. I had not anticipated that. I scarcely ducked through the stone doorway and shoved the heavy wooden door shut before I felt his weight collide with it. I fumbled with the bar, swung it down just as his hand found the latch. It rattled furiously.

"Alys," he cried, striking the door once, twice. His voice was muffled. "Alys, let me in! I must tell you, I'm not—perish and misbegotten!" A rain of blows. "There's no time for this. The dram doesn't last long. And we must be away while the moon's high. Within the hour!"

He said other things, but I clamped my hands over my ears, afraid he might be able to cast some spell on me by voice alone. I had heard of that. The door held. I felt another rush of triumph. Danna had told me once that warlocks could pass through doors like mist. Well, this one couldn't. I leaned against the wood a moment, catching my breath, then turned around.

A strangled cry escaped my lips. I had not expected what I saw: Cook slumped against the great hearth and two kitchen maids beside her. Another stood across the room, the half-full chalice still cupped in her hand. I fled the kitchen, down the long back hall. There was no one about. I wanted to shout, but the sight behind me had stolen my voice.

I found the stairs and climbed them, breathless, to my chambers. I entered, starting and turning, expecting to find the warlock awaiting me in every corner. My chambers were empty—were all the maids down at the feast? Of course they were. Everybody was. And anyone who could not get a place in the hall had more than likely gone down to the taverns in town.

Everything was very still. The little square room looked strange to me, frozen, a stranger's room. I had the overwhelming desire simply to stand and do nothing. A spider danced across the floor. I started, jarring a table, and my hairbrush feli to the tiles with a crack. A moment later, I found myself outside, descending the long, narrow steps, then hurrying down another hall.

All around me was only darkness and empty rooms. I found a door leading out into the open courtyard and tried it. Outside, the night was mild and still. The sky, for once, was clear. I could see the stars and the round moon, swollen and full of light, nearly overhead. I ran for the front gate. One of my father's guards stood sentry there.

I cried out, coming toward him, but he didn't move, didn't answer, gave no sign of having heard me. I drew near and halted dead, seeing the cup still held in his hand. I shook him, knowing it would do no good. The cup fell to the flagstones with a loud clang. I glanced back over my shoulder. Light was spilling into the far side of the courtyard from the open window of the feast.

I glimpsed no movement within, no sign of the seasinger. That only frightened me further. I wanted to know where he was. I ducked around the dreaming sentry and tried the gate.

It was barred, of course. It was always barred at sunset now. My father feared the townsfolk would steal castle stores. The bar was far too high and heavy for me to lift.

I thought of the seaward gate suddenly; it had only a bolt and no bar. Surely I could open that. Nothing lay beyond but open beach, and it was a long way around to the village along that strand, but it was better than no escape at all. I started across the courtyard toward it—then reflex froze me.

The seasinger had emerged from a doorway not far from me. He had a torch. He must have got into the kitchen by another way and been searching for me there. He did not see me, but I could not reach the seagate now. I shrank back into the shadows, stood motionless. The seasinger gazed out across the courtyard, away from me.

"Where are you?" he cried. His call was urgent, but not loud.

I remembered what he had said about departing within the hour. If his spell only lasted a little while, perhaps I need only elude him for so long. I began to hope. He shifted his torch to the other hand with a sound of desperate frustration and started across the yard toward the seagate.

A torch throws light, but also blinds the bearer to all that lies beyond him in the shadows. I skulked along the bare, moonlit wall of the courtyard, well behind his sidelong vision. If he had turned, he would have seen me. The torch's flame hid the side of his face from me. In a moment, I reached my new goal and ducked through the open doorway into the tower.

I had not been inside it in years, not since Sif had gone. No one else ever went there either. It was in ramshackle disrepair, but I needed no light. I knew the way up the winding wooden steps. A rotten board cracked under my weight, and I fell, hard forward, barking my knee. I gathered my gown and scrambled up, hurrying on, panting up the steps.

I reached the landing. Moonlight streamed in the window and fell silver on the floor. Something lay there, small and drab—I could not tell what it was. I knelt and lifted it. It was my sewing sack. I had marked it missing the day after Sif went, six years ago, and had never thought to look for it here.

The fabric was weathered thin as cobwebs. It shredded in my hand. A little mat of faded floss fell out, and then my needles—a shower of splinters, blazing in the moon's light. They bounded on the floorboards with a brief sound like rain, then rolled, some of them falling through the cracks.

I was overwhelmed with a remembrance and a longing for Sif. She, at least, had lived her life at no one's behest. She had never done what Sul told her unless she had felt like it, which was why he had so often beaten her. She had not been happy, nor had she been loved by anyone but me—but she had been free. Freer than I. And she was dead for it. But I realized now that I would rather have had that than this, to be trapped in a stone place at the mercy of lords and warlocks.

I heard a rattle and a curse. With a start, I realized I had closed my eyes. Carefully, I peered out the window. In the yard below, the singer had found the seagate bolted—obviously I had not gone that way. I saw him glance up, but not at where I stood. His gaze was toward my chamber's window. The accuracy of his guess unnerved me—or did his witchery somehow tell him where my apartments lay?

He looked at the moon, as if gauging the time, and ran across the courtyard toward the entrance that would take him to my room. I turned from the window and leaned back against the wall. My legs trembled. I sank down, hoping—hoping that his time would run out, that he would give up. Give up and go away! My breath was still coming hard, then I realized I was sobbing, dryly and without tears.

I must try for the seagate—I realized that suddenly—*now,* while he searched for me elsewhere. He had already checked that avenue of escape. With luck, he would not check again, or not immediately. My chamber overlooked the yard, but it was a risk I had to take. I had no idea how long I had sat there trembling.

I scrambled up, my breathing calmer now—and halted suddenly. There was someone below me in the tower. I heard footsteps on the hard-packed earth below. Trembling, peering over the handrail, I saw torchlight. The seasinger stood below, torch in hand. He looked up, up the well between the turns of stair, and saw me. I ducked back into the darkness—too late.

"There you are," he cried.

I heard him taking the steps two at a time. The torchlight bobbed nearer. I stood, heart pounding, then whirled and stared out the window at the courtyard far, far below. It took only a moment to make my decision. I caught hold of the gray, weathered shutter, which groaned horribly beneath my weight, and pulled myself up onto the stone sill. I crouched there, one hand upon the shutter, half turned and looking over my shoulder. The seasinger rounded the turn of the steps, and seeing me so, gave a cry of astonishment.

"Alys! Don't—" He lunged up the steps.

I didn't wait. I was completely calm. He was quicker than I expected, but I still had plenty of time. I had thought he would halt, possibly bargain or cajole, even threaten or command. And of course, he could have used witchery if I had given him time. But he tried none of these, just came charging up the steps, calling my name.

I turned away, looking out over the stones below, the light of the silent banquet hall shining into the yard, the barred front gate and the motionless guard, and beyond the wall on the seaward side, the far waves running and foaming, high on the beach. I thought of Sif, dying on the rocks, and let myself fall.

The sky spun. The rush of air against my cheek was cool. I heard a shout that was almost a scream from the seasinger. It seemed to come from just behind me, far too close—and then I felt a tremendous jerk. My gown went tight across the bodice and under the arms. I couldn't breathe.

The seasinger had caught me by the gown. I cursed my women's clothing then. My feet had not even left the sill. I tried to struggle, to let my feet slip, but I half leaned, half dangled at such an awkward angle that I was virtually helpless. With a sickening swing, the seasinger hauled me back into the tower.

He had dropped his torch. It lay on the step below the landing, the burning end swung out over empty space. The light around us was eerie, yellow and amber by turns. I struggled toward the window again, but he had me still by the back of the dress and was much stronger than I. It was no use.

He was panting, struggling to hold me and cursing under his breath. I saw him reaching for the torch with his other hand. He had to go down on one knee to get it, and he pulled me down with him. Catching hold of the burning brand, he straightened, leaning across me to set it into the wall niche by the window.

I scratched at his face, as hard as I could. He ducked, biting off a cry and letting go of the torch, but not of me. The brand wobbled in its niche but did not fall. I got hold of something and pulled, then pulled again. His beard was coming off in my hands. I stared at the dark red curls I clutched. The ends were bloodless. They had no roots. They were sticky.

I shook my head, unable to make it out. Men's beards could not be so fragile. Startled, staring, I reached to yank another clump from his jaw. The seasinger hissed in pain and got his free hand on my wrist. He forced it down, twisting till it hurt.

"By Gunnora, you little idiot." His voice was an angry, grating hiss. "Alys, stop. Stop—don't you know me even yet? It's me. *Me.* Sif."

I did stop then, stopped flailing and struggling, stopped kicking—I hadn't realized I had been till I ceased. I nearly stopped breathing. My heart seemed to stop. The seasinger let go of me. I slumped back against the wall, staring, my hands making fists in the clumps of loose hair. The one before me reached to his face, yanked and scrubbed the red curls from it—and *was* Sif suddenly, even to my bad eyes; Sif with her forward-thrusting chin with the cleft in it. Her jaw and upper lip looked red and sore where the false beard had been.

"Horned Man, how that itches," she gasped, clawing vigorously. "I had to put it on with fish glue."

I tried to swallow and could not. "Sif," I said, my voice a chirrup. "Sif."

She nodded, leaning back now and looking at me, her arms crossed. "It's me," she said. "No shapeshifter and no ghost." She had grown two inches since I'd last seen her. She must have been twenty by now. "Why'd you go out the window, little fool? That's a long drop. You could have broken your leg."

Or died. She didn't say that. I swallowed again, succeeding this time, and tried to get my breath to come back. Gingerly, she fingered the cheek where I'd scratched her.

"Did you not know me—truly? I thought if any on this isle would guess, it would be you."

I scrambled up, feeling relieved and angry now. "How could I?" I stammered, "with your face under all that hair? Why didn't you tell me. . . ?"

Sif rose, too. She looked at me a moment more, then put her head back and laughed. "Gunnora! How I tried. I thought I might meet you in the market, or on the strand—but then I learned they were keeping you close guarded here at keep, and there was no one I could trust to get a message to you. I thought I might see you if I could get into the keep, but they'd let you see no man alone, so I learned. The banquet hall—it was the only way, and I was out of time . . ."

I shrank against the wall, my blood grown cold again suddenly. "Are you a witch?"

Again Sif laughed. "No!"

"But what you said in the banquet hall, that tale you told . . ."

She snorted. "It was just a tale. I made it up. I really am a seasinger."

I shuddered, unwilling to believe her. "That dram you gave my father and mother, and all the others in the hall—"

Sif shook her head. "It's only seamilk. I swear it."

I thought of Cook and Imma standing staring in the kitchen—about the others I didn't really care. "Will it hurt them?" I cried, coming toward Sif. My hands were fists still. "If you've hurt them—!"

Sif took me by the shoulders—gently. She towered over me. I'd barely grown at all since she had gone. "Not a bit," she answered quietly, and I let myself believe at last. "They'll stand dreaming an hour or two and then awake, I promise you."

Something dangled in her sleeve. I reached to touch it through the fabric. Not a dagger, more of a tube. I couldn't make out what it was. "You meant to kill my father, didn't you? There in the banquet hall."

Sif dropped her hands from me and looked away. Her color heightened. "Not at first. At first all I wanted was to get you away. But then . . . there I was. And there he was—I don't know," she ended shortly. "I don't know what I meant to do."

I was sure then. "Would you have done it," I asked, "if I hadn't been there?"

Sif blushed outright. "I wanted to," she whispered, "but I couldn't."

I stood still, feeling cold and stiff, remembering my own thoughts in the banquet hall. Who was I to admonish Sif? I shivered. "It doesn't matter. He'll be dead soon. There's a pain in his head."

Sif looked at me, her eyes wide. She hadn't known that, of course. Her face was uncertain. "Do you love him?"

I shook my head.

Sif looked off again. "I used to envy you," she murmured, "living here, in this keep, safe and warm, always enough to eat, no rags for clothes. And then I heard the songs they were singing about you in High Hallack."

Surprising myself, I laughed. My limbs felt suddenly less

knotted. "I used to envy you." Carefully, I reached out my hand to hers. I knew beyond all shadows then that she was real. "You're not dead," I whispered. "You didn't die on the rocks."

"I got safe to High Hallack," she replied, tossing the hair back out of her eyes. I could see her brows then, how they met. "Patched boat leaked all the way. I sold your brooch for food and clothes, then signed on as a cabin boy on a Sulcar ship. I've been across the waves, Alys, and seen the eastern lands: Estcarp and Karsten and Alizon."

My breath caught. "You haven't."

I had heard such names only in stories and song. They could not be real. Sif sat down again. We both sat down.

"Estcarp is ruled by a tribe of witches. In the hills south of Estcarp live a race of hawking men who leave women alone except to visit them once a year. Karsten and Alizon"—she shrugged—"are much as here."

She drew breath, not looking at me, frowning a little now.

"The Sulcars are good people. They never treated me ill—but there is something stirring about the isle of Gorm near Sulcar Keep, some witchery. Some evil thing. I did not like the way the wind smelled in Estcarp, so after two years with the Sulcars, I came back to High Hallack."

I watched her. Still looking down, she found one of my needles and lifted it, turning it over in her fingers. It gleamed. The torchlight played smoky-dusky across the side of her face.

"I had enough then to buy my own boat, a small thing, two-masted. I coasted along the Hallack shore, trading, and when I couldn't keep myself with trade, I sang and told stories in taverns. My voice is good enough."

She glanced at me.

"That's where I heard those songs the Dalesmen sing of you." She scratched the needle across the bone dry floorboards, raising dust. "I sang a few songs of my own about you then. If they did aught to change anybody's mind, I'm glad." She smiled, a brief smile. It quickly vanished. "Then I went north."

Setting aside my needle, she worked her shoulders to get the tightness out, chafed her arms.

"Did you find your mother's Gate?" I ventured, when she did not speak.

Sif gave a laugh that had no smile in it. "I found *a* Gate, in Arvon, long deserted and unused. Burned out—it leads nowhere. Not my mother's Gate."

She sighed bitterly.

"I almost came home then. It's a strange place, Arvon, and I was very tired. I spent some months high off the coast, pondering. And then a storm plucked me far away from land—farther to the north than even my charts show. I nearly wrecked.

"But at last I made landfall, among a tiny group of islands the inhabitants call Vellas. They speak something near my mother's tongue, and they know nothing of any Gate—but oh, Alys, such a place! In the great bay between the islands, the seafoxes summer. On the inner shores they bear their young."

She leaned forward now, very intent, gazing down at the gray, wave-grained floor as though it were the bay of those islands that lay between us.

"The people of Vellas, they do not kill the seafoxes, Alys, but gather the wool of their shedding coats. It washes in to the shore like silver upon the waves. And on spring nights, they go down to the strand and sing: *Ilililé ilé ilé. Ulululé ulé ulé.* A long, strange, melodious piping that brings the seafoxes in to shore.

"Black and dappled and silver, they come, marl and burned umber and frosty white. They come to the singers as tame as children, for they know those people will offer them no harm—only comb out the mats of dense winter hair and gather the shed up in long, trailing bags. It's that they spin into the foxsilk, Alys. They showed me how—the singing and the combing and the weaving, all of it. That bolt of cloth I gave your mother—I made that."

I sat quietly amazed. I had never before heard Sif speak with pride of any of the womanly arts.

"They do not divide the work there as they do here," she was saying. "The women go out in boats and fish. The men may mind the little ones, or sing to the seafoxes and spin their hair. The children learn what skills they like—it was a boy taught me the weaving of foxsilk. It is very strange there. It is so strange." She shivered, half shaking her head. "They know little of our southern ways and have no wish to know. I like it well."

"If it is such a place," I said softly, "why did you come away?"

She smiled just a little then, and glanced at me. "I came for you," she said. "I was there, happy, and I thought of you, here. And I knew that I must come back and tell you of it. And take you there."

She spoke, her eyes shining as they had always used to do whenever she spoke of her mother's tales, of the fabulous country beyond the Gate. But this was no such land she spoke of now. It was here, in our world, a tiny clutch of isles far to the north. I sat, not quite certain what I should say or think; I had never thought of leaving Ulys, except to marry and go to a new prison in High Hallack. Escape had never seemed possible before, so it would have done me no good to think on it. Now I must.

I said slowly, "How do you mean to get me away? You've no ship of your own here, and even if you did, the harbor is chained."

Sif smiled at me. "I don't mean to go out by the harbor, Alys." She must have seen my eyes go wide, for she took my hands. "I've a little boat hidden down on the beach. But we must go while the moon's high. Now, at once."

She rose, pulling on my hand, but I held back. "We'll never clear the rocks," I exclaimed.

"I did once."

"But not with two in the boat! Your mother tried that."

"It's a different sort of boat I have this time," she said, voice growing urgent. She leaned near me. "You *must* come, Alys. Come now. He'll marry you off to anyone he can to get heirs for this place."

"But . . . what will the people do?" I stammered, clutching at straws. It was all too fast. "When my father dies, they'll have no lord."

"And what good did the lords of Ulys ever do them?" snapped Sif. "Save take half their catch and one workday out of three. It's the lord of Ulys that's ruined their fishing—by clubbing the seafoxes. It's they that eat the red dead-men's-hands. That part of what I said in the banquet hall is true."

She fixed me with her eyes.

"When the seafoxes come back, they will eat the dead-men's-hands, and then the shellfish will come back. When the shellfish return, they will strain the waters so the fish will breed again. It will take years, but it will come."

I hardly knew whether to believe her or not. It sounded so fantastical, fabulous as the shimmering cities and the self-drawn carts in her mother's tales. Sif snorted.

"The people of Vellas have no lord, and they are glad of it."

She had pulled me to my feet and was trying to get me down the steps. I resisted still.

"But Sif," I cried. "What if you can't find this Vellas again? You said it is beyond your charts . . ."

"We'll find it," she said, in a tone that brooked no argument.

"And if we don't?" I demanded. "What becomes of me? You are tall and sturdy-made, with a full voice and a fearless heart. You can pass for a man if you want. But what of me? No one would ever take me for anything but what I am. I could never be a seaman, or a seasinger, either."

My voice grew more impassioned. It was my life she wanted me to risk, everything I had.

"I won't pretend to be a man," I cried. "I can't. I'm not like you, Sif. I can never be like you. I won't don men's breeches, and I won't cut my hair!"

Sif stopped, really looking at me for the first time in some while. She studied me, and I realized I had never been so frank, with her or anyone—not even Sif could tell me what to do. If I were to leave Ulys, I must do so not because Sif wanted it, but because *I* wanted it. Sif touched my cheek, and let go my wrist. She smiled, a wry smile that was also rueful.

"Then you'll just have to come as you are."

I looked at her, and felt the fear that had been holding me back dissolve. I could go. I needn't change me, becoming something other than myself, a task my parents had been hard at all my life. And I had let them. My freedom, I realized, was not to be a hegitt's egg, falling easily into my grasp, but the hegitt itself, a flying bird that must be chased and reached after, a long time, desperately, and even then might not be caught. But I had held such a hegitt once, and let her go. Now, years later, she had come back to me. If I let her go this time, she would never return.

"I'll come then," I told Sif.

She nodded, letting out her breath. Then she fetched something out of her sleeve and gripped it. My eyes widened; I stared. I had never seen such a thing before. It looked like a hollow tube.

"What is that?" I whispered.

"Dart gun," she answered. "I got it in Estcarp. In case any of the guards missed their dram."

She took my hand. I gripped it tight. She had said she was not a witch, but she had learned such things since she left as to seem very near one to me. I shivered, and then shoved all doubt away. None of that mattered. She was Sif. We hurried down the rotten steps and out of the tower, leaving the torch still burning in the window above.

We crossed the moonlit courtyard to the seagate. Sif slipped the bolt. There were no guards, or none that showed themselves. The stone steps down the steep, rocky slope were slippery with sand, the beach beyond flat and open and infinitely more light. We ran across the dry, silvery grit to the high-water mark. The tide was going out. I could hear the surf booming on the reef.

Sif put the dart gun back into her sleeve and knelt beside a great heap of seaweed. She pulled it away, and underneath I saw a boat, but such a boat as I scarcely recognized. It was not made of planks, but of skins (or perhaps some fabric—I could not tell which) stretched tight over a wooden frame. I stared at it.

It looked far too light, too delicate, to be a real boat—more like a child's toy. Sif carried it under one arm out to the waves. It rode so high I was astonished; it had barely four fingers of draft. She held out her hand to put me aboard. I took it, but held back, looking over my shoulder at Castle Van, standing still and silent, a ghostkeep under the moon.

"The people," I said, "my father's guests in the banquet hall, and Cook, and the guards—truly, you have not hurt them?" I glanced at Sif. "They'll wake?"

She squeezed my hand. "Truly. They'll be waking very soon."

I turned away from the keep. "Will they remember?"

She smiled. "Only some muddled something—how a prince of the seafoxes came to claim the lord of Ulys's daughter. Come."

She took my arm. The waves lapped at my feet, soaking the hem of my gown. I lifted it.

"And you never found your mother's Gate."

Sif laughed. "Never—perhaps we'll find it yet."

I let her hand me into the boat. It pitched beneath me, and I clutched the sides. Sif waded out, knee deep, then waist deep in the waves. They were sucking away from shore. I could feel that in their motion. Sif pulled herself aboard, and the shallow craft bucked and yawed. Sif sat in the bow and unshipped the paddles—much shorter-handled and broader-bladed than the oars our people used. The little skiff leaped forward to her strong, even strokes.

I crouched and clung to the gunwale poles. The waves swelled and jostled beneath us hugely. I did not know how to swim. In my heavy gown, if we overturned or if I fell in, I'd drown. I tried not to think of that. I had heard others say that the motion of the sea made them sick, but I did not feel sick. I had eaten nothing at all that even. I felt very light. Ulys was slowly growing smaller, pulling away from me with every dip of my sister's oars.

I thought of Sif's mother, Zara, and her marvelous land beyond the Gate that I would never see, and of the islands called Vellas, which I might—if we cleared the reef. I heard Sif straining at the oars, biting her lip, her breathing hoarse. She sat half looking over one shoulder, her legs braced as she struggled to maneuver us—toward some gap, I supposed. I could not see it, but I sat still, trusting her. All around us, the heaving waves rose, fell, darkly brilliant under the moon, as wild and green as rampion.

Afterword

When I first received Andre Norton's invitation to contribute to her Tales of the Witch World *series, I was overwhelmed. I remember "discovering" her in the fifth grade, checking her books out of the library by the stack, and devouring them.* "This *is the kind of stories I want to write," I recall thinking. "Someday, I want to write like* this."

Of course it can't be done. No one can write like Andre Norton, whose tales bite into the reader and refuse to let go, even after the final page is turned. Her plots move; *her characters breathe and feel; her worlds, however strange, are* real. *If I could generate one tenth of the sheer storytelling power I recollect from such stories as* Moon of Three Rings, The X Factor, *and* Ordeal in Otherwhere, *I'd be content.*

How odd, then, that having savored so many Andre Norton tales, I'd never tasted Witch World *until that fateful invitation came, beckoning me to revive my old tradition of checking out great stacks of her books and to lose myself in a realm of stunning variety and fascinating contradiction, perilous magic and primeval mystery such as only Andre Norton could create.*

No one summoned to the Witch World returns unchanged. The result for me has been "Rampion," a minor offering upon the altar of one who is no minor goddess, but one of a very small and select pantheon: Grand Master of fantasy and science fiction, and grand mistress of many of our hearts.

—*Meredith Ann Pierce*

FALCON LAW
by
Judith Tarr

I

The falcons knew.

The one called Shadow lay on the hard narrow shelf that was a bed, face to the wall, and tried not to hear or heed or even remember that there were others in the room. A cold room, all stone, unlit in the night, and seven others whispering and rustling and snoring in it. They were all boys; they had no names but what they gave one another, some for insult, some for admiration, some for both together. Shadow was Shadow for quickness and silence and a talent for effacement. It was better than Grub, or Downychick, or poor Maid, who would never have come this close to a proper name if these had been the old days and this the old Eyrie that the Witches' workings had destroyed. For the land's sake and the world's saving, even the most bitter of the Brothers granted that, but the Witches were cursed here. And Maid would strive for his name and his falcon, who once would have been discarded as a weakling.

They were too few. So many had died in the wars and in the Turning; the remnants had scattered into service in the lowlands, though they hated the heat and the level land and the narrowed sky, or had taken ship over sea with chosen women and a child or two. They had only begun to come back to the Master's call, to this new Eyrie in an old, old stronghold. Perhaps it was of the Old Ones. But their Power, if it had ever lain here, was long gone; it was the falcons' now, and the Falconers', and one day it would be strong.

Shadow shivered under the thin blanket and drew into a knot. Shadow was a seachild, one of those who had sailed and come back. Sometimes, when sleep came slow, the waves' memory brought it flooding.

Not tonight.

"Tomorrow," someone whispered. Snowcat, with his pale eyes and his voice already a man's. Even when he whispered, he made it as deep as he could. "Tomorrow I get my falcon."

"Tomorrow your falcon gets you." That was Eyas, warming Shadow a little, because he was Eyas. Another seachild. A friend. Almost. Shadow did not need eyes to see him lying on his side, brows knit over the nose that in part had given him his name, telling the truth as he always did, even to haughty cruel Snowcat. "The Choosing is for the falcons. Sometimes they choose not to Choose. You have no say in it."

Snowcat growled. If it had been anyone but Eyas, he might have sprung. But in the years of their training, he had learned. He was no match for Eyas in a fight, smaller though Eyas was, and slighter, and younger. Snowcat wanted to be lord of the not-yet-men, the boys who would be Chosen or rejected at this turning of the year. Eyas did not want to be lord, and was.

"Women," Dancer said in the silence. Shadow gasped and shuddered. No one noticed. Others were making sounds of disgust or of derision. Someone hissed for quiet; Dancer laughed. "What are you afraid of? No one's listening. My tongue's as safe as it ever was. Look. Women, women, women!" He grunted. Someone yelped. "Oi! Get your knee out of my belly, idiot. What's so horrible about a word?"

"It's not the word," muttered Snowcat. "It's the thing."

Voices chimed agreement. "Animals," said Colt. He always said that, choking on it. "Do you think—when we get our names—we'll have to—?"

"Not until we're blooded, and the Master decides we're fit." Dancer sounded not at all dismayed at the prospect. "A long time yet, have no fear. Then it should be endurable enough. Cattle manage; horses do very nicely. Though I've heard that a woman has a shade more wits than a mare."

"Evil wits," Colt hissed. "Witchcraft. They snare souls. We must keep them apart; we must never speak to them, or touch them save when the Master commands, or even think of them. Else they will destroy us."

Dancer snorted. "Nonsense! They're different, that's all. Alien, like Old Ones. The moon rules them, did you know that? Their blood runs in tides like the sea."

"You speak blasphemies!" Colt gasped, appalled.

Dancer laughed. Eyas' voice came through it, soft but very clear. "The tides are true. I know it; I remember. All the rest is nonsense. She's dead, you know that. The one we had to guard against: the witch, the soul-stealer. Jonkara." They all shivered at the name; even he stumbled on it, a little. "Women are people, like men, but weaker. That weakness was Jonkara's weapon. She ruled our women, and through them would have ruled us all. And yet a woman helped destroy her."

"Yes," said Snowcat. "A Sulcar bitch. Remember what she did to Rivery. Snared him and unmanned him, and lured him away from the Brotherhood. Now he roves the world with her, he and his falcon, and whenever he meets a Brother he preaches his mad new doctrine. Set our women free, he says. Live with them. Teach them. Make them like men. And where will it end? Women riding, hunting, bearing arms. Women with falcons."

Breaths caught. Snowcat had gone beyond the bounds even of defiance. "Powers!" Colt cried. "If the Brothers could hear you—"

"They can certainly hear *you.*" Dancer yawned loudly. "Let us not wax preposterous. Falcons will never Choose a woman. I do pity poor Rivery; if he's not careful he'll be outcast, and I wouldn't wish that on anyone. Even a Falconer with a Sulcarwoman for swordkin."

Shadow struggled to shut ears and mind. They roared, both, but not with the sea. One hand closed on flesh beneath the rough tunic. Little enough yet, but growing, it and its sister. And the moon calling with her tides, and all the spells wavering, child's magic giving way to greater magic. Woman's magic.

The falcons knew. When Shadow came to the test, they would rise all together and tear her limb from limb. Because she was chosen. Because with magic and with treachery, with lies and slyness and silences, with spells and moonweavings and wieldings of the Powers, a female had crept among the fledglings of the Brotherhood.

No. Her lips shaped the word in silence. Voices murmured in her mind. Faces gathered. They flickered. Now dull-eyed, expressionless, as men must see them. Now fierce with life and wit: the secret faces, the faces which they revealed to one another, when men were far away in their arrogance and their cowardice.

One face was clearest, worn with years and pain, scarred with the violence of the Turning: Iverna who was Mistress of the women of the Falcon. "Jonkara is dead," she said. "We have waited, we have suffered, we have hidden all that we are and do, lest the men know, and through the men, Jonkara. Now we are free. She cannot touch us; she cannot bend our wills to her own, nor lure us with promises of power. Empty promises. She would have it all. We would be her slaves."

"Why?" Shadow asked without sound.

"Power. It is all Power. The Witches had it, they of Estcarp: not only magic but the rule of realms. Lords have it. The Kolder longed for it; our men fancy that it is theirs, if only over us."

"And you would have it. You chose me to win it for you. To live as a boy. To be modest, but with a spell to whisper at need, to trick eyes into seeing what a boy would show. To face the Choosing; to be a falcon's Chosen. But," said Shadow, "the falcons know. They *know.*"

"And do they hate?"

Shadow lay on her face. Her breasts did not like it. She let them protest. Iverna was no dream, and no shape of fear. She was there, in Shadow's mind, waiting. "No," Shadow whispered. "No. They don't hate me. Sometimes . . . one will let me touch him, even borrow his eyes as he flies, in secret. When no one can see and punish us. But I can't be Chosen. The falcons know the old fears. They'll never offer a brother to a woman."

"You must ask."

"Have I ever had a choice?" Shadow laughed, bitter. "I was always your obedient weapon. I let you forge me as you would. I let the Brothers hone me. Now I let you wield me. I may not even ask you why."

"Because it is time. Because we have suffered enough. Because you are not the first, but you are the only one who has come so far, and has not failed in testing or in training or in strength of will."

Shadow had little strength left. She could run. She knew ways, and she knew a witchery or two that might blind even a falcon. She knew weapons, and riding, and warfare. She had Power. For that last alone, the Witches would accept her. What a triumph that would be. A Witch of Falcon blood; a

Power out of the Eyrie. That would break the Brothers' pride, even without the Choosing.

Shadow sighed. Woman and witch she might be, and spy, and would-be betrayer, but she was Falcon. Estcarp was no land and no people of hers.

She turned her mind from Iverna's. Once she could not have done it. She did not pause to be proud of it, or even to be afraid. She was saving all her fear for the Choosing.

The night was ages long, and then there was nothing left of it. The bell brought them all to their feet, even Grub who would sleep past sunup if he were let be. Some scrambled blindly for their usual clothes, remembered, joined the rest in putting on the leather and linen of full Brothers. It was the first time for them all, perhaps the only time; they were proud in it, but stiff, part with tension, part with fear. They fell into a wavering line in the room's center. Eyas hissed; the line snapped into straightness.

None too soon. Brothers had come for them. Falconers as outlanders saw them, falcon-helmed, faceless, each with his winged brother riding hooded on his shoulder. But the falcons could see. Shadow felt their eyes like burning needles, thrusting deep into her soul.

She could not do it. She had lived this lie for a full seven years. It was too long. She would fail; she would die. She could not do it.

Someone touched her. She started like a cat. Eyas was shoulder to shoulder with her, flashing her a sidelong smile. "Luck," he said under his breath. He had always been her friend, she had never known precisely why. Perhaps because she had neither toadied to him nor challenged him; and sometimes in practice and often in lessons, she had bested him. He had asked her once to be his swordbrother. She had put him off. He had not asked again, but neither had he changed toward her. He was comfortable beside her, as a brother should be.

Maid began to snivel. Shadow stiffened her back. *She* was no girl-minded coward, to let everyone know how terrified she was.

The thought made her want to laugh. She answered Eyas' smile with one almost as steady. "Luck," she answered him, and let herself be herded to the testing.

It was threefold. First, of the body, in armed or in unarmed combat. Then, of the mind, before the Master and the eldest Brothers. And last, for those who survived that final winnowing, the Choosing. Its precise nature, no one spoke of. Shadow knew that the initiates went one by one to the Eyrie's heart, and that some came back with falcons, but some never came back at all.

Three tests, three testing grounds. The ground of flesh and steel was blessedly familiar, the same stone court in which they had all had their training, with its carving of the sleeping falcon over the gate. Shadow's eyes rested on it as she waited, standing at attention between Eyas and a pale and rigid Maid, with words of invocation washing over her. The Brothers were still as stones round the rim of the court, each with its falcon shadow. The invocation rose and fell. The voice was familiar, even coming from the masked helmet, harsh and sweet at once, like honey in barley spirit. Blind Verian, who had seen his eight fledglings through their training, would see them to the end of it. His voice rose for the last time: "May the Lord of Wings favor your hands!"

The echoes had no time to die. Weapons lay in the court's center, seven of them. Sword, spear, dart gun, axe, pike, quarterstaff, dagger. The initiates lunged for them. In the same instant, a circle of Brothers closed in. Eight of them, falconless, and seven were armed and one had only his bare hands.

Shadow's mind darted wildly, swifter even than her body.

She had long since chosen. Likewise another. Snowcat's eyes blazed into her own. Her hand flashed past his, snatched the sword, tossed it. Eyas caught it. Snowcat had the spear. For her, nothing. They were scattered, like weapon moving to like. It was the pattern and the custom. This was testing, yet it was also ritual, precise as a dance.

Snowcat was the first to strike. He faced the spearman, shaft rising in a swift smooth movement. He let it fly.

It flew wide. The Brother's did not. Snowcat was quick, else he would have taken it in the body. He stumbled to one knee. The Brother was on him, vicious as any enemy.

They were the enemy. They would kill if they must: they were fighting men. They had no room in their ranks for the weak. Perhaps Snowcat had not truly believed it. He was learning, hard.

Shadow had the Brother's spear and a stinging hand, but she paid no heed to that. If her tactic had bemused her partner in the dance, he was not showing it. Nor was he moving. She could put no name to that leathern jerkin, that faceless helm. She did not try to cast the spear, nor did she move at all, but waited. Weapons rang about her.

The weaponless man moved, a light step, forward, a little to the side. She whipped the spear about. He caught it. She laughed, a breathless bark, and let him vault her over his head. She kicked. Her foot cried pain. She landed, rolled, twisted away from a shadow, came up in a coiled-spring leap. Metal glittered. Knife. Its hilt filled her hand. Her body knew the way of it: crouched, poised, waiting. She faced a man with a face. Her foot had not won its pain for nothing; it had unhelmed him. Dimly she knew him, and she knew that she should be awed, or honored, or terrified. Almery was the best man of his hands in the Eyrie. In the Brotherhood, he had perhaps an equal or two. He waited as she waited, wary as she was wary, poised with the perfection of which she was the merest shadow. His eyes were level, and they did not condescend. Which was a very mighty honor.

And which very nearly undid her. Boy or budding woman, she was no match for him. She could not hope to try.

She did not have to win. Simply to hold her own.

She could not.

She must.

And she waited, patient, for him to begin. She knew that Eyas' sword was holding, and a staff—Dancer. And the pike. Maid had it; he was outdoing himself. The others she could not see.

She dropped the knife. Let steel contend with steel. Flesh held to another law.

Did Almery's eyes flicker?

Her body did not tarry for an answer. It danced ahead and aside, pivoted. A vise closed about her wrist. Instinct flung her back; will and training loosed her muscles, let his strength battle for her, brought her in close and close. He was a head taller than she, and stone-hard, but never stone-cold. Her knee drove upward. He sprang away. Still grasping her wrist. Snatching the other. She launched herself into his face.

Again he eluded her. He had both her hands. Twice in close—he would expect a third. She gathered her every scrap of strength. If he would wait—if he would not move—

Back. Back, down, into bruising darkness, but not utter, not yet; bring up protesting legs, call in the will and the wit, raise and roll and fling the other up, over, away. And the sky was clean and her hands were free, and a shadow loomed against the light. Now he would fall upon her and end it. She lay and tried to breathe and could not care.

"Come, warrior." The words were warm, amused, but tinged with—respect? "Here, up. Would you sleep the day away?"

It was Almery. She had not known that he could smile at a fledgling. He pulled her unprotesting to her feet, and held her up, his arm about her shoulders. Dazedly she looked about. Eyas with blood on his face but a grin through it. Maid, Dancer, Downychick, all triumphant. Snowcat snarling but erect. Of Grub and of Colt, nothing, not even a body on the stones.

Two fallen, and two tests yet to come. It was not the worst of omens, but it was far from the best. And time only to wash, cool their throats with water, patch Eyas' cheek. Rest, they must not. The Master was waiting.

The hall was not utterly strange, but it had not the ease of familiarity. They had seen it once or twice at high festivals, when the older fledglings were suffered to serve at table. It was bare like all the rest of the Eyrie, no tables in it now, no fires lit, only the falcon banner black on scarlet behind the Master's chair. The Master and four men sat below it, waiting. They wore no masks, nor any mark of rank save the badge on each shoulder: stooping falcon for the captains, falcon in flight for the Master. But their faces were masks enough, and their bearing was more than regal; it was the bearing of men born and bred and trained to command.

Their attack was of eye and tongue and mind, and it came without warning and without preliminary. Seizing Maid who was weakest, lashing him with swift words: "Each Falconer is bonded to his falcon. What need of the baubles on the jesses?"

Maid paled beneath his mask of bruises. His mouth opened, closed. Dancer made a move, perhaps to help. A word froze him into immobility. "I—" Maid squeaked. "I—I don't—" The silence was terrible. He filled it with a rush of desperation. "The—the baubles are for outsiders. To conceal the bond that is our highest secret. To speak to allies when there is need, to pass commands in battle and to warn of dangers on the march."

He stopped, gasping as if he had run a race. They had

fallen already on another: Dancer, perhaps for his presumption. "Our Eyrie once was known to any who wished. Why is it now hidden?"

Dancer was quicker of tongue, and steadier. "The Old Eyrie fell in the Turning that the Witches wrought. Our new stronghold must be a secret place until all its defenses are secured; for its valley is rich and hidden in the tumbled hills, and those rove there who would gladly destroy us to gain what we hold. Or simply to rid the world of our kind, whether because we are human, or because we live by the Law of the Falcon."

"And what is that?" They asked it of Eyas. Deceptive simplicity; he took his time in answering.

"The Law is the law of brother-in-feathers and brother-in-skin. To live in bond to one another; to look to one's brothers and to one's commanders; to fight fair wherever fighting is, and to kill never save in defense of one's life or one's brothers or one's sworn alliance. To keep the secrets of the Brotherhood, and to keep faith, and to destroy the Darkness wherever it rises. And never to yield one's self to woman or Witch, or to any enemy of the Brotherhood."

"You: How many Masters have held this seat I hold? Name them as they held it. What was the distinction of each?"

And on. Simple questions, questions less simple, questions that must be thought on but there was no time to think, only to answer. Whether there were answer or no. And never a yea or a nay, only the flashing thrust of a new demand against a new victim.

There was a pattern in it. Shadow was trained to see patterns; and this was less subtle than witchery. Where weakness was, they seized on it, and yet they seized also on strength. She was at ease with the lore of the sea, and with the histories of the Brotherhood, and with the strategies of battle; less so with the mastery of horses or with the reckoning of numbers. And when she was all but spent with the effort of answering and of waiting to answer, the Master demanded of her, "Tell us of women and the Power."

So then. She was found out. She was almost glad that it was almost over.

They waited, silent. She mustered her wits. Falconers were taught the colors of magic, for evading them; they learned somewhat of Witches and their art, for every man must know his enemy. But someone already had spoken of both. Dancer, careful to display the proper hatred of females in general and Witches in particular. "Women," she said slowly, with tautness that might pass for revulsion, "are not to be thought of. Through them were we snared, long ago, when like Estcarp we were ruled by them. Estcarp is paying even yet for that folly. We have paid, and are rewarded. She of the curse is dead, Jonkara whose name is not lightly to be spoken. Her kinswomen remain bound and apart lest she rise again within them. She is the enemy whom we cannot escape, the field of death which we must sow in order to reap the life of the Brotherhood, the shadow through whom we must come to the light. It is said," she said, and she was careful to say it so, "that no man can be strong if he entrusts his strength to a woman; and yet without a woman, he would never have been born. We are not taught to hate them, nor to scorn them, only to hate and scorn what they stand for, and to do eternal battle against it. It is the way, the teachings tell us. It must be so."

She fell silent. Her throat ached with the effort of saying only what she had been taught to say. She lived a lie, but she had no skill in lying, even for her life's sake.

The Master did not speak, nor did the captains. A falcon mantled, hissing, but in a moment it stilled. No one rose; no one leveled his sword, denounced the impostor, thundered the truth. The fledglings, for all their training, had begun to droop with exhaustion. Eyas leaned very lightly against Shadow, seeming only to stand shoulder to shoulder, a trick they had all learned in training. She leaned on him in turn, easing her aching feet. She did not look to see if he glanced at her, and she would not let herself be troubled for him, although his face on the edge of her vision was alarmingly pale. His cheek would carry a scar. He would not, she thought inconsequentially, be the less good to look on for that.

The Master raised a hand. "You." Maid started and almost fell. But he stumbled forward. Then Dancer, and Snowcat. Then a long silence. Shadow stood with the others, too tired for despair, but strong enough to be angry. Let the old fools reject her; and Downychick had not stood up well to the relentlessness of the testing. But Eyas was the best of them all. How dared they pass him over?

The Master bowed his head slightly. Eyas came, reluctant, glancing back. Shadow managed a smile. It was well enough, now. No woman yet had come even this far.

"You."

She blinked. Downychick looked as he always did, a little wry, a little morose, and completely unsurprised. He had not moved. The eyes impaled her. Her feet yielded, carrying her forward. Her mind bated, wild with relief, with protest, with terror. The one who had failed was being taken away. The Master was speaking. It had had an order, that singling out. Last to first. First and second had been very close, but in the end, the choice was clear enough.

And she was angry all over again. Eyas was the best. She was a lie. A lie and a liar. And there was no help for it. The falcons would unmask her as she had always known they must.

Even the test of the Master had had its hedge of holy words; but the utmost, the true test, the Choosing, was simple to starkness. A Brother took each fledgling apart to a cell with a lamp and a stool and no window, where he must wait, alone with his fear. If any fear was left after the harrowing of body and mind. Shadow had none. She had subsumed the last of it in patience, in the acceptance which every woman learned from the cradle. A sort of strength, that; a scabbard for the weapon which was her Power. She might go down, but she would go down fighting, for the honor of her sex.

And then she stood alone under the pitiless sky. She seemed to remember a Brother's smile. Almery's. He had given her a Falconer's gauntlet and the scarlet ribbons of jesses. His words lingered: "Be strong, warrior, and fly high. The Lord of Wings favor your hunting."

It was all the rite he gave her, and it was enough. She stood in the high and holy place, the heart of the Eyrie, the summit of its mountain: the Fane of Wings. Its roof was the sky, its walls the limitless air; its floor was living stone, shaped and carved by the wind itself. Where an altar might have been rose a fang of stone, and on it, falcons.

True falcons. Not the tiercels, the black males with their white breasts, the warriors who flew with the warrior Brothers: great birds and beautiful, and wise with the wisdom of their kind. These were the females, the falcons, larger by half than their brothers, and wiser, and immeasurably fiercer. They were as white as clouds, shadowed with silver like clouds, on the wings, on the tails, in a gullwing sweep upon their breasts. Their eyes were burning gold.

Shadow froze like a cony beneath their stare. No one had told her. They had said that falcons would Choose or refuse. Not that she must face the great ones, the queens, the untamed and untamable. They were half a legend even in the Eyrie, though it was they who had found and claimed it; they did not reveal themselves to outlanders, and seldom so condescended to the Brothers. Their nesting places were secret. No one spoke of how they mated, or of how they reared their young. That males and females lived apart, the Falconers knew, and found it unremarkable: the young tiercels new from the nest, and those who had not Chosen a Brother, hunted in companies like men. It was in companies that, Shadow had been taught, they came to the Choosing.

Laughter rang in Shadow's mind. It was falcon laughter, wild and cold, with words in it. *Ignorance! It is the unchosen who flock like starlings.*

She could not tell who spoke. Perhaps it did not matter. They all watched her unblinking: twice two hands of them, she counted, and one more.

Unchosen, the soundless voice went on, *by us. The lesser ones find mates in wingless men.* There was no scorn in the words, merely acceptance of what was proper. A falcon chose her tiercel; a tiercel, falconless, Chose his man.

Shadow almost laughed. There was irony. She wondered if the Brothers knew it, and had perforce to live with it: to be less in reckoning than a female, even a female of the falcons. "And before the tiercels Choose," she said, trying to understand it all, "you measure the man to be Chosen."

Again the laughter. Its coldness was shot through with a fire of impatience. *An eyas in the egg has wit enough for that.* One of the falcons mantled: she upon the fang's tip. Her eyes held Shadow's own. Her mind's touch recalled Iverna, strong as it was, and intent on its purpose, with no time to spare for gentleness. *But you, fledgling. You are not like the rest. Come closer, and let us look at you.*

Shadow was cold with more than wind. No falcon ever hatched had any need to sharpen its eyes with closeness. And yet she moved as she was bidden. She sensed no danger yet; only fascination. It was no comfort. Falcons killed without malice, because it was their nature.

Their eyes were jewel-hard, glittering upon her. Shadow knew beneath knowing, that they spoke to one another. They had searched her to the soul, and done it long since, before she even knew. Now the trial was past, the judgment begun. The sentence was clear enough. No tiercel had come to her hand, and none would.

Death, she found herself praying. *Let it be death.* Not the crueler punishment. Life. Maimed, blinded or crippled, sent back among the women, bound again to their life of servitude. Her Power, the falcons would take. They had the strength. It throbbed in her bones, stronger even than the Power of this place.

There was silence deeper than silence. Even the wind had stilled. Shadow stood erect, her mind's shields up and locked. If she must fail, she would fail in her own way, in a blaze of power.

Female, said the falcon, clear through her shields, scattering her gathered power. *The males fear your kind. They fear power that flies unfeathered.*

"But it is dead!" Shadow cried, reckless. "It is gone."

Yours is not. The queen of falcons stretched her wings wide, folded them with fastidious care. Her head cocked. *We knew when you came. Your magic was small then; it flew with others' wings. It has grown since.*

"Then," said Shadow, a little bitterly, "there was never any need for this. You could have closed talons on me long ago."

Another falcon spoke. She was younger, Shadow sensed, and smaller, and yet she was very proud. *So we could! The tiercels urged it. They learn to think like men; and to fear like men.*

"You let me live. As a cat would. To watch me run."

Others of the falcons cried anger; one or two rose from the perch. The queen merely blinked, a flicker of the inner lid. The young one said, *When we hunt, we kill.*

The falcons settled one by one. Shadow remembered to breathe. She gulped air, loosed it in words. "What do you want of me? Why are you taking so long to kill me?"

Do you deserve to die? the queen inquired.

"The Brothers would say I did."

We are no being's brothers.

The young falcon leaped into the air. The wind shrieked as

she pierced it. Shadow stood like stone, steadfast, meeting stare with valiant stare. Talons stretched for her. Of its own accord her arm swung up.

The talons closed. The white wings folded. The falcon smoothed a feather that had settled awry. *My name,* she said, *is Wind-in-the-North.* It was fitting. Her voice in the mind was clear and cold yet faintly sweet, like the sense of her presence: a wind off the snowfields, with the merest hint of spring.

Shadow swallowed dry-throated. The falcon was a firm weight on her wrist, a prick of talons even through the gauntlet. Stronger was the prick of talons in her mind. Awareness swelled there. Presence; power. It was strange, and yet it was not. As if emptiness had lain in the heart of her, all unsuspected, and now it was filled. She had not known that she was not complete, until she stood completed.

But this could not be Choosing. She-falcons did not Choose. They were above it.

Wind-in-the-North flexed claws as strong as steel, and spoke aloud in falcon speech. "Name yourself, fledgling."

It was Choosing. Improbable, impossible, but it *was.*

Falcons had little enough patience. Shadow tasted the beginning of their contempt. Even the least of the males had acquitted himself more creditably than this.

The least of the males had had some small hope of his Choosing. Shadow drew herself up. "Javanne," she said hoarsely, and then more clearly. "Javanne is my name."

Javanne. The falcons made of it a chorus. The queen's voice went on when theirs had faded. *Javanne our sister, our proud one has Chosen you. She does not choose idly. But there is a price.*

That was not the way of Choosing. Shadow, whose truename was Javanne, knew that much at least. It was a free bond, the meeting of mind and mind, life and life. She opened her mouth to speak.

The queen forestalled her. *It is your own price, of your own making. You are Chosen; that is right and proper. But you came veiled in a lie. For that, you must pay.*

Javanne set her jaw. There was truth in the queen's words. Falcon truth, swift and merciless and unescapable. "When I was Chosen, I was to give up my deception. I am prepared for that. I will face whatever I must."

No, the queen said. *You will not. That is your price. To live your lie until another sets you free.*

Javanne's mind struggled with sudden mad joy. No need to face them all as she had known she must. No need to know their hatred, and their bitter revulsion, and the death which they would give her with hand and blade and claw. No need—and yet—

She could not fall. Wind-in-the-North would not let her. She could not move at all. To go on. To live her lie. To take hall-oath and sword-oath. To be a man among men, veiled in her magics, as she became ever more a woman . . .

Until another should free her. Another man? Another woman? Another lie?

She swore a trooper's oath. The falcons did not even blink. They were, if anything, amused. "It was supposed to *end* here!" Javanne raged at them. "I was supposed to die!"

You were not, said Wind-in-the-North with perfect calm. *You were to belong to me. I Chose you from my egg.*

"But only tiercels—"

A falcon does as she pleases. Wind-in-the-North sprang to Javanne's shoulder, and nipped her ear, not gently. *They are Chosen, your nestmates. They wait for you. Would you have them think you a losel?*

That brought Javanne's head up. She stiffened her knees, scrambled together what wits she had. If she chose as the falcons had chosen for her, she must be Javan, Brother of the brothers of falcons. And Chosen of a queen. That would stretch eyes wide enough, even without the rest of it.

"At least," Javanne said to Wind-in-the-North, and in part

to the rest who watched, "it will not be dull living that kills me."

While I live, said Wind-in-the-North, *it will be nothing at all.*

Javanne drank deep of cold clean air. The sun was sinking; the Brothers were waiting. Almery; and Eyas and Snowcat and Dancer and Maid, who now had names and falcons and places among the warriors. As she had, now, whatever came after. She saluted the queen as a swordsman salutes one who is both master and opponent, and raised her fist. Wind-in-the-North took station once more upon it. Her mind enclosed Javanne's, as Javanne's enclosed her own.

Javanne tried on a smile. It fit surprisingly well. With head up and back straight and a grin of triumph flaring through the smile, she went to join her Brothers.

II

The dream was always the same. A falcon in flight, now black, now silver-white: poising at the summit of its ascent, centering itself, plunging down and down and down. The air tore asunder. The prey swerved, desperate. The falcon struck. Bone cracked, a small hideous sound. The body, captive, convulsed once and was still. Furred beast-body blurred into furless long-limbed shape, eyes wide in the slack face. They lived, those eyes. They burned. They were all colors and none, in all faces and none. But always, however they shifted, they settled at last into one alone: a woman of the Falcon, facing her men with dull submission, but raising behind it a white fire of Power. *Iverna,* Javanne named her. At the naming of the name, the vision shriveled. It was only a cony slain in the hunt, and the falcon only a falcon.

And there was the heart of the horror. *Only* a falcon. It was Wind-in-the-North, all white and silver and achingly beautiful, and where the bond had been that ran deeper than life, nothing. No touch of mind, no presence in the soul, only a black and aching void.

Javanne lay and shuddered and muffled her gasping in the rough familiar blanket. Her mind clutched desperately. *Here,* said Wind-in-the-North. *I am here.* With that overtone that was wholly hers and wholly falcon, of impatience with human follies. Where else would she ever be but safe in Javanne's soul, as Javanne was safe in her own?

Javanne clung to that anchor. It brought the world back, whole and solid. The guardroom in Ravenhold keep, the fire banked on the hearth, the Brothers in their beds and the falcons on their perches, deep asleep. And closest to her, Wind-in-the-North, a white glimmer and a strong presence.

Slowly the nightmare faded. Javanne rose, hunter-quiet; pulled on jerkin and breeches and boots; ran her fingers through her cropped hair. Wind-in-the-North came to her fist without even a flicker of temper.

Loric had the dawn watch above the gate. Little as there was to watch for in this sheltered valley, still he was vigilant: a falcon-helmed shadow under a sky wild with stars, Stormrider drowsing lightly on his shoulder. Javanne sat on the parapet in his comfortable silence, and let the starlight bathe her face. Her narrow sharp-chinned Falconer's face, strong for a woman's, yet almost too fine for a man's. Sometimes Kerrec called her Beauty. Kerrec could be cruel when the mood was on him; and he had never forgiven her for being the Chosen of a queen.

She could see it still behind her eyelids. The long climb down from the Fane of Wings, with the sun setting full in her eyes, and the wind striving to pluck her from the mountain-side, and Wind-in-the-North still as a carven falcon on her shoulder. But no stone, she. Warm body sleeked with feathers, wide eyes burning gold, and in Javanne's mind the flame of her consciousness. Where the mountain met the Eyrie,

Brothers waited, each with his tiercel. The falcons had regarded Wind-in-the-North with mighty respect but with no surprise. The men had forgotten for an eternal moment all that they were to say and do. One even loosed an exclamation. It was Almery who cut across it, scattering it with ritual: the full salute and the measured words. "I give you greeting, Brother. Was it fair, the hunting?"

Javanne stumbled over the response which she had never expected to give. "It—it was fair, the hunting. Is the fire warm upon the hearth?"

"The fire blazes," said Almery, "and the board is laid. Will my Brother take his rest among my Brothers?"

"Gladly would I rest," she said, and that was purest truth.

The hall that had been so grim and cold in the testing, was full of warmth and light, and Brothers. Every Brother in the Eyrie, and every falcon, and among them four who were but newly Chosen. Snowcat, Dancer, Maid, and Eyas; but now they were strangers, straight-backed stern-faced young men in full Falcon gear, with names that she must remember. Kerrec, Hendin, Jory, Loric. Yet in that first moment as she stood alone and small in the gate, she saw only eyes. They were wide and startled, fixed on her other self, who spread great wings and said distinctly in falcon speech, "I who am Wind-in-the-North have Chosen this one called Javan to be my soul's kin."

Here and there, discipline broke. Javanne caught rags of words. "A queen?" "But that has never—" "*Can* never—" And sharp and clear and yet maddeningly sourceless: "Sacrilege!"

"How can holiness defile itself?" That was Loric, managing to be both diffident and impatient. "The queen has Chosen. Who would be fool enough to gainsay her?"

"Queens do not Choose," rapped a scarred and weathered Brother.

"A queen has," Almery said, coming to stand beside Javanne. His helmet was in his hand; he was calm, almost smiling. He saluted Wind-in-the-North and addressed her in her own tongue. "Is it permitted to ask why?"

She blinked the falcon's double blink, inner lid flickering in the wake of the outer. Her hiss was falcon laughter; her answer was absolute. "It is not."

Almery bowed, and astonished Javanne with a sudden wicked grin. It vanished as quickly as it had come; he beckoned.

She followed him through all the eyes. Some were beginning to envy, or to admire. A few began to hate. In front of the dais she halted. The Master stood alone upon it, clad like any Brother in leather and in well-worn mail. His eyes were the image of his falcon's, wild and burning cold, no flicker of plain humanity to give Javanne comfort.

She drew herself up. She had Wind-in-the-North. She needed no more.

His head bowed the merest fraction. His eyes did not warm, but they considered her steadily, almost as if he knew what she hid and why, and it mattered, and he would fight when the time came; but now he would play out the game as the falcons wished it. "Will you take sword-oath, O Chosen of a queen?"

"If you will accept it," Javanne answered steadily.

There was a sword for her. Almery's. She knew what that meant. Later she would know that she was the first of the five to be oathed; they had waited for her. She knelt as she must, set her hands in the Master's, said all the words of binding to Eyrie and Brothers and Law. And again, before Almery, she swore herself into service. She did not know what she felt. She was too stunned for joy, or even for fear. Her lie must endure, with the falcons' geas now to bind it, and oaths which she would try to keep. She was sundered from those who had set her in the Eyrie: so she learned after long and baffling silence, when she tried to touch Iverna's mind and met a wall full of falcon eyes. That too was of the geas, and impassable, and no force of hers sufficed to break it down.

Time had eased her way, a little. The Eyrie's discipline had forestalled her singling out, and Almery her captain took care to use both falcon and Falconer precisely as he would use any other pair of novices. Wind-in-the-North was larger than her brothers, and swifter, and fiercer, but she was young enough to yield to wisdom where she must. Even if that wisdom belonged to a lowly male. Now, after two years' honing and training in the Eyrie and among the fighting men of Estcarp, the white falcon and her Chosen roused comment only among strangers.

No one knew her secret. No one had even guessed. Men were blinder than she could ever have conceived. She hardly needed the spells with which by care and habit she guarded her womanhood. That young Javan was modest to obsession was reckoned a simple eccentricity, of a piece with his shyness and his reticence. Had he not lived seven years in the novices' barracks where there could be few secrets? Had he not passed the Choosing, where there could be none? Even if it were a she-falcon who Chose: that was a wonder and perhaps a scandal, but it was done; there was no altering it. Javanne was accepted now, a Brother of the brothers of falcons. She lived, rode, fought beside them. Her body by fortune's favor had grown tall and narrow, its curves all gone in thinness. She had trained herself to walk like a man, and to talk like one, although her throat disliked it. The rest was in the eye and the mind of the one who saw her.

She was as safe as she could ever hope to be. And she was breaking slowly. The dreams were the proof of it. Her mind was not content to beset her with simple nightmares of unmasking and outcasting. No; she must know the full hideousness of sundering from her falcon.

Never, said Wind-in-the-North from the edge of sleep. And, stronger: *I guard you. No one can touch you.*

Tell that to my dreams, Javanne said sourly.

I tell them, said Wind-in-the-North.

Javanne sighed and shivered. Her neck was stiff. Had she drowsed? The stars were fading; the east had grown pale. Loric was more shape now than shadow.

What drew her eye upward, she did not know. Ravenhold keep boasted far more of strength than of grace; but from one corner of it rose a slender spear of stone. It was a weakness, Javanne reckoned with Falconer logic: thin-walled, ornamented with carven balconies, and weakened to uselessness by a scattering of windows. Lord Imric's women held it and the corner of the keep from which it sprang; appropriately enough, the Brothers muttered, especially those ten condemned to stand guard in Ravenhold while the rest harried the borders with the lord. Guarding was easy enough, if ignominious; and Lord Imric had men to spare for that, even if he must hire Almery's company to clear his lands of the offscourings of the wars and the Turning. But he had insisted that his castle's guards be Falconers. "I cannot rest easy else," he had said in the way he had, light, a little deprecating, but all steel beneath. "I lost my lady to a liegeman's treachery. I will not so lose my sister. From men of the Falcon at least I need fear no betrayal."

Almery had consented with little enough demur. The Lady Gwenlian kept to the tower with her women; the Brothers kept to their guardianship, not happily, but with soldierly resignation. They all knew the tale behind Lord Imric's tale of treachery. A woman alone with her lord gone to war, a captain of guards with a fair face and a white smile, and one thing led to another, and on a fine bright morning they two were gone. Eastward, people said. And Lord Imric entrusted his remaining women to the only men in the world who would not dream of breaking that trust.

Javanne regarded the women's tower in the dawn, and was soul-glad that she need not dwell there. Women in Estcarp were said to be as free as men. In the towns Javanne had seen, that seemed to be so. It appalled even hardened veterans among her Brothers. Yet in Ravenhold, whether by their own choice or by Lord Imric's doing, the ladies lived almost as prisoners.

She had heard the servants whispering. It was not only the Lady Vianna's infidelity. Some strangeness attached itself to the Lady Gwenlian. She was to have been a Witch, they said. Then had come the Turning, and the breaking of the Witches' power in Estcarp. The lady had come home without oath or jewel, riding alone through the wrack of war. She had told her full tale to no one save, perhaps, her brother. She had shut herself up in her tower, and there she remained, coming forth only to walk in the herb garden or to ride unattended in the far fields or, very rarely, to dine in hall. Since her brother left, she had done none of them.

Yet surely that was she who leaned on the windowframe above Javanne, face turned to the rising dawn. Her hair was loose about her shoulders. She wore something pale, with a shawl thrown over it, all careless where perhaps she thought none could see. She was almost frighteningly beautiful.

"I don't think we're even supposed to look."

Javanne started. Loric stood behind her; his voice was wry, and pitched just above a whisper.

"I wonder," Javanne muttered, eyes fixed on that glimmering face. And more softly still, and yet more swiftly, almost a hiss: "She is no Witch!"

"Of course not. Witches have no beauty."

"She has too much." Javanne rounded on him. "You've been looking."

"I can hardly help it," he said. "Maybe that's why she never won her jewel. Her looks were against her."

"Maybe," said Javanne, not believing it. She was very cold. It was the wind, she told herself, and the dawn chill. It had nothing to do with the lady in the window. Fair as she was, and strange, and touched with sadness, like a white bird caged. Her troubles were her own. She was nothing to Javan of the Brotherhood.

Again Javanne looked up. The lady's eyes had lowered to meet Javanne's. They were level, and very dark in the half-light. The lady smiled a very little, tentative, almost shy. *Why,* Javanne thought, *she's young.* As for her people she must be, long as their lives were, and young as the Witches took them. Not so very much older than Javanne herself, and like her, a prisoner with a secret which she dared not tell.

Javanne's face was stiff. She tore her eyes away. It was deadly, that sense of kinship. She must not yield to it.

Steel rang on steel. Hendin, come to relieve Loric. Javanne took shelter in flight.

Wind-in-the-North rode the living air, letting it carry her, with the sun warm on her back and Ravenhold's gray walls forgotten below. In a little while she would be hungry, and then she would kill. Now she was simply free.

Stormrider circled lazily below her. He waited on her pleasure, as was proper. His wings were blacker than any raven's, with a shimmer of midnight splendor. His eyes were the color of heart's blood. The curve of his beak was fiercely beautiful; his talons were strong and sure in the kill. Perhaps, when her season came . . .

Javanne thanked the Powers for the helmet that hid her burning cheeks. Wind-in-the-North was no lady; she was a queen. When she thought of loving, she spared no time for maidenly foolishness. Lately she had often thought of it. Winter was retreating from the mountains; already lesser birds were nesting. Soon Wind-in-the-North must choose her life's mate and begin the raising of her young.

Perhaps Almery had known what he did, to set Javanne among the guardians of Ravenhold. A nesting falcon had no place among her fighting kin.

I will not nest, said Wind-in-the-North with a flash of temper, *until I choose. I am no featherhead of a bird, to be at my body's mercy.*

But if your body insists—Javanne began.

My body is my servant. Wind-in-the-North gathered it. Rockdoves fed amid the stubble of a fallow field. She loosed a high fierce cry. They scattered. She laughed, chose the fattest, and struck.

Javanne untangled herself from the exhilaration of the kill. Her body was briefly strange to itself, great awkward wingless thing in leather and mail. Her gelding fretted the bit, tossing his head. He had stood still quite long enough; and there were three doves down at Wind-in-the-North's talons, and one frantic in its darting flight, but she was waiting for it. Stormrider had two on his own account, filling Loric's bag; he brought down a third as Javanne watched, and came to his perch on Loric's saddle with no little reluctance. But he settled quickly enough as Loric gutted the last of the birds and fed him the entrails.

"How fierce your birds are," a stranger said, "and how splendid."

Javanne had known that a horse approached from the castle; because its leather-clad rider was no Brother, she had noticed the fineness of the mount, acknowledged the quality of the horsemanship, and dismissed both. But the low sweet voice brought her about. Even in riding garb there could be no doubt of the newcomer's gender. Or of her name. There could not be two such faces in Ravenhold.

Javanne spoke no word of greeting. Deliberately she dismounted, calling Wind-in-the-North to her fist with a whistle and a word as one always did before strangers, gathering the slain birds into her bag. When she turned, the Lady Gwenlian had come between her and her gelding. Javanne skirted her in silence, set Wind-in-the-North on the forked perch, swung astride.

The lady seemed not at all dismayed. "It is wonderful, the flight of a falcon," she said.

Javanne set her teeth and began to gut a dove. The lady did not, as Javanne had hoped, turn pale and retreat. She watched with interest as Wind-in-the-North accepted the tribute of heart and liver. "Your bird is very beautiful. Is it a new breed? I have never seen one like it."

Javanne had sworn herself to silence. Not so Loric. "She," he said with cool precision, "is a female: a falcon. Those whom you have seen are males. Tiercels." He paused, one beat, two. "Does my lady require escort to her chambers?"

Javanne would have laughed if she had not been so desperately uneasy. As if this woman, being woman and once, almost, a Witch, could know. As if she could see what lay beneath the leather and steel.

She was lonely, that was all. Javanne hardly needed witchery to know it. It was written in her face. And perhaps she found her tower tedious, and here was a challenge to her beauty and her wit and her potent womanhood: a pair of Falconers hunting for the pot.

She smiled at Loric. It was neither simper nor snarl. It was merely beautiful. "My lady welcomes escort in her riding."

"We hunt," Loric said, flat and forbidding.

"Then you may lead, and I will follow. It is a long while," she said, "since I rode a-hawking."

Loric wavered visibly. The lady was very beautiful, and he was very young, and he was not as wholehearted a hater of women as he should have been.

"You hunt," Javanne said to him, quickly, before he could speak. "I shall return the lady to her place."

"And am I a strayed heifer, to be sent back to my byre?" demanded the Lady Gwenlian. Stung, with glittering eyes and sharpened voice, she seemed less like sheer mindless beauty and more like a mortal woman. She was all the more perilous for that.

"You are a woman," said Javanne. It was stark and reasonless terror; it sounded like hate thickened with scorn.

Loric was a little gentler. "The falcons hunt best without

distraction." Stormrider stretched his wings and hissed. He was laughing.

Wind-in-the-North had less patience. She left her perch in an eruption of wings, and sank talons into the rump of the lady's stallion. The beast screamed, lashed, and bolted.

Javanne gathered to bolt after; but a flick of the falcon's mind held her still. The stallion's path led directly to the castle, and the rider was firm upon his back. Already he was slowing under her hand.

Wind-in-the-North settled calmly on her perch and smoothed a ruffled feather. "Now," she said in falcon speech, "may we hunt?"

Falcon helm turned to falcon helm. Javanne wanted desperately to laugh, or else to howl. Loric raised his hand in the warrior's signal: *Onward.*

"Onward," Javanne agreed. Time enough later to pay for a falcon's frankness. The day grew no younger, and they had a pot to fill. She touched the gelding to a trot.

If there was a price for her abrupt and humiliating dismissal, the Lady Gwenlian seemed disinclined to demand it. She did not approach Javanne again. Javanne saw her once or twice in the window of her tower, but she did not call, and Javanne did not tarry to tempt her. The edge began to wear off the memory, although Javanne could not, yet, manage to laugh at it. She told no one of it. Nor, she noticed, did Loric. It was too small a matter, or too great, to bandy about the guardroom.

Then Javanne forgot it. She was dreaming nightly, always the same: the falcon, the hunt, the kill; and the terrible blankness of the mind behind the lambent eyes. Once she woke screaming, with Loric holding her down. Her first instinct was to cling. Her second was to fling him away with all her strength. He fell sprawling in Hendin's bed, in a tumult of startled men and startled falcons. They were all short of sleep that night, and not inclined to let Javanne forget who had begun it. She almost welcomed the three days' stable duty: she could sleep in the loft among the last of the hay, and dream her dreams without fear of shattering anyone's sleep but her own.

On the third day of her penance, Javanne stood atop the dungheap with the sun in her eyes and an emptied barrow tugging against her hands. Because it was insistent, and because she had stopped caring who saw, she let it go. It found its upward track, sprang off its legs, and somersaulted down the slope. A small madness stung her. She vaulted after it, spinning in the air. Her feet struck clean earth and a living shadow. She swayed, startled, and almost fell. A hand caught her.

Loric let go quickly. He was trying to be Falcon-stern, but a grin kept breaking through.

She swallowed her own. "I didn't mean to strike you," she said. "The other night."

And in the same instant he said, "I didn't mean to startle you. The other night."

They stopped. "I—" they both said. Stopped again. Began to laugh.

Javanne mastered herself first. She righted the barrow, set her hands to the shafts. Loric stopped her. He had sobered all at once, which was a gift he had. "Wait. I really do mean—I tried to come before, but Gavin forbade me."

"One should obey one's decurion," Javanne agreed blandly.

"I told him I started it."

"And he said that I brought force into it." Javanne upended the barrow and leaned on it. A yawn escaped before she could catch it. "Let be, Loric. It's past."

"Hardly that." His hand took in the stableyard, the redolent hill, the barrow. "And you still have the dreams."

Javanne straightened very slowly. "It was only one nightmare."

"Yes," he shot back. "Every night for nights out of count. And you running away from sleep until it catches you and ties you, and going about like a black-eyed ghost, and turning into one, too, with the bare mouthful you'll eat when someone forces it into you."

Javanne stared at him. He glared back, his dark eyes sparking gold out of his falcon's face. Anger she could understand, or impatience. But not this passionate eloquence.

His jaw set. His brows met over the swoop of his nose. "Damn you, Javan," he said. "What is there in you that won't let itself trust your own Brothers?"

"A man is strong," she answered him levelly. "He does not go weeping to his mother at every ill dream."

"Neither does he nurse a great trouble till it comes nigh to breaking him."

"What makes you think that you can ease my burden?"

She thought that she had gained his hatred then. But Loric was Loric. "Maybe I can't," he said with perfect calm. "Stormrider thinks I should try."

"Stormrider is a broody hen."

He knocked her down and sat on her. He did it without rancor, and without great effort. "Never," he said gently, "never speak ill of my falcon. Your dreams are troubling his sleep. Your self troubles his waking. He demands that I make you whole. Because, he says, you are falcon-minded, and a queen has Chosen you."

Javanne tossed him onto his back, knelt astride him, scowled down at him. "What makes him think you have any power over me?"

Loric shrugged. "Can I fathom the logic of a falcon? I can't even fathom yours. Something is killing you inch by inch. And you refuse to say a word."

"Surely the falcons know," she said bitterly.

"Only that you dream, and your dreams are dark."

She pushed herself away from him, gathering into a knot. Secrets. So many secrets. And no one—no one—

She tossed her aching head. "My dreams are dark," she said. Her voice was raw, not like her own at all; it rasped in her throat. "My dream. It is only one. My falcon, hunting. She kills. And there is no bond between us. None at all." She looked up. His face was still. Her lips stretched in the parody of a smile. "You see? There's no more to it than that. It's hardly worth a falcon's fretting, or the concern of a—" She paused. For all that she could do, the word escaped. "The concern of a friend."

She shrank within herself. He said nothing for a long while, did not even glance at her. He sat up and clasped his knees. He frowned a little still. When he spoke, at first it seemed to have nothing to do with either dream or friendship. "This morning, Gavin had a sending through the baubles. There's been a battle. Almery and the Brothers had the van. They were ambushed. They were . . . very badly beaten." Javanne sat mute. Loric considered the pattern of dust on his breeches. "Very badly," he repeated, as if to himself. "They were no scattering of bandits that attacked: there were too many, and too crafty. Renegade sellswords out of Karsten, Almery thinks, with an eye on the green lands. We pay high for what they take. Half of our Brothers—half down, killed or wounded. And the falcons . . ." His voice broke as it had not since just after his Choosing. He tossed his head, angry at his own weakness. "The enemy aimed at the falcons. It was sudden—uncanny. Our people had had no warning at all. And the falcons—just as the shooting began, the falcons went wild. Something had broken the bond. Like a knife cutting, abrupt and absolute."

"Witchery." Javanne hardly knew that she spoke aloud until she had spoken.

Loric nodded tightly. "It was witchery. Strong, but not so

strong as to hold past the first moments. It had no need. By the time Lord Imric's men came, the damage was done, and the enemy had melted away. None of them lingered. There were only our dead, winged and wingless."

"Almery?" she whispered.

"Safe. A dart grazed his hand; there was no poison in it. Those falcons who live, stay by their Chosen. But the bond, they say, is not what it was before. Like a broken pot. Mended, it shows still the scars."

Javanne was silent for a long while. At last she dared to ask it. "How many?"

"Thirty falcons. Ten men."

Javanne closed her eyes. Thirty. There had been half a hundred. Ten rested idle in Ravenhold. Only ten left. Of half a hundred falcons, only ten. Twenty men left alive, half their souls gone, torn asunder by a flight of outland arrows.

She had thought herself a veteran, blooded in battle, inured to any horror. Fool that she was. Child. She had never seen a falcon slain while his bondmate lived. Men, yes. But their brothers-in-feathers had always died with them. That was great grief, but it was fitting. She could endure it.

This was unspeakable. She wrapped her arms about the sickness in her belly, holding it there by main force.

"The dead are fortunate," Loric said. "The living are cripples, most of them. Some are mad. Revan killed himself."

He said it quietly, coolly, as if he were what outlanders deemed all his kind to be: cold and heartless, a man of leather and steel. But that was the Falcon way. His eyes were burning dry, his face carved in ice, the scar of his Choosing livid in it. And he had laughed with Javanne, suffered her cruelties, fretted over her little troubles.

He said it even as she thought it. "So you see, Javan. You dreamed true."

She shook her head slowly. Not denying it. Refusing what it meant. However twisted, stunted, bent awry by the lie which she must live, Power dwelt in her. She knew it. She could have been a Witch, had she been of Estcarp, and had she submitted herself to that stark and ancient discipline: though no less stark or ancient than the Law of the Falcon. But that she was foresighted—that she had seen what would be, and had not heeded it, and had kept it with the rest of her secrets, and by her criminal folly so many had died—

She rocked, still shaking her head, giving no thought to how she must look until Loric seized her and shook her. She looked at him and reckoned him brave; and strange, for a Brother, because he was so willing to touch and to be touched. They had hearts, the Falconers. They could love, and did, often, and freely in their own dour way. Man and falcon, Brother and Brother, soldier and captain, sometimes even man and man, though that was neither as easy nor as common as outlanders seemed to think. But they did not often set flesh to flesh. Like their falcons, they did their touching from a distance.

Loric's fingers were hurting-tight. All at once they were gone, although the pain tarried. "By all the Powers," he cried to her, "don't *look* like that!"

She swallowed. Her throat ached. But her mind was suddenly very clear. She heard her voice coming from very far away. "What will Gavin do?"

"Send five Brothers to do what they can. Not," Loric added, and that was bitter, "the five of us infants. We stay with Gavin and make a show of defending milady's virtue."

"A show," Javanne repeated. She began to laugh.

This time Loric had to strike her. She was frightening him. He had never seen her like this. Herself. Woman and witch; but he could not know that. She thought of telling him, of stripping in front of him. It was a passing madness, and she was geas-bound. She made herself sit up, arrange her face into sanity, and say, "A show indeed. That is what we must put on."

Something was awry. Perhaps she was too calm. "What are you saying?" Loric demanded, swift and fierce.

She had no answer for him. So much was unraveling in this ill-knit world of hers; the woman was part of it, because she was a woman, because she would have been a Witch, because something in her called to Javanne. Nor had it stopped calling for that Javanne would not listen.

"No," she heard Loric say. "Oh, no. You haven't let her sink her claws in you."

It was a prayer. He yearned to believe it; he feared desperately that it was a lie. He waited for her to confess that she had gone to her oathlady's bed.

Beyond hysteria lay a region of utter calm. She spoke from the midst of it. "She could never tempt me to that."

"Of course she could," he said with an edge of roughness. "She is beautiful. She rides like a man; she knows the sword; she—"

"And how do you know that?"

He stopped short. His cheeks reddened beneath the browning of sun and wind. The thin line of his scar burned scarlet. "I'm neither blind nor deaf. And I'm no less a man than you."

Javanne bit her lip until the blood sprang, sudden and iron-sweet. "Loric, I would not desire her. I could not." His eyes were adamant in unbelief. She flung truth in his face. "I *can't!* I do not—I cannot incline toward a woman."

There was a silence. Loric paled. His hand reached, retreated. "I—" He swallowed. His head tossed. His brows were knotted as if in pain. "Is that why you wouldn't be my swordbrother?"

After a moment she nodded. She could not look at him. Her cheeks were hot; her vitals twisted, racked with her treading so close to the bounds of the geas.

He did not say anything ridiculous. For a long while he did not say anything at all. Then he touched her shoulder, lightly, briefly. "You know what I am," he said. "And what I'm not." He paused. "Will you be my swordbrother?"

Her head came up. This was more than apology. She knew what he was asking, and what he was not. She had refused him once, because she knew that she must fail the Choosing. Now she was Chosen. And more a woman now than she had been then. And he was—very—

Young. Blind. Foolish. And beloved. Yes, she cried in the fortress of her mind. She was quite besotted with this her Brother, and so she always had been, ever since she saw him standing in the fledglings' barracks, awkward and bedraggled and ugly-beautiful as an unfledged falcon. That was her first terror-stark day in the Eyrie, with every moment trumpeting her discovery and her destruction; and he had been fighting: Kerrec crouched in a corner, nursing a bloodied face. But Loric had been gentle with the newcomer, the seachild brought late into the Brotherhood, and he had named himself seachild also, and appointed himself her friend. Her brother. Defender and defended, and sharer in all that she would share.

He was not a man for men. He could not be a man for women. While she . . .

"Yes," she said, defying fate and geas and her own treacherous body. "Yes, I will be your swordbrother."

The light in his face made her want to break and bolt. She unsheathed her dagger as he unsheathed his. They made the cut, held wrist to wrist, mingled blood and blood. He was steady. She struggled not to shake. Something more was passing than blood and friendship. Something potent, that would not let her grasp it.

"Sword and shield," he said, slow and solemn, "blood and bread, and the Lord of Wings over us all: be thou my brother in heart and hand, through life and through death, unto the world's ending."

"Sword and shield," she said, steady because her pride

commanded it, "blood and bread, and the queens of falcons be my witness: be thou my brother in heart and hand, through life and through death, unto the world's ending."

"So mote it be," he said, setting his hilt in her hand.

She laid her blade in his. "By the Powers of Air, so shall it be."

The air thrummed into stillness. The scent of Power faded slowly. Loric seemed not to perceive it. Her blade snicked into his sheath; he smiled at her, a little shy, a little mischievous. Yet his words were all properly dutiful. "The Brothers will be wanting their horses. Are you done here?"

"Quite done," Javanne said. He turned; she followed him into the odorous dark of the stable.

From the highest of Ravenhold's pastures, the land seemed all at peace. No wars and no Turning; no reivers in the hills. No slaughter of falcons. Even here, even after a hand of days, Javanne's mind could not dwell on that memory. It skittered round the edges. It tried to see a pattern. A plot, with the Falconers' destruction in the center.

"But *why*?" she cried aloud.

Why? the mountains echoed her. *Whywhywhywhywhywhywhy?*

Wind-in-the-North drew her back from the borders of desperation. She flew high even for a Falconer's sight; her white-and-silver body was one with the scud of clouds. *A rider comes,* she said.

Javanne's gelding wandered, cropping the new grass. She did not call him to her. From the stone on which she sat, she could see down the long rolling slope to the narrow neck of the valley. She watched the sun pursue cloud-shadows across it.

A new shadow swelled among the green. Earthbound, this one, moving at horse-pace. Javanne watched as it drew nearer.

The Lady Gwenlian wore woman's garb, the skirt divided for riding, pouring over the gray stallion's flanks. He halted neat-footed on the very edge of Javanne's shadow; his rider looked down, level, taking in the unmasked face.

Javanne let her stare. It could not matter what she saw. Nothing mattered but that some Power wished the falcons dead.

"You," the lady said slowly. "You are not—"

Javanne paid the woman's words no heed. "They are killing falcons," she said. "Do you know what that does to us? Can you even imagine it?"

Gwenlian slid from the saddle. Her eyes were intent, her fine brows knit. "I thought—you were all—" She stopped, shook her head sharply as if to dismiss a thought that had no purpose. "Who would slay your birds? What could he hope to gain from it?"

"If I knew that, I would not be sitting idle here, grieving for my Brothers." Javanne's mind was beginning to clear. There was danger in this colloquy. In coming so close to a woman who might not be blind as men were blind. And yet there was a sort of comfort in it. A sense almost of relief; a loosening of the constraints that bound her body and her mind.

The lady sat on the grass. She had made an art of beauty as did Almery of swordsmanship; it was as sure as instinct, and as unconscious. "There are ways to learn who threatens your people," she said.

Javanne met her eyes. "You are no Witch, lady."

"Not all the world's Power resides in the sisterhood."

Javanne laughed lightly enough to startle herself. "Indeed not! Though they would have your people believe otherwise. They trained you, did they not? and fell before they could bring you into the fullness of your Power."

"I left them," Gwenlian said. "I could not bind myself as they would see me bound."

"The body's pleasures are sweet, I am told."

The lady flushed faintly; yet she did not take offense. "That was not all of it."

"Surely not." Javanne ran gloved fingers through the grass. "I would be a fool to trust you. You are a woman; you were to be a Witch. What you stand for, and what I stand for, are as the wolf and the snow cat. Implacable enemies."

"Need it be so?"

Javanne glanced at her. There was no falsehood in her. "Suppose that I did trust you. What can you do?"

"More perhaps than you think. What needs to be done?"

"Something is slaying falcons. Something with Power. We must find it; name it, if we can; destroy it."

"Simple enough," said the lady with a flicker of mirth. "I have not the Power of a full Witch, but in seeking and in finding I have a little skill. If I seek and find, surely your brave sword will suffice to destroy."

"Why would you trouble yourself to do it?"

Gwenlian shrugged. She looked very young. "It is dull, this life of mine. In some matters my brother is a little less than sane; I humor him, because I love him, but he is not my master. Whatever he may think." There was steel in that. Javanne acknowledged it with a dip of her head. The lady bowed in return. "And beyond my small preoccupations, there is truth. I was taught to hear what is not said, to see more than my eyes can see. I cannot help it. Your falcons, my heart tells me, are more than trained beasts."

"They are rather more than that," Javanne said. She raised her fist. Wind-in-the-North came to it. The lady held very still: remembering, no doubt, what had come of their last meeting. Javanne smiled thinly. "If you would ally with me, you must ally likewise with this my sister."

Gwenlian regarded the white falcon with more of wonder than of distrust. Wind-in-the-North favored her with a single molten glance, and shifted to Javanne's shoulder. *We need her,* the falcon said, not with any great pleasure. *She can hunt where we cannot; her little Power can seek unmarked where our greater strength would flush the quarry. Tell her that I say so.*

Javanne did as she was bidden. The lady was not pleased to be so judged, but she mustered a smile. "The white queen is as direct in speech as in her hunting. I will suffer her if she will suffer me." She rose, shook out her skirts with the air of one girding for battle. She held out her hand. "Well, Falconer. Is it a pact?"

Javanne paused. Wind-in-the-North was wise, and more foresighted than any human seer. But it was mad, all of this. What could any of them do against a Power with strength to fell a full company of the Falcon?

They could find it and face it and take what came after. She clasped the lady's hand, and it was soft, uncalloused, yet strong. "A pact," she said. She grinned suddenly, to Gwenlian's patent astonishment. "My Brothers will be appalled."

"Are you?"

Javanne laughed and would not answer.

"There is a place," said Gwenlian, "where our seeking may be the stronger."

Javanne, once begun, refused to regret what she had chosen. She mounted her gelding; Wind-in-the-North took again to the air. Together they followed in Gwenlian's wake, by ways steep even for a mountain pony, away from the setting sun. The fighting was away eastward. The Lady Vianna had fled eastward. In the east were mysteries and memories and old, old fears.

Javanne tensed to gather the slack reins, to turn her mount back. What was she doing? She had orders: a patrol to ride and a land to protect. She had no leave to abandon her duties.

The gelding slid, stumbled, caught himself. Her fingers

loosened on the reins. Ahead of her trod her shadow, and ahead of it her guide. She firmed herself to follow them.

The mountain wearied at last of its ascent, and rested upon a high stony level. There was nothing sorcerous in it, save that magic which dwells in all high places: wind and air magic, wild magic, the magic of earth that meets the sky. Falcon magic. With a high exultant cry, Wind-in-the-North touched the summit of heaven and dropped like a stone. A bare man-length above Javanne's head, she caught herself; she settled demurely to the saddle-perch, ignoring Gwenlian's wide stare. "Begin," she said in falcon speech.

The lady scarcely needed to hear the meaning of the word. She left her saddle, taking with her the saddlebags. She set them on the ground, searching through them until she found what she needed: a peeled wand, a packet of herbs, a string of beads the color of the summer sky. She looked up from them, smiling a little. She was not as steady as she might have been. "It is a simple thing, this. With proper teaching, a child can do it."

Javanne nodded slowly. Falcon magic was more of the inner world than of the outer; it needed few trappings, demanded little ritual. She watched Gwenlian circle the mountaintop with her wand, sealing the circle with herbs and with murmured words. She sensed the raising of wards: an oddness, a cramping of Power into this small space. The stallion snorted, startling her. She gentled him. He pulled away, seeking out the thin grass which grew among the stones.

Gwenlian returned from the circle's edge to kneel in its center. Her steps were a little slower, her brow sheened with sweat. She waved Javanne away. "No, no, it is nothing. Power has its price; this is low enough. Stay by me now; watch over me. If I have not roused by moonrise, compel me. Do not touch me unless you must, and do not fear, whatever you see."

Again and more sharply Javanne nodded. Her lips were set.

Let the woman call it apprehension; that was true enough. Not since she was a little child had Javanne been forced to trust to another's Power. And this was not even a Power of her own kind. Spells, cantrips, beads and powders and charlatanry; and the wielder of them all an enemy of the Falcon, a Witch who had turned coward and fled the testing.

No. No coward. Merely one who had yearned to be free.

Gwenlian settled herself with her back to a tall stone and her face to the eastern sky. She arranged her body with care, and arranged her mind with it. She wound the blue beads about her fingers, stroking them, focusing upon them. Her face stilled. Her eyes closed.

Power gathered. It was slow; it was less feeble than Javanne had feared it would be. There was sweetness in it, but steel too, and a fierce self-centeredness that spoke to Javanne of cats. It was not a flaw in a sorceress, if she had the wit to rule it.

Javanne's shields rose with the other's Power. It was not aware of her own that yearned to call to it. It turned outward, a shadow cat with eyes like moons. A wall of light reared before it. It paced forward. A gate opened; the cat passed through, taking with it a glimmer of the wall's light. It paused beyond, head up, questing. The world had gone all strange. Dreams walked the shadowed earth; memories; ghosts, demons, flickers of alien Power. The cat took no notice of them. It sought a thing more palpable than they. A slayer of falcons. A breaker of the bond; an enemy of the Brotherhood.

Javanne was one with the shadows in the cat's wake. Part of her dwelt still in the outer world, eyes and a sliver of mind on watch against dangers of the body. She saw the sun go down; she knew when the wind rose, keen and cold. And she quested behind the lady, watching only, veiled against any Power that might come hunting.

The cat's tail twitched: a quickening of the sorceress' awareness. Javanne sank deeper into hiding. The mind-beast advanced with greater purpose now. It had found a scent. Javanne clung to control. She must not reach toward that suggestion of presence. She must trust this alliance and this ally. There had been little enough logic in the pact; in its observance at least she could take thought for prudence.

Even as she thought it, mind and body reeled. Something had risen out of the mists of the inner world. It was huge, and it was ancient, and it was nothing that had ever been at one with human soul. It was bound, but not unfree; like a young falcon on the creance, it flew as far as it might and did what it would within the stretch of its bonds. And it yearned to break them. It was a Power of the air, a winged thing trammeled, constrained to alien will.

Human will.

Great talons stretched. Gwenlian whirled to flee. Too late, too slow. Javanne caught her, mind, body. There were too many of both. She could not grasp them all.

The earth fell away beneath them. Something caught at them: the wards, feeble, toppling under the weight of Power without and Power helpless within. Mind tangled in body, body spun in void. It tore like ancient silk.

Javanne gasped for breath. She was blind, deaf, dead.

Something stirred against her. A pale blur steadied into a face, dim-lit as by a pallid radiance. She stared stupidly at it. Loric. What had Loric to do with any of this?

Her focus stretched sluggishly. Gwenlian stirred within her hand's reach. Stormrider, Wind-in-the-North, she could not see. But the white falcon was in her mind as she clutched in dream-born panic, offering nothing but presence.

It was enough. She sat up dizzily, swallowing bile. This was not the mountaintop near Ravenhold. That had held only the Power which Gwenlian brought to it. This was a place of true Power. Her bones throbbed with it.

In the mortal world it was simple enough: a ring of stones about a single central stone. Those without were newer though still vastly old, shaped and smoothed by art and hand, touched with a fugitive shimmer. Blue, perhaps. Or green. Or moonwhite. The inner stone was the heartstone, and at the first blurred glance it seemed to have no shape but that which time had given it. But it was shaped, how long ago Javanne could not even begin to guess, and that shape had about it a haunting familiarity. Like—almost like—a winged creature. A bird, beaked and taloned, its wings half spread as if it would take flight from its prison. The light which kindled in it was of no color which a human eye could encompass.

It was not of the Dark. No more was it of the Light. It was beyond either, or perhaps beneath them. And it was appallingly strong.

The others had begun to rouse. Loric was on his feet almost before his eyes opened; only Javanne's grip kept him erect. They held each other up and watched Gwenlian come slowly to herself. She saw the two who stood over her; she opened her mouth as if to speak, closed it again with care.

Javanne's knees gave way. She let them, taking Loric with her. He did not resist. Nor did his eyes leave her face. "I hope," he said, "that you know what you are doing."

Rage or terror, she could have borne. Trust made her want to throw back her head and howl. "What are you doing here?" she demanded of him.

"I followed you," he answered.

"Why?"

"I thought you might need me."

"You fool. You utter fool."

"And what are you?" he countered. "What do you call this? A child's game?"

Her eyes narrowed. "You thought I lied. After all I said, after the oathing itself, you thought I had fallen to a woman."

"I thought you contemplated something less than wise."

Neat, that evasion. Javanne glared at the ground. The truth was less than he thought, but more than she could bear to confess. It would sound too much like betrayal. Or at the very least, like madness.

The Lady Gwenlian filled her craven silence. "We made alliance," said the woman, "to find the Power that is slaying falcons. It seems that we have found it."

"Or it has found us." Loric's calm acceptance startled Javanne, and shamed her. But it was a woman who had told him, and one of Estcarp at that, from whom any madness could be truth. He stood, paused to steady his feet, approached the heartstone. He circled it slowly. But for the light in it, it seemed like any other stone, lifeless and Powerless. He walked away from it to the edge of the circle.

The outer stones waxed brighter as he drew nearer. His feet slowed. He stretched out a hand.

A hammer of light smote him down.

Javanne was beside him, with no memory of moving. Her brain held no thought at all. Could hold none, until she held him and knew that he lived. Dazed, stunned, but coming to his senses. "Guardians," he said. "Jailers. But what they guard—it grows stronger than they. It struck me. But for the guardians—"

But for the guardians, he would have died. "It wants us here," Javanne said.

"To free it." He sat up, holding his head as if it might break. His breath hissed. "*Powers!* No wonder they teach us to shun sorcery. I feel like the lure after the hawk has struck it."

"It seems to have had little effect on your eloquence."

They turned to face the darkness beyond the guardians. The one who had spoken passed the stones, moving slowly as if against the air's resistance. The stones blazed; he raised a hand to shade his eyes. Yet he smiled. "Well met," he said, "and well come. I trust your journey was not excessively unpleasant."

They were all on their feet, swaying, blinking in the strange light. "You," Javanne said, eyes slitted to make shape of the stranger's shadow. "It was you behind the Power."

He advanced a step. She knew his face then, and his light cool voice. "Indeed, Falconer," Lord Imric said, "it was I. I have been awaiting your coming."

With all her strength she held herself still. She did not turn upon the lady. What Loric must be thinking, she could well guess. The teachings were only too true. Never, never, might a Brother place his trust in a woman.

Gwenlian's voice came sharp behind her. "Awaiting us? What do you mean by that?"

"Sister," Lord Imric said. His smile showed a gleam of teeth. "You have done well. I can only wish that you had done better. These are but two; and no falcon to be seen. Where are the rest?"

Gwenlian came to Javanne's side. In spite of herself, Javanne spared a glance. The lady's face was white and rigid, her fists clenched at her sides. Her voice was a purr. "Oh, no, brother. I am no counter in this game of yours."

"Are you not? You came when I would have you come. You bring fair tribute to this my ally."

"You are not sane."

He laughed. "Sister, sister! Is it mad to seek the aid of a greater Power for the strengthening of our house? Estcarp of old is no more. The Witches are fallen; the Borders are shifted, the east laid open that was so long forgotten. This land cries aloud for the rule of a strong lord."

"What," Loric asked with perilous softness, "has that to do with the murder of falcons?"

Imric regarded Loric without fear. He was, after all, but a boy; he had no falcon to defend him. "That is the price," the lord answered, "for my ally's aid. He is, I fear, exceedingly fastidious. He will have none but Falcon blood."

"And why is that?"

Imric shrugged. "It is his pleasure. He is a Power of the air;

he exacts tribute of his own kind. It is no small price to pay, you must believe that, Falconer. Half a hundred of your brethren, even though some be green boys, do not come cheaply. There were false reivers to be bought, and true reivers to be fought, and a war that was half truth and half a lie . . . No, the payment has been neither simple nor easy."

Loric lurched forward a step. Javanne caught him. But he had mastered himself. He stood quivering like an arrow in the target, his thin nostrils pinched tight.

Lord Imric spread his hands. "Truly, Falconer, it is necessary. I have done what I can to spare your men. The birds, alas, I cannot spare. They are rare, I know, and their training is much to lose, but my ally insists. It will not aid me without its recompense in blood."

"It?" Loric asked. "Surely it is *she?*"

"It," said Imric, certain. His brows went up. "Ah. I see. That mindless fear which rules your kind. And yet I see you in my sister's company."

Despite the lightness of his tone, Javanne's hackles rose. The man was truly indifferent to the deaths of her brothers-in-feathers. But that his sister might have bedded with a Falconer—to that he was not indifferent at all. He was no more sane than the hunting wolf, and no less. What he reckoned to be his, and what he wished to be his, must be his wholly. Aught else, to his mind, was black betrayal.

Javanne folded her arms to keep her hands from trembling, or from locking about Lord Imric's throat. "We have nothing to do with your sister," she said. "We merely made use of her Power to discover what was slaughtering our falcons. She was gracious enough to grant us her aid, and unfortunate enough to be caught in the granting of it. If you will set her free, perhaps we may settle this matter of death which lies between us."

"What!" Lord Imric exclaimed. "Gallantry, in a Falconer? Astonishing. And quite riddled with falsehood. How many of your kind have had her? All of you? Do you take her all together, or does she summon you one by one?"

Gwenlian was white more with fury than with fear. Javanne dared not touch her. The lord waited for one of them to do it, willed him to venture it; then might he shed Falconer blood with a clear conscience. Javanne met his glittering stare. "My lord, your fears are groundless. We would not dream of dishonoring your sister. We are not capable of dreaming it."

Loric gripped her arm. The pain was strangely calming. She smiled at him in a way which, she prayed, Lord Imric would not mistake.

It seemed that he did not. The madness faded from his eyes. His mouth twisted in disgust. He turned on his heel, rapped a command.

In the gate through which he had come, armed men appeared, leading among them a prisoner. He seemed a youth, a stripling, small and slight and strengthless; but so were all Brothers among outlanders. Their strength was not of axe or mace but of the sword. His guards flung him into the circle and arrayed themselves just within the ring of stones.

He fell awkwardly, twisting as if to guard something at his breast. As he rolled onto his back, Javanne saw the wicked beak thrusting from the neck of his shirt, and the maddened scarlet eyes of his falcon. Had they hoped that his soul's brother would rend him?

Javanne dropped to her knees beside her Brother and captain. Almery was trussed like a fowl for the spit, motionless and barely conscious. Drugged; or beaten half out of his senses. His face, once well-nigh as falcon-keen as Loric's, was a battered ruin.

She snatched at her dagger, to cut those cruel cords. Hard hands seized her, with hard eyes behind them. They were too strong for her, struggle though she would, trained though she was. They stripped her of weapons and of her mail shirt. They set hands to the leather jerkin beneath. She began to fight in earnest.

She fought like a mad thing. And like a mad thing, she was two: Javanne who battled for her secret, and Javanne who noted with cool interest that the Power in the stone was rising. Loric was down, stripped to trews. His skin was very white where the sun did not touch it, and very smooth. Like a girl's, one might say. Her own was little smoother. He had ceased his battle: he would have seen no purpose in it.

A blow nearly reft her of her senses. She clutched them as they fled. But the hands had returned to mere imprisonment. Lord Imric faced the stone, bowing to it. He spoke words in no tongue she knew, yet somehow it made her think of falcon speech. It was as harsh, and as toneless, with a strange wild music in it: wind, and the roar of the storm, and the headiness of the kill.

And yet it was alien. It bore no love for falcon kind; it hungered for their blood. No clean bringer of death, this: raven, vulture, carrion crow. Falcons hunted its mortal kin. Falcon kin had bound it long ago.

Not her kin, human born, nor the brothers of her brothers-in-feathers. But their cousins, yes, or their like, masters and mistresses of Power before ever man set foot in this country. They had sentenced this their enemy to eternal imprisonment. And well before eternity was past, they vanished into death or something stranger than death. Their guardians grew feeble without them, until the circle would admit a man walking with firm will. Curiosity drove him first, perhaps. Perhaps the thing within had whetted that curiosity, sharpened it into a summons. And once within, he was fair prey to that ancient strength. What he wished for, it could promise to grant. Promises cost nothing, and their price was the Power's freedom. For that, it had taught him the way to loose its bonds. It had let him command it as he pleased and as its weakening prison allowed; it had prevailed upon him to give it that which served as both sustenance and revenge. Men's blood was useful, but the blood of their falcons was sweeter by far, and more potent for the breaking of its captivity.

Javanne sagged in her captors' grip. It was not blood alone. The bond between man and falcon held great Power. The severing of it poured that Power into the captive's mind. So would it do with Almery: sunder him from his falcon, and drain their souls, and drink their blood. And with Loric and herself, whose falcons had escaped its nets, the sundering would suffice, seasoned with mere human lives. Then at last would it be free.

A knife gleamed in Imric's hand. He knelt by Loric as his men held her swordbrother spread-eagled on the ground. "You," the lord said, "will do for a beginning. Your bird conceals itself; but we need not see it in order to make use of it. See, now. If it cannot be ours, yours also it shall not be."

Loric cried aloud. High above the circle, a falcon's voice echoed him. He twisted, his face drawn in agony. All his body was a scream. Lord Imric raised the knife, choosing his target.

Javanne damned her secret, damned her geas, damned all that she had ever been. Her Power roared as it came. The captive recoiled. The guardians blazed white. She almost laughed. Moon magic. Yes, it would be that. And the moon, though fading from the full, had a little strength left. She drank it like wine.

Outside of Power she was most aware, not of the enemy, but of the ally who had not known all that she was. The Lady Gwenlian was wonderstruck but unsurprised. *Witch,* she said, touching mind to mind as falcons could, *I had not guessed. But woman, yes, oh surely yes. From the moment I saw your face.*

Javanne paused. *How?*

Boys are seldom so beautiful. Gwenlian was laughing. *Yes, you are, you shall not deny it. And a woman knows a sister, even in Falcon mail.*

Sister, said Javanne, trying the taste of it. Plunging before her courage failed her. *Will you help me?*

Gwenlian's response had no need of words. Her Power stretched forth like a firm hand, clasping Javanne's own.

The Power in the stone rose to its fullest height. It shaped itself in Javanne's eyes as a great gore-crow. Its body stretched, straining. A thread glimmered through the darkness, slender as spidersilk and no less strong. The light upon it was the moon's sheen upon the wings of a white falcon.

The thread eluded the crow's snapping lunge. Wind-in-the-North came no closer. Javanne willed her to flee altogether; but that, she would not.

Javanne struck the side which the crow had left undefended. The Power whipped about. Its caw was rage, tempered with iron laughter. *See!* it exulted. *See what you have done!*

She reeled into her body. Bitter cold smote it. Her shirt was torn from her, the breastband flung away, the truth bared to the sky: full truth as hands rent her breeches. Her guards were grinning. Lord Imric's mirth pealed up to heaven. "By all the Powers of the Air! What have we here?" His eyes narrowed. "Or is that the Falconers' secret?

"Strip them," he snapped to his men.

Nakedness, she could bear. Leers and muttered comments, she had expected. But that her Brothers should see her with all her lies laid bare—that, she could not endure. And there was no mercy in the world. They were both awake and aware and able to see. Almery's stare was coldly level. Loric's . . .

It was Loric whom she could not bear. At whom she could not even look.

"Only one," said Imric, having looked long at each, and tested the reality of their manhood with a seeking hand, as now he tested Javanne's womanhood. His touch was almost gentle. She shuddered away from it. "Ah now," he crooned as if she had been a skittish mare. "It is only you. What have I uncovered then? A wonder? A secret? A conspiracy, perhaps?"

Power was her refuge. She plunged into the heart of it.

Gwenlian was there, holding their gathered strength. *The Power rises,* she said. *Arm yourself.*

The gore-crow rose against the white falcon that was Javanne's Power. Lord Imric laid hands upon her body. They all knew in Estcarp, how to part a woman from her witchery.

The lord fell back staggering. His ally spread wings of Power about her. *Mine,* it warned him. *She is mine.*

"I belong to no one!" Her voice was shrill in her own ears. It had freed itself through none of her willing; it was surely and indisputably a woman's.

Free. Yes. That was the strangeness that uncoiled in her, more even than Power or alliance or peril. The knot that had filled her center, the constraint of the falcons' geas, was gone. Gwenlian had seen it. Lord Imric had laid it bare for all to see.

It could not matter now what she did. Life, soul, sanity, all came to nothing. She was unmasked. She had nothing more to fear, and nothing more to live for.

Except, perhaps, to finish the proving which she had begun. That a woman could be all that a man was; and that a man could be as treacherous as any woman. The Brothers, refusing all Power but that which bound them to their falcons, had no weapon with which to face this enemy. Save only her ill-trained self.

They would never forgive her for that.

She had gone past any hope of forgiveness on the day when she entered the Eyrie. She drew herself up, and heard herself laugh: light, free, almost exultant. Wind-in-the-North had come down at last; and a second, darkness shot with a V of white: Stormrider in the full wrath of his kind. Javanne's captors fled the raking talons. Lord Imric cried out, cursing sudden pain.

Javanne snatched up the gauntlet which they had torn from her. Wind-in-the-North took station upon it. Stormrider circled her head and came to rest beside his soul's brother.

"Now," said Javanne. "Now we end it."

She faced the stone. Its shape was changing. It was visibly a work of hands now. Its wings stretched wider, shifting into strangeness, a sheen of feathers gleaming through the stone. In the pits of its eyes, a pale light grew. It had set aside its lust for falcon blood. Her Power would serve it far better; then at its leisure it would take its revenge.

Its Power roared upon her. It battered her to her knees. It sank talons into her will. *Come. Come, set me free.*

It did not beg. It commanded. It filled her brain with visions. Memories. Dreams. Freedom, long, long ago. The open sky and the wild wind, and wings spread wide to encompass them. It was lord of a great realm, and its will was the world's law.

But it had enemies: swift, fierce, bitter-taloned. They would not suffer its rule. They dared to fly where they chose, to hunt where they would, to cast defiance in the face of their lawful lord.

Not lawful, said Wind-in-the-North, clear and cold and contemptuous, *by any law of our kin. We had naught to do with your tyranny.*

I ruled, the Old One said, conspicuous in its forbearance, *because I was the strongest. Time has diminished you; it has but made me greater.*

In malice, the falcon conceded, *yes. You were a little lord, of little wit. So you remain.*

Free me, the Old One willed Javanne. *Give me your Power. Set me free.*

There was little enough in it of volition. Javanne's Power bled from the wounds of the Old One's assault. It drank the stream that though slow was manifold. Its will drew harder; the talons of its Power tensed to tear anew.

It twitched, startled. Denial pricked it like the sting of a gnat: infinite and infinitesimal wrath, flying in the face of its vastness. "No!" Lord Imric cried enraged. "You are mine. You belong to me. You are *mine!*"

The great creature turned at its leisure. *I am yours,* it agreed with perfect willingness. *Free me.*

"You are mine," Imric said.

Utterly, said the Old One. *Set me free.*

Imric's jaw set. Life beat in his hands, falcon-wild, bound

and helpless. His knife glittered through all the woven worlds. It flashed down.

Almery's Windhover burst free, rending the hand that gripped him, shrieking his fury. One drop of blood—human, falcon, there was no telling—fell smoking to the Power's prison. The heartstone shattered. Wings of darkness smote the sky. A bill like a lance slashed out and down, and swept up. Its prey struggled, screaming: the man but an insect in that terrible beak, a scarce morsel for its hunger.

Javanne raised all the Power she had. The earth groaned as the Old One strained to be free of it. But within her was silence, manifold. They had all come to her center. Gwenlian's grief quivered at the edge of hearing, her anger bright as blood, overlaid with coolness that must have come of her Witch's training. She was stronger than she knew, and more skilled. About her hovered the white fire of falcons: Windhover, Stormrider, Wind-in-the-North greater than either. The tiercels bore with them shadows of earth with Power buried deep and locked in chains, but there for Javanne's wielding, if so she willed.

Almery knew dimly what had befallen him. Loric was like a stone in Stormrider's claw. Not sundered, no longer. The Old One had forsaken that torment to turn all its Power against Javanne. But the shock had driven Loric deep into himself. Scarcely thinking, knowing only what Power knew, Javanne touched the stone. It hardened against her. She persisted. With infinite slowness it transmuted into shadow, and from shadow into light. Blue light, Power of ward and guard. It was strong enough to dazzle; and it swelled. It touched the circle of guardians. It made itself one of them. Their gladness was faint and sweet upon her tongue, but touched swiftly with bitterness.

Like their prisoner, the guardians had wielded Power in sleep; but now they roused. Slow, so slow. The Old One surged against its failing bonds. The earth trembled. The air caught at Javanne's throat, acrid with lightnings.

Cold horror all but severed her from her Power. The enemy

was growing stronger. She was feeding it, she and the gathered strength of her allies. The very exultation of that union was the Old One's sustenance; and through it, it could drain dry the guardians themselves.

"That is why," she whispered to the air. "That is why they chained it. Because where it was, it made all Power its own."

And to chain it with Power, luring it, trapping it, binding it for all the long ages—how mighty they must have been, those kindred of falcons. How many must have died, or sacrificed their magery, to bind their enemy in the stone.

She steeled herself. Strand by strand she loosed the woven Powers and thrust them away. Gwenlian fell back half stunned. Windhover, with Almery, retreated because they must. The guardians, embracing Loric and his falcon, wrought again their wall of light: great gift and great grace, to set her free and to shield her against the buffeting of her enemy; for without the bonding of her Power with theirs, the Old One could not feed on them.

Only Wind-in-the-North would not go. Javanne struck her fiercely with the knowledge of what she did. She was a hindrance; she was a danger. The Old One would only grow greater with the waxing of her strength. She must be wise. She must leave Javanne alone, with Power too little for allurement, but great enough for what must be done.

Perhaps.

Wind-in-the-North was a queen of falcons. She saw the wisdom and the necessity, and hated it, but at last she yielded to it. The heat of her anger fed Javanne's courage. Only the thread of the bond remained between them. Javanne could not, dared not sunder it.

The enemy had no such compunction. It slashed at the thread. The bond buckled, frayed, held. Javanne fell upon the Old One with all her staggering Power. It seized her.

She struggled briefly, madly, in purest and starkest terror. With an effort that racked her to the bone, she stilled. Black wings closed about her. The Old One's will made itself all her own. One moment, one brief instant, and the last of its bonds would snap. It would be free.

With the last vanishing grain of will that was Javanne, she shaped a thought and held it. The Old One surged triumphant. Far down in the heart of it, her thought broke free. Swelled. Bloomed. Burst in a storm of fire.

III

Javanne was dead.

Her body did not know it. It had come to life again out of the darkness that was Power's aftermath, and seen what it had wrought. The stone of the Old One shattered into dust, its prisoner gone, consumed by her Power that it had made its own. The guardians fallen. Lord Imric cast upon the ground, broken, dead. *His* death was merciful: it granted him oblivion.

For Javanne there was no mercy. Dead, she could not care. She rode among the remnant of the Brothers, her Brothers no longer. She wore the leather of the Falcon companies, because she must wear something, and she had naught else. She did not venture mail or weapon, nor ever the falcon helmet. That Wind-in-the-North rode on the perch before her, was the falcon's choice and the falcon's right; not even the most unforgiving of the Brothers ventured to contest it.

Gwenlian had tried to stop her. "Stay with me," the lady beseeched her. "My brother was never brother to me as you are my sister. Stay and be free with me, and together we will master that Power which we raised together."

"That is dead," Javanne had said.

She meant that she herself had died, and with her any hope of friendship or freedom or mastery of Power. Gwenlian chose not to understand. "I would never ally myself with any Old One. But you—you are like me. My brother has paid for his folly in death; the Honor of the Raven lies now in my hands. With another woman, strong both in arms and in Power, I may rule it as it deserves to be ruled. Will you aid me, sister?"

Javanne shook her head, remembering. Her lips shaped in silence the words which she had said then. "I am Falcon. My soul is subject to Falcon law. By that alone may I be judged. By that alone may I be set free."

"To death!" Gwenlian had cried, wild as any falcon.

Javanne turned her face to the sky. It wept slow tears of rain. She had lived longer than she had ever hoped to, and she had lived well. She had slain the slayer of falcons. Not even the Master of the Eyrie could take that from her.

She closed her eyes. *Enough,* she bade the spinning of her thoughts. Let it go no further. Let her remember only what she had gained.

She rode in a circle of silence. No Brother had spoken a word to her since she entered the ring of the guardians. None of them would raise his hand to touch her, or give her to eat or drink. She was worse than a traitor. There was no word for what she was.

She never glanced at Loric. She refused to know whether he ever glanced at her. But she was always aware of him: subtly, constantly, deep under her skin. When she woke and found food and a flask beside her, his presence lay heavy upon both. When she rode, he was most often behind her. When she slept, he spread his blankets just out of reach.

He was making her forget that she was dead. And that was more cruel than any Brother's malice.

They rode slowly, to spare the wounded. Of falconless men there were none. They were all dead or fled. And yet, slowly as they rode, they drew ever and inevitably closer to the Eyrie.

There came a morning of sun that put the rain to flight. The riders passed out of that light into a cleft like a knife-slash in the earth. Its farthest depths had never known the sun; the sky was a blade of darkness, and on the point of it a single star.

They came to the wall that was as tall as the sky, and led their horses one by one into the shadow of the hidden gate.

The Brothers, wise, had drawn their cloaks over their eyes. Javanne had not cared to be prudent. The sudden flame of the sun smote her to the ground.

Hands drew her up, set her in the saddle. By slow degrees her blindness passed. Loric was mounting, last of them all, eyes turned away from her. She looked past him to the Vale of the Falcon: and on the mountain's knees, the Eyrie. She flinched. Her chin set; she straightened. When the Brothers quickened their pace, she rode well forward among them, eyes and mind fixed upon the gray loom of the fortress.

Javanne lay in a cell, thinking nothing, feeling nothing. She was not imprisoned as an outlander would reckon it. The cell was the chamber of an elder Brother, a captain whose rank had freed him from the tumult of the barracks. Its starkness was Falcon comfort: a pallet on a frame of whipcord and leather, sheer luxury after the plain stone shelf of a trooper; a woolen blanket worn to softness; a perch on which Wind-in-the-North dreamed falcon dreams. The door was unbarred and unguarded.

There was no need of a guard. All the Eyrie stood on watch against her.

She had been fed twice. Or perhaps thrice; she was not counting. She had eaten only because Wind-in-the-North would take no sustenance while Javanne fasted. She had bathed, perhaps. She was clean; her riding leathers were gone. Nothing had taken their place. Her modesty, honed to instinct, kept raising a protest. She disdained to heed it.

The door opened. She had not heard the Brothers' coming. She would not have seen them, had not her face been turned toward them.

These two, she did not know well; they were sword-oathed to another commander. One, older and much scarred, pulled her up without a glance and dressed her as one dresses a child or an idiot. The other's eyes kept darting sidewise. He looked young. Perhaps he had never seen a woman naked.

It was he who saw what she lacked the will to notice. "Alarn. The woman. She's wounded herself."

The woman. As if she had never been Javan of the white queen's Choosing.

Alarn's scars twisted. She did not think it was a smile. His eyes, compelled, turned toward his companion's hand. He muttered a curse.

"Alarn—" the boy said.

"Bandages," he rapped. "Fetch."

The boy bolted. Javanne began to laugh softly, helplessly, with no will at all.

Alarn would not touch her. His revulsion was a knotting of her own vitals. Her laughter stilled; she regarded him with the pale beginnings of sympathy.

The boy came back. His name drifted to the surface of her memory. "Riwal," she said as she took the bandages from his hands, "there's nothing to fear. It's only the moon's calling."

He stiffened and turned his back on her. He had brought a basin, and water somewhat less than icy. She thanked his outraged back and washed herself, and finished her dressing. They had given her the garb of a Falconer. Because they had no other? Or because, until she was judged, she remained perforce a Brother?

She paused, straightening as the shock ran through her. She was waking. She was beginning to think; she was remembering how to feel. And she must not. That way was consciousness, and memory, and pain.

Sooner might she stay the tides of the sea. All her struggles only made her wits the keener. And with her wits rose her Power. She had spent it utterly, and it had come back in all its old strength and more.

"Damn you!" she cried, outraged. "I wanted to be *dead.*"

The Brothers stared at her. She was no animal that they could comprehend. She shook her head sadly. "Poor manlings. Do I baffle you?"

Alarn's drawn sword was his answer. "Out," he commanded the air somewhat beside and behind her.

Wind-in-the-North came to her fist. Together they led the Brothers from the cell.

The Brothers of the Falcon ringed the great hall, all the companies that were in the Eyrie, men and falcons both, captains and troopers, even the fledglings trying not to fidget by the wall. This would be a mighty lesson: proof positive of the perfidy of the female.

Between her courses and her fear, it was all she could do not to fall retching to the stones. Pride, and Wind-in-the-North motionless on her fist, kept her erect, led her with some semblance of dignity to the circle of trial. It was a stone set in the floor before the Master's seat, never covered and never trodden on save by some transgressor against the Law of the Falcon.

None had ever transgressed so far or so appallingly. There was a black glory in that.

Her Power twitched, rousing of itself. Someone was regretting that she had been permitted Falcon gear. She looked too much like a Brother, and much too little like a woman.

A thin smile had found its way to her lips. She let it linger. Garments alone were not her trouble; and her face was female enough if one did not persist in seeing it as a boy's. But no man there could deny what gripped her fist with fierce and unrelenting strength.

There were formalities. Javanne took little notice. Her eyes were on the banner behind the Master: the black falcon under which she had lived and learned and fought. It blurred. She willed the tears away. Fool that she was, moon-beset; she had known that this must come. Had prayed for it more than once in the black wake of her dreams. She should be glad that her long lie was done.

"You." The Master did not even favor her with a name. "Do you deny the truth of the charges against you?"

Almost she asked, stupidly, what they were. But she knew. "That I am a woman, no, I do not." Her voice was clear, with a ring in it that no man could match. "That I am traitor to my oath and enemy of the Brotherhood, yes, by all the Powers of the Air, I do deny it."

"Do you deny that you have maintained your deception with the aid of witchcraft?"

"There was little enough need of it," she said, "once men knew what they would see."

"Do you deny it?"

His words were iron. Cold iron, a fugitive thought observed, could be deadly to Power. She lifted her chin. "I cannot deny it."

A whisper ran through the ranks, more of the mind than of the body. Hatred darkened it, and fear, and ingrained revulsion. Eyes had begun to shift. If one female could have crept into the ranks, how many others might have done the same?

Wind-in-the-North stretched her wings. The eyes snapped to her. Minds struggled anew with her existence, here, soul-bound to this woman. One or two groped toward blasphemy. Female and female. How deep could treachery run? Were the queens of falcons no more to be trusted than their wingless sisters?

Javanne's spine crawled with cold. There was poison in the air, foul as a rotting wound, and more deadly. For years beyond count it had festered. Rivery and his Sulcarwoman had slain the one who wrought it. But no simple stroke of sword or Power could drain away the poison.

"Kill her," someone said, or no one, or everyone. "Kill her. *Kill her!*"

The falcons rose in a roar of wings. Javanne watched them with something almost like relief. Yes: that would be a fair ending, to die under those cruel talons. Wind-in-the-North did not even try to do battle against them. She watched as Javanne watched, as the world blurred into a flurry of black bodies, white gullwing slashes, blood-red falcon eyes.

As suddenly as the storm had risen, it settled. Javanne stood in a ring of falcons. All faced outward, wings half spread, hissing warning. One proud tiercel took station on her shoulder. The white falcon blinked once, giving leave. Stormrider dipped his head in respect. "Touch our sisters," he said, "and we strike."

Javanne found it in herself to pity the Brothers. They stood all naked, some gripping broken jesses, staring blankly at this greatest of betrayals. She had robbed them of their falcons.

Anger gusted through her, driving out compassion. "I did not," she gritted, lest she break and scream at them. "As well you should know, you at least, who knew Lord Imric's treachery." Her eye found Almery, his face returning at last to its old comeliness, although his nose would never be the fine and haughty arch that it had been. He met her stare with one which she had no time to read. "Your brother remains your brother. Not your servant, to do only as you would wish."

"And yet," the Master said, not one whit shaken to see his own brother-in-feathers among the ranks at her feet, "you are no brother of ours. Who set you here, and why?"

"The tale is long," said Javanne, warning only, not refusal.

"Tell it."

"She will not." The voice rang from the open gate. Figures stood in it. The Brothers were slow enough to know them, straight as they stood, and proud, with light in their faces, and no slightest vestige of dumb servility. Falcons came with them. White falcons. Queens. The tiercels rose up in homage.

Javanne could not move. Iverna led the women of the Falcon, and there was triumph in their coming, even if they all must die for daring it. The white falcons came as companions, and as guards; what had become of the Brothers on guard without, Javanne could well guess.

Iverna came forward to face the Master. They were of an age, and of a kind, and of a strength. He acknowledged it. His head inclined the merest fraction; he betrayed no hint of the lesser Brothers' shock, that women should have set foot in the Eyrie. "Headwoman," he said.

"Wingmaster," she responded.

"This was your doing." He was not surprised, although the knowledge was as recent as his speaking of it.

She did not answer him at once. She turned to Javanne, looking her up and down with eyes as bitter-bright as the Master's. But gentler. A very little gentler. "You have grown, daughter," she said.

She was not speaking of the body. Javanne raised her Power like a sword, half salute, half warning. "I am what I was bred to be."

"Indeed," said Iverna, seeing her with more than eyes: woman, witch, sister of falcons; warrior and hunter and swordsworn of the Brotherhood. It was a great burden, to be seen so. Javanne retreated behind her shields, seeking comfort in being simply Javanne.

Iverna turned back to the Master. "This was my doing, mine and my sisters' and our mothers' before us. Did you dream that we submitted meekly to slavery? Did you think that when you bred warriors like cattle, mating the best of your men to the best bred of our women, only the sons would be strong? Or that we would have no stake in such matings? As you bred for strength and will and wit, we bred for the same, and for Power with it." Her eyes swept the hall. The Brothers gaped at her, faces slack with shock. She shook her head as at the witlessness of children. "For many a long year we have left you to your delusions. Now it is time you learned the truth.

"You teach and are taught that all the bonds of your lives are forged by what brought you to this land: Jonkara's rise to power in Salzarat of the Falcon, and her enslavement of all her sex, whereby she bound the men and the nation; the sacrifice of Langward the king, who dying at his own queen's hand sealed the spell that bound Jonkara, and set free a handful of his people; the long fear that Jonkara would rise again in all her old strength, and take her revenge, again through us who were her sisters in the flesh.

"So you teach. So you believe. And that too has been a defense.

"For not only the women fell to Jonkara's Power. The men fell also, and as their wives and sisters turned against them in hatred and in revenge for wrongs whether true or false, so did they abhor those women whom once they had loved. It was that hatred which turned at last against Jonkara.

"A few of those women with Power, albeit no equal to their enemy's, had seen what must be, and had done what they could to arm themselves against her. With Langward, who was himself an adept of no little potency, they conceived and carried out their assault. They could not hope to destroy Jonkara, but they could cage her; prevent her from calling upon her allies of the Dark and of the worlds beyond the Gates; gather those of their kinsmen who could be compelled by Power or by the king's command or, in extremity, by deception; and take flight across the northern seas.

"We accepted subjection as the price of our freedom. It was necessary. If Jonkara freed herself and pursued us, she would strike first through the men, as she had done in Salzarat. She must not know what defense we raised behind the shield of their hatred and contempt: walls and battlements of Power, and strong weapons to defend them, honed through years of waiting and of wariness."

Iverna paused. She had a power beyond Power. The Brothers listened to her. Not willingly, not easily, but they let her speak.

Again she scanned their faces. How much alike they were, Javanne thought, following the woman's eyes. Like all the folk of the Old Race they aged almost invisibly: even the elders did not seem remarkably older than Loric or Hendin or Kerrec. Many bore scars of the battles which were the Falconers' livelihood; but beneath the scars, they all had well-nigh the same face. The face of the Falcon, bred into the line like the Power which no man would acknowledge.

And like the hatred of women which had been their preservation. "Now," said Iverna, "the necessity is gone. Jonkara's end came simply enough, and at the hands of a woman: a

Sulcarwoman at that, and hence doubly to be scorned. But Jonkara's legacy endured. Her death did not set us free. You would not even consider it. What if the ancient enemy was gone? Another might rise in her place."

"Another has!" a man cried, pricked at last beyond endurance.

A snarl rose from among the ranks; weapons glittered, unsheathed in hall against every law of the Eyrie. But there could be no law now. Women had entered the realm of the Brothers. One had gone so far as to pass the Choosing.

Here and there a captain strove to quell the revolt. The Master did not even try. He simply watched, as a falcon watches its prey before it strikes.

The falcons rose, shrilling their war-cry. They struck with wings only, without talons, but they drove back the advance, and held it back with the sheer force of their anger.

Wind-in-the-North spoke for them all. "We are not slaves. I Chose as I wished to Choose. There is no opener of dark Gates here."

More than discipline was crumbling. Men doubted the word of a falcon. Not all the blades had returned to their sheaths.

In one long leap Javanne mounted the dais to the Master's side. The tiercels came with her. From amid the tumult of their wings, she raised her voice and set Power in it. "I am not your enemy. I am of your blood and bone; I have kept the law as well as any one of you. I call the falcons as my witness."

"You have lied," the Master said, almost gently.

"There was no other way." Iverna and her companions stood unharmed, unafraid. "One of your own, Rivery himself, told you the truth. You would not heed him. Thrice we ventured it. Once you, Theron, heard me out. I tell your Brothers what you told me. 'It has been too long. The hatred runs too deep. There can never be alliance between the men and the women of the Falcon.'"

"Nor can there be," the Master said.

"Therefore," said Iverna as if he had not spoken, "we abandoned words. We chose this child to be our proof. We saw to it that she was chosen for the Eyrie. We did no more than give you to think that she was male. But for that sole deception, she was all that you could desire in one of your sons."

"That is so." Verian said it, the blind master of the fledglings. He spoke as one who confronts a bitter truth. "She was not the worst of the young ones in my care."

"Witchcraft," muttered the Brothers nearest him.

"It was not," said Verian. "She passed all the testing. She was Chosen, and by a queen. Now I understand how that could be."

Javanne's breath caught in her throat. That Verian should speak for her—that was a mighty gift. No one could question either Verian's honor or his courage. With his eyes he had bought the lives of his whole company, years agone, in the wars against the Kolder.

"It was witchcraft," the Brothers persisted. They were perhaps a little fewer. Or perhaps not. "Witches have been our downfall."

"And your salvation!" Loric thrust his way to the front of the ranks, and spun on his heel. "Does no one even remember why she was unmasked? But for her we would face as bitter an enemy as ever Jonkara was. She severed us from our women. That Power of the Old Ones would have sundered us from our falcons."

The Brothers looked at him. His hands shook; he fisted them at his sides. "She faced that enemy," he said with great care, as if his voice would not hold steady else. "She faced it alone, knowing what it could do, knowing that she dared death and worse than death. Knowing what recompense we would give her."

"We must," purred Kerrec. "Of course you would speak for her. You are her swordbrother. Or are you more than that?"

A gauntleted fist struck Kerrec down. He leaped up, knife

in hand. Almery faced him weaponless, arms folded, face unreadable. Very slowly Kerrec sheathed his dagger. Even he knew better than to raise steel against his commander.

Almery turned his back on him, advancing to Loric's side. "I will speak for the prisoner. I was part of her testing; I can affirm that she was well worthy of her training. I have been her captain, and have found her to be as strong in battle as any Brother of her age, as skilled in weapons and in tactics, as firm in her observance of our laws. I was witness to her unmasking; it was my life for which she offered her own, mine and that of her swordbrother. It was done in all honor and for the preservation of the Brotherhood."

Voices rose, tangling in the heavy air. "Lies." "She seduced them." "She is a *woman!*"

There was the heart of it. "Yes," Javanne said. "I am a woman. That is my great sin. I was given all else that makes a Brother, save that alone. What I have done is nothing to what I am." She stepped from her guard of falcons, sending Stormrider from her shoulder, Wind-in-the-North from her fist. She spread her hands. "The law is the law. I submit myself to its judgment."

"To what end?" asked the Master, as if indeed he wished to know.

She addressed her answer to them all. "You wrought me too well, O my people. You gave me honor, and you gave me pride. You made certain that I would pay for what you have done. You have cast defiance in nature's face." She braced her feet, threw up her head: a youth's bravado, and she knew it, but her body and her tongue were running all of their own accord. "Outlanders are twofold, woman and man, bearer and begetter. We were three: woman, man, and falcon. Jonkara shattered us. For one woman mad with power, we have destroyed generations of our own kin. Will she then have the victory? Must we prove beyond all disbelief, that we are no more than her hatred would have made us?" They were silent. Each tiercel had returned to his brother. There was an edge in the reunion, a tension in men and falcons alike: the beginnings of distrust. Javanne smote her hands together. "By all the lords of the air! Kill me and have done with it."

The Brothers stirred, rumbling, swaying for her, against her, in spite of her. "We have no choice!" one cried above the rest. "She is a woman, a liar, a traitor. She must die. It is the law."

But falcons did not live by Falcon law. Their high queen spoke from the eminence of the Master's seat. Her voice was flat even for a falcon's, and implacable. "We will kill the one who kills her."

"What is she to you?" the Master dared to ask.

"She is our sister," the queen responded. "She binds what was too long unbound. She makes our people whole again."

Iverna's voice was sweet after that harsh tonelessness; but it was no less unyielding. "Yes, O Brothers. That was the way of it in the days which you have forgotten. Man and tiercel, woman and falcon. Queens Chose as did their brothers, and marriages were made that mated four and not the common outland two."

"We—cannot—" The Master regained his composure with swiftness that won Javanne's envy. "Is that what you would have?"

The woman shook her head almost impatiently. "It is far too soon for that. For us as for you. We too hate, Winglord. We too have years of pain to forget. But we are willing to begin. A truce; the opening of the village and the Eyrie; the meeting of our people. We will suffer a few chosen men to dwell with us for a time, as brothers only, to learn that we are as human as they. We ask that you permit our sisters the same." Her hand forestalled an outcry. "Nor do we trust you! You looked on us as cattle, fit only to breed sons. You took those sons when they had been ours long enough to know as well as to love, and slew those whom you judged unfit, and taught the rest to hate us who had given them life. Our daughters—*your* daughters—were as nothing; a man who begot more than three was reckoned incapable and removed from the lists of herd-sires. It was a mild disgrace, release from a duty more onerous than honorable. But the mother of three daughters—on her you had no mercy. You condemned her to death."

"And you slew her," the Master said.

Iverna smiled with deadly sweetness. "So we permitted you to think." She paused. He was silent, expressionless. The Brothers were beginning to understand; she said it for them. "We acknowledge your authority only over the males."

"Which," said Loric with boldness verging on insanity, "the prisoner is not."

Javanne wanted to gag him. He was destroying himself for her. For loyalty, ill though she had rewarded it; for gratitude, as if she would not have saved the life of any Brother. "I am the Master's," she said coldly, "by my oath. It is his part to judge me."

"And how can he?" Loric cried.

Almery's hand silenced him. It did not still his mind. He beat upon her Power, insistent, incredibly strong. She walled him out.

The Master frowned. "I am asked to judge, and yet I am forbidden."

"We do not forbid," said the queen of falcons. "We warn."

Death for death. A Brother would die gladly for his people. But that one of them should die for this, and their numbers so shrunken already from the wars and the Turning and the madness of the Lord of Ravenhold . . .

Javanne's mind was perfectly clear. It wielded her body with speed and precision. She had the Master's dagger before he knew she had moved. A pause, to find the place. Just below the breast, yes. Upward, inward. A moment's pain, no more. So swift. So simple.

The storm took her. Too late, she tried to tell it. Her heart, beating, brushed the dagger's point. She gathered her waning will to drive it home.

"Hold her down."

Men's voices. Women's. Falcons'. She smiled in the gathering dark. She had brought them together in spite of themselves.

"*Hold* her, damn you!"

"Cloths, quickly."

"Never mind the lacings. Cut them."

"Yes, we can heal her. If we are swift. If she allows it. *If*"—acidly—"we are spared your gabble of questions."

She would not allow it. She would *not.*

You shall. There were many in that voice. Falcons were clearest. She refused them. They needed a death. A sacrifice, to seal the spell of their union. So did blood seal all great magics.

Not so! Anger sparked in the denial. *That is Darkness. How have you fallen to it?*

It was truth. She thrust herself away from them. She must die. She could not live as a woman. She had lost her place as a Brother. She was a weapon outworn, too deadly to keep.

Someone was cursing her steadily. He sounded strange. As if—almost as if he wept.

She paused in her descent into night. Who would weep for her? She had never mattered to anyone. She was a thing. A weapon indeed, sheathed in a lie. Wind-in-the-North need not mourn: where Javanne went, there also would she go. And falcons had no fear of death.

The cursing was louder. Light grew about her. Pain sharpened it. Faces. Falcon eyes. Her head rested on something more angular than not. She turned her head a fraction.

Loric's face was framed in falcons: black, white. He addressed his curses to the air. He did not seem to know that he wept; or that he held her in his lap, and stroked her hair over and over.

She hit him as hard as she could. "You disgrace yourself." The blow was but a brush of fingers across his streaming face. The reprimand was less than a whisper. Both earned her the flash of Iverna's temper, for what they did to the wound. She hardly noticed.

He looked down at her. His face was furious under the tears. "Why did you do it, damn you? *Why?*"

"I had to."

He heard her, if no one else could. His lip curled. "Coward."

"I had to." He must understand. He *must.*

He refused. "You run away. Leaving us to clear the field. Leaving me— Damn you, woman. Damn you."

Her eyes opened a little wider. She saw what he had no words to tell her: the waxing of Power in him, roused in the circle of the guardians, adamant in its refusal to return to sleep. Her doing, through her healing of his bond with his falcon, through her wielding of him after. He had been hiding it; it was beginning to fester in him, to swell and surge and struggle to break free. He needed training, and swiftly. Training which she above all knew how to give.

She? She was nothing beside Iverna.

She was his swordbrother.

"How can I be?" she demanded bitterly. "I am a woman."

"You are my swordbrother."

Obstinate. She hit him again. Again it had no more force than a caress. This time he caught her hand and held it to his scarred cheek. There was little enough thought in it; then there was defiance. Let them think that Kerrec spoke the truth: that he had known to what he swore his faith and his honor.

"I revolt you," she said.

He shook his head. He was a little puzzled: that comforted her. "You haven't changed. It's we who have to learn a new way to see."

Her eyes closed. But for his grip, her hand would have fallen. She was aware, distantly, of Power driving itself into her side, transmuting the pain of steel into the agony of fire. So little a wound, to be of so much moment. She thought of letting go. She could do it. In the end, her life was hers to keep, or hers to cast away.

Loric bent close above her. She needed no eyes to see his face. "We need you," he said. "Only you are the fullness of what may be."

No. Her voice was gone somewhere in the fiery dark. *The Brothers will never allow it.*

"They must," said Wind-in-the-North.

Javanne's eyelids lifted. They were intolerably heavy. She had to search, with mighty effort, to find the Master. He was close. Kneeling. Holding a basin. He looked almost human. "Judge," she whispered with all the strength that was left in her.

He lowered the basin. The mask flickered across his face. "Have you not done so already?"

She could neither move nor speak. Iverna drew back from her, raising bloodied hands in a gesture of surrender. "I can do nothing while she resists me. Judge her, Wingmaster. She will die if you command it."

"And if I do not?"

Iverna shrugged, not with indifference, but as one who knows and accepts the realities of Power.

The Master, who knew only the ways of the palpable world, stiffened in resistance. His eyes rested on Javanne; on Loric; on their two falcons. His brows met. He faced Iverna as if he found her easier to bear: less troubling to his vision of the world. "Women. Always it is women who wreak havoc with our people. Jonkara, the Witches, this youngling—whether she lives or she dies, the Brothers will not be the same. They have learned that a female can match them. They have seen the falcons turn against them for her sake. And they—we—owe her a debt which we can . . . never . . . repay."

No one spoke. Javanne sighed. She was infinitely tired. Would he not condemn her and let her go?

He took her chin in his hand, turning her face more fully toward him. He spoke gently enough to widen more eyes than hers. "If I command you on your oath to the Brotherhood, will you obey?"

Her nod was the merest shadow, but he felt it.

"Even if I bid you live?"

She strove with all her will to pull away. So much he hated her and all her sex. So cruelly. And to invoke her oath—how could he fail? If she broke it and died, she proved the faithlessness of the female. If she kept it and lived, she lived a slave, a woman of the Falcon.

He held her, eyes level. No hatred burned in them. He was too cold for that.

"Too wise," said Iverna.

His gaze did not waver. "You will live. You will remain among us. Your captain has asked it—demanded it. Your swordbrother . . ." He did not like to say it, but he firmed himself. "Your swordbrother has advised me that if you face exile, he will face it with you. He is not alone." His mind was open to hers. Jory. Hendin. Others who amazed her more: older Brothers, not all of them from her own company, who perhaps, against all law and custom, knew or guessed what a woman was.

"It is time," Iverna said. "The world changes. We change with it or fall."

The Master tensed, as if he would cry out against her. But he nodded, a jerk of the head: outrage, anger, utterly unwilling acceptance. "This is no gift I give you. You may yet win your death, and mine with it, and that of all the people of the Falcon. You will be hated; you will be tested, and tested again, and given no quarter. From me you will have no protection but what the law commands."

Javanne could see what he saw. A long hard road, with much pain, and much division among the Brothers, and much that was sown lost to the bitter wind.

She shivered. But it was a clean chill, not the dank cold of death. She met the Master's eyes. He was more than wise; he was foresighted. And he had courage beyond even the measure of his warrior kind. To judge as he judged, when her death would be so much simpler: to face what must come, and not to thrust it far ahead when perhaps he might not survive to suffer it.

He offered her no mercy. She wanted none. She was Falconer, the Chosen of a queen. She was as strong as any man.

Loric had her hands. Her body had begun to be her own again. It knew how tight his grip was, how close to pain. She mustered her voice. She spoke to them all, to Master and Headwoman, Brothers, sisters, falcons with ears to hear beyond mere windy words. But she spoke most specially to a pair of falcons, and to her swordbrother on whom they rested. "I live," she said. His joy leaped high. It made her laugh, with a catch in it, for she hurt. "I live, since you compel me. How can I resist you? You offer me a battle."

"A long one." Loric was far too joyous to be dismayed. "But in the end we'll win it. We can't fail. We have you, and we have Wind-in-the-North."

"And you have me," said Stormrider, his mind touching Javanne's, swift and proud.

"And you," Javanne agreed as the Power rose in her. Iverna was but the spark that rekindled the fire. A little while, and she would rise; and not her body alone would be healed. She had never been whole as she was now. As her people would be, now that she walked in the light: woman and witch and Falconer, untainted by any lie. First of her kind, but not, if the Powers willed, the last.

"One day," she said, "there will be many; and all our griefs shall be forgotten. By the Powers of Air I swear it. By Falcon blood and Falcon law, so mote it be."

So shall it be, said Wind-in-the-North with falcon certainty.

Afterword

When Andre Norton invited me to join her in the Witch World, I was deeply honored and slightly panicked. I had never worked in anyone else's mental universe before; I had no idea how to go about it. "Just do it," Andre advised me.

I did it. I went back to the Witch World; I reread all the books; I became *a Witch Worlder, for a little while. And, like many of my comrades there, I discovered a particular fascination with one group of people: the Falconers. The moment of truth was distinct. I read the story "Falcon Blood" in* Lore of the Witch World, *and, being then deeply into the world, I said, "That can't be all there was to it." I wrote a short story called "Falcon Law," and sent it to Andre, with a note that it seemed like a piece of a longer tale.*

Andre called me as soon as she received it. Now, the telephone and I do not get along. It took Andre, who is a lady in the fullest sense of the word, and a flawlessly patient one, some little time to convince me that, no, she wasn't one of those atrocious and ubiquitous computerized salespeople; she wasn't selling anything, she was buying. *Could I, she asked, write the whole story? Could I give her 20,000 words, preferably yesterday?*

I gave it to her, of course. It was the very least I could do for a writer who has given me so much, so freely, for so long.

Thank you, Andre, for sharing your world with us.

—Judith Tarr

Biographical Notes

BOYER, ELIZABETH H.

Elizabeth Boyer is a resident of a small, historic, copper-mining town in Utah. Since 1980 she has published five fantasy novels for Del Rey Books; the latest of which is *The Trolls' Grindstone.* Writing has been a part of her life since elementary school. A graduate of Brigham Young University, she studied English literature and writing, as well as the mythology and lore of Scandinavia, which she draws upon for her fantasy plots. The hours before dawn are her favorite hours for writing. She enjoys classical music, gardening, horses and cats, and traveling with her husband, Allan, and two daughters. She also works sporadically on the historical restoration of her 1920s house, which is on the National Register of Historic Places.

CHERRYH, C. J.

Winner of two Hugos and the John W. Campbell Award, she writes, "I have two professions: writing and trying out things . . . I've slept on deck in the Adriatic, driven Picadilly at rush hour, and outraced a dog pack in the hills of Thebes. I've dealt with horses, ancient weapons, camels, falconry, wilderness survival, archaeology, Roman, Greek civ, Crete, Celts, caves, and I handle a few languages well enough to get along . . . 'No,' 'thank you,' and 'the honor you propose is so extravagant I could not possibly accept' are some of the more useful phrases. ('Yes' should only be acquired after one attains full fluency.) I like touring this planet, as long as I'm on a stopover here . . . I enjoy the past but I like the present better and the future more than that."

PIERCE, MEREDITH ANN

Meredith Ann Pierce was born in 1958 in Seattle, Washington. She has lived in California, Illinois, Texas, and, for the last fifteen years, in Gainesville, Florida. She graduated from the University of Florida in 1980 with a master's degree in English. Her first novel, *The Darkangel,* was published in 1982. Hailed as "easily the year's best fantasy" by *The New York Times, The Darkangel* won a number of honors, including the International Reading Association's award for best novel of the year. A sequel, *A Gathering of Gargoyles,* followed in 1984, and two new fantasies, *Birth of the Firebringer* and *The Woman Who Loved Reindeer,* appeared in 1985. Ms.

Pierce now writes full-time and works part-time in a local bookstore. Her works have found audiences in Great Britain and Canada and have been translated into Danish, Swedish, and German. She is now at work on the sequel to *Birth of the Firebringer* and on the final volume of the Darkangel trilogy.

TARR, JUDITH

Judith Tarr is the author of a number of novels of high and historical fantasy, including the award-winning Hound and the Falcon trilogy, and several pieces of short fiction, including "Defender of the Faith" in *Moonsinger's Friends*. She holds a Ph.D. in Medieval Studies from Yale University; she is, in Andre Norton's own phrase, "owned and operated by" an Arabian dressage horse. She lives in New Haven, Connecticut, and is, as usual, working on a novel.

Fiction
Four from the witch world
$16.95